"SEIZE HIM!
DIGEN FARRIS IS AN OUTLAW!"

The other channels spread out, trying to ensnare Digen. He skinned free; if they got a grip on him he would die on public display—his cries for mercy broadcast as an object lesson to every part of the world.

"Don't you realize what we've done?" Digen shouted. "We saved the life of a Sime with Gen surgery. It's a step to reunite mankind!"

"He's insane," cried Beccard. "Get him before he hurts someone."

Digen eluded them again and jumped up on the makeshift operating table. All at once he saw the unbreachable wall in their minds, their hearts. In a manic rage, he ripped the double-crested ring from his hand.

"The Tecton is dead!" he screamed. "The House of Zeor is dead! And may you know what you have done before you all die!"

D1373602

UNTO ZEOR, FOREVER

JACQUELINE LICHTENBERG

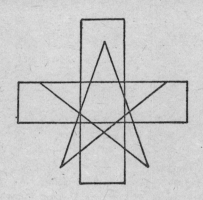

PLAYBOY PRESS
PAPERBACKS

With the exception of actual historical persons, all the characters in this book are fictitious and any resemblance to actual persons, living or dead, is purely coincidental.

DEDICATION

To my husband, Salomon Lichtenberg, who has suffered over this book more than anyone can know.

To a woolly worm called Ray Block, because every girl ought to have an extra father when the going gets tough.

To my parents, because you don't really know what parents are until you're over thirty and a parent yourself.

And
to Aunt Anna; May She Rest in Peace

AUTHOR'S NOTE

A special acknowledgment goes to Marion Zimmer Bradley. While visiting me in August 1975, Marion was sitting on the sofa with two years of notes for this book spread all about her. I came in with a cold cantaloupe in one hand, asking what she'd like for lunch, and she sat me down and forced me to answer the question "But what is this book really about? What's the story, in one sentence?"

That cantaloupe was warm before we'd hacked out three little notebook pages, which eventually—and to my astonishment—became this book. Few mortals are so privileged to sit at the feet of a true artist and learn their craft.

I would also like to thank the many Sime fans who read and criticized the various drafts, especially Betty Herr, Elisabeth Waters, and Cynthia Levine, who were during this writing the editors of *Ambrov Zeor*,* the magazine where the ardent Sime fan can always get such things as a Simelan vocabulary and pronunciation guide, genealogy charts of the succession in Zeor, how Proficiency Numbers are calculated, the mathematics of transfer, additional Sime stories and what precisely happened to poor Dane Rizdel, as well as a wealth of technical information much too esoteric to be allowed to intrude into a story.

An additional acknowledgment goes to Jean Lorrah, who had been known to me for many years through her fine writing in *Star Trek* fanzines before she wrote me an astute analysis of my first Sime novel, *House of Zeor* (Doubleday 1974, Pocket Books 1977) and then went on to an exhaustive critique on the semifinal version of this book. Do you have any idea what it's like for a chemist

---

* Published quarterly. For information, send self-addressed stamped envelope to *Ambrov Zeor*, Box 290, Monsey, NY 10952. Two other Sime/Gen fanzines can also be contacted through this address, but not through libraries or bookstores.

to have her fiction critiqued by an English professor? Don't ask. Suffice to say she uncovered many implications I had not seen, and many fruitful pathways to explore in future novels.

In fact, she began exploring those pathways immediately, producing several remarkable stories which are available in *Ambrov Zeor,* the Sime fanzine. She finally realized she was thoroughly trapped into the Sime universe and yielded to the temptation to write a Sime novel, which our beloved Pat LoBrutto has yielded to the temptation to buy, called *First Channel,* the story of the first Sime to discover he didn't have to kill to live.

Working with Jean is turning into the thrill of a lifetime and is uncovering a multitude of Sime books that "just have to be written" besides the dozen or three I had already planned on. The co-operation of Sharon Jarvis and now Pat LoBrutto at Doubleday in the shaping of this budding series—Sharon sweated out long hours editing this book and showed herself to be a true genius—has been astounding. I want everyone to know how prompt and efficient Doubleday has been in forwarding mail to me unopened. And I want everyone to know that any correct spelling or punctuation in this book is strictly to the credit of the Doubleday copy editing department, especially Fran, who made this book a labor of love.

No writer can work in a vacuum. I have been fortunate to be surrounded by the support of so many that I could go on and on with these acknowledgments, but space prohibits. May you all Live Long and Prosper,

Jacqueline Lichtenberg
Monsey, New York
December 1977

CONTENTS

CHARACTERS

SIME

Digen Farris:
Head of Householding Zeor, great-great-grandson of Klyd Farris, founder of the modern Tecton, Digen never questions the ideals of the Tecton until he meets Ilyana Dumas.

Rindaleo Hayashi:
The man who can save the Tecton, but only with Digen's help.

Jesse Elkar:
An old friend of Digen's, Elkar becomes a victim of the Tecton right before Digen's eyes.

Skip Cudney/Ozik:
A fifteen-year-old boy, born among Simes but raised by Gens, he becomes the bone of contention first between Digen and Hogan, then between Digen and Ilyana.

Mora Dyen:
She intends to marry Imrahan, but wants to bear a Farris child first.

Controller Mickland:
The Channel elected by the city and district of Westfield to be responsible for the smooth functioning of the Tecton's selyn delivery system so that no Sime should ever be tempted to kill a Gen for selyn. Mickland is antihouseholder and typical of the bureaucrat mentality that is taking over the Tecton.

11

GEN

Tchervain Rholle:
A trained Donor whose speed and capacity indicate to Digen he might be able to become a match for Digen's need.

Ilyana Dumas:
Raised to despise and condemn the Tecton and the householders, Ilyana finds herself dependent on Digen Farris for her life and sanity.

Joel Hogan:
In spite of being both fascinated and repelled by Simes, Hogan volunteers to room with Digen.

Imrahan ambrov Imil:
This Gen wants to become a member of Householding Zeor, but, in the process of qualifying, he violates the rules of Zeor to uphold the law of the Tecton.

Dane Rizdel:
A First Order Donor qualified by Mora and Digen. Rizdel has a complex history which causes him to abort transfers.

Ditana Amanso:
She proves to be Digen's nemesis, almost causing him to kill Joel Hogan.

Dr. Reginald Thornton:
Chief of Surgery at the Gen hospital where Digen seeks a Surgical internship/residency.

Dr. Lankh:
A medical researcher at the Gen hospital whose main project is to discover a way to stop and reverse changeover. He cannot understand why all his patients die.

VOCABULARY

Changeover: The process of maturing into a Sime adult. At the climax of changeover, the tentacles burst from their sheaths, ready to absorb selyn from a Gen. Children don't know if they will go through changeover unless they are channels.

Sime: An adult human whose body does not produce selyn but whose metabolism runs on selyn as a Gen's metabolism runs on calories.

Gen: An adult human whose body produces selyn but whose metabolism does not consume measurable amounts of selyn.

Transfer: The process by which the Sime absorbs selyn from the Gen, usually resulting in the Gen's death.

Channel: A type of Sime able to take selyn from any Gen without killing and later give that selyn to a Sime to satisfy need and prevent the Sime from killing.

renSime: Any Sime who is not a channel.

Tecton: The organization of channels which undertakes to provide a satisfying transfer for every Sime in order to prevent them from attacking and killing Gens. The Gens donate selyn to the channels, who give it to the renSimes, who are not allowed to take selyn directly from Gens. Only the channels are allowed to satisfy their need for selyn by taking directly from a Gen, called a Donor, who is trained to donate without endangering himself.

13

Distect: A small underground organization which holds that the Tecton channels perpetuate misery and suffering (not to mention perversion) by preventing renSimes from direct transfer with Gens. The Distect believes only the Gen can be responsible for controlling transfer and protecting his own life. It is criminal to demand self-control from a Sime in need.

Need: The urgent demand a Sime experiences when his selyn reserves are running low.

Underdraw: The sensation certain Gens experience when the body has produced too much selyn and no Sime has drawn it off. Underdraw is a pathological condition peculiar to the highest-order Donors—particularly to Gens of the Farris line.

Selyn Field Gradient: The body nimbus perceptible to a Sime caused by the presence of selyn, mathematically akin to the electric field surrounding an electron.

Nager: The nimbus perceptible to a Sime caused by selyn in motion, mathematically akin to the magnetic field surrounding an electron in motion.

Selyur Nager: The mark of the Donor. The ability to harmonize the rate of change of the nager with the Sime's selyn-consumption rate. Few Gens ever achieve any conscious control of this body function; however, it does respond to the emotions the Gen experiences. When a Gen feels empathic sympathy for a Sime's suffering, selyur nager almost invariably occurs, linking the Gen's selyn field to the Sime's selyn field. If the linkage is precise enough, the Gen can control the Sime's selyn-consumption rate, thus dispelling much of the discomfort of need and, to a certain extent, controlling the Sime's emotions. This requires great skill and is commonly considered extremely dangerous. The mathematics of this linkage are akin to that of electrical inductance, and it is thus a reciprocal relationship: the Sime can control the state of the Gen body if a precise attunement can be reached.

Trautholo: A pretransfer state in which such a precise attunement as mentioned above has been achieved. If, at this point, the Donor attempts to withdraw, the Sime's kill reflex is triggered. If trautholo is protracted, a transfer dependency may result.

Transfer Dependency: The state of being able to accept transfer only from a particular Donor. Transfer dependency always accompanies lortuen/torluen/orhuen.

Lortuen: A condition of profound and virtually unbreakable transfer dependency reinforced by both psychological and physical sexual love relationship between a male Sime and female Gen who are matchmates. (Between a female Sime and male Gen, the relationship is called *torluen.* Between the same sex, it is called *orhuen* and excludes a physical sexual relationship.)

Matchmates: A Sime/Gen pair where the Gen's basal selyn-production rate matches the Sime's basal selyn-consumption rate. Matchmates may or may not be of opposite sex, and may or may not fall into a locked transfer dependency.

In-Territory: Inside the borders of Sime country, where the laws and customs are made by and for Simes.

The Ages of Chaos: An interregnum of about a thousand years between the collapse of civilization due to the Sime mutation and the reconstruction around an armed truce, confining all Simes to their island territories.

Fanir: A Donor whose nager has a peculiar property sometimes described as akin to the musician's perfect pitch. Imrahan is a fanir whose nager is quantized in the discreet energy levels which the Tecton has adopted as a reference standard. A fanir affects every Sime near him by drawing that Sime's selyn consumption rate into the fanir's own selyn production rate. The mathematics of the quantization of rates and pitches has not been fully worked out by the Tecton's theoreticists, but most channels are empiricist enough to use even that which they don't fully understand if it works.

Deproda: A nager to nager relationship which can be described only by systems of partial differential equations which contain many singularities and many high order terms. Again, the mathematics has not yet been fully worked out by theoreticists, but channels have been using deproda balances empirically since the days of Rimon Farris, the First Channel.

Fosebine: A mild medicinal preparation made from mutated plants which appeared at about the same time as the Simes themselves. It is used quite a bit as the Ancients and Gens use aspirin, as an analgesic, but also like aspirin, it has definite medicinal qualities in proper doses and can be dangerous in overdoses. It is most effective in transfer shock and transfer burn treatment.

Pilah: A mutant citrus plant which appeared about the same time as the trin plants, i.e., concurrent with the Sime mutation and the breakdown of the Ancients' civilization.

Shen: One of the most common Sime expletives. Literally, it refers to the shock of interrupted transfer. It exists in six main degrees, in order of increasing intensity, they are, Shen, Shendi, Shenoni, Shenshay (which refers basically to transfer abort backlash), Shenshi, Shenshid. There is a milder degree than pure shen, Shuven, and a more intense degree than Shenshid, Shidoni, which refers literally to death by attrition and in some societies at various times in history was the one word never spoken aloud. Each of these expletives has been "gutter talk" at one time and risen to be acceptable in mixed company through usage which causes its shock value to fade.

Dynopter: The unit of selyn quantity.

Shiltpron: A musical instrument invented by Simes to be played with fingers and tentacles. It can be modulated in either audio or selyn field ranges, or even both at once, which can produce intoxication in Simes when done in the presence of Gens.

PART I

THE ARRIVAL

What is the House of Zeor?

Zeor is not a place or a person. Zeor is the striving for perfection, the dedication to excellence, the realization of mankind's fullest potential—Sime and Gen united.

"OUT OF DEATH WAS I BORN—
UNTO ZEOR, FOREVER!"

Klyd Farris
Sectuib in Zeor

Chapter I

BERSERKER

Digen Farris, Head of the House of Zeor, great-great-grandson of the legendary Klyd Farris, walked through the train station waiting room, acutely aware of the people turning to stare at his back. They didn't know who he was; they only knew he was a Sime.

In the dusty little farming town of Sorelton, it was unusual to see a Sime in public. Sorelton was in the heart of Gen Territory, far from the nearest Sime Territory border. All the people in the waiting room were Gen, mostly local people waiting for the big weekly event, the arrival of the train to Westfield.

Naturally, Digen told himself, the retainers, the gleaming metal cuffs peeking from his sleeves, marking him as a Sime, attracted their curiosity, apprehension, even a little fear. In a town like Sorelton, the only Simes they saw with bare forearms were the berserkers intent on using their tentacles to kill Gens.

Digen pushed open the screen door and went out to the platform, letting the door clatter shut behind him. He paused, squinting against the July sun. Before him, the track arrowed out of sight in both directions, a gleaming blue-green ceramic ribbon along which the train would slide on a cushion of air. To his left, an unpaved road wound into the distance between a scattering of houses and farms. To his right, in the only puddle of shade on the platform, one lone Gen sat on his bleached duffel bag, waiting for the slideroad train.

As Digen moved onto the platform, the Gen's attention focused on Digen. Even through the sense-deadening retainers, Digen could feel the man's idle curiosity turn to a sharp stab of alarm as he sighted the gleaming metal at Digen's wrists. But the alarm had an odd quality to it that

19

Digen couldn't quite name. It made his tentacles itch under the retainers.

Digen moved casually toward the far end of the platform, not wanting to distress the Gen any further. At that moment, Inez Tregaskio came out of the women's rest room and saw Digen.

"Oh!" she said in Simelan. "I thought you said you'd wait for me inside."

"The ambient nager in there is so thick I couldn't stand it. In fact, it's not so great out here, either." As he spoke, Digen moved to place Inez between himself and the lone Gen, using her body's selyn field to block the Gen's field.

Inez, a solidly built young woman a little shorter than Digen, was a Gen specially trained to allow a Sime to draw selyn—the very energy of life itself—from her body without harming her. Closing her eyes to concentrate, she put one hand on Digen's arm close to the edge of his retainer, and said, "Better?"

Digen nodded. Her calm, steady, confident emotions soothed him deeply. "The fellow down there is afraid."

"You shouldn't be traveling when you're in need like this."

Gen fear was the trigger that set off the Sime's attack reflex. But Digen was a channel, one of the rare Simes who could take selyn from any Gen without killing, and later transfer that selyn to an ordinary Sime to satisfy his need. Digen would never attack and kill a Gen for selyn. But he was not immune to the reflex.

"I have a nearly perfect Donor waiting for me in Westfield," said Digen. "Just get me there sane, and reasonably stable, and all my troubles will be over." He turned her by the elbow so they could stroll back toward the Gen. "Meanwhile, this fellow's nager interests me. There's something very odd—I wish I weren't wearing retainers!"

"Maybe your perceptions would be clearer without retainers," she answered, "but those nice friendly Gens inside the station would turn into a howling mob ready to kill you, and legally entitled to do it, too, if they could."

"So what should I say, thank God for retainers?" Digen checked his outburst. His frustration was partly due to need, but also to the injustice of a channel having to wear retainers, which immobilized his vital organs, making him virtually incapable of meeting his responsibilities. "Let's get a little closer. Maybe I can get a reading. He's not as afraid now that you're with me, and there's something really strange there—almost as if there were two. . . ."

When they were halfway down the long platform there was a sudden flashing blur of movement behind the seated Gen, and Digen knew what he had only half sensed before. The fearful Gen's nager had masked the low throb of a berserker Sime's nager spiraling down toward the intensity of need. The berserker was no channel, but a renSime intent on killing the Gen.

From his hiding place under the wooden platform the berserker leaped up and over a pile of cargo bales and made straight for the seated Gen. Digen yelled a warning to the Gen and launched himself down the platform, augmenting his natural speed by burning up extra selyn. The Gen had time only to perceive the two Simes coming at him faster than any Gen could move. His spiking panic was a screaming pain to Digen but a delicious promise of fulfillment to the berserker.

Digen arrived the split instant the berserker's fingers touched the Gen's arms. He swept the berserker's hands aside, letting them close instead on his own retainer. With his other hand, Digen grabbed the Gen's arm and yanked the man to his feet, thrusting him aside.

He had a moment then of eye contact with the berserker. The scrawny, mud-caked, adolescent figure resolved into that of a young girl, face twisted in a feral snarl, eyes dilated in the last stages of death by selyn attrition.

Still holding the Gen by one arm, Digen shifted his other hand to capture the girl. By this time, Inez pounded to a stop beside Digen, chest heaving. Digen could not shed the retainers to channel selyn to the berserker. And already the girl was straining toward Inez's more potent selyn field. Digen made an instant decision. "Inez, take care of her!" And he shoved the berserker into the Donor's arms.

Still dragging the terror-stricken Gen behind him absentmindedly, Digen watched the transfer.

The berserker girl's hands closed with bruising Sime strength over Inez's forearms, and simultaneously the Sime's strong handling tentacles lashed out from their sheaths—two along the top of each arm and two along the bottom of each arm—to immobilize the Gen. From the sides of the berserk Sime's arms came the tiny pinkish lateral tentacles, four of them, dripping the selyn-conducting hormone, ronaplin.

As the laterals made contact with Inez's skin, the berserker sought the mouth-to-mouth, lip-to-lip contact necessary to complete the selyn transfer. Inez made the contact willingly, surprising the young Sime.

A moment, and it was all over, the young Sime's need sated. Digen saw her then, a young girl, bruised and battered, blood mixed with the mud-covered, torn clothing. And he knew what her history must be.

Children showed no difference between Sime and Gen. But in the teens, without warning, some children—even the children of Gens—went through changeover, developing the need for selyn and the organs to satisfy that need. Here in Sorelton teen-agers were watched, and any child showing the classic symptoms of changeover was apt to be attacked, beaten to death like some crawling horror out of their elders' own childhood nightmares of going Sime. This girl had escaped during such a beating and hidden herself here under the train platform until her tentacles had matured and broken free. Then, attracted by the Gen's fear of Digen, she had attacked on simple instinct.

Raised out-Territory, she knew nothing of Simes, nothing of what she had become, save that it was loathsome.

Bare seconds had passed since Digen had first pelted past the station-room door. Now, the door came open as people crowded out to see what all the commotion was about. Sighting them, the girl gathered herself to spring for freedom, powered now with the speed and strength of the selyn she had taken.

Digen had to augment to grab and hold her with one hand while with the other he still held the Gen behind him. "Don't be afraid," he said to the girl in her own language. He let her see the retainer encasing his arm. "We'll protect you."

From the door, the Gens had begun to mutter, taking in the situation. Inez moved in front of the girl, taking her other arm. One of the Gens coming out onto the platform said, "It's the Staner girl! She's Sime!" And he made a grab for the rifle kept on the wall inside the door for just such an emergency.

Digen turned to them, raising his voice. "The situation

is under control. Please call the Sime Center and ask them to pick this girl up." *And hurry,* he thought, *because I'm not going to miss that train!*

He turned to the girl and whispered, "You run for it, and they'll hunt you down like an animal." He felt her absorb that with the returning sanity of sated need. "Now, if I let go of you, will you stay with Inez?"

The girl looked up at the Donor. Digen could imagine how confused she must be, trying to assimilate the new information her Sime senses gave her. He said, "Inez is a trained Donor. You can't hurt her, and she can help you feel better."

The girl gave one wary jerk of a nod, and Digen, sensing her decision to stand tight, let go of her arm. The crowd of Gens by the door grumbled as one of them thrust his way through to the front. It was the station-master. He called to Digen, "They're on their way to collect the kid."

"You see?" said Inez to the girl. "They know your family. They don't want to kill you. They only want to protect themselves. Don't scare them and they'll leave you alone. We'll take care of you now."

As she spoke, she took the girl back among the baled goods and sat her down, keeping her own body between the Sime and the crowd of Gens. Digen watched her work with approval, and then became aware of the tense, twisted Gen arm he still held.

The Gen had turned away, eyes squeezed shut, inwardly tensed against the scene that had just played out before them. Digen loosened his grip, placing himself between the Gen and the Sime girl. "Hey, it's all over now. Nothing happened. Nobody's hurt."

Slowly the Gen turned toward Digen and his gaze became fixed on Digen's hand where it held the Gen arm. Digen let go, watching the Gen carefully for signs of lowering blood pressure, shock. But the Gen was still dazed. Noting the mark where his hand had held the man, Digen said, "I'm sorry if I was a little rough. I didn't want you to perturb the fields by moving—uh—injudiciously."

The Gen's eyes finally raised to Digen's, searching the Sime's face. Digen said, "Forgive me?"

"You're a channel?"

Digen nodded.

"You look—Farris. I think. I've never seen a Farris before."

"Digen Farris," he answered, nodding.

"*Doctor* Digen Farris? The one who's going to intern at Westfield Memorial Hospital?"

Digen nodded again. "If I can get there by tomorrow morning so I don't get fired before I've even started."

"They wouldn't fire you just for being late," said the Gen, his voice starting to weaken. "Me, maybe, but not you." The Gen's knees started to sag, and Digen backed him up until his duffel bag was behind his knees.

"Sure they'd fire me," said Digen, urging the Gen to sit. "They'd love to find an excuse." The first Sime to intern in an all-Gen hospital was not going to be welcomed, and Digen knew it. "Put your head between your knees for a minute. You're not hurt. It's only reaction."

The Gen complied, breathing deeply, and then looked up. "I felt her touch me. . . ."

"Only a fingertip. She never got a grip on you."

"It happened so fast . . ." said the Gen in a strangled whisper, and the fear and revulsion seized him again. It was, Digen saw, a reaction far beyond the usual fear of Simes. The man was shaking, with teeth clenched and eyes staring. *He's a Sime-phobe!*

Behind them, the Sime girl had finally broken into her own reaction, crying softly, hopelessly, on Inez's shoulder. Down the platform, the stationmaster had herded the crowd back into the waiting room, shouting over the babble that the pickup wagon from the Sime Center would soon be there.

Way down the track, Digen could sense the train finally approaching.

Digen took the Gen by the shoulders and shook him once, tentatively. He was a big man, taller than Digen, large-boned, gaunt, but still with more muscle on his frame than a Sime would have. Digen took a good grip and shook him hard, saying, "It's all over. Nothing happened. Snap out of it now!"

But the man's stare seemed to have turned inward. It was almost an acute psychotic episode, Digen realized. Gritting his teeth, he drew back his hand and delivered a ringing slap on the Gen's cheek. The man's head turned with the blow, and for a moment Digen was afraid his gambit had failed, for the Gen's head just stayed there.

Then, all at once, the man seemed to shake himself back to life, one hand going to his cheek. "What happened?"

Digen drew back a little, saying, "A touch of hysteria, I think. You're better now."

Collecting himself, the Gen focused on Digen, and for the first time seemed normal. "I'm acting like a fool."

"No," said Digen reassuringly. "That was close. It could have turned into an ugly business. Look," he added, to change the subject, "here comes the train."

The long, crosscountry train was gliding into the station, blowing up dust and grit with a hissing roar until it settled gently to rest, hovering just a finger's breadth above its track its selyn-powered engines idling. Porters began opening doors at each end of the cars, and men swung down to heave the bales into the cargo cars.

Crates and boxes were being unloaded and put into hand-pulled carts, and the stationmaster was darting here and there. Passengers were getting on and off the cars at the far end of the station. As the Gen picked up his bag, offering his thanks, which Digen waved aside, Digen turned to Inez and the girl, gathering them away from the activity, searching the road with all his senses for sign of the Sime Center's wagon, until finally he saw it.

He took the two women around to the side of the station building to meet the wagon, a huge box affair built on a flatbed drawn by four horses. Digen had never seen such a thing outside a museum.

When the wagon drew up, the driver, a short Sime with long black hair tied with a band, jumped down from his perch, saying, "Couldn't get that old engine started, so I brought the horse rig. Hajene Farris? I'm Zale, channel, second order."

"This is the lady we called you about," said Digen, presenting the Sime girl in English. "Inez here will go with you. . . ."

"Digen . . . ?" said Inez. "I'm supposed to be your escort."

"You're required here," said Digen. The girl had stopped crying, and Digen sensed that the two women had established a form of understanding. "You're low field now and couldn't help me much. I want you to stay with her."

"I think," said the driver, "that our local controller ought to sort this out."

"No time," said Digen. "I'm not going to miss that train. Inez, you're released from my service and attached to the Sorelton controller on temporary duty. Stay with the kid as long as you can. I'll see you in Westfield."

The train had finished loading and the stationmaster had begun to give the engineer a signal. Digen turned and ran for the train, bounding up onto the platform and making straight for the nearest passenger car.

Out of sheer habit, the conductor held the door for the tardy passenger, and Digen sidled past and entered the car. But that car was full. He showed his ticket to the conductor and was led ten cars to the rear of the train where the last car was half empty.

Digen dropped into the last seat, facing the end of the train. He stretched out, catching his breath as the train began to pick up speed. Then gradually the strain of it all caught up with him, and between the sickening blur that the retainers made of his world and the even worse violence the moving train did to his senses, he felt suddenly and intensely ill.

He drew into himself, ignoring his need, sustaining his spirits with one thought. He would arrive in Westfield about dawn and would have a good and proper transfer at the Sime Center with the best Donor he'd had in months. Then, when he reported to the Gen hospital, he would be physically and emotionally revived enough to cope with anything they could throw at him.

Chapter 2

A CHOICE

When the train pulled into the outskirts of Westfield, it slowed for the urban traffic. Before long, a Gen came swinging along the car and stopped beside Digen.

"Respect, Sectuib," said the Gen. "I am Imrahan, companion, House of Imil. Sorelton wired ahead that your escort had been diverted. May I help?"

Digen, exhausted from the long ride, yet feeling a bit better now that the train had slowed, said, "Please sit down."

The man folded himself into the seat beside Digen. He was no taller than Digen, but had the typical Gen build, well-developed musculature padded out by a healthy layer of body fat. He spoke the Sime language with an in-Territory accent, music to Digen's ears. "Thank you, Sectuib Farris. The controller sent me to meet you and give you a message."

Digen could feel the swirl of tension in the Gen. In an effort to put him at ease, Digen said, "House of Zeor offers respect to House of Imil, but these are modern times. I don't think the titles are necessary, Im'ran."

Im'ran smiled, a bit more at ease.

Digen noticed then how the Gen had already begun to lock into Digen's nager with a casual precision. It was like a solid, steady hand offered in support of a precarious balance. Instantly Digen relaxed into the familiar hold, luxuriating in it. In seconds, the almost palpable emotions of the Gens at the other end of the car receded from his consciousness, the sickening blur of the outside world steadied, and, best of all, the insistent *do something, do something, do something* of need that had been building relentlessly for hours suddenly turned to *ah, at last!*

This caused Digen to turn his head and focus his eyes on the man in startlement. The Gen was low field, very low field. He'd obviously donated selyn very recently, possibly even within the last twelve hours. Very few Donors, even first-order Donors, could alleviate the rising tide of need in a channel while they themselves were in such a low-field condition.

The Gen sat inspecting his fingertips, searching for words to say something that was obviously very difficult. The silence stretched until Digen said, "You have some sort of bad news for me, Im'ran?"

The Donor sighed heavily. "I was to be your assigned Donor. But, as you can see, that's impossible. I've already had transfer."

Digen froze, stunned into unblinking silence. Though the deeper, more primitive part of his mind no longer screamed the panic of rising need, suddenly his conscious intellect knew he would get no decent transfer this month. *There can't be two like Im'ran in Westfield. There can't be.*

Digen became aware of the cool, Gen hands covering his own, intensifying the contact between them. The Gen's slow, steady pulse of selyn production pulled Digen into a soothing relaxation.

"Sectuib Farris, I'm sorry. I know it's been a long time for you—too long."

Struggling to come to terms with the blow, Digen absently rubbed at his left-arm retainer, just over the outer lateral tentacle.

Im'ran's hand covered his, and the Gen asked, "The scar pains you?"

"The famous lateral scar," said Digen wryly. He was the only Sime who had ever survived such a deep cut through the vital selyn-transport nerves of a lateral tentacle. "It takes a very special Donor to get a transfer into me through that scar without a series of transfer aborts."

"Controller Mickland—he's controller for the city as well as for the district of Westfield—he sent me to prepare you to make a choice."

Digen sat up straight and looked at Im'ran with his eyes as well as his other senses. "A choice of Donors?"

Im'ran shrugged. "Mickland is a very strange individual."

"Mmmm," said Digen. "Tell me about this choice."

"Mickland has been on the hotwire all night scouring

the coast for available Donor matches. It took a nine-way controllers' conference to free someone for you."

"Well then, who?"

"Ben Seloyan."

"Seloyan?" Digen had worked with Seloyan several times. The man was good, but not as good as Imrahan, and nowhere near what Digen was due. "Is he in phase with me?"

"Not quite. It will be two and a half days early for him."

"He'll be low field then." Seloyan at his highest selyn field wasn't really adequate for Digen. "What's the rest of the bad news?"

"It will take him a little more than two days to get here."

"I don't want to hear about the second choice if it's any worse than the first."

"Maybe," said Im'ran, "you should come and meet your second choice. I really don't know how to describe her."

The train was inching to a stop at its platform at Westfield Terminal. The Gen passengers were crowding into the aisles and a conductor came to open the door nearest Digen.

It wasn't far from the train terminal to Westfield's Sime Center, a towering building in the middle of town, situated right on the Territory border which bisected the city.

The moment they stepped across that border into Sime Territory, Digen stripped off the cumbersome retainers, freeing his tentacles and clearing his head. He felt much better by the time they took the elevator straight up to the controller's ninth-floor offices.

The inner office was spacious, carpeted in thick, luxurious green, with gold upholstery and drapes. A large, polished oak desk at the focal point of the room had the ornate look of modern Gen carving—a gift from out-Territory, Digen surmised. In one corner, a trophy case was lighted softly from within, displaying a number of statues and awards, while one black velvet wall was covered with plaques and certificates. The room had an unused, formal appearance, save for the rows of chart boards standing beside the desk.

Digen gained only a quick, flash impression of all this: *Typical controller's front office, a well-run Sime Center.* The moment the door opened before him, the nager within the room washed over him stunningly. Im'ran stepped in front of Digen, attempting to shield him, but the Gen was far too low field.

With his eyes Digen saw Controller Mickland, a channel of medium height, standing behind his desk. He was broad-shouldered enough to look shorter than he really was, and though, like all Simes, he scarcely carried eight per cent body fat, his large-boned frame gave him an imposing, Gen look.

Facing Mickland, shouting her outraged indignation in a clear soprano, was the Gen woman who was the source of the overwhelming nager. She was petite but had a full figure. Her dark auburn hair was long, caught up high and then allowed to spill freely over her shoulders.

"Qualify?" the woman was shrieking at Mickland. "Qualify? What makes you think I want to become one of your—your—*blensheyla eyeofi!* You think it's some kind of privilege that I have to earn by proving I can do it? You think it takes some kind of special skill to go up to a strange Sime and just let him—just passively let him take selyn? You think it would do the poor Sime any good? Look, I—I have to have transfer. You just find me a channel in need and I'll take care of him."

Im'ran said quietly to Digen, "There's your second choice. Ilyana Dumas. She's Distect."

"Shenshid!" said Digen involuntarily.

The woman turned to look at Digen, hope in her eyes.

The Distect. A myth. The shattered remnants of the House of Rior—the only real opposition the Tecton had ever faced. A hundred years ago, the Tecton was just a loose confederacy of householdings. At that time, any channel, discovering that he did not have to kill Gens for selyn, could found a householding, gathering about himself a number of Gens to provide selyn and a number of ren-Simes who swore to take selyn only from a channel, thus never again killing a Gen.

Then, Klyd Farris, Sectuib in Zeor, had engineered a coup in which the Tecton had taken over the Sime government and signed a treaty with the Gen government, accepting for the channels the responsibility of preventing renSimes from killing in transfer. Klyd Farris thus founded the modern Tecton. All the sovereign houses had signed the agreement, except the House of Rior, which held that the Tecton's avowed ideal—the reuniting of the human race, the eradicating of the mutual fear and distrust between Sime and Gen—could not be served by a society in which the only direct Sime/Gen transfers, the transfers between channel and Donor, were depersonalized and regulated by the rigid and sterile Tecton code.

The House of Rior, under its Gen leader Hugh Valleroy, had broken away from the new Tecton and founded the Distect, dedicated to giving every renSime his own Gen Donor, doing away with the channel intermediary.

Mickland said, "Ilyana, either you will qualify, taking oath as a Tecton Donor, or no channel will touch you."

She looked from Mickland to Digen, pleading. Digen, steeling himself inwardly, advanced into the room. Before he'd gone two paces past Im'ran, Ilyana's nageric fluctuations had locked in step with his own; but where Im'ran had brought Digen into one of the precisely quantized Tecton standard rhythms, this woman had locked on to Digen and let him drift into whatever natural, nonstandard rhythm his metabolism chose, following him effortlessly.

It was unsettling. Digen stood poised on the brink of dire need, controlling his natural reflex to seize and strip one or the other of these two powerful Donors, as only a lawless, killer Sime would. Fighting this predatory instinct so deep in every Sime, Digen looked from one to the other, forcing his mind to analyze their fields' effects on him.

Im'ran moved to Digen's side, trying, despite his depleted field, to fight Ilyana for control of Digen. And, strangely, though the man couldn't win, he could hold Ilyana at bay.

Im'ran is a fanir, Ilyana is a drifter—a high-order drifter but still a drifter. Given his choice, Digen would have preferred the precisely quantized, dead-true fanir to a drifter. But Im'ran had already served in transfer, and Ilyana was high field. At any rate, she'd be better than Ben Seloyan— and she was here, now. *But she's Distect!*

Legend had it that any Tecton channel who accepted transfer from a Distect Donor would end up junct—unsatisfied with anything except a kill-mode transfer.

Digen could see Mickland's dilemma. As controller, Mickland simply couldn't turn the Sectuib in Zeor over to a Distect Gen—it would be political suicide.

She was watching him carefully as he took in the situation. Digen said, "The controller is right—no channel would surrender control of a transfer to an unqualified Gen. We work too many years, sacrifice too much, to gain control of our vriamic functions to risk letting an untrained Gen cripple that function for life. But—Ilyana—if you will give me your word that you won't contest control, that you'll submit to a qualifying transfer with me, then I will let Controller Mickland assign you to me—right now."

As he spoke, Digen moved closer to her. He perceived immediately that this woman was something special. Her nager had a texture and power he hadn't felt except with his sister, Bett. But her name was Ilyana *Dumas*, not Farris. She didn't even look Farris. And then he realized what it was about her that seemed so familiar—*underdraw*.

As he approached, she stood fascinated, unable to move or speak. But, the moment Digen saw the nature of her illness, he stopped in his tracks, realizing that with every step closer he was aggravating her disorder.

The moment he stopped, she whipped around to confront Mickland, her voice rising in hysteria. "I came here begging for help, throwing myself on the much-vaunted mercy of the Tecton. And what do I get? A lousy ultimatum!"

Digen strode to the corner of Mickland's desk, trying to put the other Sime's field between him and the woman, while motioning urgently to Im'ran to step between them, to protect Ilyana from Digen's aching need, which was sending her selyn-production rate soaring, causing her the physical and mental stress which—if not relieved by transfer—would ultimately kill her, either by simply burning up her body physically, or by driving her to commit suicide. Her hysteria was just another symptom of the disease.

This put an entirely different complexion on the situation. But before Digen could speak, Mickland said, "I'm sorry, Hajene Farris, she's Distect. And she's getting more desperate by the minute. I wouldn't trust her now if she did promise to qualify."

Ilyana strode to the desk and slapped her hand down on it so hard that both Digen and Mickland flinched as they felt her pain, amplified by her wildcatting selyn nager. "If *I* made any promise," she said, "I'd keep it, though I wouldn't expect any—*channel*—to understand that." The way she said "channel," it became a filthy epithet. "Tecton!

You think you know so much about transfer, but you don't seem to know anything about life. It's just not possible for any Sime to have a satisfactory transfer where he has to control the selyn flows. I wouldn't give that kind of transfer to the most evil person in the world. I'm no—prostitute."

Digen summoned all his much-vaunted Farris control and approached her. He was at once both deathly afraid of this woman and irresistibly attracted to her. Concentrating to shift into the channel's functional mode, protecting his personal, primary selyn-transport system from the effect of her nager, he eased a little closer to her, engaging the edges of her field, reaching to control her selyn-production rate by using his own system as a governor.

As Mickland perceived what Digen was doing, his eyes went wide. He was frozen for a moment in sheer disbelief. No channel in the entire world other than Digen Farris, Sectuib in Zeor, could have thought of trying what Digen was doing right before his eyes. Digen felt Mickland's incredulity on the periphery of his mind. *Am I just showing off?* thought Digen. *No. This has to be done. For her.*

It was working, too. Her selyn-production rate was dropping slowly, and that kept Mickland silent as Digen said, his voice an octave lower as he went deeper into the delicate channel's work, balancing on the fine edge of disaster, "It is the nature of the channel to control the Gen, Ilyana. The Donor must be trained never to fear—because only if he fears can harm come to him."

Still leaning on the desk, Ilyana twisted to look at Digen, apparently confused by the relief washing through her body as well as by Digen's words. *"Trained* never to fear?" she said. "Never to fear what?"

He was close to her now, towering over her slight form, standing on the very margin of her inner core field and controlling it utterly. But it was an effort to spare attention from that to say, "Simes, of course—what else?"

Totally bewildered, she said, "What do you mean, trained? You can't *train* a Gen not to fear transfer as if you were toilet training a baby. Some do, some don't, that's all. Look, if you people are not going to talk sense . . ."

"Wait—wait," said Digen. "Hold it." He suddenly understood the magnitude of the cultural gap between them.

She really is from the Distect. It's real. It still exists some-place.

Outside of Sime Territory, the Gens who lived together without Simes around, who lived in fear of Simes, like those people at the train station in Sorelton, had been convinced that the last remnants of the Distect way of life had long since been stamped out. But apparently, somewhere in some isolated spot, it still existed. And Ilyana was a defector from that way of life—because, with her disease, she had to have channel's transfer, nothing less would do, and in the Distect there were no functioning channels—and thus no trained Donors. Yet Ilyana seemed perfectly competent and easily matched to the depth of his need. *Don't think about that, not yet.*

"Ilyana," started Digen, "I—" He broke off, turning to Mickland. "You gave me a choice between Ilyana and Ben Seloyan. I choose Ilyana. Seloyan doesn't have the capacity to supply my need, Ilyana does. Seloyan doesn't have the speed I require. In my judgment, Ilyana does. There really is no choice between them. And, in all humanity, you must admit, she—needs this as much as I do."

Looking wearily askance at Digen, Mickland said, "When you first came in here, it surely seemed you were in need. But now . . ."

A surge of anger tightened in Digen, and momentarily his control slipped. He recovered, though, before a flutter became perceptible in her field strength, and said to Mickland, his voice relaxed, "I'm in need all right. And if you'll check your records, you'll see I've been shorted in transfer now for twenty-two consecutive months, assigned—because nobody else was available—to people like Seloyan. I was promised Im'ran and I don't know or care how you botched it, but you're controller here, you're responsible for getting me a Donor comparable to Im'ran. Seloyan is not comparable. Ilyana—*is.*"

"She's Distect."

"So what? Or do you believe every silly myth and legend and fairy tale in kids' books or horror stories? Isn't it obvious that I control her?"

Mickland looked—with all his Sime senses—at Ilyana, who darted a thoughtful glance at Digen. "You're doing that?"

Absently, Digen nodded, watching Mickland. "So you

see, Controller, it's perfectly safe. But it's not just the convenience of a good transfer. In a few hours I have to show up over at the Gen hospital, prepared to go to work as an intern there. I don't expect it to be easy. I doubt I can do it at all—without a good transfer. I really am on the ragged edge."

"You certainly don't sound like it, and you don't behave like it."

Im'ran said, "You didn't see him on the train. You can't penalize him just because he's a good channel. He *can* control, sure—he had to learn it to survive that lateral injury. And—he's Sectuib in Zeor. Haven't you ever worked with a Zeor channel? Don't you know the kind of control the Zeor training builds into them? And the Sectuib—the best of them all?"

Mickland shook his head in disgust. "Householder evasions. I should have known you'd side with him."

Uh-oh, thought Digen. *Mickland is antihouseholder*. That was just the wrong kind of controller for him to have to work under. The householdings still dominated the Tecton, and Digen, as head of the most prestigious of the householdings, was the acknowledged leader of all the householding channels. Lately, though, the nonhouseholding channels had begun to accuse the householders of forming a hereditary aristocracy within the Tecton. The loudest spokesmen of this group were those whose parents had not been householders. Mickland, Digen concluded, must be one of those.

Digen shot Im'ran a glance, nodding his gratitude. The Gen had chosen an oblique but effective way of warning Digen. A quick change of tactics was in order. Technically, Digen outranked Mickland—if not by householder status, then by the law of the Tecton, simply because his proficiency rating was higher than Mickland's. Yet, Mickland was controller, and it could only undermine the already precarious structure of the Tecton if he pulled rank on his controller. So he had to win Mickland's support—and he had to have Ilyana. That was becoming increasingly clear with every moment.

Digen's eye fell on the black file with the Zeor blue stripe blazoned across it and the channel's crest embossed in the corner. He pointed with one handling tentacle. "If you'll check my file, you'll find the World Controller's special dispensation to study medicine in the Gen schools —and, now to continue that study as an intern at Westfield Memorial Hospital."

In response, Mickland flipped open the file to that beribboned and embossed page. "I never have understood how you got this—unless . . ."

"No," said Digen, "it wasn't some under-the-table, householding tradeoff deal. Simple logic. When I recovered from the lateral injury, they discovered that the scar would keep me from working again as a channel—at least for most ordinary functionals. I wouldn't last an hour in the collectorium—not five minutes in the dispensary. Collecting and dispensing selyn is simply beyond my abilities—forever. Sure, I can do some fancy and exotic specialty functionals—like this one—the kind of thing you might encounter once a month if that often. But that won't pay for my transfers. Yet it does give me the ability to work in that hospital—where any other channel would simply collapse from the shrieking nager of Gen suffering.

"So the World Controller," said Digen, emphasizing the title to appeal to Mickland's reverence for authority, "decided to use me to try to bring a new skill—a new healing technique—in-Territory."

"Surgery!" said Mickland. "You can't tell me the World Controller is in favor of this!"

Digen pointed mutely to the certificate and shrugged. *No, of course I can't tell you that. But you can assume it.* "Oh," said Digen, "you will note that I will be working here in the Sime Center eight hours a day. Administrative, not functional, work."

"And I intend to take full advantage of that. You will be in charge of the changeover ward and the in-Territory collectorium. Mora Dyen is overworked managing three departments."

"All the more reason that it makes no sense to deny me a full transfer. There's work to be done. But I can't do it like this!"

Mickland eyed Digen silently. Digen knew that the man wanted him to go into that hospital in need and be brought home on a stretcher in disgrace. It would be a quick and satisfying end to the threat of having to face surgery—the idea of cutting flesh, the ripping, tearing, flashing destruction of selyn-replete cells grating through the empathic

nerve of a Sime roused a primitive lust for the kill transfer, the kind of lust that modern Tecton culture was
designed to repress totally.

For a long, suspended moment, Digen and Mickland
faced each other across that huge, polished desk.

Ilyana said, "I don't pretend to understand your crazy
laws, but—you are choosing me, aren't you?"

Eyes on Mickland, Digen nodded. "I want to."

It was only then that he began to notice what she had
been doing. She was much closer to him now, engulfing
him in the inner fire of her nager. In a flash, his firm control over her vanished, and he became subject to her will,
control of the fields wrested from his grasp so smoothly
that he barely felt it.

Her hands slid up his arms, stroking the bulging tentacle sheaths that lay along the arm from elbow to wrist.
As her cool fingers came to the hard, swollen ronaplin
glands, halfway up along the side of each forearm, under
the lateral tentacle sheaths, Digen sucked breath through
his teeth. The ache of need spread through his whole
body, and the ronaplin glands responded, pouring their
selyn-conducting hormone into the lateral sheaths as the
small, delicate transfer organs flicked in and out of the
orifices on the side of each wrist.

Expertly then, she seized him, using gentle pressure on
the reflex ganglions to bring his tentacles into transfer
position along her arms. Dazed and giddy with it, he
found himself bending to make the fifth point contact
with his lips against hers.

Digen's need rose to transfer pitch. Glands poured secretions into his mouth, his blood, his brain, heightened all
his senses in a way he hadn't experienced in far too long
to remain aloof from it now. The room blackened around
him, illuminated to his Sime sense only by Ilyana's field.

On the edge of hearing, a voice said, "What do you
think you're doing?"

It was just enough to make Digen hesitate before the
contact would be complete. He came to normal awareness,
knowing now it was Mickland speaking. "I haven't given
you any assignment!"

Digen was unable to move. It was all he could do to
hold himself away from that unsanctioned transfer con-

tact—and he knew that if he completed the circuit, he
would draw his fill from her, despite his famed control.

In a ragged hiss, he said, "Then make the shendi-fleckin
assignment!"

Suddenly the doors burst inward, and Simes and Gens
came running into the room. The shock was, to Digen,
pure, paralyzing shen, transfer interruption, and it was
then he realized how close he had been to an illegal
transfer.

He yanked his hands away from her, sheathing his
tentacles, then massaging his arms with his hands. "It's all
right!" he called to the guards, stopping them halfway into
the office. "The Sectuib in Zeor does not have to be
physically restrained to obey a lawful controller's directive."

Digen knew Mickland had summoned the guards.

"Why?" said Ilyana. "I don't understand why you did
that."

"It's the law," said Digen.

Mickland, coming around the desk with Im'ran at his
side, said, "Am I seeing things, or—" He looked, both
with eyes and with Sime senses, from Ilyana to Digen and
back, beckoning to one of the Simes by the door, a large
man with a limp. "Rin, do you see it, too?"

The Sime, a first-order channel, compared the two of
them and said, "They're matchmates!"

"I thought so—not just close, but actually matched!"

Matchmates? thought Digen, looking at Ilyana. Yes,
that would explain it, the terrible grip she had on him. Her
basal selyn-production rate was equal to his basal selyn-
consumption rate.

Mickland looked at the new channel. "We can't expose
him to a possible lortuen with *her!*"

The man's head moved faintly in negation. He was still
studying Digen. Digen thought the man looked familiar
but couldn't place him.

"All right," said Mickland. "Then this is official. Ilyana
Dumas will be off Digen's transfer-rotation list, and she
is to be kept away from him. Rin, you have charge of her.
Keep her in your lab."

The big Sime seized Ilyana and drew her away from
Digen. Digen held himself hard against the pull of that
parting. He would not betray how difficult it was. *Match-*

mates! Locked for a lifetime in transfer dependency with a Distect woman? He shook himself, turned, and walked to the door, intent only on maintaining his control.

Behind him, Mickland shoved Im'ran after Digen. "Digen is your responsibility now. You'll have him on your therapy list—exclusive—for the next two months at least. He'll pick up slack with Ben Seloyan this month, and next month you will have him on assignment—twice in a row, Im'ran. Keep him away from her!"

That registered only dimly with Digen. All eyes in the room followed him as he went out, closing the door softly behind him. He was eight paces into the strange room before he realized he had gone the wrong way. It was the controller's inner office, the workroom/library, where the real job of running Westfield was done.

Row after row of shelving, file cases of charts, and stacks of books jammed the long, narrow room. In a crowded corner near the office door was an old, scarred desk overflowing with stacks of papers, card files, well-thumbed reference books, and an assortment of calculating instruments.

As Digen stood, astonished, the office door opened and Im'ran came in, closing it behind him. Digen began to shake all over and then sank to the floor. His control failed him all at once, sending his selyn-consumption rate soaring. Need ruled.

Im'ran knelt beside Digen, ignoring the danger to himself. With little selyn in his body to give, he could not face a kill-mode attack and live. "You're wasting yourself," he said to Digen. "We've got to get you stabilized. Relax. I can do it if you let me."

And, miraculously, he did. Careful, cool, precise, Im'ran's antidote to the Distect was the Tecton's impersonal standard applied with a tender competence. It took the therapist three hours, but at last Digen dropped into a deep, natural sleep. However much the workroom was required, no one disturbed them.

Chapter 3

'A GEN ROOMMATE

The sign on the door said, DOCTOR HOWARD BRANOFF, DIRECTOR, WESTFIELD MEMORIAL HOSPITAL. Digen rested his fingers on the handle. Behind him, Gens strode up and down the intersecting corridors of the hospital, intent on their own business. The whole building throbbed with a collective, ambient nager—overtones of pain, narcosis, worry, anxiety, and death dominated.

He wished forlornly that the hospital were as well insulated as the Sime Center. *But it's not,* he thought, *and I'll have to stand it anyway.* After a couple of hours' sleep under Im'ran's skilled care, he was again in the state of dulled, chronic need in which he had lived the last two years of medical school. *I can do it,* he told himself.

Pushing all doubts aside, he opened the door and went into the waiting room. A secretary came out of the inner office. Digen said, "I was told to report to the director. Some problem about my room, I believe?"

She looked him over, eyeing the retainers peeking from his sleeves, and said, "Dr. Farris? Won't you have a seat, please?"

Digen picked up a magazine and settled into one of the armchairs, while the woman went back inside. He was worried. He had reported to the front desk, expecting to receive his room assignment, work hours, and ward assignment routinely, like all the other interns reporting in today. Already, at the very first step, he was being singled out. Why?

His eye fell on the magazine in his lap, and he recognized its blazing orange and blue cover. It was the latest issue of *The Surgeons' Society Journal.* The lead article headlined on the cover was: SIME GRADUATES LASSER; an evaluation. He flipped to the page and began reading. It seemed to be a fair article, not shrill or hysterical, but in the end the author turned bitterly against Westfield for accepting Digen as an intern: "When the foremost surgical service in the country accepts such an intern, how can the rest of the hospitals turn any of them down?"

Digen let the pages riffle shut. *They're afraid,* he thought. *Surgery has always been the one profession no Sime could ever enter. They're afraid that if I make it, hordes of Simes will follow, taking surgery away from Gens completely.*

From the Gen point of view, it was a perfectly rational fear. Sime dexterity could not be matched by any Gen. Sime endurance in the physically arduous practice of any branch of medicine had always given Digen an edge. When his fellow students were exhausted from long hours in the lab, running from building to building, and working their stints in the hospital, and when they then had to take an exam bleary from lack of sleep, Digen was still fresh enough to tackle anything at top mental capacity. That had lost him many potential friends along the way. He suspected it would not make him popular as an intern, either.

Out-Territory Gens tended to view Simes as basically superior and therefore a perpetual threat in any competitive situation. Medicine was highly competitive, both physically and intellectually. For every opening in a good medical school there were a hundred applicants. For every internship in a great teaching hospital there were ten equally qualified applicants. Digen had won his place against a field of thousands, all Gens, and all convinced that they would have been chosen had Digen not been Sime.

What they did not know was that Digen, because of his unique lateral injury, was probably the only Sime who would ever be able—or willing—to attempt to learn surgery. Fighting his way back to life after the injury, Digen had developed a vriamic control never before seen in any channel. It allowed him to withstand the peculiar, grating shock of slicing or puncturing Gen flesh much better than could other Simes.

In-Territory, it was commonly believed that the first steps back toward the kill, toward going junct, were exposure to Gen pain, fear, or injury—inflicting such sensations on Gens—and then sharing the junct's strange gratification in these things. All through medical school, Digen had faced frequent demands that he be tested for any hint of a weakening of his antikill conditioning. He had always tested clean—so far. But he couldn't use that as an argument with the Gens, because, if they suspected surgery might cause him to turn junct, he would never complete his internship.

Digen eyed the door to the inner office. Maybe it was all going to be for nothing, anyway. Why would they call him up here on his first day?

The secretary returned, saying, "You may go in now." She gave him a tentative smile. She was an out-Territory Gen unaccustomed to dealing with Simes. Digen made a fatalistic shrug and went in.

The office was larger than Mickland's and just as formal. The man behind the desk was white-haired and had a ruddy complexion; he was perhaps fifty-five or sixty. From the large windows behind him, the early afternoon sun threw beams across the desk, spotlighting the two file folders that lay there.

"Dr. Branoff," said Digen, coming across the deep red carpet toward the desk. "You wanted to see me about something?"

As Digen neared the two high-backed wing chairs before the desk, he realized one was occupied. "Oh!" he said, as he recognized the Gen he had rescued in Sorelton.

What has he told Branoff? Digen looked back at the administrator, wishing he could read minds. He could see that the older man was tense, grave, but not openly hostile.

Branoff gestured to the empty chair. "Have a seat, Dr. Farris. Let me introduce Dr. Joel Hogan."

Hogan had his elbows propped on the arm of the chair, which pushed his shoulders up around his ears. He was avoiding Digen's gaze, and his nager was a muddy swirl of mixed emotions. Branoff reached into a drawer and pulled out an orange and blue magazine, shoving it across the desk at Digen. "Have you seen this?"

"I glanced at it in your outer office, sir."

"I've been in an emergency board meeting all morning, discussing it. It's only been out forty-eight hours, and already pressure is being brought to bear on this hospital."

Digen nodded. It was to be expected. It had been the

same when he'd finally been accepted into a medical school. Lasser had withstood it because they were the best, they had enough prestige to afford it.

Branoff slapped the magazine against the desk. "I've never knuckled under to this kind of pressure in my life, and I don't intend to start now. But I think you're entitled to know what's going on. I've just come from a meeting with a committee of our new interns. Five have threatened to quit unless you are dismissed immediately."

Digen looked at Hogan. *Is he one of the ones who has threatened to quit?*

"The board," continued Branoff, "is very disturbed at the idea of losing five interns over this. So I offered the interns and the board a compromise. You were hired as a surgical intern, to go directly into the surgical ward. Instead, you will be put into the general program."

Digen sighed with relief. It would be harder to get a surgical residency, but at least the door wasn't slammed in his face. And he would still get to do some surgery. "Thank you, sir."

"A man who's just been axed doesn't usually say thank you. Didn't you want the spot?"

"Yes, sir. You know I did. Almost every day I have to watch somebody die in-Territory, somebody who could be saved by surgical techniques. I see people survive, only to live crippled because we don't have those techniques. Sometimes—sometimes they're my patients, people I'm responsible for. And all the time I know that the skills to save them are practiced routinely. And I know that I can learn those skills. And I watch my people die. I nearly died myself, when I was fourteen."

There was a silence. The two men who had dedicated their lives to medicine could not contemplate such a situation without sharing Digen's feelings; and the Gens, projecting his feelings back at him, magnified them painfully.

"Yes," said Branoff, "I can understand your single-minded pursuit of surgery in that context. Nevertheless, my colleagues insist on seeing you as a threat. And they're going to do everything they can think of to stop you. This may be a lot harder than you expect it to be."

"I won't know if I can do it until I try. I'm grateful to be allowed to try."

Branoff eyed him thoughtfully, and then, seeming to

come to a decision, said, "By shuffling schedules around, I've managed to put together a program for you that will give you a full six months on the surgical service, a lot more than a general intern usually gets."

Digen brightened. "Thank *you*, sir."

"Don't thank me," said Branoff. "Thank Dr. Hogan, here. He gave up his own surgical internship and split his surgical-ward time with you, so you'll both have six months."

Digen's head whipped around to Hogan. "Why . . ."

Their eyes locked for the first time since they had parted to board the train. Hogan flushed with embarrassment, and said in a deeper accent than usual, "I don't like to see everybody gang up against one guy, is all. You deserve a chance like the rest of us."

"Have you really thought this through?" asked Digen. "There's such a power structure aligning against me—if you're going to take my side, they'll attack you too. It could ruin your career."

Hogan's eyes went to Branoff.

"They tried to buy him off," said Branoff to Digen. "That was when he threw his appointment in their faces and stalked out of the interns' meeting. I'm afraid you've got a friend whether you like it or not."

"I've got a terrible temper," said Hogan. "But in all my life I've never regretted anything I did on an angry impulse, and I don't expect to regret this."

Digen fell silent. *An ally can be a terrible responsibility*, he thought. *Especially if he's a Sime-phobe.*

"Well, that's settled, then," said Branoff, shuffling his folders around. "Only one more item. We have twenty-four interns on staff this year, and only twelve rooms. I know I promised you a room to yourself, Dr. Farris, but the new building won't be ready until late next spring, if then, so everybody has to double in the old building. When your assigned roommate found out who he was doubling with, he started this whole thing. So I asked for volunteers. There was only one."

"It's all right with me, sir. I've been assigned to double with someone all through college and med school." And then it dawned on him who the volunteer would be. He eyed Hogan apprehensively. The last two years his roommate had been a third-order Donor, and it had been no strain at all. He was used to the luxury.

"Yeah," said Hogan. "Who else?"

Biting his lip, Digen said, "There's another way. I've already been assigned quarters in the Sime Center residence tower—the new one, on this side of the center. It's hardly a ten-minute walk away, and I can have a direct phone patch put in."

"That would be the most reasonable solution to the problem," said Branoff. "However, the men who sit on the accreditation board were raised in the days when medicine was taught like a religion of revealed secrets. And those rules are still on the books. All interns, like medical students, have to reside on the grounds of the hospital in regulated and inspected accommodations. And in Westfield, we regulate and inspect to the letter."

Digen understood part of the rationale for that. Medicine had borne most of the blame, in the popular Gen mind, for the mutation of the human race into Sime and Gen. The irresponsible use of drugs and certification of chemicals as safe for release to the environment had come about, people had believed, through the low moral standards of the men of medicine. The medical profession was determined to see that they were never blamed again.

Branoff said, "I know it's ridiculous to hold you to the residency rule after you've already been through four years of it. But in your case, with more than half the medical profession just aching for an excuse to dismiss you, any request for special treatment, any bending of the rules, will be due cause for dismissal. If it has to come, I'd rather it came over some significant issue, something related to your competency as a surgeon, not your popularity among ignorant Gens."

"That's another thing, Digen," said Hogan. "When they get to know you, I don't think they'll be so frightened. Give it some time."

All because I saved his life—doing nothing more than my job? "You don't know me," said Digen.

"I've spent all winter studying up on you, ever since I found out you'd be here. Fifteen biographies, in English alone, and every translated article I could lay hands on. And—we met in Sorelton. I believe the biographies now."

Digen got up and paced around behind Hogan's chair.

Need was driving him to an insuppressible restlessness. He came in front of Hogan and half sat against the desk. "I don't think you really appreciate all you'd be getting into. I don't wear retainers in my room. I have a Diplomatic Corps sign I post on the door that makes it legally Sime Territory. I've been using it since I was a high-school exchange student and lived in a Gen house. I couldn't survive any other way. About ten hours in retainers is my limit."

Hogan said, "I thought you wanted to be a surgeon. But you keep trying to slam the door in your own face. Don't you have the courage of your convictions?"

"Of course I . . . !" Digen bit off the retort. His need made him altogether too sensitive for such a discussion. "I'm sorry," he said, and went on in a cooler tone, "Joel, you have no idea how many times my courage has been tested since I starterd this, or in what ways. I'm used to opposition. I'm not used to help."

Branoff broke in. "So accept the offer gracefully, and go somewhere to work out your modus vivendi. I've got work to do, and you've only got three hours before you go on duty in the emergency ward."

Chapter 4

HONEST CONFRONTATION

As they made their way through the hospital, Digen tried to get Hogan to admit his mixed motives. But the more Digen insisted, the more evasive Hogan became.

They got off the elevator on the top floor. Hogan began to stroll down the hall, gnawing his bottom lip. "I've never met anyone like you before, Digen. This actually may be a lot harder than I ever thought." An honest belligerence crystallized in the Gen. Moving with exaggerated slowness for a Sime, Digen came to Hogan's side, and reached to touch his shoulder firmly, but gently enough not to frighten. Inside, Digén was coiled to peak alertness. In his condition, he had to be very careful. "Joel."

The Gen stopped at the intersection of two corridors, permitting the touch, but inwardly shrinking from Digen. "It's true. I'm scared. You scare me. Simes scare me."

"I've known that all along," said Digen. "But I was afraid you didn't know it. Now that you can admit it, to me, to yourself, we can begin. An honest friendship. No deceptions."

Hogan looked at Digen. "But how can you—I tried to tell myself I wasn't afraid because—I— Isn't Gen fear . . ."

Digen could almost read the Gen's mind in the silence. Digen tightened his grip, touching the Gen's hand with the fingers of his other hand. "This is what channeling·is all about—being exposed to a Gen's fear and just not reacting."

Hogan stared at Digen's fingers, at the retainers visible at his cuffs. Digen said, "Somehow, I don't think the corridor is the best place to discuss this."

Hogan pulled himself up, composed his face into its usual long planes, and said, "Our room is number ten, at the end around the corner."

They walked into the side hall, passing between rows

of doors to interns' rooms. As they neared the end, one
room door was ajar, a babble of voices spilling into the
hall with hard, hollow echoes. Hogan said, "I have to get
my things. The stationmaster sent yours up already. They're
in the room."

Digen's impulse was to follow Hogan into the room
and help him carry things. But, even though he was still
keyed up, guarding himself, he didn't want to dive into
the ambient nager of that room, choked with hostility as
it was. He knew he still had a long way to go with Hogan
this afternoon and he couldn't afford to overtax himself.

Knocking perfunctorily on the door, Hogan went in.
The room fell silent. Digen was able to distinguish eleven
Gens in the room. Hogan said to them, "It's all settled. I'm
rooming with him, so he's staying."

"Not for long," said somebody.

"You're making a mistake," said another.

"We'll see," answered Hogan levelly.

In a moment Hogan emerged, dragging a footlocker
with two large cases stacked on it. Bracing himself, Digen
stepped into the direct line from the open door, reaching
for the handle of an enormous, old-fashioned record player
and a dilapidated old suitcase. He heaved the suitcase to
the floor and picked up the footlocker before Hogan really
understood what he was doing. "I'll take these two,"
said Digen. "Why didn't you say you had so much?"

Their colleagues clustered around the door to watch
them move to the end room. As they went, one of the interns whistled faintly an unsavory little tune associated
with anti-Sime jokes. Digen, without turning his head,
tried to discern which of them was whistling, but the
mixed nager was impenetrable through the retainers.
Hogan, red-faced, did not look back.

Digen was grateful to close the door behind them. He
set the two heaviest items down—he had been augmenting
slightly to manage the weight, and it left him light-headed,
a bit keyed up—and leaned against the door, saying, "Now,
this is a lovely room, at least twice the size of theirs."

"It's the only one with its own bathroom, too. They
didn't want you sharing the communal facilities."

Digen nodded. "Figures. Well, which bed do you want?"

"Flip for it?"

"No, you pick. I don't really care."

"I don't like drafts in the winter," said Hogan. "You take the window side?"

"Fine," said Digen. He was already unlatching his largest suitcase. "Last thing packed, first thing unpacked," said Digen, pulling his Diplomatic Corps sign out of the case. "I'll tack this up now, with your permission."

Hogan looked at it. He knew what it was, and what it implied. Digen let him look, waiting. The anxiety was there again. It had to be faced down or life would be intolerable —for both of them.

Hogan said, with a glance in the direction of the hall, "I'll do it for you. I have a little hammer."

He bent to where he'd unbuckled the strapping from his old case and pulled out a small household hammer. As a Sime, Digen was somewhat horrified of the idea of a Gen wielding a hammer—they hit their own fingers far too often for any Sime to watch with peace of mind. But he understood the gesture Hogan was making.

The noise would bring all eyes to the sign poster, and Hogan wanted them to see him doing it. It was sheer bravado. But it was necessary to Hogan just then.

Digen handed him the ornate plaque and watched him go out the door. *This Gen is going to make me a nervous wreck one way or another, I can see that now.*

As he listened to the tapping, waiting to feel the lancing shock of a hit finger, Digen bent to gather handfuls of underwear and install them in the drawers of the dresser on his side of the room. Somebody had left a candy bar in the top drawer and it had melted.

He chucked the things on the bed and collapsed into the desk chair, gritting his teeth until Hogan finished his deliberate pounding and came in. Seeing Digen's droop-shouldered dejection, he asked, "What's the matter?"

Digen pointed at the mess. "It's one of those days."

Hogan made an indescribable sound. "Well, see if you can get the whole drawer under the bathtub faucet." He went toward the window. "Look, we can put it on the roof and later the sun will hit it, and it'll be dry by morning. I don't think they'll inspect us until then."

Digen looked toward the window. "Good idea. Why didn't I think of that?" He knew, of course, why he hadn't. Need. The depression. The monomania. The total lack of enthusiasm for anything not directly connected with satisfying need made him feel that even his thoughts were weighted with lead.

Knowing where it came from made it just a little easier to deal with. He took out a notebook and pen, surveying the room, listing what had to be accomplished within the next few hours. The beds were, of course, unmade, linens stacked at the bottoms. Uniforms would have to be picked up at the laundry, and Digen's would have to be altered to accommodate the bulky retainers. The sticky drawer had to be cleaned, and the clothing unpacked and readied for inspection, just as in school. And it would be nice to squeeze in time for a shower. In fact, it was essential.

But first, to get rid of the retainers.

Hogan stood at the window, back to Digen, inspecting the view of the Sime Center next door and the new Sime residence tower jutting up over some trees. Digen took the opportunity to shed his retainers.

But retainers were not designed to be removed unobtrusively. The catches came open with a snap like thunder in the quiet room. Hogan turned, startled at first by the noise and then with growing alarm as he saw what Digen was doing.

With the catches released, the seals sliced open along the insides of Digen's forearms. The first searing flash of Hogan's uncut nager lanced through Digen's whole body, paralyzing him. He could sense the Gen's eyes riveted to the sparkling metal.

Hogan was strung tight, screaming inwardly, *Get it over with!*

Cautiously, Digen eased his tentacles out of the restraining pockets of the interior, releasing the pressure on his lateral extensor reflex nodes so he could sheathe the delicate selyn-transfer organs before completely stripping away the protective retainers.

He wished he could do it quickly. The Gen's anxiety level was unbearable. But the interior construction of the retainers was designed to hinder all Sime movement, especially the removal of the retainers.

Invented by the Gens during the Sime-Gen wars, retainers were meant to restrain Sime prisoners and to torture them into revealing military information. The material laminated between the outer walls interfered with the Sime sensory system sickeningly, and the interior bars and pockets forced the tentacles into extension and immobilized them painfully. After a few hours in the old-fashioned manacles, any Sime would be willing to promise anything to get out of them. The modern variety had not been modified very much. It took some learning to wear them without absently moving in such a way as to pinch a lateral. One learned to move very slowly when removing them.

Digen paused for the space of four deep breaths, adjusting his internal selyn flows to the new freedom. Then he withdrew his handling tentacles and laid the retainers open on the desk to dry. The bars had left red dents around his arms. The skin under the retainers was flushed with the heat, and his laterals throbbed unmercifully.

Hogan said, hardly breathing, "They must be very uncomfortable."

Digen nodded, rising, and made his way to the open bathroom door. "Give me a moment," he said, pulling the door shut behind him to cut the nager and allow Hogan a respite too. Running cold water over his arms—it was tepid but felt cold to him—he worked the cramps and kinks out of his arm muscles.

He hadn't actually been wearing the retainers so long this time, but the long train ride, the incessant need within him, and the draining events of the morning had all taken a toll. And the night to come would be even more demanding.

He stuck his head under the faucet and ran the water over his face and hair, adding to his list of things to do that he had to install his pharmacy chest in the bathroom. He didn't dare try the Gen soap in the dish. It would surely give him a bright red rash by nightfall, if not sooner.

He was worse than most Farrises when it came to allergies, so he was a little afraid of the towels, too. At the Gen-run medical school, the laundry had used some sort of conditioner that had given him such a reaction that the Gen doctors thought for three days it was some new infectious disease. But these towels felt all right, and there was no way to find out but to try, so he toweled briskly and went out into the room, rubbing moisture from his short black hair.

"That feels good. You should try it," he said cheerfully. Hogan was standing by Digen's desk, staring at the notebook Digen had left lying open to his list. The Gen flicked an eye from Digen to the list and back, his nager swirling with inchoate emotions.

Taking care to move with exaggerated slowness yet still to seem casual about it, Digen used two tentacles to flip the towel onto the bed beside his underwear and stepped closer to the desk. Then, looking at the notebook, he understood the Gen's feelings. He said, "Now why did I do that?"

The list was written in Simelan, a language not quite cognate to any historic human language. All the Gens used modern versions of languages of the Ancients, the pre-mutation humans. But the Simes had somewhere, somehow, developed their own language to describe the reality that their peculiar senses perceived. The Gens, of course, regarded the Sime language as a form of secret communication designed only to exclude Gens, for even Gens raised among Simes never gained more than a superficial grasp of Simelan.

Digen, in his fatigue, had made his notes in the way that required the least effort. Now he realized that Hogan had taken it as a graphic illustration of the barrier between them. Hastily Digen explained each notation, and added the last two in Hogan's form of English. Then he poked a finger at the first item and a tentacle at the second, saying, "Tell you what, if you'll go fetch our uniforms, I'll make your bed, fair trade?"

Hogan tried to dampen his lips with a dry tongue. His eyes never left Digen's arms, still showing the angry marks of the retainers. "Fair enough," he said.

Hogan picked up Digen's laundry ticket, mating it with his own. "This probably won't take too long. Everyone else has been down already."

It didn't take long, but by the time Hogan returned with two bulging packages, Digen had made the beds, partially unpacked his things, installed his pharmacy chest under the bathroom sink, and was leaning out the window, positioning the freshly scrubbed drawer so that the afternoon sun would catch the wet spot.

"You know," said Digen over his shoulder, "it looks as if previous tenants used this roof as a private patio."

Hogan, tossing the packages onto the beds, said, "Which

is understandable, rules or no rules. This floor is unbearably stuffy."

"But we've got the best room—even cross-ventilation, with a window on each side of the building corner. It seems there are advantages to being an outcast." He drew himself in the window and turned, having said the words lightly.

But, with a kind of strained gaiety, Hogan said, "The laundry has already altered your uniforms. They had them set aside with your name on them. Somebody down there likes you, it seems."

As he spoke, his eyes slid nervously past Digen's gaze. It was a peculiar mixture of fear and courage. By talking about that which frightened him, Hogan was trying to convince himself that he wasn't afraid. Digen felt his own tension level rising in response and he knew he couldn't afford much of that.

The Gen began stacking clothing in a drawer. "Joel, this won't do. I can't—we can't live like this."

Hogan, his back to Digen, continued stacking things. "I don't know what you mean."

"Turn around and look at me."

"I've got to get this done."

"Joel."

The Gen turned. Digen said, "Have you ever really seen a Sime's tentacles before? In Sorelton you didn't watch."

Hogan's face worked ever so slightly, but his eyes did not drop to Digen's arms. "All right," said Digen, "we both know you feel a certain apprehension. I can understand that. It's normal. I've dealt with it daily when working out-Territory collectoriums, collecting selyn from out-Territory Gen Donors."

Drifting to the end of the bed and sitting down, Digen considered. "Joel, it's not the fact that you're nervous about me that's getting to me, it's the way you're handling it. You haven't looked squarely at me since I shed my retainers."

From Hogan's reaction, Digen figured that Hogan had not actually been aware of that avoidance. Now the Gen forced his eyes down to Digen's arms. His pulse and respiration spiked, and a film of perspiration sprang out on his upper lip, but his selyn-production rate increased only slightly and in a rhythm wholly divorced from Digen's nager.

Sime tentacles had some sort of semantic meaning for Hogan over and above the clinical. In a wild, intuitive stab, Digen said, "You have seen a changeover—a very grisly one, right?"

Hogan's eyes locked to Digen's now and his fear was like a bolt of lightning to Digen. "No, Joel, I can't read your mind. But I've dealt with people from your background all my life. I can recognize a trauma pattern when I see one. And there are few things in this life more traumatic than being the victim of a Sime who's just come through changeover and is berserk with first need. That's what happened to you, isn't it? I mean before Sorelton."

Still unable to speak, Hogan shook his head. Then he shrugged and said, "I don't remember it."

Digen nodded. "Sometimes trauma works that way." He rummaged in the suitcase that was still on his bed and came up with a bottle of fruit nectar. It was all sudsy and warm, but it would be tart and refreshing mixed with a little water. He went into the bathroom to fill glasses, calling over his shoulder, "How old were you at the time?"

When he came out, Hogan still hadn't answered. Digen handed him a glass. "How old were you at the time, Joel?"

Hogan stared at the bright yellow-gold drink. Digen was offering the glass held in two tentacles, his own glass in his fingers, while the bottle was in his other hand. Hogan just stared at the glass he was being offered, wrapped around with two tentacles so that he couldn't possibly take the glass without touching Digen.

Digen was tempted to relent and offer his glass in his hand. But he would be sanctioning Hogan's retreat, and he had to force a confrontation here, now, or he'd never have the strength for it again. His laterals were retracted far up into his lateral sheaths, tensed against the onslaught of the Gen's nager. "You can't hurt me by touching the dorsal tentacles," said Digen. "Only the laterals contain selyn-transport nerves. The dorsals and ventrals are just like fingers—a little stronger and more dexterous, that's all."

The Gen's hand moved a bit, and Digen braced himself for the contact. *Come on, Joel, you can do it.*

It took the Gen a long time, but Digen was patient, and

at length Hogan plucked the glass from Digen's grip, the tip of one Gen finger brushing lightly against a Sime tentacle. Hogan looked at the glass in his hand with amazement.

Digen set the bottle on the closet shelf and sat down with his drink as if nothing unusual had transpired. "You'll have to tell me about it, you know. How else can I help you get over this?"

But Hogan apparently didn't hear Digen. He said blankly, "It's not slimy."

"Hmm?"

A little more distinctly, Hogan said, "It's smooth, powdery, silky dry."

Ah! "Yes, the skin of the dorsal and ventral tentacles is dry and very smooth to the touch. Only the laterals are kept moist with selyn-conducting hormones."

Hogan dropped heavily into his own desk chair and forced his eyes back to Digen. The channel said, "How old were you at the time?"

Hogan shook himself. "I—ah—they say it happened when I was eleven."

"Then you were still a child yourself, not established as a Gen?"

"No. They—the Sime Center had a truck unit at my school, testing everyone for changeover, and the channel said I'd established sometime the previous summer. It was a big relief. It meant I wouldn't go through changeover. It meant I could become a surgeon."

"Then what happened?" *Shen! Established at eleven!*

"I—I told you, I don't remember."

"You must have heard, though. Something like that . . ."

"They said—they said it was my older brother. He was hiding in the barn, sick with changeover, and my sister—she was a couple of years older than him—found him toward the—the—end. . . ."

"Breakout," said Digen. "When the tentacles rupture the wrist orifice membranes and need really hits in earnest. And what happened?"

Hogan recited the story with a glassy calm, like a thing that had happened to somebody else. "He started to attack her, but I threw myself onto his back. I'd been hiding in the loft, for some reason, and saw it. He killed my sister and turned on me. They say he burned me in transfer.

They said it was a month before I would utter a sound—
because I saw them beat him to death with clubs and hoes
and such. I loved my brother, they said, even more than
my sister, who had been a mother to me since my own
mother died."

Hogan looked up at Digen. "I can't even remember his
name, and I don't remember him at all. I never had a
brother."

"Shenoni!" swore Digen. *His brother killed, then burned
him that deeply. He must have been a channel. What a
Donor Joel could have been.* "A month to recover brain
function? Were you under care at the Sime Center?"

"No, of course not. It was much too far away, and nobody trusted them anyhow."

The question in Digen's mind was whether it had been
transfer shock or just a psychological shock that caused
the amnesia and speech trauma. Digen guessed it to be a
mixture.

"All right," Digen said. "Now I understand why you feel
the way you do. I think you've done remarkably well—
with me—so far. But I also think you're suffering uselessly.
You're not eleven years old anymore. The world is not
mysterious, inexplicable, or sinister anymore. And I am
not renSime. I am no danger to you or to anyone else."

"I know it's senseless," said Hogan, "but it just comes
—the feeling—I don't know from where. I never expected
it to be like this."

Digen took one last sip from his glass and got up. He
held out both hands, handling tentacles spread. "Come on,
Joel. There's only one way to unlearn an experience, and
that's with another experience."

"What are you going to do?"

Digen let his handling tentacles drift toward the Gen's
arms. "I'm going to touch you. Go ahead and be as frightened as you like. You're not hurting me." He let all his
handling tentacles rest lightly against the Gen's skin, saying, "All right. Now I'm going to try something. Holding
our fields in exact balance so there can be no selyn flow,
I'm going to make a full transfer contact."

Hogan jerked away. Digen moved on Hogan then, seiz-
ing the Gen's arms in the transfer grip with the lightning
speed of the attacking Sime. It was a move calculated to
evoke the very peak of unreasoning terror, to hit that

deeply buried nerve and bring it all to the surface. Digen's only worry was that Hogan might scream.

He timed his move for the end of Hogan's exhalation, and in the instant of paralyzed surprise, he made the lip-to-lip contact generally used only in transfer. At the same time, he slid his need-moistened laterals into contact with the Gen's skin, and at once his entire nervous system resonated to every detail of the Gen's anatomy.

He held position just long enough to get the readings he had to have, seeing the old transfer burn inside the Gen clearly. As Hogan began to struggle, Digen held him immobile just long enough to demonstrate that he could do it. Then he broke lip contact. "Joel, be still!"

Hogan froze, and Digen said, "I'm going to break lateral contact now. If you move, you could hurt me. Can I trust you?"

The surge of terror had peaked. Hogan now saw that he had not in fact been hurt. His nager fragmented into chaos again, but he nodded to Digen and held still as Digen drew his laterals across the Gen's skin and sheathed them. Then he released his hold on the Gen.

"You see? You did it," said Digen. "Nothing to it." Shakily, he collapsed on his bed.

Hogan sank into his desk chair, dazed. He looked pale, and Digen was about to suggest he put his head down for a minute, but Hogan said, "Why—why did you do—that?"

Digen sat up, rubbing the tension from his neck with all handling tentacles. "Joel, can you remember ever being so terrified in all your life?"

Blankly Hogan shook his head.

"That's why I did it. To scare you, good and proper." And suddenly the time had come, Digen knew, to live up to his promise in the hallway. An honest friendship. No deceptions. "You're sure now, it's not possible for you to be more frightened than you were just now?"

"Yes, I'm sure about that!"

"Good, because that was the only way to make my point. If I can withstand the very worst you can throw at me even now while I'm in such need, then you have no reason ever to fear me again."

It took a moment for Hogan to absorb that. Then he sat bolt upright, staring at Digen with white showing all around his irises. "Need! But . . ."

"There was a mishap. My Donor should be arriving day after tomorrow. Meanwhile, I wait—and not with a great deal of patience."

"Digen . . ."

A skittish flutter of fear passed through the Gen's nager. Digen said, "Look, you've been with me for hours, and you never guessed. If I'm that good, why should it bother you?" He got up, stretched langorously, and began putting his things in the closet as he talked. "There's absolutely no reason for you or anyone else in the hospital to be concerned."

"You're not going to tell them?"

"No. And I'm asking you not to, either. Remember, I said no deceptions between us. If you can't accept knowledge of this kind and handle it as privileged information, then we can't have that sort of relationship." He paused in his movements. "It's putting a burden on you, I know. Perhaps an unfair burden, at this point. I'm sorry, but it can't be helped."

Digen closed the suitcase and shoved it into the storage niche at the back of the closet, seeing that everything was arranged according to the housekeeping regulations. He went over to Hogan's side of the room and began on his closet, shoving the heavy record player under the bed.

"Out there," said Digen, as Hogan watched, "I deal with those people guardedly. I'm always on the alert, tensed for any unexpected move, so that even when I'm feeling like this, I can cope well enough. If they knew where I was in my need cycle, it would only make them constantly afraid and make it harder—perhaps even impossible—for me to cope. Can you see that?"

"I'd have to be some kind of idiot not to see it. Now. After what you did. But I'm still not sure how I feel about it. I'm not even sure if what you did to me was legal."

"Legal? Well, yes and no. Out-Territory, of course, it would be illegal. But that sign you put on our door makes this legally Sime Territory. I doubt if you'd find an in-Territory court that would question the judgment of the Sectuib in Zeor. It worked, didn't it?"

Hogan nodded.

Tentacles and fingers spread around fifteen pairs of Hogan's socks, Digen paused. "I can deal with them at arm's length, Joel, but I'm only human. I can't stay alert sixteen hours a day. I have to have someplace where I can go to unravel, unwind, and just *be*. That place is this room, and it's your room too. You have the freedom to come and go as you choose. So I have to start teaching you how to behave around me at various points in my cycle."

"That's asking a lot."

"No more than anybody expects of any in-Territory Gen, or child for that matter. Just ordinary good manners."

Digen put the socks in a drawer, shoved them into two neat rows, and began shutting things. With two tentacles, he handed Hogan both glasses of juice. After a short pause, Hogan took them. Digen grinned. "See? The worst is over. You better rinse them out while I get the drawer. There's some kind of commotion down the hall, and I think it's a Grand Inspection."

Hogan started to move toward the bathroom, but then Digen's words penetrated. He looked quizzically at the Sime. "People who can see through walls make handy roommates," said Hogan.

Chapter 5

TRANSFER DEPENDENCE

After that first day in Westfield, Digen's first month passed in a blur of frantic activity. He and Joel Hogan were on duty in the emergency ward from late afternoon until midnight, and on call from midnight until dawn. At least, it was supposed to be that way—on paper. In practice, they rarely had a moment's rest the entire night.

At first, the residents and even the attendings would turn out during peak work loads to keep Digen from doing any actual doctoring. He was allowed to run errands to the blood lab or search files for X rays. He stocked supply cabinets. Once, they let him hold an instrument tray. He bore it all stoically, refusing to let Hogan make a fuss about them treating an intern, a graduate doctor of medicine, as if he were a first-year medical student. Eventually they even began letting him take medical histories, if only from those patients who would consent to sit across a desk from him.

He did everything he was assigned to do with alacrity and his greatest precision. He took as much responsibility as he dared, always trying to make the doctors' jobs easier by thinking ahead and being there first with what was required. He was never to be found idle while others were working, nor, in fact, was he idle when others were idle.

Each morning, after making rounds with the chief resident, occasionally even with the chief of internal medicine, Digen would go back to his room with Hogan, and as the Gen fell exhausted into bed, Digen would shower and head for the Sime Center, where he would spend most of the day on the administrative work of the changeover ward and in-Territory collectorium, himself performing only those special channel's functions which were his peculiar talent.

After his wholly unsatisfactory transfer with Ben Seloyan, Digen clung to the certitude that he now had two consecutive transfers—and the intervening months—with Im'ran. Daily, the therapist would supervise Digen's sleep, insisting that he get no less than two hours' sleep in twenty-four. Digen reveled in the luxury of two whole hours' sleep every day. In budgeting for that, Mickland was virtually putting Digen on the critical list.

One day, Digen stood looking up the steps of the Gen hospital in the heavy heat of late afternoon. The air held the stillness of a gathering storm. Im'ran had stabilized Digen's condition. For the moment, all Digen had to worry about was shifting gears from Hajene Farris, department head, to Dr. Farris, intern and errand boy.

When he got to the emergency ward, the place was seething. An out-Territory building under construction had collapsed during the busy afternoon. Hundreds of people had been hit by debris. Half of them had been brought to Westfield Memorial by police wagons. Dozens of gurneys lined the corridors of the EW, and all the treatment rooms were in use.

Nobody objected when Digen pitched in, filling out charts and admission cards, ordering X rays, blood cross-matches, and asking for consulting physicians. He couldn't discharge anyone, but he could and did admit several emergency cases. He also found time to provide comfort. One little girl was hysterical, her nose gushing blood, and there was nobody to take care of her. Her mother had disappeared.

Digen was afraid the mother might lie buried in the rubble somewhere. But, equally likely, she'd been sent to another hospital. He found an icepack for the girl's nose and made some phone calls until he located the mother. He also spent time sitting with suddenly bereaved parents as they screamed out their grief and railed at their God for the death of their child. He could do nothing but sit and listen, but he did that well. He himself had lost his only two children to sudden death.

Gradually, the less severely injured were sent home, the seriously injured were admitted, and the dead were taken to the morgue located just off the EW corridor. Digen, limited in what he was permitted to do, tackled the worst of the cleanup jobs.

The nursing staff noticed his performance, and when

the head nurse went off duty, she stopped by Digen and said, simply, "Thank you, Doctor."

Months later, Digen looked back on that moment as the real beginning of his medical career. An intern can be made or broken by the nursing staff, and it wasn't long before Digen began to feel the effects of their silent support.

Many of the nurses began to wear their sleeves rolled up to midforearm in the style Digen had adopted to keep his sleeves from snagging on the catches of the retainers. The hospital cafeteria began to serve trin tea, the favorite Sime drink, which became mysteriously popular. Arguments could be overheard in elevators and corridors between those who had become his staunch supporters and those who still adamantly refused to admit that he could do the job.

Grudgingly, the residents began to permit him to take more and more case histories. Those histories were scoured for every minor flaw of form, but, try as they might, the residents could not fault him. His tentative diagnoses, entered in his own hand at the bottom of the page, always proved correct.

One day, the chief of surgery, Dr. Reginald Thornton, stopped in to the staff room where Digen was whittling away at a stack of charts. With them piled all around him, he was surreptitiously working on the changeover ward monthly report rather than legitimate hospital charts. He smoothly dealt himself a new hospital chart and laid it on top of the Sime Center folder, saying, "Good evening, Dr. Thornton."

Thornton picked up a chart, paging through it idly. Digen recognized it as a tetanus death that had been misdiagnosed as shaking plague by one of the residents. Thornton's eye stopped on the second page, bottom, where Digen's preliminary and utterly correct diagnosis had been entered and then refuted by the resident. The lab report was stapled in over it.

Thornton said, "So you want to be a surgeon?"

"Yes, sir."

"Think you'll be as good a surgeon as you seem to be at internal medicine?"

"With a good teacher, yes, sir, I do."

"Think your time is wasted in the EW?"

"No, sir. We get ten or twenty surgical emergencies a night. It's very instructive."

Thornton leaned on the edge of the chart folder, turning full to Digen. "This is ridiculous, you know. You are a first-order channel, already one of the finest diagnosticians in the world. All you have to do is *look* to tell one disorder from another." He shook the chart at Digen. "When you do some phenomenal piece of work like this, people accuse you of cheating."

Stung, Digen said, "I didn't cheat! I can't read fields very well wearing retainers. I went by the book. Truly . . ." He broke off, aware that there was no way to make a Gen sure he was indeed telling the truth.

Thornton shied back a little at Digen's vehemence. But he stood his ground. "I believe you. Branoff believes you. But if you're not cheating, how do you account for your obvious superiority to the other interns?"

There it is, thought Digen. *The Gens are afraid Simes will take over medicine.* What could he say to allay that fear?

"I'm not superior, Dr. Thornton. It's just that I'm not—really—an intern."

"What in the world do you mean by that?"

"Oh, yes, I've just graduated medical school, but—well, it seems to me that medical training out-Territory consists of a two-part obstacle course. Medical school tests the ability to absorb knowledge. More and more is thrown at the class until only the fastest learners are left. Any doctor has to have a vast store of knowledge and the ability to absorb new knowledge quickly. So that seems reasonable.

"Then, in the intern year, the stress shifts to character. The idea is to foster good medical judgment by exposing the intern to vast numbers of concrete examples of the things he's learned about in school. But it's done using a fourteen-hour workday, sometimes a straight thirty-six. It's grueling, but the intern learns to know his own limits, to know how his judgment deteriorates at the limit, and how to compensate for the deterioration. He learns to know himself in relation to medicine in a way that can't be accomplished without the crushing overwork. It's perhaps the most important lesson he'll learn in his whole lifetime."

"That's an excellent description," said Thornton. "But how does that prove you're not cheating?"

"What I have just described, Doctor, is a stretched-out, diluted form of the channel's basic training. We learn to absorb and apply information to problem solving. Then, under field conditions, we learn judgment. But, most important, we learn to compensate for the deterioration of our judgment at our fatigue limits. The work that these interns are just encountering for the first time is work I've been doing professionally for fourteen years. It's hardly surprising that I'm a little more experienced. I wouldn't have that edge in surgery."

Thornton looked at him thoughtfully, and Digen thought he had surely blown it this time. His retainer resting across the hospital chart that covered the Sime Center folder, Digen returned Thornton's gaze, wishing he could read the man's field more clearly. He moved, easing the pressure of the retainer against his injured left outer lateral.

Thornton said, "I admire your guts, Dr. Farris, but I'm not entirely sure I admire your objectives." He raised one eyebrow. "Or your manners."

Digen lowered his eyes and said, very quietly, "I'm sorry, Dr. Thornton, I didn't mean to be rude."

Thornton shook his head, grinning. "By God, I don't know how you can take the humiliation!"

He left, still shaking his head and laughing. Digen watched him go, unsure of what humiliation the man was talking about. But, as he relaxed, he realized that the backs of his knees were wet with perspiration, and his hand, where it lay over the center folder, was shaking. *If he'd caught me with this!* Digen resolved never to bring center work into the hospital again.

During the latter half of his first month at Westfield Memorial, only one incident proved of lasting significance in Digen's life.

One afternoon he came on duty to find the EW flooded with train-wreck victims, and he waded in to help sort out the chaos. He and Joel Hogan passed each other often, but hardly spoke until they both were stopped by a woman with a small family gathered around her. They were farm people, soiled and disheveled as so many who rush into the EW with a critical patient.

"My boy is dying," said the mother to Digen. "Help him, Doctor. Nobody else will."

She led them to one of the stretchers lined up two deep by the walls. The frail young boy there was as still as death. But the IV bottles strung about him dripped steadily. Digen noticed the smell, ripe and pungent. Manure.

The shoes bulging under the red blanket lay at odd angles.

"He fell off the barn roof into the manure pile," said the mother anxiously. "It took us all evening to get him out. Now they won't even look at him!"

Digen peered over Hogan's shoulder at the boy's chart. "He's been worked up, Mrs.—Cudney. He's in shock. That's why he's being kept down here, where the nurses can keep an eye on him. He'll be moved as soon as the more critical train-wreck patients have been sent upstairs. Don't worry, it's a good night to break a leg. All our surgeons have been called in for the wreck, and they'll probably have—Skip here upstairs within an hour or two, reduce those fractures, and have everything under control by morning. Don't worry."

"But, Doctor, shouldn't something be done? Shouldn't he be cleaned up?"

Digen looked around at the rapidly quieting EW. There were no more red blankets in evidence. His eyes met Hogan's. A slight nod passed between them. The two of them spent the rest of the night over Skip Cudney.

Near morning, Thornton came into the room where they were working, accompanied by the chief resident in orthopedics. Thornton looked over what they had done, glanced through the chart, and said to Digen, "Scrub in on this one, Dr. Farris."

They took the boy up to surgery then and Digen watched while they did an open reduction, scraping the ends of the bones where bits of manure were lodged, and then scraping them again and yet again until Thornton was satisfied that they had done the best they could.

As they were stripping off their scrub suits, Thornton eyed Digen's retainers. "Well, at least you didn't turn green and dash from the room the way the student nurses do." Contemplating the surgeon's retreating back, Digen decided Thornton reminded him awfully much of his own father.

However pleased he was with himself, though, Digen knew it hadn't been a real test. Skip was just a child; his nager had no power.

Digen saw the boy the next evening, and the day after that. Occasionally he'd run into Hogan around the boy's room in the intensive care unit. It hadn't taken long for infection to set in, and though the boy was still cheerful, Digen had begun to worry.

They expected the boy would lose both legs from the infection. Digen was more pessimistic. He didn't know any antibiotics, even in-Territory, that could combat all the microbes multiplying in the boy's body—and bone marrow. He said as much to Hogan, one day outside the room, which reeked with such a stench that only the boy's mother still visited him.

Hogan, hands thrust in pockets, contemplated the white tips of his shoes. "And what would you do, Hajene Farris?"

He wasn't mocking Digen. They had many long discussions on the different approaches of healing used here and in the Sime Center. "There isn't anything I could do. But if by some miracle of timing, Skip should go through changeover, now that the wounds are cleaned of all foreign matter, well, this particular set of microbes couldn't survive in the Sime metabolism. Changeover is the only chance I can see for him."

"Hm," said Hogan. "There are those who would consider that a fate worse than death."

"Oh, it's not that bad."

They looked at each other, laughed silently, and went for coffee. The next day, Digen found Hogan lingering around Skip's door. He hung back, seeing that the mother was inside, sitting by the bed, crying silently but wretchedly.

After a time, Hogan went in and spoke softly to the woman, who wiped her eyes and made a brave face. "Mrs. Cudney, we really do think we're going to be able to save both of Skip's legs. He's responding very well to the medications."

It was a false hope. Skip had responded well to every new drug, but then the infection would break out with some new microbe dominating. It was only a matter of time and they would have to take his legs. But Hogan was convinced that it was better to give hope than utter resignation.

Or is that his rationalization? Digen wondered. *Is it that he can't face death? Or is it just Skip's death he can't face?*

She raised a tear-stained face to Hogan and said, so low Digen almost didn't hear, "He said he's going into changeover. He said it would make him well. He wanted to make me feel better! I'd rather he were dead!"

Oh, joy, thought Digen. *He overheard me talking to Joel.*

Digen went in then and tried to comfort the woman, to explain what he'd said and why. He promised to keep an eye on Skip. He'd been doing that anyhow. The boy was just about the right age for changeover, and something indefinable had alerted Digen.

Over the next few days, the mother came less and less often, spent less time with Skip. And one day Digen walked into the room and found another doctor confronting Hogan, who was standing with his fists clenched, restraining himself mightily. Hogan's nager was ripe with the odd anxiety pattern that always appeared in the Gen when he was confronted with changeover. But there was no sign of changeover in the boy.

Digen knew the other doctor's name was Dr. Lankh and that he worked in the research wing, wherever that was. But Digen had no idea what Lankh did there.

Lankh said, "Dr. Farris. May I ask what you're doing here?"

"Just looking in, Doctor."

"Your assignment is in the emergency ward, Doctor. You're not supposed to be on this ward except when bringing up a patient."

"I know the rules, Dr. Lankh. But Skip doesn't have an attending doctor, and since Dr. Thornton let me scrub on the case, I've been expected to follow it."

Digen surmised that Lankh had been reprimanding Hogan for the same thing.

Lankh said, "I am his attending now. You will no longer be permitted to write orders on the Cudney case. I don't want to see you in this room again."

Digen opened his mouth to protest. He was irritable, impatient with rising need, as the time of his first transfer with Im'ran was approaching. Hogan, who had begun to grasp how Digen's temperament varied with need, stepped forward. "Come on, Dr. Farris. We have work to do."

Out in the hall, Hogan whispered harshly, "That's Dr. *Lankh,* you idiot!"

Safe in the elevator, Digen vented his feelings by barking, "And who the blazing shen is Dr. Lankh?"

"You don't know?"

Digen shook his head.

Hogan peered around the elevator as if expecting to find an eavesdropper. "Since we've been here, the hospital has turned over nineteen changeover victims to the Sime Center."

"Well, *I* know that! The center's statisticians have been going crazy trying to figure out why the sudden drop in the city's average."

"I know where the other fifteen went."

Digen stopped, suspicion dawning. "Where?"

"Dr. Lankh's laboratory. Fifteen have died in his experiments this month—fifteen kids in changeover have died here in this hospital. Digen, we've got to get Skip away from him!"

Digen stood, cold, in the middle of the elevator, trying to sort it through. "The chances that Skip will hit that point while here in the hospital are miniscule." He glanced narrowly at Hogan. "What sort of work is Lankh doing? What could he possibly want with Skip?"

"Everybody's been talking—but I guess they just don't talk when you're around. Digen, he's trying to stop changeover and reverse it in mid-course. He says he has succeeded. Parents sign their kids over to him. It's all legal. They'd rather the kids be dead than Sime."

Digen heard only the words "stop changeover and reverse it in mid-course." He went pale. When the door of the elevator opened, he plunged wildly into the dank corridor outside the pathology lab. He stopped, one hand to the rough, damp wall, a sensory link to the world. He concentrated on the feel of that wall against the palm of his hand, trying to drive away the vision of kids dying in first need.

One word wrenched out of Digen, in Simelan, over and over, until he whispered it, "Fifteen. Fifteen. Fifteen!"

Digen had seen this death altogether too often. Things

went wrong in changeover. A good Sime Center could save some. But some died. Yet—fifteen, tortured to death!

Hogan came up to Digen, hesitant. Digen shrank from the Gen. A Gen could do such a thing. Inhuman ghouls. "He's insane!" grated Digen.

Hogan's hand came lightly onto Digen's shoulder.

Hogan didn't say anything, but Digen could feel the concern in him, a sweet resonance, shattering the grip of cold horror on him. "I'm sorry," said Digen. "That's the way I almost died, you know. Attrition. I'm too sensitive to it." *Too sensitive. Too sensitive.* The thought lodged in his mind, accompanied by a strange sense of déjà vu. His brother Wyner had been too sensitive. Too sensitive to live.

"We've got to do something," said Hogan.

Nobody could reverse changeover, Digen knew, any more than birth could be reversed, or, more to the point, metamorphosis of a caterpillar to a butterfly. Lankh was lying to himself and to others, if he really believed he had succeeded. *Why? What drives a man like that? It's got to be something more than just fear.*

With an effort, Digen drew himself away from the wall. "Lankh will be stopped. Now that I know."

"Digen, if they find out I told you . . ."

"Don't worry. They won't. But he'll be stopped."

The next day Digen dropped a pointed hint to the Sime Center statisticians, and then put the matter from his mind.

It was barely a week before his scheduled transfer with Im'ran, and Digen still saw Thornton striding through the EW on occasion, briskly ordering this or that done immediately. Once Digen had seen Thornton going through a stack of charts Digen had just filed. Twice he heard his name and Thornton's muttered in conversations hastily abandoned as he approached. He began to feel like a specimen under a microscope.

Then, one evening, Digen was wrapping a sprained ankle for a little girl who was clutching her kitten and crying disconsolately, when Dr. Thornton came into the treatment room and called Digen aside.

"Dr. Farris, I'd like you to take a look at a patient in room eight."

Digen knew something was up immediately. Thornton never said, hesitantly, "I'd like you to—"; he said, "Do it," over his shoulder as he passed through. "Something interesting, Dr. Thornton?"

Walking beside Digen, Thornton said, "Looks like a classic hot appendix. Too classic. It's a sixteen-year-old girl. She has no establishment card. Sixteen's a little old for changeover—but . . ."

"Well," said Digen, "I had one who was seventeen once. He died. But there's a case in the literature of an eighteen-year-old who survived. The average changeover age seems to be going up, you know."

Thornton shrugged, ushering Digen into room eight. "You're the expert on that."

When Digen examined the girl she was unconscious, unable to give Thornton clue responses to the standard tests for changeover. He took Thornton into a corner for a fast, confidential report.

"It's both," he said glibly. "Even through the retainers, I can pick up—definite prechangeover indications. But they are not what's causing the abdomen. That could be an acute appendix."

"Well, you better get your people on it right away, because it is an appendix—on plus-time, in my opinion."

"I couldn't judge the appendix without a lateral contact examination. But if you're right about that, there's nothing the Sime Center can do for her. We don't practice surgery."

"You mean you'd just let her die from a silly little thing like that?"

"Yes," said Digen, meeting Thornton's gaze levelly. "There's nothing we could do."

"That's—that's—criminal!"

"Yes. It is. That's why I'm here, Doctor. To learn surgery and bring the techniques in-Territory."

Thornton absorbed that. Even through the retainers, Digen could feel the man's nager shifting. When their eyes met again, there was a new understanding between them.

"Prechangeover," mused Thornton. "What would happen if we did her—right now, within the hour?"

With a leap of excitement, Digen thought it over. The nerve tissues that had begun to form wouldn't carry selyn currents for another couple of days. "If you use a mid-line incision, you shouldn't be in any danger, and—she just might survive." He balanced the factors in his head, her field reading, general health, stage of changeover, age, and so forth. "It would be a better chance than if you don't do her. That is, *if* you're right about the appendix. But—I can't give you a legally binding channel's opinion without a full lateral contact examination. *I* could be wrong about her state of changeover—in a case like this, sixteen years old. . . ."

"But with a full contact examination, you would be certain?"

"Absolutely—and precisely about the appendix, too."

Thornton thought it over quickly. "You're no naïve young intern, Dr. Farris. You know what's going on in this hospital, at the higher administration levels."

"Not specifically," said Digen. "But I get the picture."

"This would blow the lid off."

"Not unless you want it to," said Digen. "You do her at eleven, and I'll diagnose her and take her over to the Sime Center at one—if you want it that way."

"What about postop? They have no experience over there. She could require a lot of blood—complications . . ."

"Changeover is enough of a complication all by itself. I'll have her on my own ward. We'll manage—or we won't. But if you're right about the appendix, which I don't doubt, then this way at least she'll have a chance."

"I've seen breakout contractions. They'll rip the incision wide open."

"She has a couple of days yet. In changeover, wounds often heal exceptionally fast. If I have to—I could rupture her membranes to avoid contractions. And—there are drugs. . . ." The more he thought about it, the more Digen itched for the challenge. He might even get permission to use Ilyana's field to stimulate the healing. But any way it went, the center would know. It would be a beginning.

But the law would have to be bent a little, to save a life. Together, he and Thornton laid plans. Digen got his full contact examination and confirmed Thornton's diagnosis, and the state of changeover, but they logged the lateral exam as taking place at one in the morning, half an hour after rather than half an hour before the operation. Since he wasn't supposed to be involved in the case at that point, Digen wasn't permitted to observe the actual surgery.

Then Digen was called in for the official channel's consultation in a room off the postoperative recovery ward.

As he came out of the locked room, easing his retainers back into place, Digen met Thornton's eyes and nodded. As he turned to the telephone to call for the center's pick-up squad, he thought he saw a familiar figure disappear around a corner. *Lankh? What's he doing here?*

Waiting for the squad, Digen began to feel nervous. By Tecton law, he had been required to phone for the squad an hour ago when he first learned that the girl was in changeover. The official record, the only record anyone at the center would see, clearly stated that his first contact with the girl had been after the operation. Only he and Thornton—and maybe one or two nurses—knew it hadn't happened that way.

A couple of days later, Digen eased the girl through changeover, cheating her of her normal breakout experience but putting her well on the path to a long and healthy life. For days the hospital was buzzing with rumors about why the chief of surgery had been doing a midnight appendectomy that turned out to be a changeover victim. Hogan told Digen some of the more bizarre explanations, ending, "I think, though, that she is really his niece, and that's why he was so interested he got out of bed to come in and see her."

"Niece?" said Digen.

"Well," said Hogan, "Thornton has certainly changed toward you since you saved her life."

Digen told him, then, the whole story.

Hogan laughed, shaking his head. "I don't know why I ever worried about you getting a raw deal here. Barely a month in Westfield, and already you've got the surgical residency sewed up!"

Digen sobered. "I wouldn't go that far, Joel. It's a long haul from here to there." *And I might not live that long.*

"You better get some sleep. I've got to get over to the center and file my monthly reports."

Everything, Digen knew—literally everything—depended on his getting his transfers straightened out. He couldn't —he didn't dare—go into surgery proper, doing all that cutting and sewing, in anything less than top shape physically.

And though things were going well at the hospital, he had problems at the center. While Im'ran was technically assigned to him exclusively, the Donor still had to spend quite a bit of time with Jesse Elkar, the channel who had gotten them into this mess. *No, that's not fair,* thought Digen. It was Mickland's incompetence that had gotten them messed up.

Jesse Elkar, like Digen, had been shorted in transfer far longer than he could endure. Every year, it seemed, there were fewer and fewer of the high-order Donors, the kind of Gens who could serve Digen's need, or serve channels like Jesse Elkar.

Mickland had released Jesse from therapy a little early in order to assign Im'ran to Digen. When Jesse attempted his transfer, he had aborted—painfully—several times, because his newly assigned Donor was inadequate. Mickland had then sent Im'ran into the room to try to pull Elkar through, but instead, Elkar had attacked Im'ran, leaving the Donor with no choice but to complete the transfer or force another abort—which would surely have killed Elkar.

Now, as a result of that incident, Jesse Elkar was deep into a transfer dependency with Im'ran. He literally couldn't take his transfer from any other Donor.

Up until now, Digen had stayed strictly out of the affair. Im'ran was the therapist, it was his responsibility to bail Elkar out of it. In fact, Digen hadn't laid eyes on the first-order channel who was contending for his Donor. Legally, Im'ran was Digen's. But—emotionally, Im'ran was torn. At last, Digen felt it was time he took a stand.

By the time Digen got off rounds at the hospital, saw Hogan tumble into bed, and changed his clothes, it was thundering. Just as he walked out the hospital doors, a warm, sluicing rain poured out of the sky, and in moments Digen was wading along the city street, leaning into the wind. He scurried up the nearest steps into Sime Center, soaked to the skin and dripping.

Finding himself in the out-Territory collectorium, walking between two benches where Gens sat waiting their turn to donate selyn to the collecting channels, Digen keyed the elevator that would let him out opposite his office door. He had a small bathroom where he kept a change of clothes just off the storeroom behind his office. As he got into some dry things, he made some phone calls and found out that Jesse Elkar was scheduled for his transfer within the hour. He had moved into the deferment suite two days ago.

Searching for an elevator that would take him up into the south tower of the huge, sprawling Sime Center building, Digen became really worried. A channel moved into the deferment suite only when he reached a state of need where he no longer trusted his self-control. If Elkar were in that condition, certainly the transfer dependency with Im'ran was the cause. This could very easily turn into a brutal business.

He found the deferment suite, heavily insulated, removed from the daily pressures and concerns of a channel's life. Elkar had the corner room, a large, comfortably furnished studio apartment, surrounded on two sides by observation booths, which were separated from the studio itself by heavily insulated, transparent partitions.

With great misgivings, Digen touched the signal button. Momentarily the door latch clicked and Digen pushed the door open. The room was decorated in forest green and immaculate white trimmed with gold accents. Heavily draped and upholstered, the room held a quiet hush characteristic of deferment suites.

On the contour lounge in the center of the room, just sitting up now that Digen had walked in, was Jesse Elkar. The two channels stared at one another for a moment in sheer disbelief. Then Digen said, "Shu-ven! *Jesse* Elkar! The name—it's common enough, I thought it must be some other—you never told me you made first order!"

They embraced, Digen shaking the other man like a long-lost brother. "When did you qualify? Why didn't you write me?"

Jesse Elkar had gone through changeover about the same time that Digen had. They had both been assigned to the same training camp for their first year, the year when the learning rate is magnified in the new Sime, often by as much as ten times the normal rate. Digen, being a Farris, had qualified as a first-order channel on his very first transfer. Jesse Elkar, a more typical channel, had had to work hard to achieve what Digen had been born with. Yet they had become inseparable comrades at the camp, as Digen tutored his friend and in turn learned from him what it was like to struggle to overcome an inability. It was a lesson that had sustained Digen through all the years after the accident that had left his lateral scarred.

Elkar was withdrawn, tight under Digen's hands. "Digen, Digen, after all you've done for me, just look what I've done to you! It had to be your Donor I intercepted—your Donor I'm in this rotten dependency with!"

"Sit down, sit down," urged Digen. "None of this is your fault. It's the Donor shortage. And—if someone had to get my Donor, I'd rather it were you. Why didn't you come up and say hello to your Sectuib? Surely in Zeor we could have worked something out weeks ago, if I'd known it was you!"

Elkar shook his head. "I'm sorry, Sectuib." Digen realized then just how humiliated Elkar was over the whole dependency thing. *He couldn't face me!* Well, now wasn't the time to tackle it. The man was primed and ready for transfer.

"Never mind, Jesse. I came up here to be of help, not—well, just relax and tell me . . ."

At that point the door signal ticked. Elkar jumped, startled, and Digen realized just how tense his friend was. He reached over Elkar and released the door catch.

As the door opened, a strange man's voice was saying, ". . . better work, Im'ran."

Im'ran answered, his head turned as he walked into the room, "It's perfectly straightforward, and Mickland said it was all right as long as we kept her away from Digen. . . ."

Mora Dyen, the channel who had managed Digen's departments before he had come, was doing a magnificent job of keeping Im'ran's very high field from dominating the room. In fact, Digen barely felt Im'ran's shock while he saw the dismay on Ilyana's face and turned to see Digen standing beside Elkar.

In synch with Ilyana and striving to control her blazing field was the large man Digen recognized as the channel who limped, whom he had first seen in Mickland's office. He had no idea who the man was, but he was obviously a very accomplished first-order channel, with every bit of the precision one expected to see only in Zeor-trained channels. Digen had heard that the man's limp was the result of a bout of shaking plague.

The group of two channels and two Donors advanced into the room, spreading out to ease the fields for Elkar. Digen's eyes came to Ilyana, and for a moment everything vanished as he slipped into hyperconsciousness, seeing only her selyn field, silky gold and perfectly matched to his need. Then a dark blot spoiled the moment, kicking Digen rudely down into duoconsciousness, and the room became visible through the fields.

It was the big man between him and Ilyana. Digen judged him to be about fifty-five, and a figure accustomed to authority. The man advanced on Digen, saying, "I'm sorry. I had to do that to you. She's—"

"Yes, I know," said Digen, with a huge sigh. "My matchmate."

"You don't remember me, do you?"

The man's nager was charged with half a dozen distinct emotions, which abruptly cut off under strict discipline. Digen shook his head. "Should I?" He was aware that everyone was watching him, but he couldn't imagine why.

"The last time I saw you—it was at Vira's changeover party. You were only four. You used to call me Uncle Rin."

"Rindaleo Hayashi!" The only channel ever to have been thrown out of the House of Zeor.

Digen stood there, assailed with a hundred memories. Vira, Digen's older sister, had died fighting the same outbreak of shaking plague which had claimed his parents and two older brothers, and which had resulted in Hayashi's disgrace. Digen remembered Vira as the smallest one in the family, tough and wiry, almost un-Farris-like. At her changeover party, Digen had stolen a whole bowl of sugar frosting from the kitchen and eaten it all at once. "Uncle Rin" had taken him out into the woods where he could be sick in private. Afterward, they had a long talk about Zeor standards, about human greed, about temptation, and about Sime need and the Zeor channels' self-control. Satisfied that Digen understood, in principle, what he had done wrong, the man had never told on him.

Digen shook his head, a quirk of a smile at the corner of his mouth. "Sugar frosting."

The warm leap of understanding between them bewildered the other channels in the room. *He's an outcast,* thought Digen. *I'm not supposed to feel for him at all.* As Digen cooled his emotional nager toward the man, Hayashi ached with such loneliness that Digen almost cried. Then that too was wiped away, as if it had never been. *Zeor discipline.*

They could work together only under the Tecton.

Im'ran said into the uncomfortable silence, "Digen, I think maybe you ought to leave."

Digen shook his head. "You didn't tell me this Jesse Elkar was *my* Jesse ambrov Zeor. He's my friend, Im', and one of my members. I can't—just leave."

"I'm glad of that," said Ilyana. "I was beginning to think this place peopled by ghouls and soulless devils, as if friendship counted for nothing."

Hayashi said, "Friendship doesn't count for much, Ilyana, not where transfer is concerned."

Digen, still stationing himself beside Elkar to manage the fields for him, said, "I want to know what you're planning."

Im'ran said, "I got him into this. I'm going to use Ilyana to get him out. Mora will balance and monitor to keep him from going after me again. Rin is here because he won't let Ilyana out of his sight."

Digen nodded. "Good idea. Who controls?"

Im'ran said, "Jesse, of course."

"Tricky," said Digen; then he looked to Ilyana. "You agree?"

Wretchedly, she said, "Have I any choice?"

It was then that Digen noticed, through the veil of Hayashi's field control, just how overcharged Ilyana's field was. He was stunned that she could stand there, rational, not fifteen paces from her transfer partner. Hayashi was shielding her but was unable to damp her production rate as Digen had done when they had first met.

Im'ran said, "There's no danger. They're not within thirty-eight per cent of being matched. No danger of a lortuen at all. I calculated it myself."

Doesn't trust Mickland's figures? Every day Digen discovered something new he liked about Im'ran. "I believe you," said Digen. "But in a straight transfer . . ." he said, turning to Elkar. "What do you think? Can you hold on to her?"

Elkar shook his head. "She's more than I could ever require. But—I don't know. This thing has such a grip on me. I'm afraid I'm going to abort."

"I know what that's like," said Digen. He turned to Im'ran. "You know what a null backcurrent is?"

Im'ran shook his head, searching his memory. "Some Zeor technique—you establish a new dependency to nullify another, and in the end, if you balance it just right, you end up with no dependency?"

Hayashi said, "Hajene, you can't! Not while you're in such need. Not with Ilyana!"

Digen kept his gaze on Elkar. "Jesse is ambrov Zeor. Legally it's permissible—within Zeor. And it's time Jesse learned the technique. It could have saved him a lot of trouble already."

Ilyana said, "Wait a minute. Nobody told me anything about breaking into a dependency. I wouldn't cut into somebody's transfer mating."

Hayashi took her aside into a corner while Digen went on discussing the fine points with Im'ran and Elkar. Im'ran stood with one arm around Mora Dyen, well away from Elkar and Digen. As he talked, Digen realized just how much deep affection there was between Im'ran and the woman.

Im'ran said, "I don't know. If we're not careful, Jesse could end up in a dependency on Ilyana!"

Digen nodded. "That's why it's not a general Tecton method. It requires a monitoring channel with the kind of performance ratings that can be built in only by Zeor training. That's just too much work for most people." He looked significantly at Elkar, wondering why the man had chosen to use his family name instead of the "ambrov Zeor" he was entitled to. Obviously Elkar had kept up his routine practice exercises. Digen could see that in the nager.

"So," said Digen to Im'ran, "I will take Mora's place opposite you."

Hayashi came to the group then, Ilyana a little behind him. "Hajene Farris, Mickland will be very upset if you're exposed to Ilyana in a transfer situation. You've already had too much exposure to her."

"I'm not worried about Ilyana. I'm worried about Jesse. I'm going to have to ask you and Mora to wait outside. We've only got a couple of minutes left to set this up."

Both channels began to protest. But there was really nothing they could say. Legally, Digen had the right of it. And he was the ranking channel, not only in that room but in all of Westfield District. He even ranked Mickland, if it came to a showdown. And as long as he didn't get involved in a lortuen with Ilyana, nobody could really say anything.

Reluctantly, Hayashi and Mora Dyen left. Digen said, "Im', I've got to apologize for doing this to you. I don't doubt that you could handle it—honestly I don't. But it would be awfully hard on Jesse."

"It's all right. I understand." Im'ran was wholly professional, distanced from the situation.

Ilyana came toward Elkar, who had leaned back on the lounge as the others left, knowing his time was almost there. Digen admired his control as Ilyana approached and he didn't move a muscle. Ilyana said, "Do you really like Im'ran so little that you want to break off with him?"

Elkar shook his head. "I like Im'ran fine. But I don't want any sort of dependency. That's the law here, Ilyana."

Ilyana shook her head, "I don't understand how they can make laws governing such a personal thing as transfer." She sat down beside the channel, reaching for his arms, where his laterals were trembling uncontrollably. Digen and Im'ran moved, then, to opposite sides of the lounge. Digen put his own hand out to intercept Ilyana's touch, and her fingers closed on the back of his hand. His own laterals vibrated in response to her, but he had himself under firm control, functioning wholly in the channel mode, using his secondary system to manage the fields.

"Not yet, Ilyana."

"I thought you wanted me to give him transfer."

"In a minute. Do you know how to link in trautholo?" She flashed contempt at him. "You think I'm a child?"

"Just link with him as deeply as you can," said Digen.

She fell easily into that special state of pretransfer readiness, which was handled with such dread respect by Tecton Donors. Elkar relaxed instantly, all the driving pressures of need removed by the linked readiness of his Donor.

Digen said, "Now, Jesse, be ready to initiate selyn flow on my signal. Ilyana, you remain wholly passive in this—*can* you do it?"

Contempt again, but she didn't answer verbally. Digen coached them through it, gauging the time spent in trautholo against Elkar's affinity for Im'ran. When he had an exact match, he called in the transfer, which went as smoothly as any he'd ever monitored. Elkar didn't flinch or waver, drawing his satisfaction in one smooth sweep, with no sign of abort.

When it was over, Ilyana drew back, giving Elkar time to dismantle the contacts. Then, standing, her body now low enough in selyn that she didn't feel sick, she looked at her arms, then at Im'ran. To Digen she said, "When I helped you heal the little girl whose stomach had been cut open, I felt good about it. I thought maybe the Tecton wasn't so bad after all. But now—I feel soiled!"

Even with her reduced field, the self-disgust and loathing filled the room, overpowering both Digen and Elkar. Ilyana turned then and fled out the door, slamming it behind her. The two Simes exchanged glances, sharing a big sigh.

Digen said, "If word ever leaks out-Territory about us harboring a Distect Gen, vigilantes will storm the walls or burn the Sime Center down."

"Oh, Digen, this isn't a householding, it's a Tecton Center. The days of raids and such are gone a hundred years."

Digen laughed. "It's a good thing Gens can't read fields. With her temper, we'd never keep her a secret."

Im'ran came over from the bar carrying a tray of trintea glasses. "Digen, would they really be so upset? One Distect Gen? I mean, a Distect Sime working as a channel, I could understand them being upset—but she's not even working as a Donor. Jesse controlled that transfer, first to last, didn't he?"

"He did," said Digen. "She let him. *Let* him, mind you. If she'd wanted to, she could have taken it away from him at any point, and he'd have had no choice in the matter. It's not just her selyn-field strength, Im', it's something about the way she—conducts herself. She's used to dominating Simes."

Im'ran said, "They don't have channels in the Distect. So I guess all the Gens are companions."

"Any way you figure it," said Digen, "Ilyana is something very—special." He was beginning to feel the ineffable fatigue as his systems strove to recover from the high-focus functional mode he had been operating in. "Move over, Jesse, I'm going to lie down for a moment."

Elkar moved, and Digen slid down onto the lounge, letting Elkar take his glass of tea from his tentacles. Elkar touched Digen's left arm with the tip of one tentacle, sensing how the scar tissue was impeding the selyn flows and slowing Digen's recovery.

Digen, sensing that this, more than anything else, was what had been bothering the channel, gripped Elkar's wrist and extended his laterals, using one dorsal to point at the scar on the left outer lateral. "It's healed nicely, see? I can do everything I could do before. Some things I'm even better at. My only problem is this fatigue. My limit is about three class-A functionals a day."

It was like a professional ballplayer now confined to a wheelchair saying bravely, "I can even play on the paraplegic team." Elkar reached for contact with Digen's laterals. "Oh, Digen . . . I shouldn't have let you . . ."

Digen permitted him the contact. "See, it's not so bad." But he knew Elkar remembered too keenly the time when Digen had measured his recovery time in seconds, when he'd carried a hundred class *A*s, seventy *B*s, plus dozens of minors every day for weeks on end without showing signs of fatigue. The channel couldn't face Digen's debility.

And Digen suddenly realized that this was why Elkar had not come to see him during his long convalescence. He'd been afraid. The healthy often fear the crippled in a peculiar way.

Im'ran said, "Let me get in there, Jesse."

Elkar relinquished his place to Im'ran. Digen felt the fanir's strong beat sink into him and sort out all the kinks and eddies in his selyn flows. Elkar said, "Do a good job for the Sectuib." And then he was gone, leaving them alone.

After a while, Digen sat up. "I don't know how you did it, but I feel ready to go to work."

"No," said Im'ran. "Actually, you feel rotten. It's just been so long since you felt even mediocre that you've forgotten what it's like."

"Well, relatively great, then. You really do have a magic touch, over and above being fanir. Who trained you?"

"My father. He made first order on his fourth transfer."

"Is he training anyone else?"

"He died years ago."

"I'm sorry. I would have liked to meet him." Digen swung his feet to the floor. "I feel privileged to be allotted so much of your time."

"Privileged? After the way I've botched this dependency thing? If I'd handled it right, I wouldn't have had to resort to using Ilyana—and you wouldn't have had to expose yourself to her—again."

"If you'd told me it was *my* Jesse you were working with, I could have saved you a lot of trouble."

"He never uses the 'ambrov Zeor'—doesn't even wear the householding ring."

"I thought I knew Jesse pretty well. I'd never have believed him afraid to face people like Mickland with his household affiliation—or I'd never sponsored him for Zeor in first-year camp."

"You've known him that long?"

"You saw—he doesn't even think of me as Sectuib Farris. I'm just 'Digen' to him. In fact, I haven't even seen him since I became Sectuib."

"I don't like to gossip," said Im'ran. And it was true. Digen had never heard Im'ran say anything personal about another. "But—well—Mora knows the girl who Jesse is going with. A renSime—Rona ambrov Zeor."

Digen nodded. "I know her parents. Good for Jesse."

"The big argument between them is whether you're going to perform the wedding in Zeor or whether it will be a civil wedding. Any wedding the Sectuib in Zeor performs will make the newsreels in theaters across the continent. Jesse apparently doesn't want a Zeor wedding—because he doesn't feel worthy of it."

"Not worthy? What's he done that I don't know about?"

"Nothing. The man's a model channel! I've never worked for better. The whole dependency mess was my fault, you know that. But Jesse feels it's his fault."

Now Digen nodded comprehension. "I should have guessed. He was always that way, even when we were kids. I'll have to have a talk with him."

"Don't let on I said anything. Mora would murder me. Besides, Imil doesn't carry tales."

Im'ran's right hand was resting on Digen's left arm, just over the lateral scar. As they had been talking, the Gen had been working. Digen admired Im'ran's smoothness in splitting his attention. He put one dorsal tentacle of his left hand on the Gen's crest ring, bearing both the seal of Imil and the Tecton Donor's identification. "You feel very strongly about your house, don't you, Im'?"

"Well, about being a householder, yes, but about Imil in particular—no, not anymore. Did you know I'm first companion now? And I can't stand—you won't tell anyone I said so?—I just can't stand Asquith."

Digen laughed. He laughed so hard and long that Im'ran said, "What's so funny? A first companion who can't stand his own Sectuib?"

"No, no, that's not funny at all. You don't know, do you? About Wyner and Asquith? You're—what—my age? You should remember."

Im'ran, bewildered, shook his head.

"Before Asquith's father died and she became Sectuib in Imil, she wanted to trade into Zeor and marry my brother Wyner, who was heir to Zeor at that time. The bargain was that she would come to Zeor and I would go to Imil to become Sectuib in Imil. The bargaining went on for months, until Wyner told me that he just couldn't stand Asquith. But Wyner—he couldn't defend himself. And one time Asquith and I met at some changeover party, and—I don't remember what happened, but I got so mad at her I threw a pastry at her. There are newspaper photographs to prove how redfaced I was—I screamed something obscene to the effect that I'd rather be fourth channel under Wyner than Sectuib anywhere—no offense to Imil, you understand."

Im'ran joined Digen's laughter then, gasping out that he remembered the incident now but had thought it was Digen's other brother, Nigel, who had been involved. "Now I understand," said Im'ran, "why Asquith is always saying that if it hadn't been for you, *she* would have become Sectuib in Zeor."

Digen wasn't sure about that. The process of choosing the best channel in a householding was often long and complex. "She might well have ended up Regent if not Sectuib."

"As far as world prestige is concerned, the Regent in Zeor is far more powerful than any mere Sectuib of another house."

Digen chuckled, shaking his head. "As a politician, I make a pretty good surgeon."

Im'ran started to answer, then stopped himself. "Uh-oh."

"What?"

"Asquith is arriving on the night train, it says on today's schedule."

"Really?" said Digen. "Well, all that was a long time ago. We've both grown up some."

"You maybe, but I'm not so sure about her."

"I don't intend to go out of my way to see her. But if I do see her, I shall merely extend Zeor's greeting in a formal way. Don't worry, the world has yet to see the Sectuib of one house being rude to the Sectuib of another —at least not in public."

Im'ran fell silent, brooding. Digen was beginning to be able to read the Gen's nager. "Im', is there something you want to tell me?"

Im'ran shook his head. "This isn't the right time."

"It may not be the right time," said Digen, "but the way life is around here, it might well be the only time. How long has it been since we've sat over a glass of tea together? You know, the only reason I'm still sitting here is that I didn't turn on my light on the roll board when I came into the building. The page doesn't know I'm here yet."

"You've got a point." Im'ran sighed. "Digen, I—I have a secret ambition."

Digen listened.

"I would—I want to be adopted into the House of Zeor. There. I've said it."

Digen considered gravely before he answered. "Im', you are good enough, no doubt about that. But—there *is* the matter of Jesse's dependency. Zeor is even stricter than the Tecton when it comes to carelessness—not that I believe you were careless, but—look, let's put it off until after our transfer. After that, I'll know you better than you can be known on paper. But—if that's all clear, and I don't see why it shouldn't be—I'll talk to Asquith about it. Tell me, how does Mora feel about all this?"

"Mora?"

"She means a lot to you. Is it mutual?"

Im'ran twirled his glass nervously between his palms.

"I keep asking her to marry me, but she keeps putting me off."

"Zeor doesn't marry outsiders, and I take it she isn't a householder at all. Is that why she's putting you off?"

"No."

"You can be so positive?"

"I know why. She has something she wants to do first."

"Hm? What's that?" It was an impertinent question, but Im'ran's request for adoption put their relationship in a new light.

Im'ran said, "I think she'd rather tell you herself. It's really more between you and her, I think."

Digen had a leaping intuition. "She wants a Farris child as her firstborn?"

Im'ran started, turning toward Digen. "How did you know?"

"A lot of women have that dream. Farris men develop an instinct for spotting it. I hadn't really thought it of her, though. She didn't strike me as the calculating or ambitious type." Digen had been propositioned many times, and had been happy to consent on several occasions, but never to those who merely wanted the social status and financial security that came with giving the world a Farris child.

"She's not like that," said Im'ran. "She's the foolish idealist type. Sometimes she goes without sex so long her proficiency numbers fall into the danger zone and the controller has to order her to straighten herself out. Since she heard you were coming, she's been impossible to live with."

"I can sympathize," said Digen. "Even though it's been a long time since I had a transfer good enough to bring me any sort of sexual sensitivity."

Im'ran set his tea aside, taking Digen's hands. "How long exactly?" he asked in his professional voice, reminding Digen more of the chief resident at the hospital than of a Donor.

"Oh, a little over two years, I guess. I stopped counting."

"Shenshid! Farrises have been known to die of coital deprivation."

Digen sighed. "Look, Jesse's all squared away now. Nothing's preventing you and me from working up to a really great transfer. Then I'll have a—talk—with Mora."

Chapter 6

IMRAHAN TRANSFER

During the next few days, as his transfer approached and Im'ran worked harder and harder to raise Digen's intilfactor—the psychological component of need—to maximum, Digen managed to get through his duties at the hospital mainly by force of will. Hogan, seeing the mounting strain on Digen, would coax him out onto their little private spot of roof to watch the sunset and unwind a bit. He contrived to make a regular little ritual out of it, which Digen found himself anticipating with pleasure.

The morning of his transfer appointment with Im'ran, Digen arranged to get away from the hospital early. He was too irritable and restless for rounds. Trudging up the hill behind the hospital, he took his usual path, angling from the top of the hill down through a little glade, and along a tree-shaded tunnel toward the side door of the Sime Center's in-Territory collectorium. As he neared the top of the hill, fairly counting the steps to the Sime/Gen Territory border marker, he at first thought his imagination was playing tricks on him. But as he neared the turn in the path at the border he looked up and saw with his eyes that Im'ran was indeed waiting for him.

The moment Digen stepped past the marker, Im'ran began helping him off with the retainers as he did almost every morning, and Digen knew he wasn't hallucinating. Laughing, Digen asked, "What are you doing here so early?"

"Hiding," said Im'ran succinctly. "Sectuib Asquith left this morning, and Mickland is in a foul mood. He's taking it out on everyone he comes across."

"Ah!" said Digen, understanding. Mickland had been using his best political tact while the center had the Sectuib of the House of Imil as a guest, but it had been too much of a strain on the man. He resented the way people offhandedly took the orders of any Sectuib. Now that the guest was gone, Mickland was back to normal.

With the retainers off at last, Digen stretched luxuriously and led the way off the path into their favorite glade. In the dewy shade of the summer morning, Digen knelt beside the brook and buried his arms in the chill water. The cold took the fire out of his swollen glands. Im'ran's nager had already begun to work its magic on him, and he felt much more relaxed.

Im'ran went to a satchel he'd brought along, saying, "I've got something special this morning." He brought out an insulated bottle and poured muddy brown liquid into glasses, offering one to Digen. "Try this."

Digen took the chilled glass and eyed the brew dubiously. "What is it?"

"Just taste it."

Digen sipped, expecting the usual nausea any food roused in him during need. But it didn't taste bad. He shrugged and sat down cross-legged on the grass, leaning against his favorite rock. "Well, what is it?"

"I'll tell you after you finish drinking it," said Im'ran, seating himself beside Digen. "Don't worry, though, it's nothing you're allergic to. I checked that."

"Never entered my mind," said Digen. That it hadn't, he knew, was a sign of how implicitly he had come to trust Im'ran. And thinking of that trust—"Im', there's something you ought to know," he said. "Yesterday I spoke to Asquith about trading you."

Im'ran, lazily contemplating the canopy of leaves, suddenly braced himself alertly. "Did she name her price?"

Digen nodded. "She said she'd trade you—for my sister Bett."

Im'ran jerked to a sitting position, spilling some of his tea. "She's crazy!"

Digen shook his head. "She just doesn't want to trade you." He measured Im'ran with an impish grin that made the dimple in his chin visible. "Actually, it would be a fair trade—if I could qualify you four-plus with this transfer. Bett's a four-plus, you know. She's one of only three Gens in the Tecton who can handle me when I go for my full capacity and speed together." With a glint in his eye, he added, "Except, maybe, you."

Catching sight of the mischievous little boy behind the

facade of the Sectuib, Im'ran made an exasperated noise and relaxed. "After all the fuss you made about trading into Imil, you expect me to believe you'd trade your own sister?"

"I'd have to discuss it with her, of course. But consider —she's not married yet, and her choices would be wider in Imil. Besides, I'd be getting Mora, too, and with her maybe an heir. Not a bad deal."

"Digen! You talk like some Sectuib of a hundred years ago!"

Putting on a hurt face, Digen said, "You don't want to be the father of my heir?"

"*Will* you be serious!" Im'ran was squirming inwardly, and Digen realized that the Gen was actually feeling threatened in some way. Relenting, Digen said somberly, "I'm only half teasing. You are capable of qualifying. And I've always been pretty good at dickering up trades to Zeor's advantage. But it will be easier for me if you do qualify. Asquith has no earthly use for a four-plus companion."

"Digen, I don't have to qualify four-plus to make this transfer work right. I can control it myself, and . . ."

"Maybe, maybe," said Digen. "I know it's asking a lot, but look, I've got to have a real Donor, somebody I can't possibly hurt no matter what I do—I've got to have that soon, Im', and for me that means qualifying someone. You're the only one—the only one in the Tecton—I might qualify. I won't—I refuse to—look outside the Tecton."

"I understand," said Im'ran.

Im'ran was Digen's protection against the all too natural obsession with Ilyana that would lead to lortuen, and they both knew it.

"Im', you don't realize how far you've come these last few weeks. I'd estimate exposure to me has brought your capacity up to within six per cent of mine; and with this appointment a full twenty-seven hours early for me, I'll only have to draw about ninety-five per cent of my full capacity. That leaves you short a mere one per cent— considering what I've had to make do with lately, that's what I'd call perfect. It's surely close enough so that if you'll go passive and let me control it fully, I can qualify you and still stop short in time not to hurt you."

"I may be close enough in capacity," said Im'ran, "but

I'm slow for you, not anywhere near the three-nine-nine-nine speeds you're tacitly rated at. And you're really a four-plus. God alone knows how fast that is!"

"My point exactly. I have to be so bloodyshen careful not to kill you!"

"Look, Digen, if I'm controlling the transfer, you won't have that 'gotta be so bloodyshen careful' anxiety to deal with. You'll get your full satisfaction. I know my business."

"That you do," agreed Digen. "But do you really know what it means to be a four-plus Donor?"

"What it means?" said Im'ran ruefully. "It means underdraw, that's what it means."

Digen shook his head, feeling that he was getting to the root of Im'ran's apprehensions. "No, Ilyana's case is pathological. All the four-pluses I know—all three of them—have no overproduction problem, at least not uncontrollable like Ilyana. The real difference with the four-plus Donors is that they actually sense selyn fields. Not like a Sime, of course, but it's what makes the biggest difference in transfer. They're not working blind the way you have to. They—participate. Haven't you ever wondered what transfer is like for us? Wouldn't you like to share some of that?"

"Digen, don't tempt me." Im'ran's voice shook.

Digen laced one ventral tentacle through Im'ran's fingers and gave a little squeeze. "You want it. I can give it to you—now. How many years do you think it will be before chance brings you another opportunity like this?"

Biting his lip, Im'ran turned his face away, but his fingers held on to Digen's tentacle like a lifeline. Digen said, "You don't have to be frightened. If we try it and then find it's not working, well, you won't catch me off guard."

"Shen you? After all I've done on your intil-factor and everything for weeks and weeks? Oh no, Digen, not this time!"

Digen sighed. *There's always next time.* "I'm willing to risk it. I have confidence in you. I've qualified enough Donors—I've learned to trust my instincts."

Im'ran, still trembling with conflict, shook his head. "No, Digen, this is your transfer. My turn will come after

I've gotten you straightened out." But there was a dark, bleak thread underlying those words.

Digen thought he understood. "Go ahead, say it. There might not be a next time. We're both pledged to the Tecton. We could be sent halfway around the world at five minutes' notice. We might never meet again—unless you become one of the three or four people who are matched to me."

"Digen, don't talk like that. You'll undo all my hard work. You've got to believe, really believe, that this is the end of transfer denial for you, or you'll hold back from commitment just enough to stifle your intil and ruin everything."

"Don't worry," said Digen. "I'm saying the words, but they have no emotional reality to me at the moment."

"They better not have, or we're sunk. Really sunk."

There was a desperation in the Gen's words that struck through Digen. "Im', you're actually worried about this transfer, aren't you?"

Im'ran was silent, struggling not to trouble Digen with his emotions.

"I'm sorry," said Digen. "I didn't realize you were so worried about it. Look, I'm not really working in surgery yet. My conditioning isn't being undermined."

"Shen! I'm not afraid of you!"

"There's been enough gossip—"

"Gossip?" said Im'ran, visibly relaxing. "But some people are even talking about how it will be after you've succeeded. Why, transfusion alone, of all the Gen surgical techniques, is going to save thousands of lives!" He went on talking about whether decreasing the Sime death rate was really such a marvelous idea during a Donor shortage when the channels could barely cope as it was.

Digen listened with one ear, satisfied that his little gamble with Thornton's niece's life was paying off.

For the first time since he was ten years old, Digen felt a quickening of real hope. Surgery would be his own unique contribution to realization of the Zeor dream. At the same time, he knew it was terribly grandiose to think like this. He was Sectuib in Zeor by default. He had never even received Zeor in the official ceremony of an heir's appointment.

"Though I must say," Im'ran continued, "as far as I'm

concerned, any Gen who's crazy enough to want to get sliced up can take his chances in a Gen hospital; when it's my life on the line, I'll only trust a channel. Statistics prove Gens live longer when tended by Simes."

"Ah, but a Sime surgeon?"

"With all respects, Sectuib—it may be irrational of me —but I'd rather die with my dignity intact and all my cells whole." He pulled a little silver medallion on a neck chain up out of his shirt. "See? I wear one of these so my final donation will be taken as quickly as possible. Maybe I'm superstitious, but I wouldn't want a single cell missing from that."

Digen nodded his comprehension, thinking, *No, it wouldn't be easy to go against a long-entrenched cultural bias.*

In a lighter tone, but trying not to sound deprecating, Digen said, "I never knew you were religious."

"I'm not. At least I don't think of myself as religious. But there is more to reality than just—this—you know."

"My father used to say so. But I kind of lost it after the accident." Uncomfortable, Digen dropped that line and went back to the main topic. "Well, if you're not afraid my conditioning has gone to pieces this last week, then what is bothering you? The lateral scar?"

"There is that," Im'ran said, "but I think I've got the trick of it now. I've been working with Hayashi's training machines." Digen grimaced and Im'ran said, "No, Digen, really. If Hayashi could get the funding, he could lick this whole Donor-shortage business—forever! Those machines are that good."

"Machines!" scoffed Digen. "I've been training Donors since I finished first year. There's a lot more to it than mere mechanics. You ought to know that."

Im'ran said, poking a little fun at Digen, "True, but if I'd used you for practice, it would have taken so much of your time that you wouldn't have been able to run two Sime Center departments—or play doctor on the side. Now, just a second ago, you were all for medical progress, and when Hayashi hands it to you all packaged and shiny, you go 'back to nature.' "

Chagrined, Digen laughed. "All right, you win that round. But truly, Im', supplemental practice is one thing— actually training new Donors is something else."

"I admit he doesn't have all the theory yet—but he's such a genius!" He eyed Digen closely. "You don't think much of him, do you?"

"Hayashi? I think about him a lot," said Digen evasively. "Especially now that I've met him." Looking back over his first weeks in Westfield, Digen realized it was true. Hayashi somehow seemed to be a focal point, constantly bringing up thoughts of his parents, of Wyner and Nigel and Vira—and even Bett, the only other survivor of his family. It had been years since he'd thought of them all so frequently. Now, suddenly, their presence seemed to shadow everything that was happening.

With a shiver, Digen took another sip of his drink and, looking to change the subject, said, "What's in this stuff anyway?"

"Oh, just half trin tea, half citrus juice—orange, lemon, grapefruit, pilah."

Digen held the glass out in one tentacle and curled a lip at it.

"Come on, drink it down. It doesn't taste as bad as it sounds, does it?"

"I think I'll just pass on this one," said Digen, putting the glass down.

"It's an old family recipe," argued Im'ran. "The theory is to balance your electrolytes before transfer to help prevent primary abort. Or," he said, raising one eyebrow, "would you prefer it—*intravenously!*" Im'ran curled his tongue around the foreign word with a certain pride, savoring Digen's reaction. Then he added piously, "I've been saving that one."

Digen picked up the glass. "With me, threats will get you everywhere." Holding his nose with two tentacles, he knocked back the remaining tea in three huge gulps. Then he juggled the glass back and forth between his tentacles, spinning it high into the air. "See, not a drop left. Satisfied?"

As he juggled, Digen kept his eyes on Im'ran rather than on the spinning glass. For several seconds Im'ran managed to hold a straight face, and then gradually it cracked like a mask into a thousand pieces. Before Digen relented, he had the Gen rolling on the ground, holding his sides with laughter. Straight-faced, Digen said, "I fail to see what's so funny about practicing my first-year co-

UNTO ZEOR, FOREVER 93

ordination exercises. One must keep these things up, you know." Then Digen cracked up, lying down to laugh beside the Gen because it just felt so good. And, he realized, the tea had made him feel better.

After a while they laughed themselves out and lay silently gazing at the canopy of leaves. In the distance, somebody began playing a shiltpron—a Sime-invented musical instrument—but only in its audible range without any selyn-field modulation. Seeking to identify the bittersweet melody, Digen imagined the selyn-field modulations that would harmonize. He remembered hearing the song once, at a Simes-only party where they had all gotten drunk on shiltpron music and householding nostalgia. "Pledge to My House and Marry Me," yes that was the title, written hundreds of years ago, anonymously, by a Sime and a Gen. It had that kind of blended vitality that marked out householding art, Sime and Gen united. Fully modulated, it could shake your teeth loose with raw emotion.

When the music had died away, Im'ran said, "Really, Digen, you don't do Hayashi justice. He keeps the Zeor disciplines. And he's so—lonely. Couldn't you—"

"Im'," said Digen, sitting up, "if you're going to pledge Zeor, you've got to realize that we are still, in many ways —well, conservative. No, the Sectuib doesn't have a lot of duties or power left. Not externally, anyhow. But the Sectuib is a symbol—a symbol of the House and everything it stands for. Hayashi disobeyed my father and thus rejected the House and everything it stands for. And so he's excluded from Zeor—and, by tradition, from every other house."

Digen sensed Im'ran's cold shudder and added impatiently, "It's not as if we'd condemned him to go junct or live in isolation like in the old days. He's got the Tecton—"

"Digen, do you really think it's the same? How would you feel—without Zeor?"

Digen didn't answer. He couldn't. He knew what he had felt when Imil had wanted to trade for him. Utter coldness.

Digen's agitation finally got through to Im'ran, who recalled himself sharply to his duties. "I'm sorry," he said, laying one finger along a lateral sheath to feel the bulge of the ronaplin gland. "Whew! You're so good at hiding it, I forget and give you a hard time as if you were normal. Just lie down here and relax so I can get to work."

The fanir's nager beat gently through Digen, taking command. With an effort, Digen let it happen. It was critical that he be in just the right psychological state of need for this transfer, and the blocks inside him were so thick—two years thick—that it took a lot to wear them away. Im'ran had a very special feel for the work, and within minutes Digen's intil-factor was soaring higher than it had in a year.

By the time Im'ran took him up to the transfer suite, Digen was counting the seconds until the appointed time. They had to hit the optimum minute, plus or minus two or three, both for themselves and in order to stay in phase with the controller's charted plans for the future transfers. Five minutes' relief this month could mean ten minutes' agony next month—it wasn't worth it.

As they came into the Sime Center's transfer wing, Digen found that Im'ran had reserved one of the larger rooms for them, complete with two contour lounges, a monitor's chair—which, Digen realized gratefully, wouldn't be required this time—its own shower, and a kitchenette. By now Digen was in no condition to appreciate nuances, but he did note at a glance that the rooms had been newly stocked with everything he might require and cleared of everything he was allergic to.

He found, after the effort of the walk, that he was again holding himself tightly against anticipation. He forced himself to relax, to let his intil-factor soar uncontrolled, depending on Im'ran completely. And, he realized, he could depend on Im'ran—that was what was making him tremble so with a mixture of anticipation and, yes, dread.

Stretched out on the lounge, eyes closed, yielding himself up to hyperconsciousness, Digen perceived his own body as a dark blot consuming selyn. Im'ran, puttering around the sink, was an unbearable brightness from which the whole room seemed to catch fire and glow; every tiny, precise movement of Im'ran's hands as he prepared medications they might require registered on Digen with a kind of tactile thrill. But there was also a strain in the Gen.

Im'ran was talking.

Digen willed himself sternly back to duoconsciousness.

Im'ran was saying, ". . . want this one to be absolutely perfect for you. It should bring you completely back to normal."

"Im', let's not try to do it all at once. It's too much, without qualifying you."

Im'ran's voice was tense. Digen could feel it in his own larynx with a sort of sensual contact peculiar to need. "Digen, don't let your nerve fail now. I know it's hard for you to surrender transfer control—unnatural, even—but you don't want to have to go through all this over again, do you?"

The last weeks flashed through Digen's mind. The time, in his room at the hospital, when he had lost his temper, hurling a tube of ronaplin-inhibitor cream across the bathroom, awakening Hogan. The time when his whole left side had gone numb and he would have fallen had Joel not been there to lean on. The time he'd accidentally fallen asleep on his bed in the hospital and had a nightmare about his years of convalescence, only to awaken and find it was really happening. Afraid even to take a deep breath for fear of setting off a convulsion, Digen had coached Hogan into using the weird little applicator to place a medicated lozenge well up his lateral sheath. He had been only half an hour late going on duty. Then there had been the time his ronaplin glands had been so swollen from Im'ran's therapy that he'd been unable to fasten the retainers. He'd used so much ronaplin inhibitor that he'd been weak and nauseated for two days afterward.

He'd been able to get through it all only because working in the emergency ward was really not much of a challenge. The surgical service, on the other hand, would be demanding.

"No, Im', I can't go through that all over again. So, you win. Go for broke. But if you're too slow, you know what I'll have to do."

"You do what you must, Digen. I can pick up your signals—if anything happens."

Digen was sure Im'ran could read the code of tiny pressures and movements used to communicate during transfer, but he was only a Gen—his reaction time might be too slow. Grimly, Digen said, "I just hope Hayashi's machines have taught you the job, because if not . . ."

Finishing his mixing, Im'ran sat beside Digen, taking

his hands. He shut his eyes in concentration, moving his fingers up the lateral sheaths, applying delicate pressure to the lateral orifices. "How's this?"

Digen's universe titled. He had spent so many years compensating for the slow filtering of selyn across the scar tissue that when the impulses were fed in already compensated, he felt off center. He caught and righted himself, swearing appreciatively about fanir talents. He felt himself begin to laugh, but it was somebody else who laughed. He was frightened. Cold and frightened. It was somebody else who was cold, dead black inside with selyn shutdown. He counted as a triumph each second of not drawing warmth.

Somewhere above the situation, he knew what had happened. For weeks he had firmly instructed his needing body to wait for transfer—to wait and wait forever. It was easy to fast when there was no aroma of food. It was easy to freeze to death when there was no warmth nearby. Deprivation would go on forever and ever and he could endure—and then Im'ran had touched him with a nager carefully compensated for the scar.

The hysterical joy of that had hit him all at once. He had made it, he had waited long enough—and then, wiping out the joy, the dread that it wouldn't work, that there still might not be satisfaction this time either. Inside, his body had shut down, dropped all selyn use to basal and below, edging into attrition. There was no physical reason for the shutdown. He wasn't anywhere near his limit yet. It was just . . .

Just too bloodyshen long! Bad transfers had become a habit.

Gradually he found himself fading back to duoconsciousness. He was still lying on the lounge, muscles clenched against one another in spasms of shivering, even though, he realized, the lounge's heaters were on high and Im'ran had covered him with a blanket.

He hissed through clenched teeth, "Trautholo—establish trautholo!"

Im'ran shook his head. "Digen, no. It's too early." Digen heard Im'ran saying words about dependency and he knew the Gen was right, but he also knew that he couldn't endure much more of this.

Through clenched teeth, words puffed out of him with

each spasm. "Must—you're—stronger now." He fought for control to plead reasonably, but it was no use. "Demand—demand you—" And then something broke.

Digen's precarious internal balance disintegrated. With his primary system low in selyn, it didn't have the strength to control the harmonics bursting loose in the secondary system, and the vibration racked Digen. Dimly, Digen heard himself begging, "Im'—Im', help me—please help me—please—"

Im'ran was saying something—distantly—something about a train. But Digen's inner strength was spent. Life slipped through his weakening grasp and he couldn't even beg anymore. There was just a distant whimper.

And then the fanir's nager caught him up strongly and firmly, gently slipping into trautholo. By stages, Im'ran dragged Digen's torn, shuddering awareness into a precise, dead-true Tecton rhythm, welding the two of them together with a perfectly balanced selyur nager. Digen's inner flows revived and his stiffened insides yielded to life.

On the very edge of transfer, they rested. For the first time in longer than Digen cared to remember, there was no tension in him anywhere, no taut, terrible awareness of voluntary denial.

"Shenoni!" he said, breathing heavily. "Don't move, Im'!"

"I know," said Im'ran, his voice professionally neutral. "I won't shen you, Digen. Relax. It won't be too much longer."

Digen knew to the fraction of a second how long it would be, but he no longer cared. Like this, he felt he could wait indefinitely. *If ever I die of attrition,* he thought, *this is the way I want to do it.* At peace, at certainty, at rest like this, Digen sensed distantly that there would be a price for the luxury, and that it might be a terrible price. But after the transfer, he felt, he would be strong enough to face any price without flinching. *Any* price—for this.

Strength returning, he said with sudden insight, "This is what you've been dreading, isn't it?"

Im'ran nodded. "We're going to end up with a dependency I hate to think about."

"Oh, Im', what have I done to you? I gave you such a hard time over Jesse that now you've become afraid to do— What has to be done?"

Im'ran shrugged. "It's done. There's nothing more to say."

"At least our basal metabolic rates are outside the limits for a selyur-nager lock, so there's no danger of us slipping into an orhuen."

Im'ran looked away.

The orhuen, only slightly less powerful than the lortuen, occurred between a channel and Donor of the same sex and involved just the single bond of transfer dependency. Nevertheless, it was just as firmly discouraged by the Tecton as was lortuen itself. And for the same reasons. An orhuen pair had to be taken off the roles.

"It's safe for us, Im'." But the Gen just focused his eyes on some object and concentrated on holding his fields steady for Digen. So Digen said, "If it bothers you that much I can mitigate the resultant dependency quite a bit if you'll let me control the transfer."

Im'ran pulled himself back to business. "No, no, I'm the therapist here. It's my job and I can do it."

"I can see that this is tearing you apart. I can't let—"

"I can do my job," Im'ran insisted doggedly. Then, with an effort, he summoned a little of the bantering tone they'd shared in the glade. "You want it to come down to a contest of wills? Ilyana would say you haven't a chance. I'm the Gen here, and I control the transfer. Digen, yield to the situation. You may not have another chance like this for a long time."

It was true. The kind of transfer where the Gen dominated the selyn flow was permitted only in therapy. It was considered very dangerous, as it was too easy for a channel to fall into the habit of trusting Gens to protect themselves. That was the way Gens got killed, and Simes went junct.

Im'ran peeled the blankets off Digen and turned off the heaters. "Better?"

"Hmm. All right, Im', if you're so desperate to get it all over with in one try, dependency or no, then we'll do it that way. There's no real harm in it. We'll have plenty of time to work ourselves out of it. I'm still on your therapy list for another four weeks."

"Digen—" started Im'ran, then broke off. "Digen, will you promise me something? After—after we finish this, will you promise to go talk to Mora? As soon as you can?"

Ah! "So that's it. Im', Mora and I talked it over, just like I promised you the day I helped Mora qualify Dane Rizdel. I thought surely she would have told you. She'll get what she wants, as soon as I'm able, whether you've pledged Zeor by then or not." Then it struck Digen. "Is . . ." *Is that why you want to finish this in one try? To get me sexually active again?* It had been so long since Digen had been clean enough of need to find his body sexually active that he'd almost forgotten what it felt like to want a woman. He knew that even under the best of conditions it wouldn't happen soon. He'd have to get through enormous posttransfer emotional purges before his nerves would be clear enough for that.

Im'ran had followed his thought, and his nager congealed with an anger he refused to acknowledge lest it hurt his patient. "I looked it up. I know it's been over two and a half years since you logged a completed posttransfer catharsis—in my professional opinion, that puts you on the critical list. In fact, I find it hard to believe you're still alive!"

"I was celibate for four years once, and survived it."

"Don't put on the tough-man act with me, Digen. We're too close for that."

Digen took a deep breath, held it, and let it out slowly, running through a relaxation sequence. "I'm sorry, Im'. I guess I'm just—too scared to think straight."

"I guess we both are. Just promise me you'll talk to Mora first chance. It'll make me feel better."

"All right. I promise. But I wish you'd tell me what's eating at you so much."

"It—it's not—important right now. Scoot over a bit," he said, squeezing down on the lounge beside Digen. "Wake me when it's time."

They had a good forty minutes to go yet. Digen knew that no one would ever believe his Donor had fallen asleep on him in trautholo. Yet Im'ran did doze, not exactly asleep but relaxed completely. Before long the deep, strong pulse of the fanir had relaxed Digen into a similar state, and Digen realized that this was why Im'ran had done it, to bring Digen to optimum level for transfer. His admiration for his Donor redoubled, but he was too comfortable to think very much. Unfocused, wholly content, he rested at Im'ran's side.

And then Im'ran was sitting closely beside him on the lounge, holding him in transfer position, bending to make the lip contact, still keeping them in that state of total relaxation. The barriers melted as if they had never been. The bright warmth suffused into Digen with almost no sense of selyn movement at all.

The flows up the left laterals held exact balance with the flows up the right laterals, neatly in phase until they reached the vriamic node, merged, and plunged down his body, awakening and warming successive nodes.

As Digen came to awareness, more and more he felt a sense of suffocation, a strangling, choking panic that engulfed him.

Too slow! He's too slow! Frantically signaling to Im'ran, Digen systematically shunted selyn into deeper storage nerves to lower his external field and increase the rate of selyn flow by increasing the gradient between them. All relaxation was lost; the cold, aching need filled him anew, overpowering him.

He began to draw selyn actively, voraciously, though he felt Im'ran's barriers raised against him just enough to impede the flow. Im'ran failed to respond to Digen's signals.

Suddenly Digen was cold certain he was going into abort.

Digen wrenched control from the Gen and savagely increased his draw speed, despite the searing flash of pain that shot through the Gen's nerves. At the first touch of that familiar pain, Im'ran went totally passive, his barriers finally going flat as he yielded all control to Digen. Together, then, they fought the abort reflex, Im'ran's resistance, and the pain it had triggered in the Gen.

When the slamming reflex of shen teetered and began to ram home despite what either of them could do, when neither of them could endure another instant of half-triggered reflex, something changed. It was as if a veil inside Im'ran had been ripped away by Digen's rough draw. Suddenly Digen knew: *He can see!*

And then Im'ran was in charge again, precisely matching his resistance to the exact rate at which Digen wanted to draw. Faster and faster, until the selyn-transfer rate peaked at Digen's lower threshold of satisfaction, and the sense of strangling panic gave way in Digen to a soaring satisfaction. Long-cramped systems stretched out to maximum in a total involvement.

He's with me! The Gen was in near-perfect resonance, amplifying and feeding back the entire experience beat after beat, until, for Digen, for just one moment, it was as if his own body were pulsing with the creation of selyn rising right out of the nucleus of each cell in his body, and for Im'ran it was as if his own need had been relieved at long last. Neither knew or cared who was controlling now.

At the very apex, an alarm rang in the back of Digen's consciousness. He terminated the transfer then, a bare one per cent short of repletion. Not quite perfect this time, but he now had a four-plus Donor, and Im'ran's capacity would grow. At the next transfer they would have the dependency whipped, and it would be perfect. He could wait now. Knowing that, he could wait.

He came out of hyperconsciousness to feel Im'ran relinquish the lip contact, letting Digen's systems begin the slow decline into need again as he dismantled the lateral contacts.

Then, without warning, Im'ran pitched forward, unconscious. Digen moved with Sime swiftness to catch him. *I burned him! I could have killed him!* That shock revived him enough to stagger to his feet. He found two glasses with liberal doses of fosebine already measured. He had to cling to the sink, dizzy with the recovery transients coursing through him. Somehow he got the water into the glasses, and after what seemed like years he reeled back to the lounge where Im'ran lay draped over the edge and struggling feebly to get to his feet to help Digen.

Digen propped the Gen up and made him swallow again and again. The fanir's strong, steady nager was weak enough to frighten Digen. He heard himself whispering, in a wild mixture of English and Simelan, "Im', you—you—don't dare die on me, not now!" He shook the Gen. "Im', listen to me, we made it! You did it! We did it!"

Im'ran came to a focus on Digen, reached to take the glass from Digen's tentacles, cupping them all between his fingers. He sat up shakily and gulped down the potion without even making a sour face. "I'm all right, Digen. Nothing to worry about, honest. I've had worse just practicing outfunctions. What about you? Did I hurt you?"

Digen, seeing Im'ran's field strength and coordination return, slumped. From somewhere came an unaccustomed prayer: *Dear God, thank you. Thank you.* And, to his own shame, he knew it wasn't all relief that Im'ran was safe, but something more selfish, more personal.

It's over, the waiting, the aborts, the chronic cellular starvation, the whole Donor shortage for me is over. With Im'ran every third or fourth month, Digen knew, he could survive, he could do anything he had to, even surgery. *It's over. I'm going to be all right.*

Deep inside, a wall crumbled. He let the tears come, shameless before Im'ran, surprised that it had held off this long. Ordinarily, the moment transfer was completed, all the emotions that were blocked off during need surged back, leaving the Sime highly unstable for hours, sometimes for days. Digen gave himself up to it, knowing that this emotional upsurge was part of the channel's stock in trade, that he had to experience it fully in order to produce it in the Simes he treated. And it had been so long, so very long, since he could savor this to the full. He was only dimly aware of Im'ran leaving him, of the shower running in the other room, of Im'ran coming back in a fresh coverall. The Gen sat by him for some moments, and finally, when Digen showed no signs of calming, he reached out to touch his arm.

"Digen. Don't talk, just try to listen to me. I don't have much time, and there's no easy way to say this. I wish— oh, God, I wish I didn't have to do this to you!"

Digen didn't want to hear, didn't want to do anything but abandon himself to the luxury of posttransfer syndrome. The real thing, this time, after so many months of stunted reflexes and incomplete reactions.

But Im'ran—instead of encouraging the catharsis—kept on talking in that neutral, therapist's tone, which Digen began to hate. "I have to tell you now, Hajene Farris, exactly what's been bothering me all day. But I want you to understand first that I had to keep it from you or it would have ruined the transfer."

Digen let go of his tenuous hold on the postsyndrome and sat up slowly. "What are you talking about?"

The cool therapist melted before his eyes. "Digen, you're going to hate me worse than you hate Hajene Hayashi. I don't know how I'll live with that."

Digen frowned, reaching for Im'ran's hands, the ronaplin still active on the Gen's skin, giving him deep contact. Im'ran slid his fingers up Digen's arms, savoring the contact, and then, as if relinquishing forever something infinitely precious, he slid away and stood.

"Digen, this morning I found some doctor from the hospital in Mickland's office. With a three-Gen escort, no less. He told Mickland you had examined that little girl they operated on before the surgery . . . that you knew she was in changeover and anyhow you left her to be— cut open. Is that true, Digen?"

"Yes. It's true. She would have died in changeover, Im'."

"Then there's nothing we can do," said Im'ran bleakly. "The law is very specific. The minute you know a child is in changeover, it is your duty to have them brought in-Territory. That's Tecton law, and it's binding on you even when you're out-Territory. There's no way to contest Mickland's reprimand. I knew there wouldn't be."

"Reprimand?"

Im'ran handed Digen a yellow card. "This was in your box this morning, with your mail. By controller's edict, your special transfer privileges have been withdrawn, including your extra month on my therapy list. Since I'm not required here now to treat you, they're sending me to the islands. I—I can't—even sit out this postreaction with you. I have a train to catch, right now."

He backed toward the door a pace or two, but his attention was wholly on Digen, waiting for the concepts to sink in and register.

Digen rose, blankly, stunned, and then shook his head in disbelief. "No . . . no! Mickland can't do this. Nobody can." Backing away from Im'ran as if to block his rising hysteria, he said, "You're sensing fields now, you're a qualified four-plus. There are maybe three others in the world who can do what you've learned to do today! One in a thousand—a hundred thousand—one in a million! I did it, I did that, and now they have no right— You're mine, *God damn it all*, mine!"

In that colorless, neutral tone, Im'ran said, "I'm sorry, Digen." But the mask slipped and his nager shattered on the last syllable. He turned away, face twisted in unformed sobs. He made for the door, but Digen seized him by the shoulders and spun him around. "You lied to me. You deliberately lied to me."

"No, Digen. I helped you lie to yourself, that's all. It had to be that way. At least—at least this much we have. I'm one of those few now, and we're bound to meet again —someday. If you'll have me."

Digen picked him up bodily and shook him until the Gen's teeth rattled. He shook and shook, and his voice rose to a cry, "What kind of companion are you that you could do this to me?" He was augmenting slightly, taking out all the frustrated impotence on the limp Gen, until finally Im'ran cuffed him roundly on the ears.

Shocked, Digen came to his senses, staring at the Donor. He'd never attacked a Gen before in his life. He wanted to fall on his knees and beg forgiveness. But he couldn't move. He just stared through a veil of dulled horror until Im'ran, running fingers through his hair, said, "You want me to behave like a companion in Zeor. But I'm Imil. You and I work together only under the Tecton—and the Tecton doesn't recognize—personal loyalties except within a house. I'm not in your house, Digen. What shall we do? Disband the Tecton? Run away to the Distect?"

With bitter irony he picked up his jacket and dusted it off in three vicious slaps. "Would you accept the pledge of an oath breaker, Sectuib?"

Digen found it in himself to turn away, to stand stiff and tall, locked against himself, showing only an impassive mask. Then, with unexpected gentleness, Im'ran said, "I was sure that if I didn't do the transfer this way, you'd die in abort trauma or eventually have an even messier death because of coital deprivation. At least you're alive. So maybe someday you can find a way to forgive me."

Forgive me. Digen had begged for trautholo. He had been so sure that he would gladly have paid whatever price was asked of him. He made himself say steadily, "I got one decent transfer, anyway. It was—worth it."

His own words came back to mock him: *At least there's no danger of orhuen.* Oh no, no danger at all. Just an ordinary dependency to be cold-ripped out of him. If it had been orhuen, he'd have a legal claim on Im'ran. They wouldn't be able to do this to him, disciplinary action or no.

He could feel the Gen behind him, wanting desperately

to say something more. The Gen was deep into his own first posttransfer syndrome. *It's our qualification! We have a right to this time.* Digen felt about to break down, plead, cry, scream, kill himself—if Im'ran said another word. Without turning, he snarled savagely, "Get out, damn you! Get out while you can!"

He held himself very stiff, eyes closed, until he heard the door close. Then he flung himself down full length on the lounge, but he could not even weep. Everything inside him was hard, dead, destroyed, and the wall within him was back, as if it had never been breached—as if the transfer had never happened.

Why didn't he just let me die?

PART II

THE DEPARTURE

What is a Sime?

When life first came forth, there were one-celled creatures, and then colonies of cells cooperating.

The next big step was the polarization into male and female, adding adaptability, mutability, flexibility, and, above all, an explosive vitality to the biosphere.

The further differentiation into Gen and Sime —energy producers and energy users—is an evolutionary step of the same magnitude as sexual specialization, so far appearing only at the end of the evolutionary chain—humanity.

The vitalizing effect of sexual polarity can function only when male and female join. The value of the Sime/Gen mutation will be evident only when mankind is reunified.

"OUT OF DEATH WAS I BORN—
UNTO ZEOR, FOREVER!"

Muryin Alur Farris
Sectuib in Zeor

Chapter 7

DR. LANKH WINS

For hours after Im'ran left, Digen wandered aimlessly through the halls of the Sime Center. When he came to a stairway, he went down because that was easier. When he came to a turn, he went left, for no particular reason. Eventually he came to the second subbasement level, under the cafeteria and above the selyn battery packing plant.

There was only one room on this level, the Memorial to the One Billion. Every householding had been built around such a room—a remembrance of the countless millions who had died during the fall of the civilization of the Ancients, during the ensuing Sime/Gen wars, during the thousand years of chaos and darkness of the human spirit.

Digen found himself in the memorial hall, standing on the inlaid spiral of names, feeling the emptiness of the place. He didn't bother to turn on the light. There wasn't much selyn field to see by, but he didn't want to look at anything anyway.

Here were inscribed the names of the martyrs of all the householdings, of the Tecton, and those of Westfield, too. He stood on that floor of long-dead martyrs and said the words that had been meant to express the responsibility so heavy it claimed his life whether he consented or not. "Out of Death Was I Born . . ."

He was Sime. He lived because so many Gens—a billion or more—had died under the tentacles of his ancestors. Always before, when he lost his sense of purpose in life, he'd been able to turn to the memorial and its pledge, "Out of Death Was I Born—Unto Zeor, Forever!" When all else failed him, there was always that. The fact of his existence invested him with a certain inalienable responsibility.

But this time it didn't work.

He stood alone in the dark cavern beneath the Sime

Center, a duplicate of the Memorial of Zeor, and stubbornly said the words over and over, trying to flog their magic
to life within him. "Out of Death Was I Born—Unto Zeor,
Forever!" But they didn't rekindle the spark of vitality in
him.

Only one thought came to him: *No wonder it doesn't
work. I'm only an imitation Sectuib. I've never properly
received Zeor. I don't even know what it means to receive
Zeor.* And under it all, like a litany: *Why didn't he just
let me die—die—die.*

He hadn't felt like this since he'd come out of his injury
to be told that his family had died.

After a time, the huge double doors opened a crack. A
Sime registered startlement. The door opened wider to
admit—Jesse Elkar.

"Digen?" He came into the hall, his nager coruscating
off the walls, then moderating in deference. "Digen? I'm
sorry—you didn't have the 'occupied' light on. I didn't
know there was anybody in here—Digen?"

Digen tried to ignore him, knowing custom would force
him to go away. But, perversely, his concentration was
shattered, his meditation ended spontaneously. *You see,*
he thought, *I can't even hold a simple focus.*

"I guess I didn't turn the sign on. It's not your fault,
Jesse."

"They've been paging you all over the building for
hours. There's somebody in your office—from out-Territory, something-or-other-unpronounceable Hogan—terribly
anxious because you're overdue at the hospital."

At Elkar's urging, Digen let himself be put on the service
elevator that came out near the back door of his office. He
found Joel Hogan pacing restlessly.

"Digen! Where have you been? Branoff and Thornton
are about ready to can you! Come—" He broke off, frowning. "What—what's the matter?"

Digen became aware that he'd been staring at the Gen
listlessly.

"Didn't you get your transfer?" asked Hogan.

"Oh." Digen felt obliged to reassure his friend. "Sure.
I'm fine."

"Well then, what's the matter?"

Digen's will, paralyzed since the moment Im'ran had

walked out on him, finally came to life, flooded by the pain of conscience.

"Nothing," he said dully. Then, shaking himself, he repeated, "Nothing at all." He wiped his sweaty hands on his coverall, suddenly noticing he was dressed in Sime Center uniform. "Ten minutes while I shower and change —can't turn up for work all grubby and used. Who's covering for us? I owe them some time."

In the days that followed Im'ran's departure, Digen avoided the little glade on the hill. He used the front doors to go from building to building, telling himself that winter was coming and the back way would soon be impassable with snow and ice.

But he didn't like parading through the Sime Center's front door every morning wearing hospital whites and retainers. There was always a crowd of out-Territory Gens waiting to donate selyn to the channels or waiting at the accounting windows for their donation payments. He found himself more and more reluctant to return to the center after a night's work on the emergency ward.

Then one day Mora Dyen cornered him in his office, and, remembering his promise to Im'ran, he talked with her, a discussion that went on for hours, and then, in disjointed snatches, for days.

Mora took to making sure Digen consumed enough basic nutrients to replace worn-out cells and keep his electrolyte balances just right. She also made sure he got a good sleep at least every other day. And bit by bit his system rebounded to normal function. He began to believe he had merely suffered a perfectly normal posttransfer depression.

Soon he was walking through the Sime Center's front doors on the balls of his feet, bidding a cheery good morning to the lines of waiting Gens, many of them with lunchboxes in hand, on their way to work.

It was bravado and he knew it. One day he caught himself ostentatiously stripping off retainers in front of a group of nervous Gens waiting their turn. The lines were moving —Gens coming and going in a steady stream—and he was causing an eddy in the traffic.

Disgusted with himself, the next morning he made himself use the back trail to the little glade where he and Im'ran had spent so many restorative hours. He sat against his favorite rock and let the sun creep over his toes, summoning one of the Zeor exercises he'd learned even before changeover.

As he relaxed each set of muscles in turn, clearing his mind of all the distracting chatter of worded thoughts, he became more and more aware of one central emotion— like a steady clarinet tone hidden within the voices of a symphony orchestra, emerging as each instrument fell silent around it.

He knew he had been playing the orchestra of his daily thoughts louder and louder to drown out that steady emotional note. In the quiet of the glade, where he had come closest to Im'ran, he knew it for what it was. *I miss him.*

But there was more to it than that. Hundreds of Donors had passed through Digen's life, there one month, gone the next. That was the Tecton way, to prevent deep personal ties from forming between channel and Donor, to prevent any shadow of dependency that would keep them from working smoothly with whoever was available. That was the best way, the only way, to run the Tecton.

But there in the little glade on the path from the hospital to the Sime Center, Digen found himself rebelling, for the first time in his life. *It's wrong.*

Next transfer—without Im', without any Gen capable of breaking a dependency for me . . .

He knew what was in store for him. They were setting up to double monitor—Mora Dyen and Cloris Agar. They'd get the selyn into him, over or through his reflexes, this time, next time, the time after, however long it took for the dependency to simply fade away. It wasn't an orhuen. It would fade. But Digen still couldn't help feeling that it was wrong. Im'ran should not have been sent away.

Digen had done his best for Thornton's niece, and as punishment for that the Tecton had taken away the one and only source of strength in his life. *Is it so much to ask, an hour or two of his time every couple of months? Haven't I earned that?*

But Digen knew he'd violated Tecton law with the girl. The punishment, by Tecton scales, was just. Discipline had to be maintained. Society could not tolerate anarchy. It had to be that way. Better a few should suffer—even die —because of inflexible laws than that all should die for lack of law.

It had been many years since Digen had been punished.

It was almost a new experience for him. But he came out of it with new insights, rededicated to his oaths and vows. Follow the law scrupulously and the Tecton will never let you down.

One afternoon shortly after coming to terms with the loss of Im'ran and his bleak prospects for the future, he went to the hospital to find Hogan in their room, wrapping a present in gay ribbons. Digen closed the door behind him and set down the bundle of laundry and the package of ronaplin-culture dishes from the center's shaking-plague screening lab.

Because of an isolated case of shaking plague that Digen had found at the hospital, the center screening lab had doubled its routine culturing of all channels' ronaplin secretions to four times daily—so Digen had to do one each night at the hospital.

Shaking plague was one of the rare diseases vectored from Sime to Gen and Gen to Sime only. A Sime could catch it only from a Gen's skin. A Gen could catch it only from a Sime's lateral tentacles. Thus, the Tecton was wide open to epidemics of the killer disease via the hundreds of Gens a channel could infect every day.

Stripping off his retainers, Digen separated the laundry, asking Hogan, "Whose birthday?"

"Little girl over in pediatrics. Lankh's got his clutches on the parents and the poor kid doesn't get any visitors because of it. Dr. Muskar diagnosed kidney disease, but Lankh says it's a prechangeover syndrome, so they're not even treating the kidney disease. Damn all internists!"

Hogan finished tying the bow with a flourish, and said, absently gathering things into his pockets, "I'm glad you're back. I've only got a few minutes, so if I'm late you can cover for me, all right?"

"You going to take that over right now?"

"Well, a birthday present is best when it's your birthday —or don't they celebrate birthdays in-Territory?"

"Hmm," said Digen. "If you don't mind, I'll just come along with you." He snapped his retainers shut and gathered a few things he'd have to have on duty.

Hogan paused by the door. "Lankh lays eyes on you, and you'll be in big trouble."

"He forbade me to follow Skip, not this one." Digen

grabbed a clean jacket and followed Hogan. "And I check on Skip every day anyhow."

"True," said Hogan. "All right. But we have to hurry."

In the farflung pediatrics building, they threaded their way through the back corridors to an isolated wing. "This is Lankh's territory. His lab is back down that way. You sure you want to come?"

"Just lead the way, Joel."

Hogan pulled open one of the heavy swinging doors, then turned back. "What are you going to do if she is in changeover?"

Digen stopped. He hadn't really thought about that. He shrugged. "One thing at a time, right?"

When they entered the room the patient was dozing fitfully. She woke at Hogan's step, beaming. "You remembered! I cried all morning when you didn't come! Oh, give me . . ."

Hogan handed over the present while Digen hung back, studying the eleven-year-old girl. She was small for her age, very thin—naturally thin, Digen thought—and there was a faint hint of jaundice to her skin, which looked the worse for her platinum-blond hair and pale blue eyes. She wasn't beautiful, she was cute.

Digen closed his eyes to concentrate on her nager through the retainers. In just the few seconds it took her to tear open the box and pull out the frilly bed jacket, Digen saw the characteristic dip in her selyn field. As she reacted to the present, he watched the emotional nager interact with the selyn nager, and he was certain.

He approached the bed, saying, "Why don't you put it on? That shade of blue becomes you."

She saw him for the first time. "Do you really think so?" And then her eyes riveted on his retainers. She froze.

Digen sat down on the side of the bed and slipped the little cape over her shoulders, fastening it at the neck for her, letting her get a good close look at the retainers. He stopped with his fingers just brushing her chin, holding her eyes with his own. "Yes, it does."

By that point he had almost tied down the pathology, and he wanted to cry. *It's not hopeless,* he told himself. *She has a chance.* He had to get a lateral contact to be certain, and there really wasn't a lot of time left.

He picked up one of her hands as if to kiss it gallantly,

but instead he ran one finger along her arm. She winced, finally coming to herself enough to shrink away from Digen. "What are you doing here?"

"Trying to be helpful," said Digen. "How long has that spot been tender like that?"

"Oh, it's nothing. I must have bruised it this morning."

That long? Digen studied her nager again.

"Why are you looking at me like that?"

"Trying to pick up the timing," said Digen. "As you have noticed, I am Sime. Even through the retainers I can sense your nager—a little. My name is Digen—Hajene Digen Farris. What's yours?"

"Didi," she answered guardedly.

"You aren't frightened of me, are you, Didi?"

"You're the doctor who's a channel. We studied about you in school."

Digen nodded. "Some of the doctors here thought you might be in changeover, so I came to have a look. Did they tell you about that?"

She nodded, eyes wide. She was afraid now, afraid of what he was going to say next.

"Do you know what it's like to live in-Territory as a Sime? Do they teach you that in school?"

She shook her head.

Shen! swore Digen silently. "People in-Territory go to school, and have jobs and families, and generally do mostly the same things people do here. When someone from here goes through changeover, they're sent to a boarding school for a year, to adjust to being Sime, and then they're adopted by a family where Simes and Gens live together. When they finish school, they get jobs and go out on their own—just like you would here. Did you know that Simes make friends a lot faster than Gens do?"

"Why—are—you—t-t-telling me . . ."

Digen took her hand again and placed his other hand over the swelling tentacle sheaths. "You know. You can feel it."

"No! They're going to stop it!"

Digen shook his head. "That's not possible, Didi."

"Dr. Farris!" said Dr. Lankh, coming into the room on those last words. "Dr. Hogan! Who gave you two permission to interfere . . ."

Hogan was braced at attention, but Digen didn't even

turn to look at Lankh. When the Gen had entered the room, Didi had stiffened, reacting to the discordant screech that was Lankh's nager. Digen held her eyes while his hands sought her arms and he attempted to shield her from the worst of Lankh's nager. His whole concentration was on the girl. He knew Lankh only as a vague zone of Gen outrage somewhere at his back.

"I know, Didi, he hurts me too. That's better, no?" Digen felt clumsy, trying to work through the retainers.

"Dr. Farris! Get away from that girl!"

In just the few minutes Digen had been in the room, the newly formed tentacle sheaths had begun to fill with fluid. He had the timing now, and the pathology. He turned, at last hearing Lankh's demands, but brushing them aside. He was a channel serving changeover, and the situation was critical.

He looked up at the two Gens, forcing his eyes to focus, his brain to think in English. "There isn't time to move her to the Sime Center. If you'll go out and lock the door from outside, and post a guard, I can give first transfer here. . . ."

"You didn't hear me, *Doctor*," said Lankh. "Get away from my patient."

For the first time Digen noticed the treatment cart behind Lankh and the two nurses behind it, a man and a woman, both Gen. He realized that Lankh knew very well what was going on with Didi. He had come to "arrest changeover" with his experimental treatments.

Slowly Digen stood up, keeping between Lankh and Didi to handle the fields for her. "I'm sorry, Doctor. I didn't mean to interfere with your patient's protocol. But it's too late, sir. Her laterals have matured to the point where she is sensing fields. I expect breakout within half an hour."

"Get away from that girl! I'll have you sued from here to . . ."

"Your pardon, sir. Perhaps I wasn't clear enough. There's nothing you can do for her now." *If there ever was.* Digen told himself he was humoring a madman and had to be forbearing.

"Dr. Farris, Didi Rill is a key patient in my program," said Lankh, assuming the same tone as Digen, but the twisted hatred for Digen showed through clearly. "If you don't leave immediately, you'll set my work back years. She's going to be my first real success, the first to survive the treatment. Now stand aside so we can get the restraints on her."

"Success?" said Digen, eyeing the pair of retainerlike gauntlets attached to the treatment cart by insulated cables, pulled out now by the male nurse. He had to stall for time. There was no way he could allow those things to be put on a changeover victim. "You've had some extraordinary success with this patient?"

"Well, you saw! We've had her changeover stopped for the last three days."

"Seventy-odd hours, in stage five, and no change in her condition?"

"The biggest triumph on this protocol. If you interfere now, I'm going to have you blacklisted in every hospital —and Sime Center too!—in this country!"

Digen, however, wasn't listening. He went back to the bed, where Didi had laid her head back against the pillows. Pale and drawn, eyes closed, she tossed fitfully. Digen nodded, wishing he could get a full lateral contact. He had learned to diagnose blindly in the hospital, but he hated to depend on deduction alone in something as tricky as changeover.

"It fits, yes. Renal shutdown, an arrested stage five followed by a sudden onset of breakout, the whole texture of her nager . . . Dr. Lankh, this is a classic case of Noreen's Syndrome." He turned to Lankh. "You didn't think *you* caused her to stop in stage five?"

Lankh, hands on hips, gazed at Digen in wonderment. He could not believe that any intern, but especially one whose appointment was as precarious as Digen's, could ignore a threat of blacklisting. Yet, at the same time, he was caught up in what Digen was saying. There weren't many men in his field who could or would talk about his work. And Digen did have an advantage Lankh didn't have —actually perceiving the nager. Lankh said smugly, "Of course we stopped her. She's the fourth we've been able to stop, and the longest to date. We're going to save her, if you'll get out of the way!"

"Four!" Noreen's Syndrome was rather rare, and Digen knew enough about the total number Lankh had treated to be shocked. "That machine is inducing Noreen's Syndrome!"

"So! You concede we know what we're doing, Dr. Farris? Now, if the intern will move aside and allow the senior attending to treat the patient . . ."

The sarcasm was lost on Digen. "How did the others die, the ones you stopped?"

"They just died. Autopsy didn't turn up a thing, except a few minor lesions that couldn't possibly have been fatal."

"Nerve-sheath lesions are characteristic of Noreen's Syndrome," said Digen, just to keep talking while he absorbed the shock. "Your patients died of attrition—before breakout?"

"Attrition? No such," said Lankh authoritatively. "Only Simes die of attrition. My patients were all Gens."

"Your patients," said Digen coldly, "died of lack of selyn before their bodies were mature enough to receive transfer. The most ghastly death known to mankind. I don't intend to permit you to do that to Didi."

At that point, Didi yelled, the open-throated, inarticulate grunt of air being forced from her lungs by the first breakout contraction. Digen gave her his hands to grip. "Good girl. Hard as you can."

As the spasm abated, Digen said to Lankh, "That's it. You've lost this one to me, Doctor." *Even a madman should be able to concede that at this point,* Digen thought.

Before the first full spasm had completely dissolved, the second hit the girl, and then on its crest a third, and again a fourth. As often happened in Noreen's Syndrome, the breakout contractions were premature, the tentacle sheaths not filled completely with fluid, so the pressure would rupture the membranes.

Digen counted six waves of contractions, wishing mightily that he could shed retainers and get a solid field reading he could trust. But, by the terms of Sime/Gen law, he couldn't do that unless the Gens would seal the room and give him their permission. He had to make a decision that could cripple the girl, and he couldn't get the data.

As the next wave of contractions began, Digen said, "Joel, is there a sterile scalpel on that cart? Bring it here."

Hogan, who had been following everything silently, jumped to comply as if he'd been waiting for an order.

"What are you going to do?" he asked as he slapped the instrument into Digen's palm.

Digen rolled the narrow haft in his fingers, watching the girl. "An act of total desperation," said Digen absently. Then to Hogan, but also to Lankh, who had come a few steps closer and was watching indecisively, Digen said, "Watch closely, you may have to do this someday. It's the only surgical procedure you'll ever see a Sime use."

Digen had never done it with a sharp instrument before, but, wearing retainers, he couldn't use his tentacles. "I'm going to rupture her membranes for her. Will you help me, Joel?"

"What do I do?"

A trained Donor would probably have argued. To steal the moment of breakout from a changeover victim was, morally, a crime. But Hogan didn't know anything about that. And if he had known, it probably wouldn't have bothered him. He was a doctor, used to unpleasant alternatives.

"Put one palm on her forehead and one here on the breastbone," said Digen, placing the Gen's hands. "Think reassuring thoughts," said Digen, capturing one arm.

The breakout spasms seized her again, still futile. Her nager was plummeting. Digen ran his hand down toward her wrist, hoping to squeeze the fluids against the membranes and rupture them in a more or less natural way. But, as often occurred in Noreen's Syndrome, the membranes themselves were too thick, even if the fluid pressure had been right. She was dying.

"All right," said Digen, "with the next contraction, hold her still."

As the contractions rippled through her again, Digen pushed the fluids against the membranes so that they belled out visibly, and then he nicked each orifice in turn around the arm, as quickly as he could. Then he shifted to the other arm. But as soon as the first lateral was freed, the spasms ceased. Now Digen had to deal with lax muscles, a flaccid sheath.

"She'd dead!" said Hogan.

"No, unconscious," said Digen, working his hand down her other arm until he could nick the membranes there. He pressed the fluids out of the now opened sheaths and felt for the ronaplin glands. He could feel them swelling under his fingertips. "You can let go now. She's going to be all right."

Digen had figured that the sight of the completed changeover would bring Lankh to his senses. There was nothing more he could do but allow transfer or have a berserker on his hands. "When she comes to," said Digen, "she'll be ready for transfer. It may only be a few moments. Will you clear the room now?"

Lankh, who had watched the entire procedure with clinical absorption, backed away from the scalpel Digen still held casually. "If you think you can get away with this, you're crazy. That's my patient you've—wasted, Dr. Farris."

Digen looked to the two nurses. "I suggest you leave now. I don't think you want to face a berserker."

They started for the door, Hogan crowding after them. But Lankh somehow didn't get the message. "You can't order my staff around like that."

Feeling Didi begin to stir to consciousness, Digen wanted to lift the Gen up and put him out bodily. But that would surely create a border incident that would go down in history beside the proverbial Battle of Leander Field. Lankh might be insane, but his type of insanity was considered the healthy norm by most out-Territory Gens. By their standards, it was Digen who was dangerously insane until proved otherwise.

The girl came awake all at once. She drew herself up to her knees, scuttling around Digen to launch herself at Lankh with all the speed of a hunting Sime. Digen, caught off guard, didn't intercept her until her frail body was in mid-flight.

The two of them went down in a tumble, and Digen contrived to come to rest with his body between her and Lankh. His back to Lankh, he held her by the shoulders, augmenting to match her struggle. "Didi, don't fight me, you're only killing yourself! Doctor, will you please get the hell out of here!"

Digen had dropped the scalpel. Behind him, Lankh picked it up. "Maybe it's not too late," said Lankh. "We can still get some good data. Help me get the restraints on her."

Digen swung around to face Lankh, putting the girl between them. He still held her by the shoulders securely, but he knew his grip didn't look secure to Gen eyes. He was hoping the sight of raw need would finally get through to Lankh.

But as he saw Lankh coming at the girl with those two retainerlike gauntlets, Digen realized that the man had no fear of the kill. And his attitude toward death by attrition was clinical curiosity.

I'll give him a good show, thought Digen. *I'll strip off my retainers and serve her right before his eyes.*

Digen was on the verge of doing just that. But it was against the law. A Sime out-Territory without retainers could be killed on sight.

Suddenly Digen realized that Didi was a Sime out-Territory without retainers, and thus if Lankh chose to kill her like this, he was within the law.

Digen's systems were primed and ready to serve first transfer. He had fully expected to do so. But Lankh would not yield. Something held Digen in the instant of irrevocable decision, held him to loyalty to Tecton law, and held him and held him as he struggled to make the decision, to offer transfer because—in spite of everything—it was the right thing to do.

And then, suddenly, he was holding a corpse.

Chapter 8

DEATHSHOCK

Too late.

Heavy Gen feet pounding into the room.

Too late.

Branoff's voice. Digen forced himself to focus on the hospital director.

"All right, Digen, we're sealing this room off so you can—can—"

Hogan came skidding to a halt behind Branoff, half into the act of grabbing Lankh to remove him bodily from the room. He froze there, then said, "Too late. What happened, Digen?"

Digen raised haunted eyes to Hogan, making no effort to conceal what he felt.

Branoff turned on Lankh. "Well, that's it, Doctor. Twenty-five deaths out of twenty-five attempts. I'm closing down your lab, no matter how many friends you have on the hospital board and in the city government. We won't have human experimentation in my hospital."

Lankh somehow shook off the emotions of moments before and confronted Branoff. "The board won't permit your meddling in my . . ."

"You may have had a majority on the board," said Branoff, "but after this, Whitring and Shyr will vote with me, and you're finished."

"We'll see about that!" said Lankh, and stalked regally from the room.

All this barely registered on Digen, who was still locked to Hogan's eyes. The Gen, absorbing the fact of Didi's death, was resonating with Digen, emotionally, in a way Digen had never felt before.

Hogan knelt before Digen and gently took the small, frail body from Digen's arms. He held her head cradled

against his bulging Gen biceps and shared Digen's stinging grief as if he were the girl's own father.

Branoff let them have their moment, understanding without sharing. As Hogan at last stood and laid the body on
the bed, Branoff went to Digen. "Should we call help for
you, Hajene Farris?"

The title got through to Digen as nothing else could
have. He got to his feet, wiping the palms of his hands on
the seat of his pants. "No, I'm all right. The retainers
shielded me from a lot of it."

"I can see you're pretty badly shaken, you and Joel
both. I'm not going to ask a lot of nosy questions right
now. You can write me a full report tomorrow."

"Yes, sir," said Hogan.

"Uh," said Digen. "Will I have to face the death committee?"

"I doubt it. You didn't do anything wrong. But she was
Lankh's patient, and it's time he was called to account
for all this. You may have to testify. We should have it
all down on paper while it's fresh."

Branoff turned to Hogan. "You two get somebody to
cover for you and take a few hours off. I don't want EW
staff on duty in anything less than top condition." He
went toward the door, then paused and added as an after-
thought, "But no more than three hours. I want you to
recover your edge, not develop a phobia, understand?"

"Yes, Doctor," said Hogan for both of them.

Digen let Hogan escort him out the front door of the
pediatrics wing and across the grass of the rotunda toward
the Sime Center. The sun was low in the sky, shadows long
across the circular drive leading up to the emergency
entrance.

They were turning from the sidewalk onto the footpath
between the hospital's old building and the Sime Center
before Digen realized they were not going to their room,
but that Hogan was taking him to his own people to be
treated for shock.

At the Territory border guard's kiosk, set just a few
yards back from the street, Digen stopped short. "Joel, I
don't require any special assistance. I'd just like to get
these retainers off for a while. There's a little spot up on
the hill there. No telephone, no page system. If I go into

that Sime Center, it will be one thing after another, and I'll never get out all night. What do you say?"

Hogan eyed the lush trees. "Well, if you're sure . . ."

"Come on," said Digen, and started off. Hogan caught up to him at the border marker, where Digen paused to shed his retainers. Hooking them together, he parked them on his belt. "Just up this path," said Digen, taking the brick walk that curled up away from the Sime Center.

Luck was with them. The little glade was deserted. Digen had half expected to find picnickers there, but it had rained earlier. There were still tumbled fragments of stormclouds in the sky, blotting out the sun from time to time.

Digen dropped gratefully onto his own favorite spot and began to massage his tentacles. Hogan drifted over to look for fish in the brook. He wasn't, Digen noticed, avoiding the sight of Digen's tentacles. They had come a long, long way together since that first day.

Hogan came over to where Digen was and hooked one leg over a nearby rock.

"The hospital should have something like this."

"Yes, it is refreshing to get away from the—the pressure, the atmosphere of the hospital or the center. You see," he said, holding out his hands, tentacles extended, "steady as a surgeon already."

Hogan worked his own hands against his thighs and then held them out, inspecting them critically. "I'm still shaking inside, but at least it doesn't show. Digen, what happened while I was gone? How could she just—just die like that?"

"Come here," said Digen, indicating a place beside him, the place where Im'ran used to sit. "I'll tell you. If I can."

Hogan moved down beside Digen.

Come on, damn you, match with me! But of course Hogan wasn't able to respond to Digen's field fluctuations. Their moment of resonance over the girl's body had been a coincidence. *I want something from him he's not able to give. That's dangerous.*

Digen recited exactly what had happened during the moments Hogan hadn't been there. "So you see," he ended bleakly, "it was my fault. I killed her. But it's all so damn legal, nobody's blaming me. That, I think, is what I can't quite stand. I think—I think I brought you here because

I want somebody to blame me. I want you to hate me for it. You cared—for her—as much as I did, more maybe because you knew her longer."

He got to his knees, taking Hogan by the shoulders, and said, "Joel, I was—I was . . ." Digen fumbled with the English, "primed to serve first transfer. I was—you don't know, you can't know. . . ." But somehow, if only for an instant, it seemed that Hogan did know.

Digen gave in to the wrenching sobs that had been in him since the deathshock had hit him. "I didn't *ask* to be born a channel!"

It lasted just a few moments and then cleared, like a stormcloud passing the sun. Kneeling on the damp grass, his arms wrapped around himself, Digen looked up at Hogan, who was angrily scrubbing away a single tear. *He can't let himself cry.*

The out-Territory Gen culture held that crying was for children, and shameful for adults. It was one of the biggest barriers to out-Territory Gens aspiring to become Donors.

"Joel, I just realized something. I am the duly constituted agent of a social order in which the most heinous crime known to humanity is not only legal—but heroic and admirable."

Hogan shook his head. "Digen, after what you've been through in your life, there's no way you'll ever be able to think rationally about attrition. Now, let it alone. There's nothing to be gained by flagellating yourself."

"Isn't there?" Digen felt he was onto something very significant.

The retainer laws were the base and substance of the Sime/Gen union. They were made not for the convenience of the individual, but were there to give all Gens the confidence they had to have to associate with Simes. Eventually, this would make Territory borders—and retainers—disappear, and mankind would be reunited. One ill-considered act, such as saving a little girl's life, could set humanity back from that goal a generation or more. The retainer laws were the absolute that the Gens could rely on. They had to be. Didn't they?

Weren't retainers, and an occasional death like Didi's, a small price to pay for all the progress the Tecton had made? *What progress?* Digen asked himself. He remembered Ilyana's scorn when he had told her how nicely his changeover courses for teen-agers were spreading in the Gen schools. *Three new schools in twelve years. That's not progress, that's stagnation.*

How very desperately, thought Digen, *this world requires surgery, or something like it, to blast it loose and get that progress going again—before it's too late.*

He raised his head from his knees and looked at Joel Hogan. And he felt better instantly. Hogan was a living example of his real and immediate progress toward his personal goals. No Gen could be less suited to fraternizing with Simes, yet here Hogan sat, attending Digen as if he were a companion born.

"What are you thinking?" asked Digen.

In the long silence they had each followed their own thoughts. Hogan said, "Trying to figure out what drives a person like Lankh. You once said that a channel has to risk his life for his patients. Doctors don't, but they do risk a kind of pain—the pain of losing the battle against death. Maybe Lankh is battling changeover because to him it hurts worse than death."

"I'm not sure I follow that."

"A doctor has to accept death as the *inevitable,* as fate, and just stave it off as long as possible. But changeover isn't inevitable. Only about a third of the kids are lost to it. And they are lost—gone in-Territory never to be heard from again even by their families. It's worse than being dead—because they're out there somewhere, cut off, alone and beyond all reach."

"But it's not like that at all. . . ."

"To Lankh—to *us*—it is."

"They aren't held incommunicado, you know. People can write or phone their families out-Territory. There's a lot of traffic."

"But they don't."

"The out-Territory kids cross a tremendous cultural gulf, often fighting every bit of conditioning their parents drummed into them over the years. I suppose they feel they have nothing in common with their parents after a few years. It's more the parents' fault, for not preparing the child more carefully for what he might have to face as a Sime."

"Well, that's a fine attitude for the Sectuib in Zeor to

take! 'Look how the nasty Gens abuse us!' No wonder the world is going to hell!"

"I didn't . . ." Digen cut off his retort, stunned. "But I did," he said. "Look, Joel, don't be angry with me. We have to learn to understand each other—better than we understand ourselves. We even have to learn to understand Lankh and his kind—or the Tecton will never make any real progress. I watched him when Didi tried to attack him. You would have run screaming from the room—no offense—"

"It's true. When I finally did get out of there, I thought I'd have to run and puke like some kind of lowly intern, but by the time I finished calling Branoff I felt better."

"Lankh didn't react like that. He stood there as cool as if— I'd swear he's never been touched by a Sime, has no conception of what it's like, and he considers ordinary Gen fear beneath contempt. It's not repressed fear with him. It's something else, just as powerful, but I can't name it. That bothers me. I wish I could have watched him without my retainers on."

"It must be terrible to go around half blind all the time."

"Turn off the sarcasm. I'm serious."

"Digen, you depend so much on—whatever you call it—that you don't use your eyes or your brain. Lankh is as transparent as they come. He resents Sime superiority, only he refuses to admit you're superior."

Digen was taken completely by surprise by that and let out a guffaw that startled Hogan. He laughed and laughed until Hogan was laughing at him for laughing like a hyena.

When their laughter finally sputtered to a halt, Hogan said with some dignity, "I can't imagine what I said that was so funny."

"It wasn't what you said so much as how you said it. Dead earnest—'He resents Sime superiority, only he refuses to admit the fact that you're superior!' "

"What's so funny about that?"

"Ooohhh, don't start me off again," said Digen, holding his sides. "The one prime requisite attitude for out-Territory Gens who want to become technical-order Donors is exactly that—the refusal to admit that Simes are superior. You want to know why? Because, Joel, Simes are not superior—Gens are. And you just proved to me that I—

the goddamned Sectuib in Zeor, for shen and for shame—
am not entirely free of resentment of Gen superiority!"

"Whew!"

"You said it."

"But, Digen," said Hogan a few minutes later, "you
people are superior. You are everything everyone wants to
be—graceful, dexterous, sure-footed, strong, fast, you can
see in the dark or around corners or through things, you
never have to carry a watch or a map—there's nothing
you can't do better, faster, and longer than a Gen. You
don't even sleep like we do. How could any Sime resent
a Gen?"

"Because," said Digen, and he was grave now, "for
everything we are, we're only tools in your hands. When
your hands are skilled, we feel safe. But when your hands
are not skilled, we are—terrified of you. Just what you
said—I see it now in myself like I never saw it before. I—
resent a Gen who holds such power over me yet doesn't
take the trouble to learn how to use me properly. It fright-
ens me to be exposed to such a person. I have to work
hard not to let him grab hold of my insides and turn me
against myself. I know he wouldn't do it on purpose—
most people wouldn't. But deep down I do consider such
a person morally corrupt, and his laziness—well, consider
a doctor lucky enough to own one of those microsurgical
sets you were drooling over the other day, and he's too
lazy to read the instruction manual, so all the fine-honed
edges get hopelessly pitted and bent. How do you think
the set would feel if it were alive?"

"But you're not a tool, you're a person!"

"Yes, I'm a person, but I'm also a tool—that's the nature
of the Sime/Gen relationship. I wouldn't have said so before I came to Westfield, though I'd certainly read it often
enough. But here I've finally met someone who can handle
me. It's changed me an awful lot."

"Im'ran?"

Digen started to say no, he hadn't been thinking of
Im'ran. But he realized he couldn't talk about Ilyana to
Hogan. However, Digen's hesitation said it all for him, and
Hogan sat up straighter. In the thickening dusk under the
trees Digen could barely see him, but Hogan's nager shone
like fire to Digen's Sime senses. "That's wonderful, Digen!
What's her name?"

Digen shook his head, but Hogan persisted, "Don't worry, I won't tell on you."

The celibacy rules of the medical profession were still in effect in conservative places like Westfield. It was the one rule Digen broke, when he could, without a qualm.

"No, no, it's not like that," said Digen. "Actually, I prefer my women to be channels. This lady is a Donor. I've never even had transfer with her, but she handles me as if I were her glove, tailor-made. It's a whole new experience for me. She doesn't frighten me—and I've never met a Gen who affected me like that before."

"I don't frighten you. You don't resent me."

"You did at first. But I never resented your inabilities because—it just hit me, because you're like me, crippled in a strange way that very few can understand. And you don't frighten me anymore because you take seriously your responsibilities toward me. You're not—never have been—lazy. You struggle against your handicap. You're a good friend. I couldn't ask for better."

Hogan said, "I like being a friend better than being a tool user. I'm sorry, but I just can't buy that idea."

"Well," said Digen, looking toward the tunnellike entrance to the glade, "I think it's time we got back to the hospital."

"Someone coming? I didn't hear anything."

"Couple of renSimes," said Digen, as the man and woman stopped outside the screen of bushes.

"It's all right," called Digen in Simelan, "we were just leaving."

He got to his feet and helped Hogan up as the couple came in with a picnic dinner and a small selyn-glow lamp.

"Oh, Sectuib Farris!" said the man. "I'm sorry, we didn't mean . . ."

"No, no, really, we were just leaving."

Digen exchanged a few more words in Simelan with the couple, then escorted Hogan out onto the path. The Gen stumbled, unable to see in the dark, and Digen took his elbow to guide him, using the Gen's nager to "see" by.

When they paused by the border marker for Digen to put on his retainers, Hogan said, "I couldn't see a thing, but I got the impression that they were staring at me very oddly."

"Well, your nager is weird, to say the least, especially

for a friend of a Farris channel. We confused the hell out of them. It should make some interesting gossip by tomorrow morning. I can hear it now: 'Zeor adopts out-Territory tich.' I didn't want to spoil their fun by introducing you. Come to think of it, that might have added fuel to the fire! Next time, I may."

They went to work.

Chapter 9

SURGERY

The closing weeks of summer were difficult for Digen. He found himself drawing strength from his work at the hospital in order to endure his life at the Sime Center. As his first transfer since Im'ran left came nearer and nearer, he often found himself daydreaming about Ilyana, or even talking about her without consciously intending to. But they were now keeping him away from her very assiduously.

He found himself tensing in dread anticipation of that transfer, and Ben Seloyan, his appointed Donor, was unable to help him relax. Seloyan, Digen found, was not so much less skilled than Im'ran as he was lacking in Im'ran's sense of humor.

The transfer itself turned out to be worse than he had expected. Even with both channels, Mora Dyen and Cloris Agar, monitoring, he thrashed through four aborts before they could get the transfer into him. When he returned to the hospital afterward, Hogan commented sourly, "You look like a terminal cancer patient with just moments to live."

Digen said, "Thanks," in a gruff monotone and refused to discuss the matter for three days.

The death committee met to review Didi Rill's death and Lankh's procedures. Digen, called to testify, waited outside the closed doors for three hours, then was told to go back to work. He never learned what politics went on above the director's level, but Lankh was back in business a week later. Dr. Branoff went around tight-lipped and as foul-tempered as Mickland for a good ten days after that.

Digen brooded over it, still determined to stop Lankh, but he was powerless to do anything. Lankh, operating out-Territory, was not only within the law, he was viewed by many Gens as a savior of humanity and a genius.

131

Digen made sure the Sime Center statisticians notified Mickland about it, with copies to the World Controller, and then just watched to see what would happen.

Once or twice he saw Mickland coming or going to see Branoff. Always the controller came into the hospital with two first-order Donors escorting him, shielding him from the hospital's ambient nager. Seeing him on these occasions, Digen wondered if the man had some deep-rooted psychological problems. It wasn't rational to be so terrified of contact with Gen pain.

The hospital staff was now firmly divided into two warring camps—those for Digen and those against him. For the most part, none of this touched Digen personally. People were afraid to say anything about it to his face. Occasionally, work he'd done, such as filing Xrays, would be sabotaged. Several times, orders he had written or messages he had left disappeared mysteriously.

But for every negative incident, somebody would do something nice to offset it. The stockroom ordered a shipment of surgical gloves styled with wider than usual cuffs so that they fitted neatly over his retainers. One of the nurses in pediatrics spearheaded a successful Donor drive and signed up twenty-five new general-class Donors for the Sime Center's out-Territory collectorium. (Digen didn't have the heart to tell them that that wasn't the kind of Donor shortage the newspapers had been talking about.) The hospital's auxiliary volunteers circulated a petition to have a Final Donation Room opened in the hospital—where a Sime Center channel would collect selyn from the recently dead who wore the tag of the Final Donation Society. They got fifty-two signatures before a weekly newspaper wrote an article calling them ghouls and the hospital board forced them to quit. Shortly after that, as if in protest, the doctors' lounge suddenly subscribed to a Simelan newspaper, which nobody but Digen could read.

Digen continued to look in on Skip Cudney, bringing him puzzles and games from in-Territory. There were times when he was well enough to take an interest in things, but more often he was battling some new infection. The stench in his room was so bad that the rooms on both sides had to be vacated and extra fans installed by his windows. By timing his visits carefully, Digen was able to avoid Dr. Lankh. But he knew it couldn't go on like that indefinitely.

The day the first breath of autumn was in the air, Digen came on duty with Hogan just as a police ambulance screamed up to the dock and began unloading red blankets before it had rocked to a halt. In all, five shooting victims, three of them police officers, were wheeled into the EW.

Before they all had their names taped to their wrists, Thornton was there. Digen and Hogan waded in, getting the patient who had the most critical brain injury up to surgery. By the time Digen finished with the last admission form, turning away from the nursing station to look for more work, the others had all been taken to treatment rooms or to surgery.

A resident came by and, seeing Digen idle, handed him a couple of units of blood plasma. "Room five. Jump!" He sped away and Digen took off in the other direction. He pushed open the door without knocking and stopped dead in his tracks. The nager was overwhelming.

The patient on the table was surrounded—Thornton, an orthopedics resident, and a neurologist on one side, Joel Hogan and half a dozen nurses and orderlies on the other; at the patient's feet, two police officers blazed with anxiety-fueled anger.

"What do you mean, you don't know if you can save her? The mayor went out on a limb to get her assigned to this case—those in-Territory sonsabees didn't want to risk one of their precious Donors on a raid of a Distect hideout! Not even to wipe out Distect influence in Westfield! Said it was our imagination! Well, it wasn't—Pirot Street has always been a hangout for them—and you know what will happen if she dies? With them all yelling 'Donor shortage' all the time! They'll . . ."

At that point somebody spotted Digen and moved to take the plasma. "Well, it's about time!"

As Digen surrendered the two containers, the policeman who had been delivering the tirade saw his retainers and fell silent.

Hogan said, "Dr. Thornton, I think she's coming around."

Thornton nodded. "Get those IVs set." Then he briefed Digen crisply. "Two bullets, one lodged near the spine, I think. Profuse hemorrhage, not sure of the source yet. We've got to get her up to surgery immediately."

Hogan whipped a tourniquet around the patient's arm. Her head rolled from side to side as she struggled to focus on her surroundings. Gleaming white tile walls, intense light, upright poles, and dangling tubes. Then she came to Hogan—face, arms, uniform whites—and suddenly she twisted her arm out of Hogan's grasp, staring at the needle he held, screaming, "No!" in English, and then in Simelan, "No! No! Get me out of here! Help me, somebody!"

As she began to thrash about, an orderly threw herself across her legs while a nurse drew the pelvic restraining strap tight. Hogan grabbed the patient's shoulders and said, "Stop it! You'll bleed to death if you don't lie still and let us get some fresh blood into you!"

It was the wrong thing to say. She went totally hysterical, wildly fighting them. The red stain on the sheets spread visibly. Digen leaped to her side, grabbed her hands tightly, and shook her hard. "Stop it!"

As he touched her, the shock of her pain lanced through him, driven by the power of her Donor's nager. His breath caught in his throat. Then she ceased in mid-scream and let out a ragged cry of relief, her nager falling into crude synch with Digen, drained now of the wild panic. Faintly, she said, "Hajene Farris, help me. I hurt so."

Digen switched to English, trying to make a point. "I can't help you. There is nothing—at all—that channels' science can do to save your life. Understand that: *nothing*. You've lost too much blood, and the damage is too severe to be corrected by the usual method."

"I'm dying, I know. Stay with me, Hajene—As One First, All Firsts."

"There's still a chance. Let the doctors try. I've seen them save people with worse injuries."

Eyes fixed on the needle Hogan still held, she twisted aside. "No!"

"You're too precious to waste like this. Trust me, they know what they're doing."

She was fading fast, shock and blood loss catching up to her again. "I can trust you, Hajene. Not them."

Digen met Thornton's eyes, then said to the woman, "I'm one of them. And I'll stay with you every minute. I won't let them harm you."

Her eyes were closing inexorably, but she was driven by such panic that she managed to insist, clearly, "Pledge of Firsts—"

Digen hesitated, pleading to Thornton with his eyes. *I can't break a pledge like that.* Thornton gave a slight nod. Digen turned to the woman and gave her formal channel's commitment to see her through the crisis.

She dropped into twilight consciousness, relaxed at last, and allowed them to insert their needles and wheel her up to surgery. Digen helped them swath her in sterile drapes and install her in the operating theater.

When at last she succumbed to sedation, as the anesthetist applied the mask to the patient's face, Thornton said, "The board is probably going to consider this some sort of intricate plot to get you into surgery."

"I can't leave her, Doctor. I gave my word."

"I won't ask you to break it. A doctor has to have a certain integrity—despite what you might think from observing my colleagues upon occasion. But I won't have spectators in my operating theater. You'll scrub in as an assistant. Jump!"

The nurses were efficiently preparing the room while one of Thornton's residents was prepping the operating field. Digen considered and decided that stepping out to scrub didn't constitute abandoning his patient.

Digen had lost track of Hogan. He realized it only when his friend half poked his head into the scrub room, holding two dripping X-ray films, to say, "Your sterile retainers are in the autoclave." And then he was gone with the Xrays for Thornton.

When Digen rejoined his patient, Thornton was already making some progress with increasing her blood pressure. A whole-blood bottle had been attached to the IV stand. Thornton said, "Stand here, Dr. Hogan. You there, Dr. Farris. I'll want the retractors in two minutes."

With that, he continued to peer alternately at the X-ray film displayed off to one side and at the blood-pressure indicator, which the anesthetist read off at thirty-second intervals.

As Digen and Hogan took their places, Digen said, "I never even found out her name."

"She knew you—I thought you knew her," said Thornton, holding out a hand, into which a nurse slapped a scalpel without being told to.

Somebody said, "Everyone in-Territory knows a Farris, and they're all Hajene Farris."

Thornton grunted, studying the blood pressure and respiration. Then, eyeing the Xray again and positioning his scalpel carefully, he said, "A little more light on the field, Nurse." And to Digen, "Name's Ditana Amanso. I understand she's a first-order Donor."

"That she is," said Digen, once more overcome by her nager. Ditana Amanso wasn't above a 3.0, but she was definitely high field, and Digen couldn't help but feel it. He braced himself as Thornton lowered the scalpel to slash open the wound, saying, "We're going to have to do some fancy repair work in here, Doctors, now observe carefully."

Digen could barely stifle a gasp. Amanso's body had been responding to Digen's nager, increasing her selyn production to her maximum. This was, Digen was sure, one of the prime reasons she was still alive. Yet, that same powerful production now drove the shock of sliced tissues, sundered cells, deep into Digen's body.

". . . I said, *retractors,* Dr. Farris!"

Thornton, struggling to catch every bleeder, to save every ounce of blood he could, didn't look up. If he had, he might have thrown Digen out of the room rather than risk having him faint.

Digen extended the retractor. The assisting resident placed the cruel-looking instrument along the incision and pulled back to hold the wound open, saying, "Now, just hold that tension, just like that, no more, no less, until I tell you to stop."

Thornton bent over the wound and swore. Then, offhandedly, he said, "What I don't understand is how she's —hemostat—still alive, let alone—hemostat—how she managed to regain consciousness downstairs. Sponge. Clamp. And you better have enough of those on that tray."

Digen only half heard him. He could see, over the resident's shoulder, just one corner of the operating field. What he couldn't see he could perceive, etched in fire within his own guts. Against that, the resident's occasional revulsion at the sight of Digen's retainers hardly registered at all.

Placing a vacuum tube into the incision, Thornton drained the fluids that had collected, had the light adjusted a few times, and then said, "Maybe it's not as bad as it looked at first. Get comfortable, gentlemen, this may take a while." And he began, painstakingly, to dissect away the damaged portion of her liver.

While his fingers flew through the work with deft precision, Thornton went on, "If she survives the first eight hours or so after surgery, she'll have the psychological shock of finding that she may never have the use of her legs again. That will probably kill the last spark of her will to live, which is the only thing that's sustained her this far. Yes, gentlemen, you will find as you go on in medicine that 'will to live' is a very tangible factor, often decisive."

Thornton went on and on, lecturing to the interns on one level, then to his resident on another. Some surgeons had to have a radio playing while they operated, others swore and threw things on the floor, others blamed every little problem on the incompetence of the nurses, and others told gruesome jokes. These were the colorful legends among surgery teams. By and large, most surgeons put in a day's work and went home satisfied. But Thornton was a born professor, lecturing casually, easily, constantly, but in a wholly uninvolved monotone. And he expected to be listened to.

Digen could not listen. As internal organs were sutured back together, as muscles were mended, and cells destroyed in the tedious process, Digen, whose only responsibility was to stand perfectly still, pulling on a retractor at a steady rate, drifted on her selyn field inexorably up into hyperconsciousness, snapping rudely back down to duoconsciousness every time Thornton attacked a high selyn-field zone.

The first few times that the transition to duoconsciousness hit him involuntarily, it was an unpleasant shock. But then it didn't feel too bad, and Digen congratulated himself on getting used to one phenomenon of the surgical theater. After a time, he found himself waiting with anticipation for the forced snap back to duoconsciousness. There was a certain electrifying thrill to it that was totally different from anything he'd ever felt before.

After a while he let it happen and just ignored it. But toward the end he suddenly found himself wishing to guide

Thornton's hands toward a zone of high-density selyn storage in the Gen's body—*there, right there*—anticipating the resounding snap to duoconsciousness it would cause him.

Then he was thrown abruptly all the way down into hypoconsciousness, losing all touch with the selyn fields.

The world stood out around him in stark, too bright colors that hurt his eyes, with sounds that were merely dim clicks penetrating like needles in the brain, and he could almost feel the polka-dot weave of the Sime Center undershorts he was wearing. The stinging smell of the room seared through his sinuses, bringing tears to his eyes.

He staggered under the impact of it, and swore silently, *Shen!* He suddenly found that he was shaking, with real tears flooding his eyes now. The thick walls of emotional callus that had held him since Im'ran's departure were dissolved, gone as if they'd never been. For a few moments he thought he was going to collapse in postsyndrome.

But Thornton's voice shocked him back to reality. "Dr. Farris! *If* you please!"

Digen realized that his retractor had become dislodged. Still swaying on his feet, he replaced it and resumed his stance. It wasn't long before the surgeons had completed the work and released the two interns from holding retractors.

During this time, Digen gradually faded back to duoconsciousness and stayed there, not comfortable but less affected by the superficial suturing that closed the wound. His internal balances had been badly disrupted, and he knew that he required some time with a good Donor to set himself to rights.

Yet, he had given his word to stay with Ditana Amanso —and Thornton had said it might take eight hours or more in the recovery room before she regained consciousness.

As they were all stripping off their gloves and gowns, Thornton said, "I presume, Dr. Farris, that you intend to sit with her until she comes to?"

"Yes," said Digen. "I'd like to. I'm obligated to."

"Hmm," said Thornton. "Well, since I'm having you two assigned to my staff, effective immediately, I may as well send a couple of my interns down to cover for you, and let you get some experience following post-surgery patients. Report to the recovery room—"

He saw the surprise on Hogan's face and added, "Oh, you can take time out for coffee first. I'm not a slave driver. You did well enough—for green interns. If Dr. Farris can learn to pay attention the way you do, and if you can learn to stand still the way he does—no, Dr. Farris, I don't blame you for freezing up at first sight of a real, living incision—I did, too—nor for getting tired and dropping your retractor—even Simes must be human, sometimes—well, we'll see if we can make surgical residents out of you in five months."

At that, Thornton left, the swinging door flapping shut behind him. Digen and Hogan looked at each other, then at Ditana Amanso being wheeled past. With one accord, they eschewed the coffee and followed the stretcher off to the recovery room.

There were actually three recovery rooms on the surgical floor. The most critical patients, who were expected to linger for a day or more instead of the usual hour or so, were taken to a special ward at the far end of the wing. The particular four-bed ward where Ditana Amanso was taken had only one other occupant, who was being removed—deceased—when Digen and Hogan followed the nurse into the room.

Digen slumped into a chair and let Hogan deal with the nurse and the assorted routine traffic in the room. His head was ringing, and he was having periods of acute hypoconsciousness again—as if he were definitely post-, even though there had been no selyn flow into his system. His internal circulations were severely disrupted in some very odd ways that worried him; but there it was, at last, the reaction that had begun after the transfer with Im'ran and been shut off so abruptly.

He clenched his teeth, gripped the chair arms tightly, and forced himself to stillness. Every Gen moving through the room was a screeching discord that further disrupted his internal flows.

And there was something else, a throbbing ache, a gathering of tension at the base of his skull that was still only a ghostly shadow. He wasn't sure how long he'd been ignoring it when he finally named it. *Entran! Shen! It's not possible to be post- and entran at the same time!*

He began to giggle at the ridiculous things happening inside him. Dimly, he realized how it had happened. Entran, the prime nemesis of the Farris channel, was a condition set off by not exercising a channel's secondary system vigorously or frequently enough. Digen, during his first year after changeover, when all physical capacities grow at their fastest rate, had had his secondary system forced to maximum development, as did every channel. After his accident he had become unable to work at that capacity, and as a result lived in the constant shadow of entran.

Somehow, and he wasn't sure how, Ditana Amanso's field during the operation had broken down some resistances, unblocked certain functional pathways, and cross-connected his primary and secondary systems. And now, the long-cramped and abused primary system, rebelling against the transfers that had been forced into him, was responding with both the postsyndrome *and* entran symptoms—a contradiction in terms, but there it was.

Giggling, Digen tried to invent a word to describe what was happening to him, and his attempts were such atrocious puns—or seemed so to him in his giddiness—that he laughed out loud.

The sound of the door closing sobered him momentarily. Hogan, standing by the closed door, was looking at Digen with a mixture of curiosity and outrage, but at the same time he was grinning. They were alone in the room with Ditana Amanso.

"Digen, I know it's ironic, how we finally got to the surgical ward and all—but *really*, a doctor ought to be dignified and all that—especially around the critically ill—at least when they're conscious." He glanced at Amanso, whose breathing was stronger and more regular now than it had been.

Digen shook himself out of it and got to his feet. He was exhausted as no physical exertion could make a Sime. He felt as if he'd just been through three consecutive A-prime functionals. He went unsteadily toward one of the vacant beds. "I agree absolutely," he said, "but right now . . ." His feet betrayed him and he grabbed at the end of the bed, hanging on for dear life as the room tilted around him.

Only a moment, and Hogan was there supporting him.

"What's the matter with you? You've been acting strange ever since you dropped that retractor—"

Digen groped toward the bed, letting Hogan help him climb up on it. His knees had turned to water as the entran symptoms grabbed hold. It was like nothing he'd ever felt before. Some muscles contracted hard, shaking in spasm, while others let go, completely flaccid—but they were all the wrong muscles. His head throbbed with exploding migraine, but he somehow was wholly hypoconscious, still flying in the grip of postsyndrome, and he should have felt great.

"Digen?" Hogan was enough of a doctor not to panic. His brain was still ticking off diagnoses, and in a moment he added it up. "Some kind of seizure?" Hogan fumbled in a bedside drawer and came up with a thick object that he attempted to force between Digen's teeth.

Digen resisted. He knew, as Hogan didn't, that those sticks were not strong enough to hold against a Sime's jaw muscles, and he had no desire to have a surgeon pick splinters out of his tongue.

Then, suddenly, pain like he'd never felt before in his life flashed through every fiber of his body, and the world went black.

He came to moments later, the entran broken yet still lurking as an undefined tension gathering at the base of his neck. "Digen?"

"Joel, listen . . ." But he couldn't find the strength to finish the sentence.

"I'll go get help. Just hang on—"

"No! No time." Digen gathered himself, realizing that he was in serious trouble and might as well be on the moon for all the help the Sime Center could be. "Must get the retainers off before next seizure. Then—I think—you can help me stop them."

"Digen, you should have a Donor—"

"No *time*. This one is sudden death." He couldn't explain vriamic fibrillation or how a simple thing like entran could induce vriamic malfunctions in the Farris mutation strain. "The retainers—the laterals—that's why I fainted. Got to get them *off*, Joel."

Hogan looked at the door, lips tight. It had a lock. He went toward it decisively. "If they catch us, it's your career. But if you're dead, who cares about a career!"

Hogan snapped the lock home and returned to help Digen divest himself of the retainers. It was a slow, painful process that further disrupted his selyn flows. When it was over, he pulled Hogan down to sit beside him on the bed.

Hypoconsciousness had disappeared under the slamming torture of entran. "Quick course in doing entran outfunctions, Joel. Ready?"

"I guess," said the Gen.

"I'm going to use your—selyn field—you don't know what that is. Well, you have a—a force about you that I can push against to regain control of my internal flows. You're going to—provide me with—traction, internal traction, understand?"

It was badly stated, but Digen didn't usually train out-Territory Donors, and he had no other analogies ready. "All you have to do, is—well, just what we've talked about so much—just be a doctor who cares. You won't feel any selyn movement—"

With the next seizure gathering like a dark cloud, Digen slid into lateral contact. At first Hogan flinched, and Digen paused, saying, "I have to have a full contact to make this work—your field is so weak. I'll let you initiate the lip contact when you're rea-dy!" The last syllable exploded out of him as the next spasm claimed him.

Hogan steeled himself inwardly and completed the lip contact. That was the moment, Digen realized later, when he should have broken off, recognizing that Hogan's defensive courage was operating again—a courage used to suppress fear, not banish it. But Digen was involved in a life-or-death struggle against a strange sort of entran seizure, and Hogan was offering a Donor's empathy despite the fear curled within him.

For quite a while it seemed to be working all right. But for Digen it was something like dying of pulmonary edema and trying not to wheeze. He succeeded up to a point—and then reflex took over.

The first two or three times it happened, Digen managed to keep the vibrations in the fields between them from inducing perceptible currents in Hogan's system. But then, at the highest crest of the entran seizure, Digen was locked against himself and helpless. His show field oscillated uncontrollably. To Hogan it felt like a transfer draw, though no selyn was exchanged between them, and the Gen panicked.

The fear lanced through Digen like a spear of white fire. In one instant, the shock wiped away the entran and the postsyndrome, leaving him cold level. The entran he could gladly live without. But the loss of the last trace of the postsyndrome, the newly awakened hope of banishing the stubborn dependency on Im'ran, which was causing him abort after abort on his transfers, was more than he could stand.

In a last-ditch effort to save it, he reached out to Hogan, blindly groping for that oh-so-vital sensation. Instantly Gen panic struck through them both.

By an act of will, before his conditioning could even engage. Digen brought about an abort—taking the entire backlash from the suddenly broken contact, into himself, protecting the Gen from all but the most minor selyn flux.

It was almost as bad as the entran attack, leaving him convulsing, senseless, for minutes. When it was over, with only a dull thudding ache left somewhere in the region of his vriamic node, Digen found himself alone in the room with Amanso. The door was unlocked, standing slightly ajar.

Hastily Digen slipped on his retainers, looking toward his patient as he did so. The severe perturbation in the room's ambient nager had not damaged her at all, but then Amanso wasn't a terribly sensitive Donor like Ilyana. Digen dragged himself off the bed and peered out into the hall.

At the nurses' station, several of the women nurses were gossiping, watching their signal boards with half their attention. A couple of interns headed for the stairs, shoulder to shoulder. There was no sign of Hogan.

Digen went to the house phone beside Amanso's bed and punched his own room number. He let the phone ring for three minutes, then quit. *Where has he gone? I've got to find him—now—before he does something foolish. But I can't leave here. I can't.*

Chapter 10

INJUNCTION

For twenty-four hours Digen kept vigil beside Ditana Amanso. Twice Thornton's resident checked her, and once Thornton himself came and stood over her chart, shaking his head and muttering his bewilderment at her stubborn clinging to life. He left, saying, "Maybe you're a good-luck charm or something, Dr. Farris. If so, you'll do wonders for our mortality rate."

Digen got another intern to cover for Hogan, and then sat expecting a Sime Center pickup team to descend on him with a warrant for his arrest. During the first hours he hovered over his patient, frantically nursing the spark of life in her with his nager, and praying that he wouldn't be taken away before she regained consciousness. Time and again he played the scene over in his mind—they would come bursting into the room and he would refuse, on channel's privilege, to go anywhere until she opened her eyes and released him.

Sometimes, in his imagination, he got away with it. Sometimes, though, they tore him away from her, insisting that his act of defilement had lost him all channel's rights.

The hours went by and nobody came. Gradually the scenario in Digen's mind changed. He began to see the incident through Hogan's eyes, and he began to understand that Hogan would not—could not—press charges against him. Betrayed by his closest friend, disturbed to the very core of his being, where lay hidden memories too horrible to face, Hogan would walk the streets, torn up inside, too groggy from transfer shock—however mild—to think it all through. He'd be easy prey for any thug who came along.

Time and again Digen picked up the phone to call EW receiving—but he couldn't *ask* if Hogan were a patient.

144

He wouldn't commit suicide—not over something like this—he's not the type.

Eventually Digen's ordeal ended as Amanso's eyelids fluttered open and she whispered, "Hajene—" Digen held her hand, fingertips brushing her face reassuringly. There wasn't much else he could do without lateral contact. But somehow it was enough.

"Thank you," she said. She managed to swallow, flexing her throat muscles well. Pleased, Digen logged it all down in her chart, checking her IV and writing up the orders for the rest of the day. Then, released from his vigil, he went directly to his room and checked for signs that Hogan had been there, but there were none. He then headed for the Sime Center's out-Territory emergency receiving unit, where all the out-Territory Gens who survived berserker attacks were treated.

It was an ultramodern three-bed facility, much larger than Westfield actually required. As soon as Digen walked in the door, Cloris Agar stepped out of one of the cubicles partitioned off by heavy insulating drapes. Digen said, "Hajene Agar, have—"

She cut him off with a wave of a tentacle, saying briskly, in Simelan, "Hajene Farris—we have a patient here who claims transfer shock. Our thirds and seconds couldn't find any trace, and we called Hajene Mickland. He found an old burn scar, but nothing recent, and called me. I can't find anything either, but the patient insists—it's probably delusions and hysteria, we get enough of that, but since you're here, I thought . . ."

Digen listened with a growing sickness in the pit of his stomach. He knew who was behind that curtain. Nodding absently, he stepped around the drape and stopped, not at all surprised to find Hogan sitting up on the bed, searching frantically for his shoes, as if to flee.

Their eyes met for a long, searching moment.

Without retainers blocking his perceptions, Digen could feel Hogan's throbbing, bursting headache—the kind that seeped down the spinal column to nestle, burningly, in the lower back. The transfer-shock headache.

I didn't hurt him that badly.

Behind Digen, the door swung open to admit Mickland, who came up beside Agar, saying, "Where have you been all day, Hajene Farris? I have a patient here who claims he's been— Oh, I see you've met."

The tense silence between Digen and Hogan finally penetrated to Mickland. He switched to his thickly accented English, addressing Hogan: "You must not be frightened. This is Hajene Farris, our best channel. He will examine you just as the rest of us have, and—"

Hogan's emotional nager spiked terror all through the three channels. Mickland turned, wide-eyed, to Digen, grasping that he was the focus of Hogan's fear—while none of the others had roused quite that much reaction from the Sime-phobe. The implication was at once obvious and absurd.

Over his shoulder, Digen said to Mickland, but in English, a dull monotone, "I don't have to examine him. I already know the precise nature of his injury—and its cause."

Hogan, tense with conflicting emotions, forced himself to accept Digen's touch passively. "Digen, you—I never said a word. You—didn't have to—I would never have told them. . . ."

Digen took Hogan by the shoulders and shook him once, roughly. "You fool. You should have told them. They were ready to lock you in the psych ward for the night."

Letting his hands slide down Hogan's arms, Digen turned to Mickland, carefully staying in English as he said, "I was using him for an entran outfunction shunting field, when he hit me with a panic and I took an abort." Digen gave Mickland the exact figures on selyn movement, saying, "What shock he may be experiencing is so minor, I doubt that even I could find it under the sympathetic awakening of the old injury."

Mickland frowned, considering that, while Digen moved to draw a glass of fosebine from a fountain tap labeled, in Simelan, eight per cent. "Drink this down, Joel. It tastes awful but will make the headache vanish."

"Digen—" Hogan was still immobilized by conflicting fear of Digen and fear for Digen.

Digen held the glass out with a tentacle, just as he had that first day in their room, and said, "You trust me that much, don't you?"

Hogan made himself take the glass, deliberately lingering to touch Digen firmly. "I failed you. How can—"

"Just drink it," said Digen impatiently. "Drink it all down before we go out of our minds with your headache!"

Hogan drank, and Mickland said to Digen, "You aren't training him, are you?"

"No," said Digen. "That's obviously impossible. We're —friends, that's all."

Mickland looked at Digen in astonishment, and Digen could imagine him thinking, *Friends, with a nerve-injured Sime-phobe from out-Territory?*

"Tell me, Hajene Farris," said Agar, "how did it happen that you were caught out-Territory by an entran attack?"

Digen wanted to say, flippantly, "Don't ask me, ask my controller." But Mickland said, "Yes, and how is it that an abort pulled you out of it?"

Digen looked to Hogan. "Perhaps we should discuss this upstairs," he said to Mickland. "Joel, you'll have to sleep here, where the channels can monitor you."

Hogan shook his head. "I feel better already."

"The fosebine is acting now as an analgesic. The underlying condition still exists, though you don't feel it so sharply. I want my thirds to keep tabs—it isn't wise to ignore even the slightest symptoms in your case. I have some business to conduct, but I'll be back to—"

"You're not going anywhere, Hajene," said Mickland, "until I get a straight answer. I'm not giving you time to—"

"Controller Mickland," said Digen softly.

Mickland dropped into Simelan, saying, with a deadly nager, "His system wouldn't react to an attritional death-shock at two inches, so we can't possibly be doing him any harm. Now answer the question."

Digen paced out of the cubicle, squaring off against Mickland. "I can't document this—I doubt if you'll even believe it—but, near as I can figure, it was a primary-system entran complicated by all the transfer aborts I've been having lately."

"Primary?" said Agar, shaking her head.

"Subjective impression," said Digen, "but that's what I come up with. I—"

"What triggered it?" asked Mickland, shrewdly.

"I think it had been coming on for a long time."

"If you had that much warning, what were you doing out-Territory?"

"Name me two other channels who'd recognize the warning signs of primary entran," countered Digen.

Agar suppressed a smile, but Mickland brushed that aside. "I'm not falling for any of your legalistic diversions this time. I want to know what you did that triggered an entran attack."

"What difference does it make? It's gone now."

"Hajene Farris, if you don't come up with a straight answer right now, I'm going to suspend you pending test."

That could be a long suspension, without anyone like Im'ran to play target. "I took the abort, so obviously my conditioning—"

"Obviously nothing! Answer the question."

Digen sighed. Mickland knew. Undoubtedly reports of Ditana Amanso had come to him almost immediately. So he told Mickland about the operation, leaving out the odd perceptual oscillations he had experienced—primary entran was enough for the man to swallow in one gulp. If Digen added a story about postsyndrome and wholly unknown sensations, he'd not be believed at all, or, worse, he'd be locked away as having completely lost his mind. Besides, now that it was over, Digen himself wasn't sure that it really had happened.

"So, surgery made you burn this Gen," said Mickland.

"He's not burned, just—bruised a little on an old wound. And he saved my life. He's a good friend."

But Mickland wasn't listening. "I knew it! We've all known it all along! Surgery! By shen and by shid, it always comes back to that. I won't have it—not in my district I won't!"

"You have no choice, Controller Mickland. I hold a dispensation from the World Controller to pursue a surgical education in the Gen hospital."

Mickland, eyes blazing, rounded on Digen. "But I'm controller in this district, and I'm serving notice right now, Hajene Farris, that you are under my personal injunction against performing any sort of—surgical—procedure on any citizen of our Territories—whether you find them in- or out-Territory. If I could, I'd pull you out of that hospital so fast—"

"But you can't," said Digen. "I'm free to—"

"*Not* in my district and not on my people, you're not! You'll be served with my official papers in the morning, and you know what will happen if you violate an official controller's injunction!"

Mickland swung around and stalked out of the room, oblivious to the little knot of attendants gathered at the side of the room, watching it all. It wasn't every day the staff was treated to a full-blown confrontation between the Sectuib in Zeor and a district controller.

Digen stood, staring after Mickland, unable to assimilate the controller's attitude. The man was too hysterical even to examine the facts. Finally Hogan said, "Digen, what was that all about?"

Digen realized that it had all been in Simelan. He went to sit beside Hogan, to monitor his nervous system, more as something routine to do, something real and concrete to grapple with, to get himself moving. He said, "Near as I can make it, it's Mickland's turnover day. He's always a little more irritable than usual when going into need. Maybe he'll get over it by morning."

Digen sat with Hogan, talking softly for a while, trying to regain his trust—and discovering that he'd never actually lost it. Hogan's fear was nothing but the last gasp of an old reflex triggered by the familiar headache. During the night Digen left to attend to his departments but came back at every spare moment. Hogan, unable to sleep, talked and talked until at last he got Digen to tell him of Mickland's injunction. "And what will they do to you if you violate the controller's injunction?"

"Joel, you have to understand the original purpose of the controller's injunction—as a legal document. Under the First Contract between the Territories, the Tecton is responsible for controlling the—asocial behavior of all our Simes. Considering that Simes are only human, that can be a tall order."

"Yeah, but surgery isn't my idea of an asocial act, so what will they do to you if you do surgery on an in-Territory citizen?"

"The penalty for violation of any controller's injunction is—death—by attrition—publicly."

Hogan blanched, his shock alerting half the room. Hogan knew Digen's exaggerated sensitivity to attrition, and most of his shock was sympathetic reaction to what he imagined Digen felt. Digen waved the third-order channels away, saying to Hogan, "I have no intention of violating any controller's directive—let alone an injunction. But I doubt if Mickland will actually do it."

Digen was wrong. The papers were served on him while he was signing Hogan out of the Sime Center treatment facility. Digen stood numbly staring at the little folded packet of papers with the official Westfield seal, while the messenger, a Gen, turned to Hogan and said, "You're Dr. Joel Hogan?"

"I am."

"I am required to ask if you wish to press charges against the Sime who attacked you."

Hogan met Digen's eyes.

Digen said, "Joel, you are in a position to make all channels tighten up on their casual interactions with out-Territory Gens, to make sure such a thing never happens to anyone again. All you have to do is say that I've failed the trust you placed in me."

For one long, pregnant moment, Digen looked into Hogan's eyes and thought, *A huge step backward into stagnation; another rift in the unity of mankind.*

Hogan looked at the messenger and said, "Nobody attacked me."

Reaching out a hand, he laid it over Digen's tentacle sheaths. "It was I that failed the trust, Digen."

Neither of them noticed the messenger shrug and withdraw. "Thanks," said Digen roughly. "I don't know what else to say."

"Why not just say where we can get a good breakfast. Anyplace but the hospital cafeteria."

After that, Digen and Hogan tried to go back to their old relationship, but from that moment on, their friendship became deeper and deeper. As the first snow flurries sifted down over the city, they were both under more and more stress: Hogan, as his battle to become a surgeon brought him longer and longer hours, and more and more of the critical or terminal patients became his responsibility; Digen, as the continued bad transfers and gradual loss of hope of getting Im'ran back took their toll.

The only bright spot for Digen was the rapid progress

he made at learning surgery. He spent several weeks on the recovery wards, changing dressings, pulling drains, giving injections, replacing IV needles that infiltrated, and writing routine orders.

From time to time he was allowed to hold retractors on an appendectomy, and, just once, a gall bladder. But Thornton's lectures ranged through every possible variation of Gen anatomy—and there were many variations, because Gens, like Simes, numbered dozen of submutations among them. Digen found to his relief that operating on a non-Donor out-Territory Gen was simple compared to what he'd been through with Ditana Amanso.

After a few weeks, Digen was following several dozen patients, making rounds with as many attending surgeons as he could, and scrubbing several times a day. The day passed in a delirium of fulfillment, for suddenly, after all the years of boredom and frustration, plodding through Gen schools merely to obtain the credentials—suddenly, all he had read and studied came to life under his hands. It was real now; he knew he could do it.

Gradually his duties began to center on the operating theater itself. Sometimes he scrubbed five or six times a day, and he often got cases that the other interns—ahead of him in the rotation—coveted jealously. Thornton was amusing himself, trying to find out just where Digen's limit for absorbing new knowledge and skills might be.

And Thornton also kept close tabs on the mortality statistics, finding that the patients Digen spent a lot of time over tended to survive. He never said a word about it on the wards, but even the other patients noticed, and, despite their aversion to a Sime doctor, they began asking for Digen, claiming his time even when he was supposed to be elsewhere.

Life was not all deep fulfillment, though. Once, Digen came back to the hospital after a long night at the Sime Center during which he had lost a changeover victim to brain hemorrhage. He found Hogan in their room, prone on the bed, in the deepest state of despondency he had yet seen in the Gen.

Easing off his retainers, Digen sat on the edge of the bed and placed one diagnostic hand on the back of the Gen's neck. Hogan's misery was paralyzing.

"You haven't slept a wink all night," said Digen. "You'll

never make it through the year—never mind another three years of surgical residency—like this."

"It doesn't matter," Hogan said, then rolled over and sat up to face Digen. "Tell me, how do you do it? How do you survive it all? Where does the strength come from?"

Digen frowned, shaking his head in puzzlement. Hogan amplified, "I mean, well, look, you're in worse shape than I am. What happened when you tried suturing the first time, remember? And after Ditana's surgery. And all these things, they keep happening to you, yet you keep coming back for more. How? Why? Where does it come from—the—the courage to go up to a patient and say, 'I'm a doctor. Let me help,' when you know you're on the edge of collapse—when a patient has just died on you—and you don't know if it was your fault—and—and you might make another mistake—and—and you have to go and tell a bunch of kids their mother just died when maybe it was your fault—how, Digen, how?"

Digen said, "I shouldn't have left you alone with Mrs. Korand last night. She died, didn't she?"

"I had to tell her kids—after we bought them candy and jollied them into confidence in us. I can't go down there again today, Digen. I can't. What if it happens again?"

"It will happen again," said Digen, with a kind of gentle brutality. "And again, and again. It's what being a doctor is all about. You can't fight death, Joel, there's no way to win that battle. You can only enhance the enjoyment of life."

"But when they die, and it's your fault . . ."

"It's never your fault—when you follow the dictum 'do no harm.' "

"But how do you *know?*"

The vibrating torrent of pain and doubt bottled up in the Gen all night came flooding out onto Digen, and for once he was grateful that Hogan wasn't a Donor.

"That's the worst part," said Digen, "not knowing if maybe you'd done this or that instead, maybe the patient would have lived."

There was no way Digen could share with Hogan the intricate series of decisions that had led to the death by brain hemorrhage in changeover, but it had been substantially the same situation he and Hogan had faced the day before with Effy Korand. He and Hogan were only interns

—rigorously supervised by residents and attendings. At the Sime Center, Digen made the decisions alone.

"How do you do it, though, Digen? How? Because I can't anymore."

"I cry a lot," said Digen. "Desolately, disconsolately, even—if necessary—hysterically, like after Didi Rill."

In a moment of shared silence they both thought of the lectures at medical school where they'd been exhorted to make every death count, to learn something from each one that would be of value to the living—and then they thought of the real world here at the hospital, in which people died and nobody could find anything to learn from their deaths.

Digen knew what was bothering Hogan. He'd gone through it in first-year camp. Every physician worthy of the title went through it during transition from school to the real world. Loss of self-confidence.

"Joel, if you think too much about the mistakes you might make and the terrible consequences you might face, you end up causing yourself to make those mistakes. It's only human—when you're gambling for more than you can afford to lose, the game isn't fun anymore."

"Who can afford to lose a life?"

Who indeed? "I have a friend," said Digen. "Jesse Elkar. He's a channel—we—went to school together. He asked me that same question once, when he was trying to qualify second order and kept failing because he was always brooding on the responsibilities the higher orders take on. But then he found—religion—a religious attitude, anyway—that life is not ours to create or take away, and that death is not the end of a soul's existence. It helped him. He qualified first order recently—that's like, well, equivalent to finishing a residency, I suppose."

"I'm not religious. Where I come from, the only religion is Church of the Purity—and you know what they teach—that Simes have no souls, and all that. I was raised in that, Digen, and I— No, none of it makes any sense to me."

"I don't consider myself very religious either," said Digen. "But it seems to help more people to lower the stakes by giving the responsibility to a Higher Power."

"I guess that's it—the responsibility. I'm just not strong enough to take it. I'm just not cut out to be a doctor."

Digen had worked with Hogan long enough that he

could not accept that analysis. "No, Joel, I don't think that's it. You got to know Effy too well, became emotionally involved with her kids, and she became almost a mother figure to you. You could feel how her family would feel—without her. That preyed on your mind until you were afraid their loss would be your fault, and you just froze up inside at that. You couldn't function—as a physician—because you were too closely, emotionally, involved —the stakes were too personal for you."

"It's never too personal for you. Take Skip, for example. You treat him like he was your own son. What will you do if he dies?"

"It's not the same. I'm not on his case. I don't make decisions about him."

"But one day you may have to—like with little Didi Rill. Or what about Ditana Amanso? Thornton's practically made her your patient. What if she'd died because of something you did or didn't do?"

Digen knew there was a rumor around the hospital that he and Dita had some sort of romantic involvement going. In the celibate atmosphere of the interns, such rumors were inevitable.

"Joel, this discussion isn't getting us anywhere. The way I handle my emotional problems has to be different from the way you handle yours. Or don't you understand yet what a channel is?"

"But aren't we all human? Isn't that what you keep telling me?"

"Our problems are the same, the way we handle them is different. Look, what we're talking about basically is the fear of getting hurt—emotionally or physically. As a Gen, you have to arrive at a state where you know you will not be hurt. As a channel, I have to live with knowing I will be hurt and come to a state of mind where I offer no resistance. Every time I treat a patient—as a channel—I risk being affected by the patient's disorder, even killed by it. It's not unlike the Donor's skill. The less resistance I offer, the less risk I take. The only way I can reach that state of unresistance is via my utter confidence in my Donor therapists and assistants. That's the secret of my strength, Joel, the whole secret.

"Just two hours ago I was—a basket case, from losing a little girl to a brain hemorrhage during breakout. I'm here now, reasonably calm and sane, only because my Donor has strength enough for both of us."

"Then why don't I have strength enough just for me?"

"I don't know," said Digen, but he was beginning to suspect. "Unless it's just the basic difference between Sime and Gen. In-Territory, only the channels are physicians. I've always thought that was because we have keener, deeper perceptivity than a renSime, or a Gen. But now I see something else. Joel, you can't do what I do, and there's no reason for you to try. There's no reason for you to become—emotionally involved with your patients. I do it because it's part of the—nageric linkage that induces healing in the Gen. But you don't work with nager, so there's no reason to expose yourself to such—pain. The exposure itself prevents you from functioning as a physician—because when you care that deeply, when you understand your patient's emotions so well that you can feel them yourself, the stakes are too high, the fear of being hurt keeps you from thinking clearly. The only solution for a Gen who's a physician is to remove himself from that deep knowledge of the patient's emotional life, from the knowledge of who they are and what their illness means to them. They have a name for it in this hospital. Clinical detachment."

"Digen, do you know what you're saying? You know what you're telling me to do?"

Digen nodded. "You have to build your inner defenses so strong that you have no fear of being hurt. Otherwise, your judgment will always be in danger of being paralyzed by that fear, or by the pain of a loss. And one day somebody's death may actually be your fault because of it."

"Digen, I swore an oath—on my aunt's deathbed I swore that the day I couldn't *care* for my patients anymore, I'd quit medicine."

"That was a little boy who swore that oath."

"There are some things of childhood worth preserving."

"Joel, don't you see you have no choice?"

Staring bleakly at his hands, Hogan retorted, "What do you think I've been facing—all the damn night?"

Digen slumped. "I'm not much help, am I?"

"I can't go down there anymore, Digen, I can't make myself do it. I'm afraid to care, and I won't *not* care."

"I can't let you quit—not now, just months away from

the finish line. There's nothing in all the universe you want more than surgery."

"Yes there is," said Hogan, with an oddly dull determination. "I just never knew it before I came here. And when I knew it—I couldn't face it, couldn't admit it to myself. That's why I ran away—after the Amanso surgery. I walked and walked, trying to bury it. But it won't stay buried, it just won't."

Digen was silent, choking on the Gen's roiling emotions. Finally Hogan raised his eyes to Digen's and said, "I want to be a Donor."

Digen's cold shock blocked out Hogan's nager for one frozen moment. Then Digen gathered himself, recognizing—after months of studying Hogan—the Gen's fear of rejection, of ridicule, of failure. And the earnestness in the man gave Digen a real scare. *He doesn't know. He hasn't the faintest idea it's impossible for him.*

"Digen, don't laugh at me."

"I'm not laughing. I'm touched. Deeply, desperately touched. I had no idea I'd had such—an effect on you."

"I think it's the best thing that has ever happened to me—meeting you. Digen, I didn't tell you—maybe I should have, but I couldn't—but—after the Amanso surgery, while I was walking around out there, I found I—I could almost remember—just flashes—of what they say I saw. I remember my brother. His name was Dorian, but we called him Carrots because that was about all he'd eat as a baby. I remember him—killing my sister. I remember wanting to kill him, trying to, and I remember—what it felt like—when he—he—tried to kill me. It happened. It really happened—what they said—and I feel all different about everything now."

Digen sat, trembling. *What have I done? Oh, dear God, what have I done?*

Digen felt an insane laughter rising within him, and buried his face in his hands. He rose, paced around the bed, and then sat on his own bed, stifling that laughter and the wrenching sob that followed it. He dared not seem to mock Joel now.

Digen shook his head and met Hogan's eyes. "The work isn't that different, Joel. The Donor is physician to the channel, applying knowledge to sustain life while maintaining a rigid, clinical detachment, yet at the same time using emotional resonance as a healing agent. But closeness be-tween Donor and channel is even more dangerous than between doctor and patient, dangerous in ways I couldn't begin to explain to you—and illegal, too. Not only that, but it's a much greater temptation. And the responsibility —the decisions—it's all the same. If you can't hack it as a doctor, you can't hack it as a Donor." *But what a Companion he would have made!*

"It's not that I'm trying to—avoid a struggle, Digen. It's that I've finally found something worth struggling for."

Digen could feel the truth of that. *I have to tell him—there's no way I can dissuade him.* He took a deep breath, then another, steeling himself inwardly.

"Joel, our friendship has survived—a lot—and grown stronger all the time. That friendship means more to me than I can tell you—and not just here in the hospital; it's important to me in my life as a whole. Now you've got me at a point where the stakes are too high, and I'm afraid of —losing your—esteem. And no Donor will be able to help." *At least nobody short of Im'ran . . . (Ilyana?).*

Hogan shook his head, bewildered by Digen's shift of mood.

"Joel, I swear to you—Unto Zeor, if you like—that I didn't know you didn't know, or I would have said something a long time ago. I'm sorry if I ever gave you the impression I thought you could ever qualify—even third order."

Hogan sat, furrows deepening across his brow, soaking up the implications of that. Confused, he shook his head. "But, why—why not? I learn fast, I'm willing to work hard, I'm not afraid—at least, I can get over it now. . . ."

Oh no you can't. You still just bury the fear.

"Digen, just think what it would mean to have a Donor who can assist you in surgery!"

If only!

"Why not, Digen? Why not?"

God damn the Church of the Purity and—and the Tecton too! The warped, twisted, broken lives! Damn them all to hell and back!

Digen reached out his hands and tentacles to Hogan, beckoning him across the gap between the beds. "You want to do this. I know, I can feel it, and it is genuine. It's true —being a Donor is more to you than being a surgeon.

You've found yourself, Joel, the real you under all the scar tissue."

As the Gen touched his hands, Digen shuddered with the intensity of it.

"I can do it, Digen, I know I can. I just want a chance to try."

Digen shook his head and turned to sit cross-legged on the bed, facing Hogan. "You would have made—a great Donor. But you've been crippled, Joel—like me, permanently crippled. I've never seen your field vary even fractionally in response to any external selyn field—not even mine. You have no selyur nager—not a trace."

"Handicaps can be overcome. I never said I thought it would be easy."

"You don't understand. It's impossible, not just difficult. Look, if you took a newborn and bound up one of his legs and kept it that way all during his teens, would he be able to walk when you unbound it as an adult? Or put it another way. You were injured, paralyzed at a very critical age. Instead of growing, strengthening, maturing, that paralyzed capacity has atrophied, withered beyond reclaiming. Joel, you and I are both cripples, after a fashion. I sometimes think that everyone is, one way or another."

A long, long while later, Hogan said, "I'll never be a Donor." He shifted a bit, and for the first time Digen noticed a fine silver chain around the Gen's neck. Just peeking from the open V of his shirt was a little silver medallion. With a rush, Digen recognized it—Society of the Final Donation. *Oh, Joel.*

Very quietly Digen said, "But you can still be a doctor, and a good one, too."

Sometime later the phone rang. Digen took it, muttering softly into the mouthpiece. He changed his clothes and went out the door, saying, "I'll cover for you. Come on down when you feel better." But Hogan didn't move, barely registering Digen's voice.

Torn, Digen forced himself to go, knowing he could do little good for Hogan at that point.

In the following days Hogan clung to his work, grimly determined to see his internship through, but no longer talking about a surgical residency. In time, some of his old buoyancy returned. The solid walls of courage, so much a part of Hogan's daily armor, had won out over the pain and fear. At least on the surface.

One rosy afternoon later on in the fall, Digen was taking a break out on their private patch of roof when Hogan came clattering into the room, calling, "Digen?"

"Here. It's summer again for a few minutes. Come enjoy while it lasts."

Hogan clambered, feet and elbows, out the window and tossed down a blanket to sit on. He was more animated than Digen had seen him in a long time. "Digen, did you know they've scheduled Ditana for surgery again?"

"No, when?"

"Oh, not until spring, at least. They want to give her a few months of physical therapy to build her up. But they think they may be able to restore her legs, at least partially!"

"Marvelous," said Digen, sarcastically. "Have they discussed this with her?"

"Not yet. I just overheard Thornton talking with Branoff in the coffeeshop. They figure she'll go for it if you're into it. Rumor has it that Thornton is putting you to work under that orthopedics resident—what's his name, McBryde—just so you'll be ready when they do her. Some people have all the luck. I'll probably be on the internal wards by then. Or—obstetrics."

He's completely forgotten the injunction. Dita is an in-Territory citizen. How am I going to get out of this?

"Speaking of which," continued Hogan, oblivious to Digen's sudden gravity, "Skip's mother was admitted a few hours ago to the OB floor—miscarriage. And guess what?"

Automatically Digen said, "What?"

"She's not really Skip's mother! I got a look at her chart, and she was never pregnant the year he was born!"

Digen sat up, abruptly alert. "Does he know?"

"I don't know. Rumor has it Mrs. Cudney's younger sister ran away in-Territory with some Sime and came home eight months' pregnant and died giving premature birth to Skip—which explains why his family abandoned him to Lankh so readily. He's just an unwanted bastard, poor kid."

Digen was getting to his feet, hastily brushing the gravel off himself.

"Where you going?"

"Just keep talking," said Digen. "How did his mother die?"

"Who knows—it's just rumor—"

Digen was already in the room, clamping on retainers and heading for the door. Hogan called, "Where you going?"

"I haven't seen Skip in almost three days, what with Lankh hanging around all the time. If I'd only known—shen!" Digen swore as one of the catches on his retainers jammed, slowing him down. But in that time Hogan caught up.

"Known what, Digen?"

"All orphans are suspect—you of all people should know that! And he told us—weeks ago, he told us he was going into changeover, and I just chalked it up to overhearing you and me talking that time—remember? But he's convinced, and he's still convinced—and that's the way it is with channels, you just know, deep down inside, beyond all logic or argument, you just know it's going to happen."

"Channels? Digen—"

"What?" Digen stopped by the door, grabbing his jacket and a worn notebook he used for scut work.

"Digen, something new happened this morning with Skip. He's spiking a fever again, vomiting, complains of vertigo, the works—could be just another infection, could be—"

Digen ripped the door open. "Coming?"

Chapter 11

TURNABOUT

Channels tended to go through the sequence of changeover a lot faster than renSimes.

When Digen and Hogan arrived at Skip Cudney's room it was already too late. Panting, they hung in the doorway for one timeless instant. In the middle of the room, Lankh's treatment cart was overturned, electric circuits burning, smoking. Beside the cart, crumpled in a heap, was a man's body—one of the nurses. One of his outstretched arms clearly showed transfer burns.

In the far corner, Skip, tentacles extended, was in the act of leaping at Lankh, who was backed against the wall, terrified by the first of his patients to attack him.

Digen bounded across the bed and dived at Skip, his outstretched hands closing on Skip's shoulders just as the young Sime began to draw selyn. Even through the retainers, there was no mistaking the unfathomable depths of selyn hunger of a new channel. The boy had killed one Gen, and still it raged in his fragile body. *A junct channel!*

As Digen's feet sought the floor, he knew he would have to shen the boy—to save Lankh's life, he'd have to. There was time enough for Digen, in augmented motion, to rebel inwardly at what he had to do. Then his feet were on the floor; grimacing savagely, Digen ripped the boy away from his victim.

Digen flung the stunned Sime across the room and threw himself over him, hastily quelling his augmentation to concentrate on antishock-treatment for the boy. Distantly, he heard his own breath coming in great gasping sobs as he fought the total chaos he'd created in the boy's nerves. *He's still in need.*

Digen's every instinct cried out to strip off his retainers and feed that need. But he could only work at controlling the turbulent shen currents until the boy, weakened by his long battle with infection, lapsed into a deep coma. A moment later, Digen heard the *whoosh* of several fire extinguishers and the chaotic nager of many Gens rushing into the room.

Hogan's hands peeled Digen off Skip's lax body. Reeling, Digen knelt to examine the boy, cursing the retainers. "He's not dead, Joel, not yet. It might be better—if . . ." *If we just let him die?*

Digen shook himself. "Call the center, get a pickup crew over here, jump!" *Let him die, oh, please let him die first!* Digen, better than anyone else in the Tecton, knew what faced a junct channel. Disjunction had always been the Zeor specialty—and the odd or unusual problems still fell to Zeor's channels.

"Digen. Digen? Digen!"

"Wh-what?" Digen turned to see Hogan bending over Lankh.

"Digen, Lankh's still alive! He has to have help!"

Digen pulled himself up and stared uncomprehendingly at Hogan, then at the crumpled heap of Gen flesh. Yes, there was life there. Dimly at first, and then with growing guilt, Digen realized he had been wholly concerned with Skip, knowing intimately the agony he'd put him through, forgetting that there was another survivor to attend to— also suffering.

Digen moved to Lankh's side. "He's hurt pretty badly," said Digen, probing blindly through the retainers. "The pickup crew from the center—they should be here in a few minutes."

"*If* the orderly I sent got through on the phone—the phone company is working on the hospital lines again today."

Grimacing, Digen said, "Then, just as insurance, dash upstairs and bring my pharmacy case, the locked half." Wearing retainers and without the pharmacy case, there wasn't much Digen could do for Lankh—or was there? As Hogan left, Digen picked up the Gen and put him on the bed.

"Nurse, get me a number-three respirator cart!"

The major dangers from severe transfer shock—if the victim lived through the first moments—were cardiac arrest, brain hemorrhage, and simple respiratory failure. The hospital had its own odd but sometimes effective means of dealing with such things.

Digen felt sliced in two. The transfer-shock drill had been etched into him during his first year after change-over. He'd learned the hospital drills more slowly but just as thoroughly. There was no reason you couldn't treat transfer shock effectively in a hospital—at least on a first-aid basis.

Shen! It's no different from the idea of doing surgery in a Sime Center!

Hogan and the orderly with the respirator cart arrived at the same time. Sweeping the things off the nighttable, Digen took the pharmacy case and motioned Hogan to take a pair of shock paddles from the cart. "Stand by," he said, while the orderly connected the line from the cart to the wall receptacle.

At that point Branoff arrived, surveying the swirling chaos of nurses and orderlies in the room, and for the first time Digen heard the page saying, "Paging code green to six-eleven." They were in six-eleven. And they definitely had a code green on their hands.

Branoff said, "What's going on here, Dr. Farris?"

Fumbling through the retainers, Digen opened his case and began preparing a full therapeutic dose of fosebine in an inhalant aspirator as he told Branoff precisely what had happened, ending, "Where's the Sime Center pickup squad I asked for?"

"I sent a runner. Phones are out."

Shen! mouthed Digen silently as he closed the inhaler and applied the mask to Lankh's face. "Lankh's critical, and I have to work in these damn retainers! Can you get this room sealed off?"

Branoff looked to the smoldering treatment cart, where two fire-control monitors were poking at the remains, muttering their total lack of comprehension of what had caused the fire. The pall of smoke in the room was choking, and only the cross-ventilation from the windows and the door let anyone breathe.

Branoff shook his head. "Let's move him, bed and all, next door. But I don't know if I should leave you alone with him. If he dies—well, everybody knows you two aren't on the best of terms."

"That—" started Digen, then broke off. "No," he said,

retreating behind a formality he hadn't used in years. "I will not take offense where none was intended."

"None was intended. But people talk."

Digen took the inhalant mask away, concentrating suddenly on Lankh, raising one finger to alert Hogan with the shock paddles. Digen had no idea what the shock paddles would do to a transfer-shock victim, but if he had no choice he'd order them used.

He put one hand on Lankh's chest, monitoring the heart function as best as he could through the retainers, completely forgetting the stethoscope sticking out of his hip pocket. The faltering heart skipped a beat but then settled into a firm rhythm, and thoughts of heroic procedures dissolved from Digen's mind.

"I don't understand it," said Digen. "He should have been conscious minutes ago." But he lowered the alerting hand, and Hogan relaxed.

"Maybe," said Hogan, "he inhaled too much smoke. Some oxygen—"

"No," said Digen. "Because of the way I terminated the transfer, we may have more than a simple transfer shock to deal with. Let's just get him out of this smoke."

As two women in striped orderly's uniforms began to move the bed, Lankh tossed and moaned. Digen put out a hand to restrain him, and Lankh's hands closed over Digen's retainer. The feel of hard metal against flesh brought the Gen to full wakefulness, wide-eyed.

Branoff bent over Lankh, saying, "Trust Dr. Farris, he knows what he's doing. He's going to take care of you. You're going to be all right."

He went on softly, but Digen didn't hear him. He was distracted by a couple of nurses getting ready to put Skip on a stretcher. He shouted, "No, don't move him! The pickup crew will be here before he comes to." *I hope.* "That's an order!" Moving with Lankh's bed out into the hall, Digen didn't have time to see if they obeyed.

Out in the clearer air of the corridor, Lankh's breathing improved, and he said, "Get your hands off me, Dr. Farris!"

Digen said, "I can't. You've been very badly hurt, Doctor. We're going to take you to the Sime Center, where we can treat you more effectively."

"No!"

"You're feeling all right now because I gave you something for the pain. The initial effect will wear off in a few minutes, and you're going to require a lot of help. I've already saved your life twice, why not again?"

And Hogan, who was carrying the pharmacy case, said, "The survival rate of transfer-shock victims here in the hospital is about one per cent. What is it at the Sime Center, Digen?"

"About ninety per cent."

Branoff caught up with them, having used the wall phone. "Pickup crew just entered the building."

"I won't go!" said Lankh, struggling.

"All right," said Digen, removing his hands from Lankh's chest, relinquishing what small measure of nageric field interaction he'd established. "Let's go, Joel. There's another victim who'll welcome our help."

Hogan followed Digen to the door, too stunned to word his protest. Digen was in the hall before Lankh felt the first chill closing in. He yelled out, pitiful in his sudden panic, "Don't go! Don't leave me!"

Digen paused just outside the door, where Lankh couldn't see him. Branoff was at the bedside, calling out, "Dr. Farris!"

Digen said to Hogan, "Wait. He has to realize how badly hurt he is before he'll cooperate, and there isn't much I can do without cooperation."

"Help me, please help me! I'll do anything you say!"

"Now let's go," said Digen to Hogan, and went back into the room.

At the Center, Digen had Lankh placed in the ward presided over by Mora Dyen. He looked in on Lankh twice a day until the Gen was up and around, and then only once a day. Together he and Mora administered lateral-contact therapy, often having to use sedatives to keep Lankh calm enough to accept it.

After a while he ceased fighting them, ceased caring enough to fight them. Over the weeks, he lost weight precipitously, and seemed twenty years older almost overnight. He lost all his old confidence around unretainered Simes and was unable to summon the energy to be terrified. He became timid instead, crouching at the edges of corridors or rooms, frozen physically and emotionally as Simes passed.

For hours Lankh would sit in his room, hands dangling between his knees, and mumble to himself. Whenever anyone tried to talk to him, no matter what was said to him, he would answer only his internal monologue. "It's not possible, is it?" "I was only deluding myself." "There's no way to rid the earth of the damned." "So many years—wasted, wasted."

While Digen brooded a great deal over Lankh's condition, still the Gen was only peripheral to Digen that winter. His major problem was Skip Cudney. The authorities, on investigating, found that his father had been a channel by the name of Ozik, and that became the family name used for Skip at the Sime Center.

Ordinarily a junct would have been sent away in-Territory to one of the isolated camps that specialized in disjunction of berserkers. But this was a junct channel, almost a contradiction in terms. Digen, as Sectuib in Zeor, was the recognized authority on that problem. So, Skip was kept in Westfield, in the ward behind Digen's changeover-ward office, while Lankh was in the ward on the other side of the changeover ward, connected with it via a small, armored door beside the elevators that fronted Digen's office door.

Neither Skip nor Lankh knew of each other, and Digen preferred to keep it that way. Neither of them was yet ready to tolerate emotional stress. Skip was on the critical list for a week before his transfers and for a full week afterward. Systemic dysfunctions would come and go without warning during those days. Pretransfer depression often kept him lying almost comatose on his bed.

In the posttransfer state he was often so manic that it took two channels to restrain him. And it didn't get better. It got worse.

He's going to die.

Digen came to this conclusion during one particularly difficult transfer in which Skip had gone to the brink of abort three times, with Digen hauling him back by force each time. Afterward they both were exhausted, and Digen again considered altering the therapy to include transfer from a Donor. But he knew it wouldn't work. It would give Skip no deep-seated inhibition against transfer from a Gen, and that would eventually lead him back to the kill.

So Digen hung on, month after month, watching Skip move closer and closer to his disjunction crisis—the point at which he would have to make the conscious decision to give himself wholly to a channel's transfer. Deep down, Digen hoped that the boy wouldn't survive to die in crisis, or to fail and start all over again, having taken transfer from a Donor. Digen couldn't stand what he was doing to Skip, denying the boy his rightful due as a channel.

As Digen's own transfers improved—twice he managed with only one abort and by mid-winter he was using only one monitoring channel—Digen felt guilty for having what was denied to Skip. They were both, in their own way, crippled by the Tecton system. He knew it was ridiculous to feel that way. Skip was growing and thriving under the regimen of channels' transfers despite the difficulties, while Digen's own health was deteriorating noticeably because his transfers were not improving fast enough.

Mickland, Digen had to admit, did his best—scouring the countryside and bargaining like a householder to get Digen Donors in the three-nine-three to three-nine-five range, the best available. Some of them, long out of test, were even better than their ratings; and once, a very good Donor, Tchervain Rholle, was kept as Westfield for three weeks after Digen's transfer.

Digen wasn't permitted the luxury of a full-time therapist, but he did manage to spend quite a bit of time with Tchervain, loosing the hold the Im'ran dependency had on him. But again and again after the halfway point in his cycle Digen would find himself turning to his left, reaching out unconsciously for Im'ran and coming up short against the chill realization—always new—*he's gone!*

Digen continued to drag his way through his obligations, trying to convince himself it couldn't go on like this forever. During the winter weeks, that was all that kept Digen going—hope.

And then one night, on the eve of one of Skip's transfers, Digen was sitting in the changeover-ward office trying to make sense of the figures on Skip, thinking that it was almost as if he'd been regularly exposed to a fantastically high-field Donor, when suddenly Ilyana Dumas came tearing through the back room and into the office, yelling, "Skip's gone! He's not in his room, he's not anywhere!"

Digen wanted to ask what she'd been doing in Skip's room—indeed, what she was doing on this floor at all—but the question seemed silly in the face of the numbers before him. *She's been visiting him!* Digen just sat there, looking at her, feasting himself on her nager, with not the least impulse to reprimand her.

"Digen!" she said, slamming him out of it with a nageric clap of thunder.

He grabbed for the phone, muttering, "He's in need—hard need, at that!" He ordered up building security squads and was half out the front door of the office before the voice on the phone finished answering, "Yes, Hajene Farris."

Two strides into the hallway, Digen stopped short. Skip Ozik was crouched in front of the elevator doors, facing a Gen woman who was backed against the wall, fist to her mouth, too paralyzed to utter a sound. The heavy armored door, with its small reinforced window—the door beside the elevators that led to the ward where Lankh was being kept—was closed, but, Digen noted, not secured, as it should have been.

Halfway between Skip and the terrified woman, Digen stood poised, evaluating the situation. Skip had always been so docile in pretransfer that his attendants had probably not watched him closely enough. Digen himself had not expected Skip to try hunting his own transfer. It was too soon for his disjunction crisis, but that indeed seemed to be upon him.

As Digen pondered, ready to leap between Skip and the woman, Ilyana moved out to Digen's right and around the receptionist's desk toward Skip. Her nager was so strong that Skip turned, following Ilyana with his eyes.

Digen, assuming her move was to protect the woman, circled to his left, placing himself between Skip and the woman. He beckoned to her. "Come here. You're in no danger now." With a little coaxing she came, and Digen said, "See that little door by the elevator? Go through there and down the little tunnel, and on the other side you'll find another bank of elevators. Go down to the ground-floor lobby and wait there. I'll send for you when we've secured this floor. Don't worry. Everything's under control."

Still wide-eyed, the woman sidled through the armored door. Digen's attention returned to Skip and Ilyana. "Ilyana, not so close to him!" he called, moving to the third point of an equilateral triangle with Skip and the Gen.

"Skip," said Ilyana, "you've no reason to torment yourself like this. What have they ever done for you?"

"Ilyana! You are a guest here. Don't forget that." He turned to Skip. "Relax. It's too soon for you to make this decision. We'll take care of you—"

"Take care of him?" yelled Ilyana, turning on Digen. "This is how you take care of him, killing him cell by cell!" She turned to Skip and pleaded, "They'll never let you on their sacred rotation rolls, and I'm not on them either. What possible harm . . ."

"Il-ya-na!" It was Hayashi, emerging from Digen's office to catch the drift of what she was urging Skip to do.

Digen turned to him. "It's premature. Block her."

Hayashi circled Ilyana, juggling the fields expertly. Ilyana turned to Digen. "Let me have him. It's life or death for both of us. And I can prove it's nothing so terrible. It's a bold step, Sectuib, but the Tecton can't just stagnate, cringing in fear at every chance for progress. Simes and Gens belong together—can't you, of all people, see that? Or are you a coward like all the rest of them?"

"You don't understand," said Digen. "He's a channel, and he's killed once—almost twice. We don't dare let him touch a Gen—"

She tossed her head, glancing from Hayashi to Skip and back to Digen. He could feel the intense effort it cost her to say calmly, "And how many junct channels have survived your methods, Sectuib?"

"We can discuss the mathematics later," said Digen.

"We don't lose *any* in Rior. I can give him his kill and not get hurt. It'll do me good—won't it, Rin?"

Rindaleo Hayashi shrank from answering that, but they all knew it was true. Ilyana's field was a blazing ache begging to be tapped and drained. She needed a channel.

They were arguing in Simelan, a language Skip was still not fluent in. It would have made no sense to him in any case. Need ruled body and brain, and all at once he leaped at Ilyana, tentacles extended primed for the draw.

In that same instant Digen and Hayashi moved in concert. As Hayashi scooped Ilyana up and spun clear, Digen intercepted Skip in mid-air, joining lateral to lateral, his own systems primed to offer transfer.

Skip, in spontaneous kill mode, was unable to stop himself, and simply drew and drew selyn from Digen deep into his aching systems. It was the first trouble-free transfer the boy had had at the Sime Center, and for Digen it was both thrilling and satisfying, a vicarious sharing almost as good as having his own transfer.

It was all over by the time their joined bodies rolled to a stop against the elevator doors.

A moment later the elevator doors flew open, spilling security guards onto the ward, followed by Mickland. The controller eyed Hayashi holding Ilyana, and then Digen and Skip at his feet. The nager told the story clearly enough, and all the guards heaved a sigh of relief.

Mickland bent to help Digen to his feet, remanding Skip to the guards. Digen was still a little dizzy with recovery transients by the time he found himself in his own office, with Mickland, Hayashi, and Ilyana. Mickland was still giving orders out the door—"And get that patient back to Mora. He's in severe postburn depression and shouldn't have been allowed to see something like that—especially not involving Skip Ozik!"

Digen was only half listening. Hayashi was meticulously blocking Ilyana out of synch with him, and it hurt.

"Now," said Mickland, closing the door firmly, "let's hear it. And it better be good."

Dimly, Digen heard Hayashi telling how Ilyana had overstepped the bounds of her freedom of the top floor—again. He heard Mickland giving out a good reprimand and Hayashi throbbing with guilt and apology. With an effort, Digen shook his head to clear the buzzing in his ears and said, "It's a good thing she did get down here, Controller Mickland. Thirty seconds later and Skip would have killed a mother in our out-Territory waiting area. Imagine what the Gen papers would make of that!"

"You mean," said Ilyana, "that I saved the shendi-fleckin Tecton?"

She met Digen's eyes. Simultaneously, they smiled, then laughed. "Yes," he said, "you did that. At least you saved us some embarrassment, not to mention a woman's life."

"I only wanted Skip to know he doesn't have to die, not like this. He's just a kid—"

"He's no kid," said Mickland. "He's a grown man. And you'll stay away from him, or your welcome will be over. Understand? Now you, Digen. You're responsible for this department. How did Skip get loose among out-Territory visitors?"

Digen shook his head, dropping heavily onto the lounge. He felt strange. "I'll have to talk to my staff, investigate. I'll see that things are tightened up by—"

Digen broke off, wrapping himself around the churning in his middle.

"What's wrong?" asked Hayashi, limping to Digen's side, struggling to discern his fields through Ilyana's blazing nager. Digen shook his head, waiting for the spasm to pass. He knew that dull, pregnant tension at the back of his neck, the odd, giddy sickness. He got the words out at last. "Touch of entran, that's all."

"What!" said Mickland. "You're still in recovery from a secondary functional!"

Hayashi, kneeling down before Digen with laterals extended, said, "Let me."

Digen shook his head, withdrawing. "I'm all right. It's nothing."

But Hayashi had made a brief contact, paused, then seized Digen's tentacles. Digen was too busy fighting to maintain his internal balances to object again. Hayashi hissed between his teeth, "It's the *primary* system, Dee. Come look at this."

Mickland came to Digen's other side, probing curiously. "Shen and double shen!" He knelt, concerned now for Digen. "I never heard of such a thing."

Hayashi eased Digen down onto the lounge. "It's that Farris vriamic. His brother Wyner had the same problem once or twice."

"I— never—knew that," gasped Digen.

"At changeover," said Hayashi. "Then maybe another time, but we were never sure of the diagnosis. Wyner— Wyner was a law unto himself."

"I know," said Digen. In one quick flash he was a child again, looking up at the tall, tall figure in Zeor blue and Farris black. "I worshiped the ground he walked on."

Hayashi worked at Digen's clothing, exposing his chest.

"Will you stop trying to talk?" Over his shoulder, he said, "He's allergic to apronidal. Get me some nikinimin."

Digen felt the cool cream laved onto his chest, the lateral contact warm as Hayashi probed for a more direct reading on his vriamic node. The long, tense, building spasm gathered and gathered, and at last he admitted to himself that it wasn't "nothing." It was happening again, the same thing that happened after Ditana Amanso's surgery.

Bending over him, watching Hayashi work, Mickland said almost compulsively, "Digen, I'm sorry. I didn't believe you the first time. I'd never heard of such a thing. No wonder you burned that kid. It's amazing you didn't kill him!"

Hayashi brushed Mickland aside, beckoning to Ilyana. "Put your hands here on the chest and give him a good, solid, high-bounce deproda—just like I taught you on the machine, remember? I'll take the laterals, and when I call it, we'll bring him down easy."

Mickland watched blankly as Ilyana moved to obey. But as she actually touched Digen, Mickland stepped in, blocking her. "Rin! He's wide open. You know what will happen! Look what she was just doing to Skip Ozik."

"I'll keep her out of synch. Now either match with us, Dee, or get the blazing shen out of this room!"

Mickland backed off, fading his nager into a rough match, but the turbulence triggered the gathering spasm and Digen went rigid. Hayashi grunted as he said, "Now!" and he and Ilyana went to work over Digen, bringing the jammed neural currents gently but firmly into perfect adjustment.

But, under it all, there was a screeching pain such as he'd never felt before. As he came back to normal he squirmed inwardly to stop the pain, then fell into synch with Ilyana, starting to drift with her, soothed by it. Suddenly she was wrenched away and the pain was back, flaring and then subsiding to a dull ache.

"Digen, no!" said Hayashi. "Ilyana, go upstairs. This once, let me trust you to do as you're told."

Digen felt her looking at him, responding to his incessant need—a need that had become so constant a part of him that he barely noticed it anymore. He knew now what the pain was—the forced desynchronization with Ilyana.

"Rin, don't make me—" she protested.

"I'll get someone for you. I promise. Now, go before you undo all we've done for him."

Reluctantly she edged out the back door as Mickland called after her, "I've moved Skip's room. Don't go looking for him."

Digen felt her contempt for Mickland, but Ilyana left without saying another word. However, she lingered outside in the storeroom, fussing with her disheveled clothes and hair.

Hayashi turned to Digen, frowning. "Let's see if you can get up on your feet now. Give me about half-per-cent augmentation, just to clear out the fog." Backing away, he held out his hand to steady Digen.

Just touching the tips of Hayashi's fingers, Digen bounded to his feet, then cut the augmentation abruptly. "I feel—perfectly normal," he said. *And now that he's saved my life, what am I going to do?*

In an awkward silence, Digen felt compelled to say, "Thank you."

Hayashi smiled with an attempt at remote formality and said, "As One First . . ." Then he made a big to-do, slapping the wrinkles out of his uniform coveralls, running tentacles through his sparse hair. Digen paced around behind the desk and sat down, staring at a stack of requisition orders.

Hayashi, limping across the office to confront Mickland, said, "Well, Dee, that's it. We've *got* to do something. He can't go on like this. His primary system has to be fully stretched—on a regular schedule, or—or—well, or else . . ."

Mickland paced a circle around Hayashi. "I'm doing my best! You don't know how hard it is—"

"Come off it! I've been district and regional controller often enough to know what the job entails!"

"You want the job back, maybe?"

"I've served my time. Now it's your turn, and you're going to *do* the job!" said Hayashi.

"And just what do you suggest?"

"Well, for a start, give Digen to me. I've been yelling for another therapist for Ilyana for weeks now. She's got to be put on a tri-month schedule soon, or she'll jump off the building one of these days. That's why she went after Skip."

"Rin, you know why we can't do that."

"And I know why we've got to. Look, I'm not asking this just to save two lives. I'm trying to save the whole blazing Tecton. It's this theory we're using—it's wrong somewhere. Maybe with a little more data on the far ends of the curves, like way out where Digen and Ilyana are, maybe I can do it."

Exasperated, Mickland paced over to the hotplate and plugged it in, pouring water into the pot from the pitcher. Digen concentrated on the man's nager, trying to discern how his thinking was going. He felt his whole life depended on this.

At last Mickland turned to Hayashi. "Maybe—maybe you'd have something to relieve the Donor shortage, and maybe you wouldn't. But for sure I'd have a red-roaring scandal on my hands. I'd go down in history as a traitor, for turning the Sectuib in Zeor over to a Distect Gen."

"You'd go down in history as the man who was brave enough to save the Tecton, and every first in the world would worship your memory for generations. If that's what you want out of life, you'd have it, but I don't want any part of that. I just want to shore up this rickety structure we're all depending on."

"I don't know what you're worried about. I haven't let you be shorted—much—recently."

Hayashi's eyes rested on Digen as he spoke to Mickland. "It isn't personal. I wouldn't expect you to understand. Call it—call it an unusual upbringing."

Hayashi captured Digen's eyes for a moment, but Digen tore away. He knew deep down that Hayashi wasn't just saying this to impress the Sectuib in Zeor. But he was not going to acknowledge the tie between them, which his father had wanted obliterated.

Ilyana slid back into the room, indignation around her like a cloud. "Just what makes you people so glibly certain I'd accept him? You're killing Skip, you've destroyed that doctor fellow without the mercy of killing him, you're torturing Digen to death, and you're tormenting me like a rat in a maze—and all in the name of your precious Tecton! And now you expect me to submit to experiments to save your hides?"

Hayashi, moving to her side, said, "It would be good for you, and with precautions—"

"Precautions? You're going to let me have him but not let me have him? More torture? Rin—I—I *won't,* don't you understand that yet?"

"You came to us for help," said Mickland. "We're doing our best for you."

"Are you?"

"It's merely academic," said Digen. "They have to have my consent too on something like this. And I won't play games. You and I are matchmates—and Zeor doesn't marry out of Zeor, let alone out of the Tecton. If I got caught in a lortuen with you—as you stand now—I'd be worse off than I am now. You'll pledge and qualify, Ilyana, or I won't touch you."

They were brave words. Digen didn't know just how far he could actually back them up. Her nager was like silk on his raw nerves and somehow made him want to cry.

"Is that some kind of an ultimatum, Sectuib Farris?"

"You could call it that. I prefer to call it an act of mercy. Now get out of here."

"Oh, I will. But first I'll tell you what I think of you. Hypocrite, that's the word. You profess that you'd do anything for this almighty Tecton of yours, but you haven't got the courage of a Mickland-cringing lorsh! Sime/Gen unity, the shining Zeor dream! Well, I'll tell you something, Sectuib ambrov Zeor—the day I actually see the Tecton *do* something toward unity, that's the day I'll pledge and qualify. But that day will never come, because the first one of you to so much as bend one of your precious rules for a chance to end all this—this—human wreckage—would be torn to bits by the ravening mob of cowards you've let take control of your world. People's souls are bleeding to death in the streets out there, and you sit there talking about acts of mercy and bowing down to that lorsh you call a controller, who couldn't even control his own bowels without a law to tell him to! And you call yourself Zeor! You ought to be shenned and shidded into attrition!"

She whirled and ran from the room, slamming the door behind her with a vicious crack.

The three channels expelled long breaths in unison.

"Well, I guess that idea's out," said Hayashi.

Mickland was stunned. "What do we do now?"

"Give me a minute," said Hayashi. "I'll think of something." He went to the hotplate and carefully measured tea into three glasses, pouring boiling water over the fine grounds, then setting each glass in a holder and handing them out. The little ritual settled all their nerves. It was becoming a habit for all the Simes to resort to some steadying ritual when Ilyana left a room.

As Hayashi placed Digen's glass on the desk before him, he hovered a moment, scrutinizing the Sectuib. "If she'd slammed me with that one, I think I'd be nothing but a shattered heap of colored nager fragments you could sweep out with a broom."

"I'm all right," said Digen with a wave of a tentacle. "There's a certain truth to what she's trying to say, even if she does overdo the vehemence a little."

"Digen!" said Mickland, offended.

"Oh, I didn't mean the name calling, but I think you can rise above that. Chalk it up to underdraw pathology." *But she's right. He's a coward of the worst sort. It's what makes him a good politician.* "She sees what we do without understanding yet why we do it. When she understands our motives—emotionally—which she can't learn by being *told*—then she'll pledge and qualify."

Hayashi paced to the middle of the floor. "The problem still remains. We've got to do something about Digen, no more fleckin around with one tentacle. Dee, you've got to drop everything and get Im' back here—and—" he said, looking at Digen speculatively. "We've only got maybe— three weeks?—to do it in."

"Two and a half," said Mickland. "Can't be done."

"Don't tell me that. You've spent your life building this political network of yours. You can do anything once you decide you're going to. Call in some favors, pull some strings, make some trades, just get it done. It's his right now—not a privilege. And it's your duty to see he gets Im' back—at least once."

"Well . . ." temporized Mickland.

Hayashi planted himself in front of the man and said, "He's earned it, and you know it."

Digen got up from his desk chair, shaking his head. "No. No. Mickland can't get Im' back—nobody can. Im' is working with that first who's holding things together down in Alia—Rogzin is his name. Since that hurricane knocked out the Alia seaport, the area has been listed critical. I'm not even earning my own keep these days, let alone the sacrifice of half a continent for my convenience."

"It's a little more than convenience—in my professional opinion, Hajene Farris," said Hayashi. "And though you may not be earning your keep now, the Tecton trained you —made you into a first without even asking your consent. Now, even though you were injured—and, as I recall, it was in the line of duty—the Tecton has a certain obligation to you. We can't let you die—or none of us will be able to live with the system."

"It's still not worth sacrificing the economy of half a continent," said Digen. "I can piece something out—maybe with a channel therapist or something. Rogzin is working; he requires Im's services constantly. I don't, because I'm not working. I'm only on maintenance to avoid entran."

"Your maintenance," said Hayashi dryly, "is what most channels call overwork."

Digen laughed. Mickland said, "Digen does have a point. He takes us into the red about half his capacity every month, despite what he's done for this department. The only thing keeping this Sime Center solvent is Ilyana's contributions offsetting Digen's losses."

"It's not his fault. The Tecton developed him, and now the Tecton is responsible for his support. He's entitled, or none of us are."

"Well, I agree with that, naturally," said Mickland. "What channel wouldn't? But—it's just not possible."

"Well then," said Hayashi, limping up and down in annoyance, "get Im'ran here next month, or the month after. Meanwhile, Digen—what do you think of Ilyana and I in tandem? We could—" Hayashi slipped into rapid jargon, embroidering creatively on some basic Zeor techniques not in the Tecton manuals.

"Now wait a minute," said Mickland. "I can't authorize you two for—"

"The shening shay you can't! Don't you realize—"

"Hold it," said Digen.

"You can't object, either," said Hayashi. "You'd have to accept from any Tecton channel, and that's all I am, just a Tecton channel doing a job on another channel. First to first. Nothing more."

"She's not a first," said Digen. "When she is, I'll consider it. Meanwhile, forget it. Or—no, don't forget it. It's brilliant. Write it up somewhere. Somebody may require it sometime."

"Well then, what are you going to do?" asked Hayashi.

Digen had been thinking about just that, and he started talking with assurance before he was even aware of what he was going to say. "Controller Mickland, do you remember that Donor you got for me a while ago—Tchervain something—Rholle, I think his name was?"

"Hmm. The fellow I almost got a permanent on. Kept him three weeks before Biderfeld stole him. He wasn't bad."

"He was flaming good," said Digen. "Functioning three-nine-six-four when he came—nine-six-seven or so when he left. Young. Lots of potential. I talked to him some, about qualifying four-plus. He's game to give it a try. If you could get him back—put him on my list as a student, instead of me on his therapy list—"

It was a subterfuge unworthy of the Sectuib in Zeor. Digen found himself glancing at the closed door, wondering whether Ilyana might have heard that. But—what other choice was left?

Mickland leaned against one corner of the desk. "I might—I just might be able to get him, but it would take a few weeks. He's been rephased. It would be expensive to crash phase him for you—he'd have to skip a transfer."

"Shenoni!" yelled Hayashi, flinging his arms in the air. "Will you ever learn when to count pennies and when not to? Get him, then, if he's the only one Digen will accept. But get Im' back too, just in case."

"Why, if Digen can qualify us another four-plus?"

"Zhhh!" said Hayashi. "Look, I know the Farrises, and I know the Zeor mentality. Just get them both, unless you want to get mired down in a scandal that will last a hundred years."

Hayashi limped across to Digen, searching his face and his nager. In a kind of resignation he shook his head. "You and Wyner!" Briefly he laid one hand on Digen's shoulder —a fatherly gesture that Digen bore without exactly knowing why he didn't slap the man down. Hayashi said, "Digen, you're a credit to Zeor and to your office. I just wish—oh, shen!"

And Hayashi stalked out the back door, mumbling something about checking up on Ilyana before she got into more trouble.

Digen looked at the half glass of tea in his hand. He wanted to squeeze it until it crushed into shards. Carefully, he put it down.

"Controller Mickland, there still remains the problem of Hajene Hayashi's experiments. According to the charts I've seen, and to what I know of Jesse and Dane, I think maybe you could pair them and let Rin study their interactions. It might work—and it ought to keep him busy until—well, until something is resolved with Ilyana, or Im' gets back."

"Rizdel and Elkar? What gives you that idea?"

"I've known Jesse since first-year camp. He has a lot of potential that doesn't show. And Dane Rizdel—well, I watched his qualification. I tend to trust my instincts in something like that. He may not be quite ready yet for Jesse, but—Rin did a great job with Im'ran for me, he can probably do as well for Jesse with Dane."

Mickland picked up the glass of tea Hayashi had left on a file cabinet. He swirled it contemplatively.

Digen said, "I don't have time to kick it around with you. I've got a kid on the out-Territory ward with Noreen's Syndrome, and another who's been beaten. I've got to go check on them—and that woman is waiting downstairs—and some other things."

He stepped around Mickland and went out to discipline his receptionist for not being there when Skip got loose.

Chapter 12

FAITH DAY

On the day of the worst snowstorm of the season, Jesse Elkar took a suicide abort off Dane Rizdel in Hayashi's lab.

Digen was giving a ronaplin smear for a shaking-plague culture when he heard of Hayashi's call to the Sime Center morgue. He ran up the fifteen flights of stairs to Hayashi's penthouse laboratory, seeing visions of Ilyana dead, in a lax heap on the floor.

But, when he arrived, Ilyana was nowhere in sight, and Jesse Elkar's body was laid out on a lounge, surrounded by humming and clicking machines. Off to the side, on a high table, Hayashi was coaxing Rizdel back to consciousness. Digen stared at Elkar's body for a full minute before he realized that the man was dead. Then he brushed the morgue attendants aside and seized Elkar's body up in his arms, desperately searching for any flicker of selyn movement a non-Farris might have missed.

But there was none.

He was beyond need.

Jesse!

Digen was suspended between shock and defeat, willing time itself to stop, thought to freeze, selyn to congeal. But he knew what he didn't want to think, knew it without thinking it. The Tecton, with all its rules and regulations governing transfer, had killed Jesse Elkar. And Digen himself, as a first-order channel, and as Sectuib in Zeor, supporting the Tecton way of life, was morally responsible for Elkar's death.

Digen had always urged Elkar to fulfill his potential as a channel. But why? For what? To work night and day to the exclusion of all your other interests in life, only to have the Tecton deny you the fulfillment of your basic needs? If Elkar hadn't strived so hard to become a first-order channel, he'd be only second order, but he'd be alive.

There was no second-order Donor shortage. In the Distect there were no Donors at all—and no overdeveloped channels whose bodies demanded more than humanity could supply.

Hayashi's hands gripped Digen's shoulders, pulled him gently away from the corpse, up and out of his suspension. Digen turned on Hayashi, thrusting him roughly away. "What did you do to him? How could you have driven him to this!"

Hayashi said, "Dane panicked in mid-commitment. He's done that before, but I thought I had him over it—or I wouldn't have risked him with Jesse. You know Jesse'd been treated too roughly for too long. He couldn't manage an ordinary abort and chose suicide to avoid hurting Dane. Give him a hero's burial—in Zeor."

Digen felt his tears coming then, the blessed release of frustration, rage at the universe, sorrow over all the things done and undone, said and unsaid. Seeing the cocoon of recorders and monitors clicking and blinking around the body of his friend, he struck out at them to silence them, to destroy that which had destroyed Jesse Elkar.

Hayashi spun him around in mid-blow, taking the impact of Digen's fist on his own shoulder to protect his machines. "No! Digen, I've got the whole thing recorded —the first time in history we've been able to make such a record. We'll learn so much—Digen, he didn't die in vain. Don't make him die in vain."

Struggling feebly, Digen choked out words that burned. "Why didn't you stop it?"

Hayashi let go of him. He was shaking too. "Don't— don't think I didn't try. Please don't think that." He displayed his arms with angry burn stripes across the gnarled old flesh. "I lost him, and that record's all that's left."

Digen touched one of the burn marks, then met Hayashi's eyes. Their grief met and merged and choked them both to silence.

. . . *Wreckage of human lives . . . souls bleeding to death in the streets . . . crippled . . .*

The Tecton is killing us all!

Isolated and alone, victims of the loftiest ideals ever conceived by man, our souls are being bled to death and there's not enough courage among the lot of us to call it wrong. We have to do something. Somebody has to do something—fast.

Digen looked at the man who had been banned from the House of Zeor and pulled himself away from the nageric linkage, so very familiar, so very Zeor in texture. He could not offer sanction—not even now. Something had to remain unstained by the blood of souls. Something in life had to retain some meaning.

Digen turned toward Rizdel, who was sitting up on the edge of the treatment table, groggy but alive. "It wasn't your fault, Dane. You have to believe that. Jesse misjudged his limits, that's all." *Mickland misjudged Jesse's limit.*

Rizdel shook his head. "I killed him."

"No," said Digen, trying to sound reassuring. "It's always partly voluntary—the abort reflex has to be permitted to work, by an effort of will."

"He was protecting me. I—"

"He was protecting the Tecton," Digen heard himself say. "We don't hurt our Gens—not ever. That's our most sacred vow, and it's an absolute, Dane, an absolute every Gen in all creation can trust. It has to be that way. It has to." *Doesn't it? Doesn't it?*

Of all the things that happened that winter, Elkar's death hit Digen the hardest. For days afterward he held himself hard against thinking about it, but the knowledge thrummed vibrantly through every nerve, whether he let it come into words or not.

He would sit at his desk in the Sime Center, signing routine papers, and the panic would hit him. He would be holding retractors for Thornton, and the surgeon's lecturing voice would recede under a swelling cry of *Doesn't it?* Or he'd be with Mora, and suddenly Im'ran would come into the conversation, and the overwhelming loneliness would paralyze him. He and Im'ran hadn't been quite close enough for any danger of an orhuen, but Digen gradually began to suspect that their dependency had been something more than a simple one, because while the physical symptoms abated, the *pain* never diminished. And now it was worse than ever. *But it has to be like this, doesn't it?*

He would be in the Sime Center screening lab, giving a routine ronaplin smear, and suddenly he'd remember

Wyner or Vira, or Nigel, or his parents, dying to keep shaking plague from sweeping out-Territory and devastating the Gen towns. *It has to be—doesn't it?*

He'd be treating a changeover victim who had been beaten by his family and left for dead in a dirty alley, and it would hit him like a tidal wave: *We've got to do something!*

He'd be sitting at the little desk in the surgical-ward office, working through a stack of charts, entering post-operative notes or writing follow-up orders, and he'd curse Mickland's injunction out loud, not caring who heard.

He'd be going over Lankh's progress with Mora Dyen, seeing the vast and unexplainable improvement in the man since Lankh had seen Skip that time in front of the elevators. He toyed with the idea of trying to get them together —hoping for a miracle—because despite Lankh's physical recovery, psychologically he was a broken man. Indecisive for the first time in his career, Digen delayed returning Lankh to the Gens.

Invariably these conferences over Lankh would end with Digen seeking refuge in the Memorial to the One Billion. More and more, as the winter passed, it became clear to him that he was living amid atrocities. He knew that things just exactly like these—Didi Rill, Lankh, Joel Hogan's neglected injury, and Jesse's—suicide—had gone on all about him all his life. He asked himself why they suddenly seemed to take on new significance. But he was afraid of the answer. Ilyana Dumas—the idea that there exists another way of life. And then one day in the memorial the question formed unbidden: What if—what if it doesn't have to be that way?

And he knew what had really killed Jesse Elkar. The Tecton's fear—drilled into him since changeover—the Tecton's abject terror of going junct. Digen had studied Hayashi's recordings of the suicide abort, and he knew Jesse had been perfectly able to get out of it with only minor burns to Rizdel—provided he had kept his nerve. But Jesse had panicked—and now Digen knew why.

Jesse Elkar had died because of the Tecton's exaggerated fear that burning a Donor, even a bit, contributed to the desire to go junct. *Gen pain can make you go junct.* That was the attitude that had killed Jesse.

But it just wasn't true. Sime satisfaction didn't depend

on Gen terror. It was Sime fear that made a Sime attack a Gen who would deny him selyn—fear of attrition and death, fear of his own helplessness, fear of Gen superiority.

As the weeks of winter passed, Digen came gradually through his grief and reached a new determination to see surgery take a good bite out of the prevailing Tecton fears. Wasn't his success under Thornton *proof* that it was Sime fear, not Gen pain, that drove Simes junct?

Eventually Tchervain Rholle turned up to begin studying with Digen. This eased a lot of the pressure on Digen, giving him a good many hours with a fairly competent therapist. Tchervain was a taciturn man who worked steadily but contributed very little of himself to the Sime Center. He was, in a word, the ideal Tecton Donor.

Digen admired him for that—the more so when his own doubts were raging in him—until one day Joel Hogan asked offhandedly, "What about Tchervain? Is his family out-Territory?"

Digen felt blank for a moment, answering, "I—I don't know. His accent is—odd. Could be out-Territory."

With Im'ran, Digen had felt he knew all he had to about the man merely from his Imil affiliation. Rholle wasn't a householder, but still Digen hadn't thought to ask, and Rholle hadn't offered anything personal in their relationship.

After that Digen began to feel more and more uncomfortable around Rholle, and the month that he would have been assigned to Digen to qualify four-plus, Digen let Mickland send Rholle away—for a while, they had said, but they all knew it would be a long while.

Im'ran had been sent to the Orient, but Westfield's claim on him had been gradually working its way to the top of the bidding list. Digen felt he could hang on that long. *At least,* he thought, *now that Rholle has gone, I won't be plagued by visions of Jesse's body becoming my own.* And then, *Did the man really disgust me that much?* And, *Why should that make any difference?*

Even with Rholle gone, though, there was no way Digen could escape Jesse Elkar's name. Some press syndicate picked up on Elkar's suicide, playing it as a concrete example of how close to the brink of disaster the Tecton really was. Day after day, papers and magazines carried stories with Jesse's picture featured beside Hayashi's.

Hayashi and his new Donor-training method became a rallying point for those who felt the urgency of doing something about the shortage. Overnight, funding began to pour into Hayashi's project, and the whole city bulged with the press, delegations of researchers, salesmen, inventors, and volunteers for Hayashi's experiments.

The spring holidays came with the first rains of the season, and the whole city got decked out for the celebrations. Ditana Amanso's second surgery was scheduled for just after the holidays, and Digen had not yet found a way out of Mickland's injunction. But he was determined that somehow he was going to scrub on that case, if no other. He also knew there was no way he could survive another surgical procedure on such a Donor without somebody like Im'ran to back him up. He was now convinced that with a good Donor working at hand, surgery would be easy.

As Digen wrestled with all this, the whole city, in- and out-Territory, laid plans for the celebration of Faith Day, commemorating the first true act of trust between Sime and Gen.

Historically, Klyd Farris, then Sectuib in Zeor, had led the combined in- and out-Territory Sime and Gen armies against the last and biggest of the roving bands of Sime raiders who preyed on Gens. They had laid winter siege to the town the raiders had occupied, and, at spring thaw, the combined Sime and Gen armies were just about beaten. Then Klyd Farris had given to the Gen army all the food his army of Simes had on hand, in an act of faith that the Gens would support them with selyn donations. The Gens did, and the Gen Territories were rid of the worst menace they had ever faced.

Every year Faith Day was celebrated, with the Simes giving gifts to the Gens, and vast numbers of once-a-year general-order Donors descending on the Sime Center until, on Faith Day itself, a full holiday was declared, the householdings in formal conclave, families gathering from all parts, and the spring season was joyfully launched.

It was the emotional peak of the year, with brotherhood keynoted throughout the land, and all Digen's most cherished ideals were given public expression—even if only once-a-year lip service.

Digen had looked forward to the day, the first time in four years he'd be able to preside in Zeor. But just as in medical school, he'd been listed as on duty for the holiday and so could not travel to the local Zeor gathering point. Digen was left alone on the holiday, the only member of Zeor in the city.

Restless, he found himself prowling the Sime Center halls, finding excuses to look in on this or that patient and generally getting in the way of his own staff. *Shen! It's supposed to be a holiday! Even out-Territory it's a holiday!* Which brought to mind the loneliest patient in his care— Skip Ozik; a junct channel denied his just heritage of Gen transfer, an out-Territory kid trapped in foreign surroundings without even the support of a first-year camp full of kids in the same plight.

He turned on his heel, went out, and bought Skip the unabridged, illustrated encyclopedia of horticulture, which he'd been wanting for weeks, and had it gift wrapped.

With the package tucked under one arm, Digen bounced into Skip's room, radiating holiday cheer, and was three steps into the room on sheer momentum before the ambient nager hit him full force. "Ilyana!"

In the moment of silence that followed, Digen mentally replayed the few words he'd heard her saying as he came in. ". . . have to do is go to eighteen Pirot Street, and tell them Roshi's . . ." *Pirot Street.* That sounded vaguely familiar, but at the hospital Digen dealt with so many out-Territory addresses that he couldn't keep them all straight.

At the same time, his doctor's eye raked Ilyana's emaciated body, the discolored hollows around her eyes, the too prominent knucklebones. His channel's vision gathered the texture of her nager. His physician's intuition—all too often accurate—told him that she was not going to survive. She was burning herself up in selyn overproduction.

She gathered her shrunken, withered body to face him, and Digen noted that her reaction time was unusually slow, even for a Gen. She said, "What are you doing here?"

The lack of resonance in her voice bit into him. *Changed so much! In only a few months!* Something Hayashi had said came back to him. Ilyana was on transfer three times a month now. It wasn't helping her at all; it was increasing her production, eating her alive.

With an effort, Digen unkinked his frozen muscles and moved to hand Skip the package. "This is for you." And in English he added, "Your first Faith Day on this side of the border, Skip. It should be something special for you—I'm sorry it's not."

Skip took the package on his lap; then, clasping his hands over his breast, he said, "Hajene Farris, would—would you—"

He was looking sideways at Ilyana. He was in need; she was high field, and the tension in the room was unbearable. Digen stepped between them, pulling the fields down for Skip's comfort. "You shouldn't be in here, Ilyana. You might precipitate his crisis, and it's still just a bit early for him."

He took Ilyana's arm, feeling her resistance. "Skip, I'll be back later," he said, propelling Ilyana toward the door. She went a couple of steps with him, then drew away with a snap to her nager that forced Digen to let go.

"No! Skip and I are not on your precious rotation rolls! Why shouldn't we share a transfer?"

"It's for his protection, Ilyana," said Digen patiently.

"Protection? Can't you stop torturing him even on Faith Day? Or is it that you won't let anyone else have what you deny yourself?"

Pained, and urgent that she understand him, Digen said, "He could kill his best friend—or his lover—if he's not utterly conditioned to channel's transfer. It may be callous, but it's his only hope for any happiness in life."

"His only hope for happiness? You haven't come to your senses yet, have you?"

The image of Jesse's body floated before Digen's eyes: . . . *not your fault, Dane* . . . *a hero* . . . *the bleeding wreckage of human lives* . . .

"Ilyana—"

"No. It's no use. I should have known that all along." She grabbed the book from Skip's hands and shook it at Digen. "This is what you give him for Faith Day when what he—needs—is a warm—human touch!" With her last strength she hurled the heavy tome at Digen, saying, "*This* for your miserable Tecton! I can't stand the stench anymore! I'm leaving!"

Digen caught the volume and passed it neatly to Skip

while Ilyana whirled and made for the door. But her frail body, shaking from the intensity within her, betrayed her. She sank to her knees and Digen scooped her up, shocked at the wispy, weightless arms and legs, horrified by the wildcatting selyn production eating her alive. Over his shoulder, he said, "Ilyana is not well, Skip. I'll see to her. Mora will be in to see you in a while."

Outside, he carried her through the storeroom to his office and laid her down on the lounge. All the while she was crying softly, "It was all for nothing! I should have known you'd never change."

With the door shut behind them, Digen said, "In here you can rant at me all you like. But wouldn't you prefer some tea first?"

Preparing the brew, he let her fall into that dead-perfect synchronization he had only half remembered during all the months of winter. He told himself he had to do it in order to bring her production rate down or she'd die right then. But inside he knew that this was what he'd been aching for all these weeks. This was what was missing from his life. He didn't want to train Tchervain—or even Im'ran. He wanted this, and nothing else.

But he couldn't have it.

He shoved all that aside, addressing himself to the problem at hand. He had to get some food into her, and bring her production rate down in a hurry, or nothing else would matter. He cast about, and remembered that Im'ran had always kept some candy on hand for emergencies. Rummaging in a drawer, he found a box of candy bars and offered her one with the tea, which he'd laced with cherry syrup. "Good Faith Day, Ilyana," he said. "Come on, take it."

She sat up, saying sarcastically, "I suppose you'd be offended if I refuse?"

"Yes," said Digen simply.

She grabbed the candy bar from his tentacle and flung it across the room as hard as she could. "That's for you and all your shidoni-be-f—" She broke off, throat constricted with unshed tears, and then slid off the lounge to her knees, curling around the impossible, shuddering ache, and sobbing helplesly. "I give up! I don't care what you are, just help me. Oh, please, don't fight me like this, don't make me die. Not like this. Let me have it right, just this once, and I'll die tomorrow willingly."

I'll die tomorrow. Yes. I know. Digen had felt just this so often at the brink of attrition, at the gathering of a fourth primary abort, at the lip of sudden death. *With nothing left to live for, we die gladly, but not like this.*

He sank down and took her in his arms, engulfing her within his nager, seeking a controlling grip on her fields—an impossible task, as her body stored more selyn than his at that moment. He had to quell his transfer impulse again and again, managing only because she had no control at that moment, and he was desperate not to increase her production rate but to will it to slow down.

Her head rested on his chest, her field penetrating deep into his vriamic node. Drowning in her nager, he floated to pure hyperconsciousness, commanding her systems as if they were a part of himself. She offered no resistance, joining to him, drifting with him beat for perfect beat. *She can see. Of course.*

After a time, he got her to drink some of the tea and to eat a candy bar she picked out of the box herself—not a formal Faith Day offering, just food to keep her going.

Then they sat for a long time, holding each other. He became aware of her touch on his arms, doing the splendid but unsanctioned things only a Gen such as she could do for him. He started to withdraw, but relented, thinking, *Just once more—what harm in it?*

Aaahhh! She'd touched that deep channel Im'ran had opened in him, and Digen's need suddenly bloomed as it hadn't since Imrahan had worked for weeks to bring it up. Ronaplin poured from aching glands, and his laterals danced in the sudden flood of it.

Ripping himself back to duoconsciousness, he pulled himself free, knowing that one moment more of that and he simply would not refuse it. He was too far into need to refuse. "I can't permit—unscheduled—"

"Don't . . ." she said, grasping his arm just over the ronaplin gland. With the lightest of touches she held him immobile. Her precision was so great that she inflicted not the slightest pain—in fact it was intense pleasure—but Digen dared not move. She controlled him utterly.

"Digen, let this be our act of faith. I'll accept your food if you'll accept my selyn—mankind unified in us?"

"I can't."

"Why *not?*" She damped her frustration so it wouldn't paralyze him through her touch. "We can't control what all the people of the world do with their lives, but with our own lives we can exemplify what life should be."

Put that way, it seemed so reasonable. Doggedly he repeated, "I can't. I can't. Don't you feel what we are to each other?"

"What we are—you're the only one in all the world who could resist me like this. That's what we are to each other."

Digen knew just how precarious his resistance was at that moment. He himself wasn't even sure why he was resisting, and he was afraid of the question. He knew that resisting her had been causing the primary entran, the lousy transfers, everything. It was killing them both.

Her hand tightened on his arm. "Just do it now, Digen —our act of faith on this day—and I'll gratefully lay this body down to its grave."

"And me beside you," said Digen. "No, Ilyana, we can't die before we've lived."

"We can't live like this. Perhaps our deaths would be a symbol—"

A suicide pact on Faith Day—how melodramatic—and how utterly typical of underdraw. Digen felt her desperation deep in his bones. He eyed her fingers spread around the vital nerve plexus under his lateral. The right pressure, and she could kill him so easily. Yet he knew she would not. He knew it. She had no fear of him, and thus not the least impulse to harm.

"Free me, Ilyana."

Their eyes locked in a silent clash of wills. He held fast, at her mercy yet commanding her.

She said, "You hold my life, moment to moment, with your will. I—I need to touch you." Her use of the word "need," reserved for the Simes' sensation of selyn hunger, touched Digen as nothing else could have. It was the literal truth. She was one of the few Gens ever to live who knew what that word, "need," really meant.

He took a firmer grip on her nager, damping her selyn-production rate with his will. "I won't desert you, Ilyana. But you must free me."

She took her hand away. He got up, reaching to help

her up. "There is a way for us to live under the Tecton laws. No, let me finish!" he said, forestalling her indignation. "Lortuen is recognized. It happens—it will surely happen to us the moment I touch you in transfer, and there's no way short of the grave we can avoid transfer. We have to make Mickland see that and give us a legal assignment. Then we can apply for a lortuen exclusive and be taken off the rotation rolls completely. If I have to—" Digen broke off, then took the plunge, "If I have to, Ilyana, I'll use my Demand Rights to get you. But for that to work, you must pledge to the Tecton and qualify to be put on the rotation rolls."

She was shaking her head, lips compressed, eyes wide and leaking unheeded tears.

Digen took her by the shoulders. "There's no other way for us, Ilyana—because I am still Sectuib in Zeor, whether I will or no—and you are—what you are. There simply is no other way out."

"Yes, there is. You could come home with me."

"I've taken oaths that I will not betray. Especially not on Faith Day. Ilyana, the whole world looks to the Sectuib in Zeor. As long as I hold true to the dream of unification of mankind, the world believes it can really happen. It's intangible, but it's very real. And with the Tecton—in the trouble it's in—it's very important that people continue to believe."

"I have also taken oaths—Unto Rior, Forever!—to the unification of mankind—to lortuen or at least a strong dependency as the inalienable right—not privilege to be applied for, but inalienable right of everyone. And now that I've finally found lortuen for myself—on my deathbed —it's denied me—by some law I don't even acknowledge."

After a long silence Digen said, "Ilyana, I can't be— other than what I am."

"Nor I, Digen." She turned to the lounge as if to lie down and die right there and then.

The phone rang. When Digen heard it, he realized it had rung before, and rung and rung, ignored. Digen gathered her into his arms again, willing her body to life. "My shidoni-be-flayed Tecton conscience won't let me ignore that phone. Wait for me, Ilyana. You've got to wait for me."

She let him go to the phone. It rang twice more under his hand before he could bring himself to pick it up. Then he raised it slowly to his ear and said, "Hajene Farris. Yes? . . . What! Be right there!"

He slammed down the phone and headed for the back door of the office. "Hayashi's been shot. Come on."

Chapter 13

HAYASHI'S PLEDGE

Digen arrived at Skip Ozik's room well ahead of Ilyana. In the stark clarity of shock, he saw it as if he'd never seen such a room before.

To his left was the wetbench, a long, free-standing counter with sinks and hoods where instant lab analyses could be done. In the far corner was the bed, surrounded by all the paraphernalia of a treatment room. The door to the adjacent library/sitting room was ajar, admitting a splash of cheerful yellow sunlight to the dim, shaded room. To Digen's right was the contour lounge where Digen had managed Skip's transfers, but Skip was nowhere in the room.

On the lounge lay Rindaleo Hayashi, arms across his abdomen. Mora Dyen was trying to stanch the flow of blood from Hayashi's arm, but she herself was half hysterical. Digen could see why. Hayashi's blood loss was negligible compared to the profuse selyn voiding, a plume of brilliance spewing high from one torn lateral.

Seeing Digen, Mora said, "We've got to have a four-plus therapist! He's dying in attrition."

"Calm yourself, Mora," said Digen, but actually it was himself he was admonishing. "Don't even think about attrition. We have plenty of time. We're going to save him."

Holding himself rigidly apart from the grisly reality, Digen took a place opposite Mora and put his hands over hers. "Shift control to me—I've got it now." He then examined the wound visually. It was a long gouge aslant one lateral sheath and biting deep into the lateral tissue itself. Digen couldn't tell how deep, but, from the intensity of the voiding, he guessed it was pretty close to the core. It was very similar to the injury Digen himself had survived.

"I'd like two pairs of matched anchor teams on this

one," said Digen, hearing his own voice as if it belonged to a stranger. "Who's available?"

"Nobody! Digen, I've been calling and calling all over for fifteen minutes. It's a *holiday!*"

"There must be a Donor in the Sime Center you could use! Mickland couldn't have given everyone off!" Digen knew only one way to handle this type of injury, using carefully balanced channel/Donor teams on each side of the patient. He and Ilyana would make one pair, and Mora was half of another. "There must be someone!"

"There's nobody I could use except maybe Chanet, and she—"

"Forget Chanet!" said Digen. "She could never do this." Digen own sense of panic was rising now. He knew what had to be done, but there was no way to do it. Meanwhile, his fingers and tentacles moved automatically to apply a backfield to the wound to slow the selyn loss. Covered with Hayashi's blood and ronaplin, Digen probed deeper and deeper, seeing now that there was voiding in both the primary and secondary systems.

Despite all Digen could do, the selyn and blood losses continued. *He's going to die,* thought Digen, with rising paralysis. *Right under my hands, he's going to die of attrition.* The thought echoed in his mind, blocking all other thoughts. *He's dying of attrition.*

Suddenly the room was slit with intense nageric brilliance. Unconscious beneath Digen's hands, Hayashi moved spasmodically toward that selyn source. Digen cut the field, desperate to hold everything in stasis as long as possible.

Now that Digen was taking the brunt of it, Mora had recovered her normal poise. "Ilyana," she said, "get over here and help Digen. He can't tolerate attrition—because of his own injury."

As Ilyana glided into place at Digen's left, he said, woodenly, "I'm all right, Mora." And he took Ilyana's enormous field strength, meshed so perfectly with his own field, and used her strength to control the voiding. "See?"

Mora, on the verge of taking back the responsibility Digen had assumed, relented. Because of their disparities, she couldn't use Ilyana the way Digen was. She retired to arm's length and said, "Attrition isn't something you should have to face, Digen. I'm sorry I called you. There's nothing either of us can do anyway—it would be kinder just to let him die."

Digen shook his head. "We've bought some time with this," said Digen. "I'll think of something." *I hope.*

Ilyana laid her left arm along Digen's left, placing her right around his waist, her body against his, her head on his shoulder. She was controlled, relaxed, a source of infinite, steady strength. Soaked in her nager, attrition seemed like a fairy tale.

Mora said, "Ease up a little, Ilyana. You're removing him from reality."

Her fields lightened and Digen's mind cleared. Mora said, "Digen, he's going to die. There's nothing we can do. Just look at his fields, the turbulence. The blood loss alone—you can't hold that pressure forever—cells in his lower arm are already dying for lack of blood."

Digen examined the wound more carefully. The bullet had driven across the lateral and then somehow passed between the bones of the forearm, nicking the main artery to the tentacles. Digen concluded that Hayashi must have been moving under augmentation when he was shot. Bullets do not ordinarily follow such curved trajectories.

"How did this happen?" asked Digen, probing the wound.

"I didn't see it. When I got here, Lankh was on the floor, unconscious, with a gun in his hand, and Rin was—like this. Lankh must have— Oh, Digen, ever since that day he saw you and Skip by the elevators, he was so much better. He must have been planning revenge on Skip and had the gun smuggled in to him . . ."

Digen's eyes met Mora's. "Don't blame yourself. We all missed it. Now we've got a life to save." He looked at Hayashi's heavily lined face, lax in unconsciousness. "He's really on to something with those machines of his—ever since Jesse's death. He really is the key. The Tecton—it all depends on him."

"I thought," said Ilyana, "the whole principle of the Tecton was that no single person be irreplaceable."

"Maybe he's not irreplaceable—and then again, maybe he is. We've got to save him."

"I'm not a Zeor channel," said Mora, "but I know there's nothing—not even among the householdings—that can save him now. Digen, it took four perfectly matched channel/Donor teams to save you. We can't even muster two teams—not in time."

Digen loosened his hold on the artery to let blood down into the lower arm. But blood gushed freshly from the wound in little spurts. Suddenly his fingers itched for a suturing needle. His hands knew what had to be done.

"It's got to be repaired surgically," he said.

Mora looked at him, eyes wide. Then she looked at the wound. "You can't. You're under controller's injunction —violation is summary execution by attrition, no appeal, even for the Sectuib in Zeor!"

Digen shook his head. "Mickland was scared that surgery on Donors would make me go junct. Surgery on a Sime—a channel—should pose no such problem. Mora, don't you understand yet—this is what I've been working toward all my life. Mickland will tear up his injunction when he sees this. He's got to. This will change *every-thing*."

"If he dies . . ."

"If he dies," said Digen, "there's going to be a revolt in the ranks somewhere before the end of the year. People see themselves in Jesse. We've all been shorted lately; we've all had the nightmares. Where will the Tecton be if the firsts and high seconds quit?"

"The renSimes will be shorted; they'll start raiding Gen Territory, killing . . ."

". . . For the first time since Klyd Farris signed the First Contract. Five generations of sacrifice—for nothing. And on Faith Day . . . ? We're just going to sit here and let that happen? Ilyana," said Digen, "get me an out-Territory line on that phone."

She hesitated, then moved to punch in the number Digen gave her. "You two," said Digen, propping the handset against his shoulder and waiting for the connection, "are going to help me. You will help, won't you, Ilyana?"

"To cut Rin up?"

"No. Just handle the fields, help me keep him from voiding to death. You don't seem to faint at the sight of blood."

With a measure of offhanded pride, she said, "I'm a trained midwife."

Digen was a little startled. That was no job for a Gen. "Well, good, then this should be fairly easy for you."

"You mean, save the Tecton—again?" She tried to muster an ironic smile through a veil of tears.

"Not for the Tecton," said Digen. "For Rin."

"For Rin. I owe him that much at least."

Whatever her motives, Digen knew she would again be credited with saving the Tecton, and on the strength of that he could make them grant a lortuen exclusive. She'd come around to his way of seeing things, eventually.

A distant tinkling indicated that the phone on the other end was finally ringing. *Answer, damn it!* thought Digen. The tinkling began its second one-minute repeating sequence before there was a long beep and a groggy voice mumbled something.

"Wake up, Joel, I've got a case for you!" snapped Digen. He could imagine Hogan sitting up amid tangled bedclothes, palming his eyes and peering at his watch.

"Digen? Whatimesit? Where—we're not on duty—"

"I'm at the Sime Center. It's happened, Joel, what we've talked so much about. Now wake up, a lot depends on you!"

More crisply, Hogan said, "What? What's happened?"

"You've heard of Rindaleo Hayashi?"

"Who hasn't?" He was attentive now, completely awake.

"He's going to die unless you get over here with a full field-surgery kit and about five units of plasma—and, just in case, bring the thoracic-instrument package too." *But I hope I won't have to try* that!

Hogan made disbelieving sounds, but Digen cut him off. "I give him about fifteen minutes. If I don't get something into him by then, he's not going to make it."

"I've got my pants on; I'm on my way. Hang tight."

"Don't forget the venipuncture and IV set. We have nothing of that sort here." Then Digen gave him directions to the door where Mora would meet him and escort him upstairs. "You can trust her as you trust me."

With Ilyana punching phone combinations, Digen organized the materials he would require to turn the room into an impromptu surgery. With Mickland out of town for the holiday, Digen was senior in the district, so all his requests went unchallenged.

By the time Mora brought Hogan into the room, the wet-bench had been turned into a fair imitation of a surgical table. "Set up over there," Digen said to Hogan; then he described the injury and what he planned to do.

Hogan never paused in his work as he said, "Why not bring him over to the OR? Thornton would let you do him."

"Not without retainers. That artery is inside a basket-weave of selyn-transport nerves. Try this blind, and none of us would live through it."

Hogan did stop then, absorbing the implications.

"That's right, Joel, you're assisting."

Hogan half turned his head as if in negation, looking at Hayashi. "Digen, you know I can't tolerate selyn movement . . ."

"You won't have to. Ilyana here will handle the fields. But I can't do this alone, Joel."

Hogan stared at Hayashi, summoning every shred of courage he owned. "He's the one with the miracle Donor-training machines, right? I suppose it's poetic justice, somehow. All right, what's the plan?"

"That plasma heated yet? Sime body temp, remember?"

"Almost."

"Let's get this IV set up, then." While Hogan screwed the pole together and ripped open the field tray, Digen had Mora help him move Hayashi onto the makeshift operating table. Hogan approached with the tourniquet in hand, looking at Digen. "Where . . . ?"

"At the ankle. You'll have to do the cutdown, but there's no problem as long as you just expose the vein, going no deeper than that."

Joel went to work, Mora Dyen standing back, struggling to keep herself unaffected. But the moment Hogan's scalpel bit into flesh, Mora's gorge rose and she dashed from the room, mumbling an apology. Digen said, "Let her go. Ilyana's holding his orientation well enough."

The commotion jolted Hayashi back to consciousness just as the first of the plasma worked its way into his veins. Digen leaned over him, saying, "Hajene? Hajene Hayashi?"

The channel's eyes blinked open, squinting against the lights Digen had rigged. "Where's Skip? Is he all right?"

Digen said, "He's disappeared. Mora put out an alert to have him picked up. Lankh has a concussion—he's in the doublescan room for the thirds to watch."

Hayashi, his immediate anxiety relieved, began to take note of his situation. "Digen?" he said, focusing on his right arm where Digen held the wound. Then he became aware of the needle taped to his ankle, the hanging bottle of plasma, selyn-dead as it dripped into his veins. "Digen!"

"It's gruesome, I know," said Digen, deliberately in English. "But it will save your life. Can you understand me?" Hayashi's assent was a weak nod. Digen went on describing the nature of the problem and what Hayashi had to do to help them. Working with Digen, he could control much of the bleeding, the pain, and the tension in his muscles.

When Digen told him, Hogan said, "You mean you're not going to use anesthetic?"

"It would kill him," said Digen. "Those instruments ready yet? At least the small clamps?"

"Right here," said Hogan.

Hayashi caught at Digen's hand. "No! There's no way you can get selyn across that severed lateral. I'm dying—I won't let you risk your life for a lost cause."

Their fields were so entwined that Digen felt the bleak resignation that gripped the channel. He bent over, saying, "I'm going to repair that gash, and then I'm going to get selyn into you. I have a plan. I can do it. I'll have to put you into suspension. . . ."

But Digen's words weren't quite registering. Hayashi was in a deep inner struggle. "I—I'm dying. Accept—accept my pledge, to Zeor and to the Sectuib in Zeor. I can't—you can't let me die alone like this."

Digen was shaken by the plea. "I—can't do that. You know I can't do that."

"If I'm going to die under your hands, it's going to be under the hands of my own Sectuib." His voice was reedy, but Digen heard every word. "Accept—my pledge—or—or I'll take myself out right now—the easy way."

"We've no time to argue now. We'll take it up after," said Digen, knowing that it would be altogether too easy for Hayashi to let himself die at this point. "There's a chance, a good chance, that you won't die if you'll let me do this."

"I—won't let you—violate a controller's injunction. Not for a nonmember. Your father—would never forgive me.

Take my pledge, Sectuib, and you can do anything you want to me."

It would change the legal picture drastically. The Tecton recognized the peculiar personal loyalties between members of a house. But never, to Digen's knowledge, had that recognition extended as far as a violation of a direct controller's injunction. Still, it was a temptation, one more factor in his favor. *But no!* "Hajene Hayashi," said Digen stiffly, "I—loved—my father. I was pledged to him and to Zeor. I—can't—go against his wishes. No matter how much I'm tempted. You should know that."

Digen was bearing the weight of both his own and Hayashi's emotions, joined as they were for Hayashi's life. His heart grew almost too heavy to beat, thickened by almost two decades of Hayashi's unrelenting pain. "Sectuib—it would not be—against—Orim's wishes. He never meant—it to—be this way. Believe that. You've got to believe that. I have kept the standards, remained loyal. Don't make me die outside of Zeor. Don't . . ."

Hayashi truly believed, Digen saw, that he had done nothing to incur a banning. But the testimony had been clear. Several people had heard Orim issue an order which Hayashi had deliberately disobeyed. Im'ran had said it: "Would you accept the pledge of an oath breaker, Sectuib?" Yet, Digen must do just that to save the Tecton—for Hayashi, in his current mood, would surely suicide to prevent the Sectuib in Zeor from violating a controller's injunction for the sake of a nonmember.

"Do you know what you're blackmailing me into?"

"I am no oath breaker, Digen. Zeor is my life."

Digen twisted off the ring he wore bearing the double Tecton/Zeor crest, and thrust it into Hayashi's left hand. "Pledge then," he said, "and may father forgive you this —and Vira, and Nigel, and Wyner, and Bett too! Because I can't guarantee I ever will!"

Taking the ring, Hayashi said, gathering his last strength, "Unto the House of Zeor, I pledge—my heart, my hand, my substance. And unto Digen Farris—heir to Orim Farris—Sectuib in Zeor, I pledge my life, my trust—my—undying loyalty. I commit my life, my substance, and my children—Out of Death To Be Born—Unto Zeor, Forever."

Forcing the words through tightened throat, Digen said,

"Unto Rindaleo ambrov Zeor, I pledge—my—substance, my—trust—my undying loyalty, in my own name—born from death, Unto Zeor, Forever."

In the faintest whisper Hayashi said, breathing heavily, "Do what you will, Sectuib. Sectuib Farris, I rest content."

Digen eased Hayashi into the suspended state necessary to simulate anesthesia, and, true to his word, Hayashi cooperated fully. Hogan and Ilyana scrubbed as best they could, but Digen's fingers and tentacles had already been as deep into the wound as possible, and there was little sense in him trying to scrub now, except to rinse the blood and ronaplin from his fingers so that he could handle the suturing needle.

Digen positioned Ilyana beside him, Hogan across from them, and began to repair the artery. Hogan, watching, said, "Ilyana, hand Digen the suture in the blue box. I think it would be best for this job."

"She doesn't speak English," said Digen, translating to Ilyana. A little later, a clamp that Digen had placed on a minor artery slipped. Hogan reached to replace it while Digen was wrestling with a delicate stitch. Digen dropped what he was doing, blocking Hogan's hand. "No!" And he replaced the clamp himself.

"Well," said Hogan, "I don't know what you want me here for!"

Digen was shifting back and forth from duoconsciousness up to pure hyperconsciousness, concentrating as he'd never done before in his life. He had to hold down the selyn voiding while at the same time not interfering with the vital nerves around the nicked artery. He paused in duoconsciousness, and snapped, "I can't talk now! Wait!"

Hogan's reply was lost as Digen slipped back to hyperconsciousness, planting the last two, tiny sutures to secure the artery. The way he was using his hands, he had to let go of the tight control of the selyn voiding. The selyn flows in the little nerve fibers were shutting down in attrition, and Digen, as he finished, could barely see them to avoid hitting them with the needle. The plume of voided selyn was fading alarmingly.

Tight-lipped, Digen threw the needle back on the tray and picked up his post at the lateral. With all the field gradient at his control, he could not force selyn into Hayashi. He knew he would have to take his most desperate gamble. "Quickly, Joel, the thoracic kit," said Digen, and named the incision he would require, straight down to the vriamic node. "Expose the lungs," said Digen, "you're safe to that point. I'll take it from there."

Hogan froze. He had begun to understand what surgery on a Sime—with the whirling energy currents—entailed. "We've got ten minutes," said Digen levelly, "and he's dead."

Hogan tightened up on his courage and began to open the chest. "I've never done this before, Digen, only watched."

"I've done it," said Digen. "Now I'll teach you." And he began talking Hogan through it, splitting his attention between that and holding down the selyn leakage as much as he could. Ilyana, eyes closed, lending her field to Digen, was seated on a tall chair where she could reach Digen's instrument tray.

Hogan, working steadily, sweating, without any nurse to wipe his forehead, said, "He's going to take another unit of plasma."

"Not until I get a selyn infusion into him. It would kill him."

"So will circulatory collapse."

"We can only do our best, Joel. Just keep working." Then Digen turned to instruct Ilyana. She roused herself, glimpsed what Hogan was doing, and turned aside with a grimace. "Just a few minutes more, Ilyana. Give me your hands now."

Ilyana steeled herself inwardly and thrust her hands at Digen's. "No, no," said Digen. "Barriers down. This is where you've got to bridge for us in perfect mesh."

Digen placed her hands across the lateral gash he could not repair until he had enough selyn flow to see what he was doing. "If you're close enough," said Digen to Ilyana, "when I let go here, I'll still be able to use your field to block that selyn loss. It won't be long, Ilyana, just until I can force selyn into him at the vriamic node."

She looked at Digen through tears, bit her lip, and came into the closest bridge synchronization Digen had ever seen. *It has to be good enough*, he thought, loosening his hold. He didn't wait to see if Ilyana was securing the leak, but plunged his hands, wrist deep, into the chest incision, groping for the vriamic node, with his laterals extended.

The instant he contacted Hayashi's vriamic, the three of them—Ilyana, Hayashi, and Digen—meshed into one extended system so perfectly that Digen could barely distinguish one from the other. The selyn he had summoned high into his secondary system poured into Hayashi's primary without the usual resistances of lateral-contact transfer. Digen struggled to regulate the speed of that infusion, feeling as if it were Ilyana herself who was delivering selyn into him.

He wanted it to go on and on, but at the right moment he snapped off the delivery, holding the contact to damp the terminal transients. He felt Hayashi's body beginning to vitalize the plasma that had already been run into his veins. "All right, Joel, the next unit of plasma—now!"

Digen's knees sagged and he found himself still clutching Hayashi's vriamic node. Through that contact he could feel Ilyana's selyn field across the lateral gash as if the gash were in his own right inner lateral. He could feel the throb of her—*need* to donate. Hayashi's near attrition had sent her selyn production spiking upward again, and Digen—resonating much too sharply with the channel—was feeling both his physical and psychological need drowning out his conscience and his will.

Dimly he heard Hogan say, "Want me to close?"

Digen knew, as if it were superimposed on his awareness of Ilyana, that in a moment Hogan would reach out to take over from Digen. He shook his head and forced his laterals to retract, breaking the physical contact with Hayashi. But he was still part of Ilyana's field; he still had to use her to maintain that pressure on Hayashi's wound so that the selyn he had given would not all leak away.

"Suture," said Digen, holding out one bloody palm.

Hogan placed the threaded needle in Digen's hand. "Suture."

Digen closed his eyes to concentrate on the tracery of deeply planted nerves lacing outward from the vriamic, and then began to close the incision. At first he worked swiftly, fingers flying faster than the nerve pulses carrying the pain signals could travel from Hayashi through Ilyana and, magnified, come back to him through his linkage with her.

But then those pulses began to arrive faster and sharper as he drove his needle through living cells—not selyn-producing cells, but selyn-enriched cells nonetheless. His own hands, soaked in Hayashi's ronaplin, and ungloved, acted almost like exposed laterals at a skin contact. Every punctured cell was, to Digen, as if he were puncturing a cell of Ilyana's own body.

He realized distantly, that she was experiencing it just that way, and unconsciously transmitting that empathic experience via her nager to Digen. He found himself pausing to brace before each dip of the needle, relishing the pauses when Hogan would hand him a different needle. He had begun sweating and his hands were shaking. His own systems were still in secondary recovery, no condition to be taking this kind of abuse. But he dared not turn it over to Hogan yet. If the Gen should slip and hit a transport nerve with the suture needle, he could suffer a selyn flashburn that would be worse than transfer shock.

He began to have more and more trouble maintaining hyperconsciousness. Every flick of the needle kicked him down to duoconsciousness, where the physical pain met the bursts of selyn—little bursts emitted by Ilyana in sympathetic linkage with the dying Sime cells. To her, this was a mixture of physical pain with the subliminal relief of tiny increments of selyn drained off her overcharged system.

The last five stitches around the drain tube he was implanting kicked him all the way down to hypoconsciousness, and on the last one, he stood there dumbly staring at the operating field as if he'd never seen the like before——in fact, he hadn't, not since Ditana Amanso's first operation. *This is what it looks like to a Gen. No wonder it's so hard for them to learn.*

But that was a bemused thought in the back of his mind, while his whole body resonated to harmonic mixtures of pleasure, pain, and the shrieking death of Hayashi's selyn voiding.

Hogan was working along behind Digen, tying off each suture where Digen had cut it, until his flying fingers caught up. He paused, watching Digen, seeing exactly what had to come next, knowing the clock was running out, even though he himself couldn't see the plume of selyn issuing from Hayashi's arm around Ilyana's fingers. He said something, but Digen couldn't resolve the English words.

The Gen's hands closed over the threaded needle. The instant Hogan's skin touched him, Digen whipped into a transfer attack on Hogan, thrown hyperconscious by the reflex that had built and built with every stitch. For the first time in his life, he knew there was nothing—not one shred of conditioning—left to stop him from the kill.

Suddenly, before he could make lip contact, a sheet of fire swept up his left arm. The three-way contact between them shattered, slamming Digen into a primary abort.

Ilyana's voice came through the dizzy fog. "Get *over* here, Digen, or Hayashi will die."

Digen reeled. His secondary system was still in recovery, he was knotted up with primary abort, and the pain— Gen pain—possessed him totally.

"Digen!"

Ilyana's dominant field rose around him. She was there, but she didn't touch him. He felt the strength of her fields soothing his shen-shattered nerves. His vision cleared. "Digen! You've got to finish what you started."

Digen looked at her, shaking his head to clear it. There was a long abrasion on her left arm, just where he felt the pain. She held the bloody scalpel in her right hand. She had scraped her arm with it to break him out of the attack.

Across the table, Hogan flexed shaking fingers and steadied down to finish with the chest incision.

Ilyana said, "Sectuib Farris, one of your members is dying!"

Digen moved then, his feet like sodden weights. But once he was in position over Hayashi's arm, he became once again a physician working against time. Second after second, all the selyn Digen had infused was spewing out of the gashed lateral. He took up the suture needle, forced the selyn fields to an unstable neutrality, damming up the selyn in Hayashi's system, and began to repair the rent.

He matched the edges of the gash, nerve fiber to nerve fiber. He had seen this done by Thornton once on a leg that had nearly been severed. He had read how the Ancients could take a big toe and graft it to a hand to replace a lost thumb. Now he was doing it—in a context they had never envisioned—inventing the techniques as he went along.

It was the last, finishing stage of the long, complex operation, and that thought was the only thing that kept Digen on his feet those final few moments. He didn't dare think or feel anything. He was an automaton completing a program, nothing more.

By the time Digen finished, Hayashi had faded from the deep suspension into true unconsciousness, and Digen was again working almost blind. Even so, the repair was masterful compared to the butcher job that had been done on his own lateral.

As Digen finished, Hogan had applied the last dressing to the chest and was looking with bewilderment at the Sime arm. "Can I bandage that?"

Digen stepped back, seeing the plume of voided selyn now reduced to a mere haze that faded almost perceptibly *(Or is that wishful thinking?)* as he watched. He shook his head, waving away Hogan's bandages.

Hogan mumbled something about it not mattering. The patient was septic as hell anyhow. And Digen drew forth words, saying, "He has a better chance against infection than against death by attrition."

And then Ilyana touched him.

The thin crust over his blazing need melted away. Dropping the last suture needle on the floor, not even missing the droning voice of a nurse counting needles, sponges, and clamps, Digen seized her wrist just below the long, bloody scrape she'd inflicted on herself. "We did it!" he said. Then, not sure he'd spoken in Simelan, he repeated, "We did it. Whatever happens now, we've brought surgery in-Territory. On Faith Day. And the world will never be the same again."

It was his goal. His life's purpose. And he gloried in it. She came close to him, wiping his sweating face with the towel she held in her other hand.

Trautholo.

Just like that, it was there between them, as easy as slipping into a surgical glove. "Don't move!" said Digen.

"I know. You didn't want me to let you attack me—the way you attacked the doctor? You—we—don't approve of kill-mode transfers—do we?"

"We?"

"We. Digen, I'm sorry I ever called you a coward. You're not like Mickland—not even like Rin. Digen, you're —I see it now, what you've been trying to do with surgery.

You've known all along what's wrong with the Tecton. However misguided, you've been trying to fix it. I don't think it will work—they don't have your vision—but, Digen, if it does, I'll pledge and qualify and never look back. Unto—Unto Zeor, Forever, Sectuib, if you'll permit it."

Digen scooped her off her wobbly legs, realizing now for the first time that in his desperation over Hayashi he had let her selyn-production rate run wild, burning into her last reserves.

"Joel," he said over his shoulder, heading for the adjacent sitting room, "keep an eye on Hayashi. Give us an hour—maybe two—I don't think anything will happen with him in that time."

Hogan said something, but it faded from Digen's consciousness before he could make sense of the English words. In the sitting room, Digen kicked the door shut, and, seeing by Ilyana's nager, found a large padded divan among the bookshelves. He put her down and settled wearily beside her, on his back, letting her field soak through and through his battered systems.

She too was tired beyond her endurance. Digen cradled her in one arm, saying, "Rest a moment, let me damp your production a bit. There's no hurry."

But she was already asleep, holding the trautholo by some subconscious mechanism. It reminded Digen sharply that she was a very sick woman. His need drew strength into her, but it came from her very substance, from her flesh. She seemed pounds lighter to him than she had earlier. He wanted to put her aside, to take himself elsewhere to recover, trautholo or no, but of course he couldn't. And he too was tired beyond measure. He contented himself by planting a conscious command in himself—like a fist clenched over some valuable—to keep down her selyn-production rate. And then he too drifted into slumber.

Their systems were locked from the deepest rhythms layer by layer outward to the most fleeting and superficial bodily rhythms. Hours of intense exposure had sealed them, and now, asleep, they healed each other.

Neither had known a moment's surcease since the first day they had met. But Digen had been unaware of that extra tension in him that resisted his natural response to his matchmate. Now, when Digen awoke, all that was gone, the whole weight of it, which had sapped his strength, was lifted. The depression that had gripped him all winter had disappeared without a trace; he was flooded with a new strength of spirit that felt like his old, pre-injury self. It was like waking from a terminal illness to find oneself in a new, healthy body, with all the vitality of youth.

She slept in the crook of his arm, the premature lines of her face smoothed at last, and he could sense the same ebullience within her. He kissed her gently on the cheek. The contact, even without a direct lateral touch, threw him soaring into giddy hyperconsciousness.

As he was just beginning to discern visual images again, he felt her awaken, responding to his state, moving in his arms to transfer position.

He wanted it. He needed it. He had used selyn recklessly in his efforts for Hayashi, and since Im'ran he hadn't had a real transfer. In fact, with Ilyana in his arms, he knew he hadn't ever before in his life had a real transfer.

They owe me this. Shen and Shid! We've earned at least this!

Her hands slid softly into full transfer contact, gently teasing his laterals from their sheaths, still coated with blood and ronaplin. As she made the full transfer lip contact, her fields slid off kilter to compensate for his scar, but somehow she avoided the odd, tilting sensation Im'ran had evoked. She was holding him firmly in trautholo so that not a trickle of selyn moved across their contacts.

"Ilyana!" He groaned, trying to initiate the flow.

"You're still in secondary recovery, I can feel it. I'll have to control this, Digen, or you'll abort, and I couldn't stand that. Qualify me some other time." She sought the lip contact and suddenly Digen realized that somehow she had gotten his ronaplin on her lips.

The selyn, when it came into him, came at his highest kill speed, way above his satisfaction threshold, and it came and came and came, forced deep into him, down and down to that newest level that Im'ran had touched with such a feather-light flicker compared to this solid, sure, unrelenting deluge. Through and through, down and down, even deeper, selyn coursed until, with a bursting flash, Digen felt as if a whole new area of his being had been burned clear. He knew there was no physiological structure corresponding to what she had touched—but it felt as if there were. His control barriers fell flat before the onrushing pulses of selyn, pulses matched so perfectly to his own body rhythms that he could scarcely tell they originated outside himself.

And when it was over, and he was full, primary and secondary systems alike, so full he felt as he had always supposed a Gen must feel, the selyn flow did not end, leaving him to begin the long, slow, but subliminally terrifying decline into attrition.

This time, at satiation and beyond, Digen rested on the terminus, and Ilyana's body supplied him selyn at the exact rate at which his body was using it. For every pulse that went through him, consumed and dissipated, a pulse entered so precisely on his rhythm that he never felt it enter.

As a result, for a time, at the peak of satiation, he was held forcibly at constant field. His whole body sang a euphoric bliss, a crescendo chord of a symphony, every voice of sensation within him precisely attuned to all the others and caroling his joy.

It lasted a long, long time, and gradually, without the sudden, shuddering shock usual to termination, the world faded in around him and he slid gently from full hyperconsciousness, through duoconsciousness, and gently on down to the posttransfer hypoconsciousness in which the Sime senses were blocked, leaving the world etched in painfully bright tactile, audio, and olfactory sensation.

Hyperacute from long disuse, tactile nerves registered the ineffable Gen skin against his—and the areas of painfully coarse clothing between them. Digen loosened the long zipper of her uniform and she undid his. Somehow the unwanted clothing fell aside, forgotten. He was wholly concentrated on the incredible feel of her skin. It was as if he'd never felt human skin before.

The aroma of her body teased his long-unused glands until they ached. The taste of her mouth raised him to new heights. He was surprised that he could have been near her all these months and not *noticed*. He had to touch her everywhere at once. His greed for her knew no bounds.

Somehow she contrived to keep lateral contact as they slid together. She held him at constant field again, through that contact, and tipped him back to duoconsciousness, so that his awareness of her went deep, deep into her body, luxuriating in its nager while at the same time he retained his keen, hypoconscious awareness of her touch. It was a combination wholly new to him, and before he realized how powerful it was, together, in perfect unison, they came. She had turned the drab physical necessity of post-transfer systemic realignment into a sublime work of art.

His whole body thrummed to the glory of it, too much to bear. He began to cry—in unutterable sadness for all the wasted years—in joy too great to be endured by mortal flesh that at last, at last, he was alive.

"No, not like that," she said, breathing heavily. "You'll spoil it." And with skills Digen had never known existed, she quelled the tide within him and turned it into another fresh, unique consummation—as keenly felt as if it were their very first.

The third time, Digen turned her aside. "I must. I must cry, let it come. I'm a channel, Ilyana. I must clear myself."

"Channel!"

Her frustrated outcry was like a slap in the face to Digen, hitting him on all senses at once. He sobered instantly. "Ilyana, you'll pledge to us now. You'll learn to live with—channels. Whatever we've accomplished today, the Tecton won't change much within our lifetimes."

She shook her head, casting all that aside, and groped for a lock on his fields, guiding him toward another peak, collimating all his turbulent energies into a pure sexual arousal. "This is better for you, Digen, the natural way."

She's still Distect. She'll always be Distect. No matter how hard she tries, always Distect.

The full sense of what he'd done finally hit him: lortuen consummated—with a Distect Gen. *It will take time,* he thought, *but it will be all right. It has to be all right.*

Gathering himself together, facing now the practical situation, he wriggled loose from her and stood to pace across the room. "Enough for now, Ilyana. There are things that must be done."

She drew herself to her feet and padded up behind him. Her nager flowed sensuously over him, satin to his ravaged nerves. "If you must, then I'm with you, Sectuib."

But what she really wanted was to focus all the surging

energies within him on purely sexual release, leaving his secondary system unrelieved. He couldn't permit that. Too many renSimes would suffer for it. *Oh, Im'ran!* The fanir would have allowed the full hysterical postsyndrome to run its course, guarding him from all destructive pain, and when it was over Mora would have been there to take up the rest.

That part of my life is over, gone forever, thought Digen. *Mora will never get her Farris child now*. In lortuen, he could be potent only with Ilyana.

He turned to Ilyana, buried his face in her hair, and said, "There will be time to finish this later, but first I— we—have obligations—to—to Rin and Joel—it's been close to four hours—and you've got to eat and rest. I couldn't bear it if anything happened to you."

"I don't want to sleep—I'm through being sick. I want to run and dance in the sun."

Digen nodded. "But first . . ." he said, and drew her toward the door. Turning his attention back to the world, he suddenly noticed the low-level turmoil in the other room, realizing it had been going on for some time. Hayashi shouldn't be exposed to anything like that!

Digen grabbed up his coverall and stepped into it. The underlining had been torn, somehow, in their struggles, and the zipper jammed on the edge of the torn fabric. He worked it loose while stepping into his shoes and walking toward the door. Still zipping the coverall, he opened the door with two tentacles and stepped into the outer room, Ilyana also dressing at his side.

The first thing Digen noticed was that Hayashi, still unconscious, had been moved to the bed. But Digen's alarm at this evaporated when he saw Mora and Joel working with the IV setup and the more ordinary bone-marrow stimulants and transcutaneous nutriment packs, panspectrum antibiotics, and precision field management.

With that worry off his mind, Digen's attention went to the tight knot of arguing people in the middle of the room. Phrases had come to him as he opened the door. ". . . Doesn't matter what he's done, you don't shen a channel . . ." ". . . No question he's guilty, problem is he's the Sectuib . . ." ". . . When this gets out, if we don't take immediate action . . ." ". . . But even if we do, they'll crucify us . . ."

The last was from Controller Mickland, his nager shredded between conflicting anxieties, his voice tight. Cloris Agar and Controller Hume of Eastfield District were also there, along with a channel Digen recognized only from newspaper photographs, Regional Controller Flemis Beccard, one of the most powerful women in the Tecton, and Mickland's immediate superior.

She was stately rather than pretty, austere in a provocatively sexual way—or, wondered Digen, did he see that merely because of his condition?

As Digen and Ilyana took in the scene, the other channels quieted in growing astonishment. At last Flemis Beccard advanced on Digen, focusing minutely on his field. Digen knew he was presenting an entirely new aspect to the world, knew the consummated lortuen was clearly visible in his entwinement with Ilyana's field—as well as the spectacular improvement in her condition—but he was entirely unprepared for Beccard's shocked accusation: "The Sectuib has gone junct!"

They had been prepared for the illegal transfer, the lortuen, and the violation of the controller's injunction on doing surgery. They had not been prepared for a junct channel.

Mickland, Agar, and Hume edged closer to Digen, probing cautiously. Agar and Hume were mumbling their confirmation of Beccard's observation, when Mickland said loudly, "I knew it! I knew it would happen all along! This is why I issued that injunction. I wanted to protect him, and the Tecton, from this. You see what happens when you allow people to worship hereditary aristocracy? You see what happens when one person is allowed too much power? There's only one way for the Tecton to survive this. We must show that even the Sectuib in Zeor is not above the law! Seize him!"

Drawing Ilyana with him, Digen evaded their encirclement and faced them again, still not quite able to believe that this was happening. "You can see," said Digen, "I have not harmed anyone." His hands on Ilyana's shoulders, displaying her glowing health and their indissoluble link, Digen said, "I don't glory in Gen pain. I've not suddenly become evil."

Beccard turned to Mickland. "I'm sorry, I didn't believe you. But I'll back you now. He'll have to be incarcerated and displayed to as many as can file by—so that people will not accuse us of any antihouseholding sentiment. If they see it with their own senses, they'll know—the Sectuib in Zeor is a Distect outlaw!"

The other channels spread out again, trying to ensnare Digen in their fields, neutralize him for capture. Digen skinned free, knowing that if they once got a grip on him he would never get another transfer but would die on public display—in attrition—his cries for mercy broadcast as an object lesson to every part of the world.

"What is the matter with you?" shouted Digen. "Don't you realize what we've done? At a price, sure, but it was worth it. We've saved Rindaleo Hayashi's life, saved the Tecton with Gen surgical techniques. We can halve the death rate in-Territory among Simes *and* Gens. It's a small step, but a real one—to eradicate the fear that keeps Sime and Gen apart, to reunite mankind. What else is Faith Day all about?"

"He's insane!" cried Beccard. "Get him before he hurts someone!"

Digen eluded them again and jumped up on the makeshift operating table to get above their fields. All at once he saw the unbreachable wall in their minds, their hearts, and, like comparing a picture with its negative, he saw through the Tecton as it was today. If Klyd Farris could see this, he knew, his esteemed ancestor would cry tears of blood for this perversion of his ideals made in his name.

The whole argument between Tecton and Distect had originally hinged on Hugh Valleroy's prediction that just exactly this would come to pass—that the Tecton, which Klyd had designed and enacted into law, would come to victimize the sincere channels and reward those who sought only personal glory and power. And with the power of the channels inherent in the Tecton structure concentrated among the glory seekers of humanity, the grip of the Tecton could never be broken. No slavery in the history of mankind had ever been so unbreakable.

Ilyana—and all her people—have been right all along! Klyd Farris himself was wrong—wrongwrongwrong! He meant well, but he was wrong!

On a rising crest of manic rage powered by the post-syndrome still in him, Digen screamed, "The Tecton is dead! Your Tecton is nothing but a travesty of the human spirit, and Zeor will have none of it!"

He ripped the double-crested ring from his hand and flung it down on the marble bench top, stamping it flat with his heel. "The Tecton is dead! The House of Zeor is dead! And may you all know what you have done before you die!"

The anguished rage beating from Digen, powered by the selyn he had taken from Ilyana, drove the channels to their knees. The nageric resonance between him and Ilyana caught up the beating anguish and amplified it until the channels were groaning helplessly on the floor.

Digen leaped down from the countertop, caught up Ilyana, and swept out of the room without a backward glance.

Out on the streets of Westfield, Digen made Ilyana stop for a moment. "Where can we go now? What are we going to do?"

She took his arm over her shoulder, giving him all the strength of her nager. "You just leave that to me. The train station is right here. We're going—home."

"Rior?"

"Where else? Who else would have us—now? At least there we can live in peace."

PART III

THE RETURN

What is the Distect?

The Distect is an idea. You can not kill an idea by killing the people who hold it.

"OUT OF DEATH WAS I BORN—
UNTO ZEOR, FOREVER!"

Orim Farris
Sectuib in Zeor

Chapter 14

SHILTPRON PARTY

It was a holiday in the Distect, the anniversary of the founding of the House of Rior. The sky was scoured clean and the russet and gold leaves of fall were sprinkled among the evergreens of the high mountains.

Digen had been in Rior for six months.

Yet, on this day he could not join in the festive mood. Instead, he walked the paths between the little fields of shoulder-high wheat that surrounded each house of the mountain settlement, listening to the clink of utensils against sinks and dishes as the holiday meals were prepared. He watched the swarms of children playing tag up the mountainsides to the berry patches. He savored the ambient nager of the whole settlement, steeped in a vibrant contentment he could only envy from the outside.

Life here in the House of Rior was very different from anything he'd ever known before. It seemed as if there were no rules governing transfer. People did as they pleased, and they seemed—happy, in a way Digen hadn't ever seen before in a group of people. There was a deeply committed family life, usually with four adults who were mated in transfer and separately in sex. And they raised their children without regard to whose natural children they were. Nobody seemed to care whether a child would become Sime or Gen. And changeover or establishment was hardly even an occasion.

In fact, Digen hadn't seen a single case of pathology in changeover since he'd arrived, though he knew they happened. Rior had no channels because Rior had precious little use for channels. Overall, it was a tough life, a frontier existence, but it was a healthy one.

In his own little house, surrounded by his own little field of ripe wheat, which he'd planted so joyfully with his own hands, Ilyana was singing to herself, putting the finishing touches on a new dress she would wear to the party that night. She had made him a cape of Zeor blue adorned with the Rior crest—and he had rashly promised that to please her he would wear it to the party.

But he dreaded the moment when the sun would set and he would have to put it on.

He climbed a little hill and sat on a sun-warmed rock overlooking the small settlement. He counted thirty little houses like his own and the huge main hall at the center of the valley. To one side of that was the laboratory building, with Roshi's lab, the one place Digen was forbidden to go. On the other side of the settlement valley, over a ridge of hills, a cliff fell off nearly a thousand feet straight down. In the hazy distance Digen could just make out the descent of the mountain peaks to the foothills where Zeor and Rior had both been born.

But Zeor is dead. It could not survive in a world where fear ruled supreme. Zeor was dead. It was all over and done, a closed phase of life. Rior lived, and somehow so did he.

Digen didn't recall much after he had stormed out of Westfield's Sime Center with Ilyana. A merciful fog shrouded those weeks, binding up his mental wounds until, somehow, in Rior, he had healed and emerged.

The turning point had been the day that they had planted their own wheat field near the house. He had plowed and sown the field with his own hands. Day by day, as the little green shoots emerged and grew, he too emerged and grew. And now the wheat was almost ripe for harvest.

All summer he had lived each day as it came, noting with contentment how his physical condition had improved. Under constant exposure to Ilyana's field, his bouts of entran had become less and less severe, need was never more than a passing sensation, his allergies became dormant, and his strength seemed boundless. Physically he had never in his entire life been so strong and healthy.

Mentally, though, he still shied away from thinking about the past. He kept his mind quietly in the present, never ranging far into tomorrow or yesterday. Yet, as his general vitality increased, he knew such stillness of mind would no longer satisfy him.

Behind him, the sun dipped below the highest peaks sending afternoon shadow lapping across the valley. He experienced a sensuous delight in the sunset, and the glow of happiness emanating from the houses about him bathed him with contentment. Could anyone ask more out of life?

Just a little longer, he thought. *Let me hold on to this just a little longer.*

Off to one side, a little jagged peak of shadow touched the windows of his own house. Ilyana, a tiny figure in the distance, came out on the porch, disturbed that she couldn't see him anywhere.

He didn't like to see her disturbed. He gathered himself and ran down the mountainside toward home, striding full out for the sheer joy of the movement. He would wear the cape for her and her happiness would be enough for them both.

As Digen arrived home, all over the settlement families were already emerging from their houses, singing together as they walked the winding pathways to the main building where they assembled for the official celebration.

Ilyana made Digen wait until the last of the singing had died away before they started out of their house. "Roshi isn't due back until the day after tomorrow," she told Digen. "So this year I'll have to lead the sing."

Roshi, Ilyana's older brother, and Head of the House of Rior, had been acting strangely ever since Digen had begun to recover. "Odd," said Digen, "that he'd be away on such an important occasion."

"I don't understand it myself," she replied. "Not only is he deliberately staying away with about a third of our men, he's actually forbidden the celebration."

"Then why are we having it?"

"Digen! What would happen if you tried to forbid the celebration of—oh, Union Day in the Tecton? Instant demoralization, right? Just what we require to face a long hard winter?" She shook her head. "I don't know what's become of Roshi lately. He's all wrapped up in something and he won't even talk to me about it."

"Maybe it's just what people have been saying—that he's having trouble with his Donor—I mean transfer mate. If Fenris were to leave him, where would Roshi turn for transfer?"

"Fen wouldn't do that. He's been Roshi's transfer mate

since they were kids. They're practically in orhuen. And their spouses are in orhuen. It's a perfect Distect marriage."

There was just a tinge of bitterness in her voice, which she managed to keep from her nager. The main reason she had left Rior to try for a life in the Tecton was the powerful attraction Roshi had for her as a transfer partner. She had almost broken up that "perfect" Distect marriage by taking Roshi away from Fenris. She'd bear the scars of a nearly fatal fight with Dula, Roshi's Sime wife, for the rest of her life.

"Look," said Ilyana. "It's time for us to go down."

They walked hand in hand along the pathways to the central hall. Emerging from a stand of trees, they approached the huge double-sized barn doors, which stood open. Inside, the hall had been decorated with gay paper hangings and parti-colored lights. At one end, a buffet table was heaped with elaborate but edible artistic creations, beautiful enough to make even a Sime's mouth water. The Simes and Gens stood in segregated groups, Simes to the right, Gens to the left, along both sides of the hall, leaving an aisle for Digen and Ilyana to walk along to the stage.

Ilyana took Digen's arm firmly and began the march up that aisle, saying aside to him, "You sing like a lead bell, so you're going to play the shiltpron for me, and keep your mouth shut."

That was the first Digen had heard of this plan. "I can't play . . ."

"Don't argue," she said. "I heard you playing out by the waterfall yesterday."

He whispered, aware of the people staring at them, "Only on audio range. And I haven't played in public since the injury."

"Don't worry," said Ilyana. "If the scar gives you any trouble, I'm here."

And then they were on the stage and Ilyana was handing him the shiltpron.

"It will do you good, Digen. Trust me."

The instrument fitted neatly into the curve of his arm, his fingers resting lightly on the strings. He kept his tentacles away from the resonating pipes and prongs that would pick up the audio resonances of the strings and translate them into selyn-field harmonics. The shiltpron, an ugly instrument at best, looked like a cross between a harp and a bagpipe, but was played by finger plucking, or with mallet or bow—or all three at once. It was the first truly Sime instrument invented.

This particular one was made of antique rosewood, polished by long decades of use. It came against his shoulder with a soft, gracious feel. And when he sounded an experimental chord, it filled the room with rich, warm tones perfectly attuned.

Before the chord had died, Ilyana raised her voice and sang out a joyful note. Then all the gathering was singing and Digen concentrated on following the tune. It was a simple tune, somehow distantly familiar to him, but with verses that told of the founding of Rior. Soon Digen was embroidering around the melody with more confidence, thinking that Ilyana had been right. There was a definite healing quality to this, and he was enjoying it.

As they finished the last verse, recounting the names of the charter members of Rior, the aisle dividing the Simes from the Gens disappeared in a whirl and suddenly the company mixed and then reseparated out in family groups.

"Come," said Ilyana, "dance with me, Digen!"

A Sime woman took the shiltpron from Digen as Ilyana drew him down onto the dance floor. A chord rang out audibly, and then as the shiltpron player exposed her laterals to the vibrating tines of the instrument, an exquisite shiver brightened the ambient nager. Every Sime in the room groaned a little with it. Even Digen gasped. In three expert strokes, the shiltpron player struck up a cadence to which Ilyana began to move.

Modulating the throb of the shiltpron field with her own body, Ilyana wove through it, casting streamers of pure sensation out over the Sime dancers. Digen found himself slipping into hyperconsciousness, entranced by the beauty of it.

He had never seen anything like it before. In the Tecton it would be considered obscene for a shiltpron to be played in that manner in the presence of both Simes and Gens. No Tecton Gen would use his body to stir a Sime to need. It would not be pleasure to the Sime but torture, and there was always the risk of sparking a kill-mode attack.

But here, the stirring of need was a joy to be shared,

not a torment to be feared. No Sime in that room, himself included, harbored one thread of repressed need. Until that moment Digen hadn't realized just how much of a residue even the best Tecton transfers left.

The entire room danced with Ilyana and Digen as if they all were extensions of their own bodies. There wasn't a person not in perfect tune with the rhythms of the shilt-pron. *It's like living without effort,* thought Digen. And for him, that moment became the very definition of being alive.

That was the last clear memory Digen had of the next few hours. Ilyana became a pinwheel of modulated colors, focused and projecting through his own body field. Digen let it happen. He felt beautiful inside and he wanted to share it with everyone in the world.

Sometime the family groups broke up and people began dancing with anyone and everyone, changing partners with or without reason. Ilyana was whirled away and replaced by a high-field Gen boy flushed with peaking selyn production and eager for Digen's tentacles. To his own surprise, Digen enjoyed the attention, letting it stir his need, and he was vaguely disappointed when the boy was snatched away by a Sime girl. He knew the boy was not the transfer mate of that girl, and he watched, strangely fascinated, as they completed a transfer right on the edge of the dance floor.

He realized that all about him Simes and Gens were pairing off across the normally strict family lines, and even the Simes who were not ripe for transfer were enjoying intimate lateral contacts they would ordinarily shun.

His Tecton scruples twinged in dismay, but as a cuddly Gen woman came into his arms, he laughed at himself and seized the waves of shiltpron music, taking them through himself and flinging them to the far corners of the room, bidding everyone joy. Before long he found himself again dancing with Ilyana, she gathering and focusing the shilt-pron fields for him to grab and send outward in a corus-cating display of hyperconscious pyrotechnics. They were so perfectly attuned it almost hurt. Digen became caught up in the intense gratification.

He retained a flashing memory of Ilyana's face, rosy and sweat-streaked, exuberant with the bursting vitality pos-sible only to a Gen. And she was his. Love and need moved and mingled as he had never thought possible. He was drunk on it and he knew it and didn't care.

Digen danced harder and harder until Ilyana, breathless, bent over, saying, "I have such a stitch in my side!"

Someone came and took her to the sidelines, but Digen was still wild with the newfound joy. Before he knew it, he was drawn up on the bandstand and the shiltpron player thrust the instrument into his hands. Digen began to demur—he wanted to dance. But the musician reached over and touched off a chord among the tines that hit Digen stronger and deeper than it had when he'd been way out on the dance floor. He sat down slowly, cradling the shiltpron in his arms.

His hands and tentacles fit themselves automatically among the upright tines and webbing of taut strings, and the anticipatory shimmer from the people in the room sent Digen off into hyperconsciousness.

Once or twice, during his first year after changeover, Digen and some of the channels at his training camp had held secret orgies of deliciously wicked shiltpron music. But, of course, they hadn't allowed any Gens near them. Remembering those nights, Digen let his laterals just grace the tines here and there as he played.

Each time he made that contact, the music seemed to penetrate his inner core a little deeper, to possess him a little more strongly, to open out layers of tensions he would have sworn were not there. He seemed to be thinking more clearly, understanding his own nature more profoundly. Each time he touched the tines, his own body translating the audio music of the strings into nageric harmonics, the audience begged, "Again—again—faster—more —again!" Soon he was daring longer and longer lateral contacts, using both his primary and secondary systems to modulate the music as nobody else had ever been able to at Rior.

He let the music flow through his vriamic without fear that his lateral scar would cramp on him. Without fear. The Simes were blind drunk on the music, but the Gens were in control. Nobody was being hurt; nobody was in danger.

As Digen played, he realized that hours had passed. The younger children had stuffed themselves from the buffet and fallen asleep in the hayloft or been sent home to bed. The Simes who had nursed their need, conserving it for this occasion, had taken transfer, and the drunkest of them had already sought out their spouses and settled down to enjoy postsyndrome. The rest were simply reveling in the expanded capacity of their senses under the shiltpron.

Little by little his channels opened. He was pouring energy into the ambient nager—beat and ebb, beat and ebb—until he was commanding the inner flows of all the Simes in the room. It was not any of the channel's functionals he'd mastered in the Tecton, but it was what a channel was really for in a way he could never put into words.

Through the shiltpron, he was in deep contact with the Simes, and through them with the Gens they touched, little bright sparks embedded in a dim ruddy glow of half need. Without conscious decision, Digen was feeding into them all the newfound bliss and glory of his lortuen, celebrating it beat after insistent beat.

The power of the ambient nager took hold of him, lifting him to new heights of ecstasy, which he magnified and fed back to them, enjoying the pure need without fear.

Ilyana was before him, gathering and bathing in the shiltpron field, spewing torrents of bright wavefronts in every direction, a pinwheel to the hyperconsciousness.

Digen knew there was no stopping it now. The Simes had all paired off with Gens, moving deeper and deeper into lateral contact, trautholo, and verging right up to transfer, even for those not actually in need. He was a part of that network, central to it as all the fields blended and focused through his vriamic. It was as if, via the shiltpron standing wave, he was about to give transfer to all those Simes at once.

His secondary channels opened wider and wider, selyn rose from his depths and poured out into the ambient-nager beat and ebb—beat and ebb—harder and harder and harder until, at one crescendo beat, the room *surged* with selyn movement—deep—beautiful—perfect.

It was over.

The couples folded in on themselves, sinking to the floor, stunned and breathless. The shiltpron fell from Digen's hands as his secondary system went into recovery transients. He hadn't performed a secondary functional in months, and now he reached for Ilyana's steadying nager, shaking with the unexpected strain, and suddenly cold sober in the flickering colored shadows of the hall.

Ilyana folded him up in her arms as they, too, sank to the floor, exhausted. Only then did he realize that he had played the shiltpron fully, and without so much as a twinge from his lateral scar. He let Ilyana's silken field bring him down, down, down to normal, as he thought over and over, *This is what it's like not to be crippled.*

All at once, outside in the yard there was a great clattering of horses' hooves and wagon wheels, men and women yelling, and the snapping crack of longwhips.

Roshi ambrov Rior, Head of the House of Rior, had returned with saltfish and provisions for the winter. Almost before anyone could stir out of exhaustion to meet him, four or five men burst into the hall, shoving before them two mud-spattered Gens who stumbled and sprawled into the crowd on the dance floor.

Roshi, a tall, slender Sime with black hair and the high forehead that made him look vaguely Farris, stormed into the room and bellowed. "I left orders the celebration was canceled this year! Do I hold your pledges or not?"

Ilyana climbed to her feet and in her clear soprano said, "I ordered the celebration." In Rior, Head of House was usually the Gen in direct descent from Hugh Valleroy. Because of Ilyana's illness, Roshi had taken her place, and Ilyana had never before seen fit to challenge that. But now she was well again.

Roshi strode over prone bodies, some of them so absorbed in postsyndrome they didn't even notice him, and confronted Ilyana. Everywhere, Simes and Gens were picking themselves up, focusing on the battle of wills. "So," said Roshi, "I come home a little early, and what do I find? This place blazing like a Tecton city, enough to be seen all the way to Valley Station—half the guards partying in here while two Gens have broken through our perimeter! And one of them from out-Territory!"

Everyone turned toward the two helpless Gens. Digen, clinging to Ilyana for strength as he fought through the recovery, watched the gathering mob converge on the interlopers and begin to shove them around from group to group, seemingly to provoke their fear for the fun of it before killing them. Around the outside of the group of

Simes, Gens gathered to yell insults and dire threats at the Gens.

Digen could scarcely believe it. The joyfilled people had become a savage pack of barbarians. *Living secretly in an armed camp like this would do that to people. They can imagine what the Tecton—or the out-Territory Gens—would do to them if ever this place were found. And it doesn't help that I've gotten them all into postsyndrome at the same time, nor that Roshi interrupted it.*

The Simes who'd been on the trail were not post-; many of them were in need. They sensed what they'd missed by not being here. All together, there wasn't an emotionally stable Sime in the entire room. And they were bent on taking out their frustrations on the hapless prisoners.

Digen got up onto his own feet and made his way through the crowd. The two Gens had been separated, and he went toward the most frightened one. He got to the edge of a cleared space where two Simes were literally throwing the terrified Gen back and forth. The moment he laid eyes on the Gen, he recognized him.

"Joel! Shidoni!" Digen pushed and shoved his way through the ring of bystanders and out into the cleared space, catching Hogan as he reeled toward one of his tormentors. Glaring at the two Simes, Digen said, "This one's mine. Or would you care to contest that?" His voice held a deadly threat.

For a moment the two Simes seemed about to contest it, then the larger one waved a tentacle and said to the woman from whom Digen had rescued the Gen, "He's not worth it." In a moment the circle had broken up and many had drifted away to watch the play with the other victim. Few Simes in all the world would care to take on Digen Farris.

Digen held Hogan slumped against his shoulder, becoming more aware of his worn but essentially healthy condition, and his terror. Simultaneously, Hogan became aware that the punishment had stopped. Dizzy, he raised his head and began to struggle onto his own feet.

Digen let him go but kept a hand on his shoulder. Hogan focused on his captor. "Digen!" There was a surge of joy in the Gen, but it was swamped out by a new wave of fear. Hogan's eyes went to Digen's hand on his shoulder.

"What's the matter?" asked Digen. "You can't be afraid of *me?*"

"Is it true, what they said? Are you—junct?"

As much as he wanted to, Digen could not say no. "I have never killed in transfer, Joel, and I never will. That's all that's left of my life."

Joel searched Digen's eyes, judging truth as best as a Gen could. He finally relaxed. Then he stiffened in sudden memory. "Digen, they'll kill Im'ran!"

"Im'ran? He's here?"

"We came looking for you together." Hogan was pulling Digen toward the knot of Simes who surrounded the other captive Gen. Digen restrained him.

"Joel, Im'ran can take care of himself. We've got to get you out of here. Some of these people are in need, and the others could turn ugly at any moment."

"I'm not too sure Im' can take care of himself. He's been suffering from underdraw—at least we think that's what it is—ever since the channel who was guiding us got killed in a rockslide."

Digen dragged Joel toward the door until he encountered Ilyana. He thrust Hogan at her, saying, "You remember Joel. Take him home. I'm going back. They've got Im'ran in there."

"I'll go with . . ." she said.

But Digen plunged back into the melee of Sime and Gen bodies, yelling over his shoulder, "No! You protect Joel!"

He pushed through the crowd, saying over and over to himself, "Im' can take care of himself. None of these renSimes could ever hurt a companion, let alone a Tecton-trained fanir."

In the far corner of the room, surrounded by a throng of Simes and Gens, Digen found Im'ran faced off before Roshi, who was in need. Digen could sense it despite the dense nager. It was the first close look at Roshi Digen had had in several months. And he began to see what the trouble was.

Roshi was a channel, although, being Distect, he had never performed any secondary functions other than perhaps playing the shiltpron. Now in his middle years, his secondary system had begun to stir to life. He would,

Digen realized, have been feeling sick, out of sorts, and perhaps even a bit irrational, especially during need.

Behind Roshi, at the edge of the crowd, stood Fenris, the man who was Roshi's regular Donor. On Im'ran's side of the circle, beside Digen, stood Fen's wife, Ora, and her transfer partner, Roshi's wife, Dula—one of the most beautiful renSimes Digen had ever seen. The whole foursome were grimy from the trail and tired from the long ride.

Dula grabbed Digen's elbow in her handling tentacles. "If you're really on my side, you'll get that Tecton Gen away from him."

Ora grabbed his other shoulder, saying, "Fen can satisfy Roshi, if he'll only give him half a chance. I know it."

Digen looked from one woman to the other. They were locked in orhuen, both in postsyndrome. Where lortuen attracted during postsyndrome, orhuen repelled. The static between them was almost unbearable. Digen broke loose and plunged into the cleared space, coming up beside Im'ran, grateful for the fanir's clean nager.

"Digen!" said Im'ran. Then he tossed a glance around the room. The steady fanir's rhythm drove into and through Digen, powered by the Gen's overcharged selyn field. "Digen, Joel Hogan was with me. They took him—"

Digen flipped a tentacle, wiping away Im'ran's concern. "He's all right. Now, what about you?"

Im'ran paused to consider, as if he hadn't thought of that. "Well, I seem to have an assignment for transfer. He's not much, but I admit I'd be glad for anything right now."

To Im'ran alone Digen said softly, "You could overcontrol him easily. But he's Head of the House of Rior. If you survive the transfer, you'd become his permanent Donor—until his old Donor—or his wife—kills you for it. The political ramifications could bring the roof down on us before we can get you and Joel out of here."

Roshi bellowed, "I said get away from him!"

Digen turned. "I heard you, Sectuib Rior." In the Distect, "Sectuib" was a gross insult, not a title of respect. Digen had made his tone a model of deference.

Roshi, tense with need, turned livid.

"You're a channel," said Digen. "Everybody knows that shameful secret. What they don't know is that you've lately found a strange quality to your need. You're not satisfied with Fen anymore. And now you're after a Tecton Gen who happens to be a companion to the Sectuib in Imil. What kind of a Sime can only be satisfied by a companion, Roshi? An active channel, Sectuib of this House."

"No!" said Roshi.

Im'ran stepped up beside Digen and their eyes met. "Please, Digen—don't . . ."

Digen put his arm around Im'ran's shoulders, falling into synch with him in the old way, feeling now from Im'ran the same sense of desperation he'd felt from Ilyana all the months in Westfield. He worked to control the Gen's wildcatting production rate, and said to Roshi, "Let me teach Fen to help you. You don't really want a Tecton-trained fanir in your family—and you don't believe for one moment you could kill him in transfer. So let me help."

With a roar, Roshi flung himself at Digen, going hyper-conscious and into the Sime hunting mode. At first Digen thought Roshi was attacking Im'ran for a kill, but then he knew that he, himself, was Roshi's target. He shoved Im'ran aside and yelled, "Fen!"

Then Roshi was upon him, tentacles digging into Digen's arms, forcing a vicious Sime/Sime lateral contact to strip Digen of all selyn. Digen rolled with the momentum, struggling to bring his secondary system—still in recovery from the shiltpron—up to transfer pitch. He felt a searing lance of pain through his vriamic node as he switched to secondary functioning while Roshi had just begun to force selyn movement in his primary system. But Roshi had no vriamic control at all, and Digen took control, handling the channel as if he were any berserker Sime, providing him just the right amount of resistance to induce the necessary satisfaction, and giving selyn to repletion. It didn't take much, but it was a lot more than Digen had expected for a mature but undeveloped channel. A lot more.

It was all over by the time Digen's shoulders hit the floor and they rolled to a stop at the feet of Dula and Ora. Fenris pulled Roshi off Digen and started ministering to his transfer mate. Digen came to his feet and went to Im'ran.

"I'm sorry, Im'. I had to keep him off you—I know you wanted it—but I had to. Come on, let's get out of here."

Behind them, Dula was bending over her husband, sharing his postsyndrome. Suddenly, Ora went wild, and attacked Dula, screaming incoherently. When Fen tried to pull her away from the Sime woman, she turned on him and threw her shoe at him.

Shuddering, Digen started toward the door. Im'ran swayed on his feet. "It's so hot in here. I think I'm going to faint."

Digen swung one of the Gen's arms around his neck and walked him through the muttering crowd and out into the fresh night air. "It's not far to the house. Think you can walk now?"

Revived by the cool air and Digen's firm grip on his nager, Im'ran said, "I think so."

They took a downhill path through some shrubbery and off between the wheat fields. After a few steps Im'ran said, "Do they always behave like that?"

"No," said Digen. "It's just that here—they take transfer very personally—even more personally than sex. And I'm afraid the ambient nager in that hall was enough to drive anyone crazy."

Im'ran paused to look at Digen in the dark. His emotional nager ran the gamut from shock and disbelief to censure of Digen for making excuses for them. He shook himself and continued along the path. "Are they just going to let us walk away like this?"

"Why not? Here, transfer is a private matter, not regulated by laws."

"But isn't channeling illegal here? And you gave him channel's transfer."

"Not illegal so much as immoral. In the morning, Roshi will probably be very ashamed of himself."

Im'ran stopped. "Shen! You're in recovery. I should be . . ."

"Ilyana will take care of me. I want to get home before my knees start to shake—and before you collapse. This way." Digen turned into another path and shortly they stepped onto the wooden slats that led across the often muddy ground to the front porch of Digen's house. Digen stopped for breath, saying, "As soon as my insides stop churning, I'll take care of your problem with underdraw. Come on."

Ilyana opened the door and came out on the porch, framed by the light behind her. Then Joel limped into view and Im'ran hurried up onto the porch, saying, "What happened to your leg?"

Joel said, "Must have sprained it down in that hall sometime, but I didn't notice it until just now."

Digen gathered Ilyana up in his arms, burying himself in her field. In the light from the doorway she noticed the livid marks on Digen's arms. "What happened?"

Digen told her.

"Roshi did that to you?"

"Don't blame him too much," said Digen. "I provoked him on purpose." He explained his diagnosis of Roshi's developing secondary system, saying, "I'll teach Fen how to handle it and all will be back to normal in a month or so."

Digen had been leaning more and more on Ilyana, and now his knees did begin to buckle. Im'ran came up on his left side and together they got him into the front room and laid out on the couch. For nearly an hour both Ilyana and Im'ran worked over Digen's systems.

Chapter 15

NEW CHOICES

Later, over trin tea and steaming soup, Digen said, "Well. It's over."

"You're not normalized already?" asked Im'ran.

Digen shook his head. "No. I'm stronger than I've ever been, but I'll never have a decent recovery time again. In fact, my head's still spinning from playing that shendi-flamed shiltpron. No, it's what I was thinking this morning." He explained his train of thought as he had sat overlooking the valley, not wanting the peace of life here to end.

"And now the world and all its questions comes pouring in on my head. Yesterday I could have welcomed you and not asked. Now I've got to know. How is Rin?"

They were seated at a little round table in the middle of the front room. Hogan put down his tea, almost untouched, and stood to pace up and down. "He's fine, Digen. Completely recovered from the surgery."

Digen released a breath he hadn't known he was holding.

Im'ran said, "He has a lot less scarring than you do." Then he ran through a technical list of channel's functional parameters that had changed for Hayashi, ending off, "Other than that, Joel's right, he's fine."

Im'ran and Hogan took turns filling Digen in on all the happenings of the last six months.

After Digen and Ilyana had disappeared, Im'ran had been called back to Westfield to manage Hayashi's convalescence. He had asked Hogan to stay on as surgical expert. Together they had pulled Hayashi through an infection, pneumonia, and a grueling assortment of transfer dysfunctions.

Sometime during the convalescence, Hayashi had wakened one morning with the sudden knowledge of exactly what had gone wrong with Dane Rizdel's training that had caused Jesse Elkar to take a suicide abort. "Or, rather," said Im'ran, "he figured out a new equation with some universal constants nobody's ever heard of before—" Im'ran broke off, looking at Ilyana. "This may not be the right time to say it, but, Digen, you and Ilyana—you can come home."

"No!" Digen shook his head. He realized he had said it louder than necessary. *What am I afraid of? A choice?* "No, this is the only home we have. It's all over, finished. I—I am—for all practical intents and purposes—junct. I can never work as a channel again. What have I to go back to?"

"Surgery," said Hogan.

"The House of Zeor," said Im'ran.

Digen looked from one to the other and said, "Don't be cruel."

"The House is not disbanded," said Im'ran. "Your sister took over as interim Head of Householding. They voted to wait a year and then, if you didn't come back, to look for a new Sectuib among the Farris families allied to Zeor. Bett has pledged to marry any man they choose as Sectuib in order to keep the family line unbroken."

"She can't!" said Digen, lunging to his feet. "She can't marry a Farris! Our father was a double Farris. If she tries to have a child by a Farris, it will probably kill her."

"That's what I told her," said Im'ran. "We all did. But she's determined. She says Farris women always die in childbirth anyway, so what difference does it make."

He knew his sister pretty well, and he could see this as her way of forcing him to return. "I can't go back, Im'ran. I'm under a death sentence several times over."

"No," said Joel. "Not anymore. It's all—fixed."

Then Digen noticed that Hogan had been speaking Simelan—haltingly but understandably. At his quizzical stare Hogan shrugged. "I've been trying to pick up the language," he said in English. "But I'm not any good at saying important things yet."

Im'ran said, "Hayashi's made a deal with the World Controller. If you and Ilyana will come back and let him use you to evaluate those new constants, he says it will give him the key to the safe wholesale training of Donors. And the World Controller says that if you'll do that, all charges will be dropped. You may not get your out-Territory license back, but you could do almost anything you wanted to in-Territory."

"Like, for example," said Hogan, "surgery."

"It won't be easy," said Im'ran. "World opinion is against you. People are more scared now than ever before about introducing any surgical techniques. But Hayashi is living proof that it can be beneficial, and he's working on a paper that proves mathematically that you got into trouble basically because you'd been shorted to the brink far too long."

"You could open a little clinic," said Hogan. "For terminal cases. When I finish my residency I'll join you. It could be a good life and we could all accomplish something worth doing."

"If we could just establish the use of blood transfusion, Digen, think of the lives we could save."

"Wait. Wait," said Digen.

"You can't refuse," said Hogan, carried away in his enthusiasm. "We're giving you your whole life back."

"But," said Digen, "you're assuming that what you're offering is better than what I've got. I've been happy here. This has been the very best time of my entire life."

"I can see that," said Im'ran, glancing at Ilyana. "The vacation has been good for you. And—and you'll come back to an official lortuen exclusive. Nobody will ever be able to separate you."

Ilyana was biting her lips, watching Digen. He got up to stand looking out the window into the night.

Im'ran added, "Hayashi's a genius, Digen. And since you accepted his pledge—he's become maniacal in his loyalty to you. He'll find a way to get you disjuncted—eventually, he'll find a way."

Digen whirled on him, blue cloak flying about him. "You're assuming that I want to be disjunct! Can't you see what this has done for me? I haven't taken a single medication since I've been here. There isn't a rash anywhere on me, no watering bloodshot eyes, no sinus congestion. And functionally—don't you realize—I played the shiltpron full range for over two hours and then performed an A-prime functional for Roshi after six months of secondary dormancy and here I stand on my own two feet, not one drug in my system and no therapist hovering over me, expecting me to die any minute. Now I should want to go back to a world where health is illegal?"

There was a silence in which Im'ran's eye fell on the cloak Digen still wore, Zeor blue ornately embroidered with the Rior crest. After a space, he said, "Have you then pledged to Rior?"

Digen became aware of the cloak for the first time since he'd painfully donned it that afternoon. All the unanswered questions that he had been shunting out of his mind flooded back to overwhelm him. What was right? What was wrong? What should the world be? How much personal responsibility did he have to make the world over into what he thought it should be? What did he really want to do? And why should he do it?

He loosened the clasp at his neck and let the cloak fall from his shoulders. "No," he said. "The cloak was just for the festival—to make Ilyana happy. But now," he said, turning to Ilyana, "I see why you wanted me to wear it. To make me confront the problems, the decisions yet to be faced."

"Digen," she said, "I can't go back. If you go, you go without me." She turned to Im'ran. "I grew up here in this valley. And for years, all I wanted was to get out of here and see the real world. But when I got there, I found it was insane, cruel, vicious, and sick. Most of my memory of that time is mercifully hazy or blank. I did have a few lucid moments, though, and I saw what your precious Tecton was doing to Digen. I saw him meekly accepting living death as the lot he was born to—so that others might also live their tortured half-lives. I used all the strength in me to stick it out until he would see the evil of the Tecton and come home with me. I don't have the strength to face that again, and I won't."

"I won't defend the Tecton," said Im'ran. "It's a hard life, and the channels are never given a choice about the sacrifices they make. But that's why I'm in the profession. If they can do so much, how can I do less? And I'm not the only Gen who feels that way. Ilyana, Digen suffered not from the Tecton so much as from the Donor shortage. And with his help, Hayashi can solve that problem once and for all."

Joel said, "I grew up in a little town not too unlike this one. Except only Gens lived there. If you want to know what's insane, cruel, vicious, and sick, Ilyana, it's a community without any Simes at all, a community of Gens who beat their own children to death in changeover. That's what the real world would be like without the Tecton and its channels."

"We've learned a terrible lesson from what happened to you, Digen," said Im'ran. "The Micklands and Beccards are being removed from public office. The transfer code and penalty clauses are undergoing a complete revision. There's even been some question about whether Mickland's injunction on you was ever legal in the first place. People are asking themselves the hard questions about the purpose of what we're all doing. And Zeor is leading it."

Hogan said, "Im', tell them about the strike."

"Strike?" said Digen.

"Just after you left, when the condemnation on you was published, the entire House of Zeor went on strike. And the next day all the firsts—channels and Donors—went out too. Then all the householding-owned businesses closed their doors. The seconds and thirds wanted to join the strike, but we wouldn't let them. We wanted to dramatize a point, not destroy the Tecton. If the law permits the Sectuib in Zeor, the best channel in all the Tecton and the one Sime in the whole world with the greatest measure of control, to be shorted beyond his endurance, how can any of the rest of us live with that law? If the Sectuib in Zeor can sacrifice—well, his integrity—for the life of the man who can save the Tecton—how can we condemn him?

"We won our point, Digen, in just forty-eight hours. You're not a criminal, and you haven't been for almost six months. You don't have to hide here. You can come home —in lortuen exclusive, and stay junct if that's what you want. But we've got to have you and Ilyana so that Hayashi can get the data to solve his theoretical equations and start relieving the Donor shortage."

Hogan said, "It's much worse now than when you left. The situation is critical."

"He's right," said Im'ran. "The incidence of suicide abort is way up. The firsts are counting the days until your return. You are their only hope."

"And the Tecton is our only hope," said Hogan.

"You can't tell me," said Digen, "that the fate of the whole world depends on how I order my private life."

"The Sectuib in Zeor doesn't have a private life. Whether you like it or not, Digen, in some kind of metaphysical way, you are the Tecton. Too many generations have sacrificed more than you're being asked for. Zeor has a life of its own. You can't abdicate."

Digen turned to look out the black window. Everything in him cried out to answer that summons. He'd been born to it, raised to it, and he had invested all the years of his adult life in it. In a strangled whisper, he said, "I can't— I can't do it."

"Why?" asked Im'ran, standing to pace restlessly.

"I—I don't know why. There's just no strength in me. Not for this."

Ilyana picked up the cloak from Digen's feet and took station by his left hand, facing Im'ran. "Leave him alone, can't you?"

"No, I can't leave him alone, Ilyana, and I can't leave you alone either. Too much depends . . ."

Im'ran broke off. He suddenly crumpled to his knees, weak, dizzy, and sweating. Digen was at his side instantly, scooping the Gen onto the couch. "Don't talk, Im'. You've got your production rate way up again."

Im'ran wiped his forehead with the back of one hand and said, "I don't know how you ever stood this, Ilyana."

Hogan said, "You were all right a minute ago. What happened?"

"He only has a slight touch of underdraw," said Digen. "His governors were working fine there for a while. His net field was actually bleeding downward. Im', how long has it been since you had transfer?"

"Six or seven weeks. Somebody open a window."

"They are open," said Hogan.

"I'll get a cold towel," said Ilyana, going toward the kitchen.

Digen considered. "You began to feel it when you were about a week overdue?"

"Yes. But it's getting worse."

Digen nodded. "It would—about now, your body is expecting transfer again."

Ilyana came with the towel and began sponging Im'ran's head and arms. He said, "I thought you told me I wouldn't be likely to have this problem."

"Well," said Digen, "you didn't exactly level with me that day, as I recall."

Im'ran seized Digen's hands with all his strength, suddenly flooded with all the remorse and pain of their parting. "Digen, I did the best I knew how for you. I was under orders. . . ." His selyn-production rate began to climb precipitously.

Digen had, despite Ilyana's presence, automatically fallen into synch with Im'ran's dead-true Tecton standard rhythms. Now he used all his new strength to gain control of the fanir's body fields and bring down the production rate. At the same time, he said gently, "I know, Im'. When I finally shook loose of the dependency—Im', I would have done the same in your place."

"If I'd been able to get back, though—you wouldn't have been—your conditioning wouldn't have—I could have prevented this. Oh, if I'd handled Jesse right and kept you away from Ilyana, none of this would have happened."

The Sectuib in Zeor—junct.

Ilyana, waving the towel over Im'ran to make a breeze, said, "You mustn't blame yourself. That's just underdraw depression. Take it from me, I know."

"Im'," said Digen, "I wanted Ilyana from the very first moment her field touched me. Nothing could have kept us apart much longer—not even you. Lortuen—lortuen is stronger than orhuen, you know—and you and I aren't quite close enough for that, even."

"That's what I mean—for us it would have been relatively safe." He looked backward and up at Ilyana, then back at Digen. With a rueful, bittersweet ache, he said, "I can't say I'm not happy for you. You've got what ordinary people only dream about—and—and never did anyone deserve it more. But—why did it have to turn out like this! Oh, don't listen to me. I need a good transfer!"

Im'ran squirmed restlessly on the couch. Digen frowned. "Haven't they been using you four-plus at all?"

Im'ran shook his head.

Criminal! thought Digen. *But, to be expected from the timid little rulebookers like Mickland who have taken over the Tecton without understanding what they are really supposed to be doing.* "Well, that's probably why you've run into this trouble, then. But you should normalize in a week or two, if you avoid getting so intense about things—and stay away from Simes in need."

"A little difficult to do around here," said Im'ran.

"True," said Digen. "They'll be chasing you all over the settlement, with your field the way it is."

Hogan said, "What's to keep us here? There are no fences. We could just walk away." And then he had a sudden thought. "You wouldn't set those—people—on us again, would you?"

"I wouldn't have to," said Digen. "They have Sime lookouts posted all the way around the perimeter. You might get through by yourself, Joel, but Im'ran's field— even when he's at his lowest—would be perceptible to any renSime for almost a day's ride in any direction."

"You mean," said Hogan, "they're keeping you prisoner?"

"No," said Digen. "It's just their normal security procedure. You can imagine what the Tecton or out-Territory Gen government would do if they could locate this place."

Ilyana said, "They'd raze every building to the ground and execute us all—publicly."

"Digen," said Im'ran, "would they *let* you go back?"

I never thought about that. But Digen couldn't say so, or Im'ran's production rate would soar again. "I'd never reveal the location," said Digen, "and everyone here knows that. These people have never done anything to deserve destruction. They don't raid or steal or kill Gens. Though they're against the Tecton in principle, they're not foolish enough to do anything about it."

"I don't know about that," said Im'ran. "They've nearly destroyed the Tecton just by holding you here."

"I stay here of my own will. The Tecton was going to execute me—remember?"

Im'ran struggled up to rest on his elbows. "You don't believe that Beccard and Mickland could have gotten away with anything like that?" His field began to climb again.

Digen wasn't so sure. He'd met many people in his life who positively enjoyed seeing any householder, but especially Zeor members, suffer humiliation, degradation, or defeat. Pushing Im'ran back down, Digen said, "Let's drop it for now and just deal with your immediate problem. I can see that there's no way to hold your production down long enough for nature to take its course. I can't offer you a full primary transfer." Digen looked at Ilyana, knowing he'd never be able to take transfer from anyone else for the rest of his life. "And there isn't a Sime in this settlement who could even total your TN-2 level. So, in my—professional opinion—I think the best thing for you is to attain transfer dormancy."

Im'ran tilted his head back at Ilyana and said, "Now I know why you kept saying you'd rather be dead."

"Im'," said Digen, "once normalized, you won't feel this way. Your governors are functioning beautifully. Given time, your production rate will equal your diffusion loss rate and you'll feel completely normal."

"I haven't missed a transfer since I established," said Im'ran forlornly.

"You may find a hole in your life, but physically you won't suffer from it."

Hogan crossed the room to kneel beside Im'ran's shoulder. "Im', we can try to make a run for it. Get you back to civilization . . ."

"I'm not leaving without Digen," said Im'ran. "And Ilyana too. Otherwise, I wouldn't mind making a run for it. I might get a transfer out of it, anyway."

"All right," said Digen, "I can see you running around here seducing every Sime in sight and getting some transfer mate to kill you for it. Ilyana, you can sympathize with how he feels."

"Digen," said Im'ran, "do you have to be insulting?"

"Sorry," said Digen. "It seems my manners are in transition or something."

Ilyana asked, "What do you have in mind?"

"I can't strip him," said Digen. "That would only stimulate production and he'd have to go through it all over again."

Im'ran, who had surged with hope, collapsed again. "I don't care about tomorrow. It's now I've got to get through. Digen, if you're worried about entran, I can handle anything that might develop from this."

He probably could, Digen thought. Ilyana was a natural but wholly untutored talent, and though she had put him neatly into secondary dormancy, she really didn't have Im'ran's exacting and meticulous discipline.

"No," said Digen, "stripping would just aggravate your

problem. What we should do is tap your GN levels, just to relieve the immediate pressure but not to stimulate production. Now, to do that, we have to maneuver so that no selyn disturbance propagates down into your TN levels. Follow?"

Im'ran nodded. It would be a low-level functional for Digen and probably would not aggravate the entran he'd already invited by serving Roshi's need. It would make Im'ran feel better immediately and still not slow his progress toward transfer dormancy. With no selyn movement in the TN levels, there would be no sensation of transfer, and, incidentally, no sense of satisfaction either.

"It's all you can offer me," he said. "It's all I deserve."

Digen wanted to say, "Self-pity is unbecoming to a companion in Imil." But nothing would be accomplished by chastising him for an underdraw-induced mood. At the same time, he also realized that Im'ran was expressing a deeply held conviction—one that he might otherwise be too proud to voice.

"Im'ran, I'm going to give you the sole responsibility of holding your TN barriers."

"No, Digen, you do it."

"No, I won't let you be lazy. Besides, if you do it, it will strengthen you. You'll attain dormancy a lot faster—and there's less chance of accidentally stirring your deeper levels."

"I don't trust myself. I'll take you if I'm tempted."

"I trust you," said Digen, taking Im'ran's overheated forearms in his hands and laying his handling tentacles along them. To Hogan, Digen said, "If this is going to disturb you, why don't you step out on the porch for a moment?"

"I'll stay," the Gen said. "I've grown up a little in the last few months. I can behave myself."

"All right. Just give us a little room."

Hogan and Ilyana moved away as Digen narrowed his concentration to the job before him. A Donor was not ordinarily adept at flattening the GN barriers while holding the TN barriers tight. Digen had to coach Im'ran for two or three minutes before he finally got it right, but by then Im'ran had become so wrapped up in the learning of a new technique that he forgot his apprehensions. *He's a therapist,* thought Digen.

Then Digen made lateral and lip contact, fields balanced to a gentle flow, the kind he would use on an out-Territory volunteer Donor. He carefully drained off the superficial selyn-storage—gleaning about four times what an out-Territory volunteer would have provided. Then he dismantled the contact.

Im'ran went limp. "Shenoni, Digen, you're good. I didn't feel a thing. How can a channel like you stay in a place like this?"

Digen pulled a coverlet over the Gen, saying wearily, "It's late. Why don't we all get some sleep and talk about it again in the morning."

But, inside, he was wondering the same thing. Working with Im'ran had suddenly brought back all the key satisfactions of functioning at the channel's craft. The joy of saving a life or easing suffering. The purely personal, physical gratification of using his body as it was meant to be used. The distant echoes of all his oldest and dearest ideals.

The channel is the medium through which the human race can be reunited. How can I sit here in Rior with Ilyana and all the satisfaction she gives me and never again lift my hand to share that satisfaction with the isolated Simes and Gens of the world?

I cannot go back, and I cannot stay here like this. What am I going to do? I wish they hadn't come.

Then he saw that the coverlet he had drawn over Im'ran was the Zeor blue cloak with the Rior crest embroidery. He wanted to laugh or cry or both—but he dared not make a sound. Exhausted, Im'ran had fallen asleep.

Chapter 16

HARVEST

The morning dawned brisk with mountain chill. Before the sun had cleared the eastern peaks of the valley, grain-harvest crews had set to work in all the ripest fields—including Digen's. As the first wagonload was sent to be threshed, the field foreman came pounding on Digen's door.

In the back bedroom, Digen disentangled himself from Ilyana and padded barefoot to the door, worried that the commotion would wake Im'ran, who was still asleep on the couch. Hogan, bleary-eyed, came shuffling from the side bedroom, struggling into a robe, as Digen opened the door to the cold morning air.

Without greeting, the Sime woman who ran the harvest for Rior said, "Well, you want it to rot on the stalk?" Then she turned her back and swept down the steps, two Gens and a Sime following her. At the bottom of the steps she turned and said, "I hear you got two new hands last night. Let's have a full turnout."

Digen gave her a tentacle-to-finger gesture of agreement and shut the door. Im'ran had come to his feet, shaking himself awake. Ilyana was poking up the fire, saying, "Hot cereal and sweet buns in five minutes. It's going to be a long day."

Digen explained the Rior custom of trading field labor while he dragged out coveralls for the two Gens. "If, as it seems, you may stay here awhile, it's expected that you'll work for your keep. Personally," said Digen, "I consider it a crime for such top professionls to have to do field labor."

Hogan slipped his shoulder straps into place over the rough shirt Ilyana had found for him and said, "I was raised on a farm. And harvest is harvest. Be fun, I expect."

243

Over hot cereal and trin tea, Im'ran said, "I've never done anything like this before. But I'm willing to learn."

When they came out onto the porch, a row of Simes wielding scythes was already far into the stand of ripe grain. Behind them, a line of Gens was gathering the felled stalks and bundling them onto flatbed wagons, all under the watchful eye of the Sime woman foreman, labeling every wagonload.

Digen joined the scythe wielders, working between a woman he knew only slightly and, at his left, Skip Ozik. Skip had made his way to Rior with the help of some underground sympathizers to whom Ilyana had directed him. He was now a provisionary member of the House, under the protection of Roshi's family—which made him an unofficial member of Digen's own little family, and unconsciously Digen had come to think of him as a son. Skip had not yet noticed Im'ran and Hogan working some yards behind them. Skip said, "I heard about what you did last night with the shiltpron."

"You weren't there?" *No, of course not, he hasn't had transfer, not recently.*

"I'm here on probation, Digen. I wouldn't dare go against Roshi's orders—where else do I have to go?"

Digen looked at the boy. He had grown two hands taller in the few months since his changeover and had begun to fill out with a mature Sime build. But it was more than that. His whole nager was aglow with pure health now, whereas the Tecton would surely have killed him—despite all Digen could do—trying to disjunct him. Yet here he hadn't actually harmed anyone, and he was happy. "You do have a point."

"You should have seen Roshi's face this morning when he heard what you'd done! It's got to turn into a hundred-year legend, for sure—imagine, everyone in transfer at the same moment! Roshi heard Shurban and Aliase snickering in the dining room—you know how those girls are at their age. He called them in and gave them the stern-father routine and made them tell what was so funny. Then he went all stony and said, 'That's an example of what happens when you turn a Tecton channel loose in Rior! Consider yourselves fortunate you weren't there.' So they pulled long faces and went outside to snicker some more, this time over what you did to Roshi. Before I left, they made me tell them all about what channel's transfer feels like!"

Digen enjoyed Skip's oh-so-grown-up amusement, while at the same time thinking, *He's just a kid himself yet. First year can be the best year of your life.* They worked in silence for a while, then Digen caught a glimpse of a moving nager over Skip's shoulder. "It seems," he said, "that we are going to find out how Roshi feels about it all, right now."

At about the same time, the others became aware of the approaching horsemen and stilled their scythes. The Gens caught up with them, and they all stood in a group, awaiting Roshi. Suddenly Skip whirled and shouted, "Dr. Hogan!" Arms wide in eager greeting, Skip went toward Hogan.

Not recognizing the boy, Hogan stepped backward, his fear plain to every Sime. The Gens around him melted away, leaving him to face Skip alone. In English, Skip said, "Don't you recognize me? I'm Skip!"

Hogan's face lit with a smile and most of the fear vanished. Most, but not all. Digen moved between them, saying hastily to Skip, "Joel isn't used to being around Simes." At about the same time, Im'ran worked his way through the crowd toward Hogan and took charge of the fields. Digen stepped clear to give him room to work.

Hogan, still in the grip of surprise, said, "I see you— made it, Skip. We all wondered, you know."

"Well, I couldn't very well send a telegram home," said Skip facetiously.

Digen saw the boy's emotional hunger for contact with home, with his old life. It was normal for changeover victims from out-Territory. Hogan's fear had given way to his usual curiosity. For him, too, this meeting was a touch of a past so distant that it had already become nostalgia.

At that point Roshi arrived on his roan stallion, kicking up dust and spooking the wagon mules. Staying mounted, he said, "Digen Farris!"

Digen stepped out before him. *He's afraid of me. But he's not admitting that even to himself.* None of the other Simes had the acuity or training to read Roshi's nager in such fine detail. They saw only his righteous anger whipped up over the preceding hours.

"You are a houseless man," said Roshi, "come among

us on sufferance. But you have betrayed our trust—subverting my sister—and then, last night, using your physical endowments to manipulate my members, exposing them all, shamelessly, to the part of you that has been made into an abomination.

"Leaving aside the atrocity you committed upon me, I have sufficient reason to demand your banishment or execution."

Ilyana, mouth agape in stunned amazement, finally pulled herself together enough to believe her ears. She stepped out in front of Digen. "Roshi! Subvert me? Betray trust? Digen? He's been a model guest in this House. I gave the order for the celebration—you never said why there shouldn't be one—and I got Digen to play the shiltpron." She gestured at the crowd around them. "As far as I can see, nobody's complaining about the results!"

There was a general murmur of agreement, which only provoked Roshi's anger to greater heights. "Well, you ought to complain!" He focused on Digen. "I have to protect my people. We've sheltered you in good faith. Now I think it's time you returned that. Pledge Rior, now, to me, with the understanding that your life is forfeit should you use that—body—of yours again on any of us, and your —indiscretion of last night will be considered an accident of drunkenness, a fluke never to be repeated."

Pledge Rior?

Ilyana stood, lips compressed, hands clenched together. Digen guessed she was thinking that if any pledge was to be given, it should be to her, not Roshi. Roshi had not, to Digen's knowledge, ever been called upon to accept a pledge. For Digen to offer his pledge to Rior unto Roshi would be to acknowledge—with all the weight of the traditional position of the Sectuib in Zeor, parent house to Rior whether or not he was acknowledged here as such— Roshi's right to head the House of Rior and the Distect.

But, by custom, Rior was always headed by a Gen, and by right the position was Ilyana's. She had never revealed that during her stay in the Tecton.

"If I were to offer any pledge to Rior," said Digen, "I would offer it to Ilyana—as Sosectu ambrov Rior under Rior's charter from my great-great-grandfather, Klyd Farris. No Sime may be more than Regent in Rior."

There was a stirring that gathered into a firm, bright

approval among the onlookers. But there were others who supported Roshi in place of the slender, often ill, sometimes temperamental Ilyana.

Roshi noted the crowd's approval. "This is not the time or the place to discuss the succession in Rior. It's your crime that's being considered, not Rior's politics."

Digen was beginning to feel a sense of desperation. He had not yet fully assimilated the news that he could leave Rior and go back to the Tecton. He could not—now—confront the idea of pledging Rior and leaving behind him forever the life of the Tecton. To him, a pledge was far too sacred a thing to be entered with any quiver of uncertainty.

Digen turned to the group around them, tentacles spread in open appeal.

"What I did to you all was wrong," he said. "By everything I believe about the dignity of the individual, the right of consent, and the ethical use of the power I carry in this Tecton-molded body—what I did was truly an atrocity. I—am—sorry. I didn't know it would happen like that. I'd never played in a mixed crowd before. I didn't know any such thing was even possible. Had I known, I would not have entered that hall—even to please Ilyana. But I did go, and I did play, of my own free will. I accept full responsibility for the consequences of my choice. If there is anyone in all of Rior who would have my life for this—then my life is forfeit without argument."

He stood before them, wholly open, his nager in true contrition and repentance. Im'ran gasped, then turned aside and translated to Hogan. A murmur rose as the Simes told the Gens how they read Digen's nager. Some thought he might be using Tecton tricks to present a false reading to them. Over the sound of argument, Digen said, "I have nothing to offer as bond but my bare word that I will never touch the shiltpron again. But—Rior seems willing to accept my pledge, which is tacit endorsement of my word. Forgive me. Please forgive me, and accept my word."

As Roshi saw that Digen had gained a consensus, manipulating Roshi's own members against him, his anger rose another notch. "Your word is not good here unless you pledge Rior!"

The general discussion among the onlookers surged in another direction, and someone suggested that a houseless man had no honor and thus no word to offer on anything. It was an attitude that had been valid before Klyd Farris had founded the modern Tecton.

Pledge Rior? No! I can't! But—not to pledge—to take Ilyana into exile? If they'd let us go? To leave—all this, which has been so good, and go back to—the old life. I can't.

Turning back to Roshi, hands falling lifelessly to his sides, Digen was torn beyond endurance. But as his eyes came to the man on horseback, something Im'ran had said the night before floated to the top of his mind and locked into place within his sense of reality.

"Roshi, I can't pledge Rior. Zeor is not disbanded, as I thought it had been when I came here. It lives. And as long as it lives, I am not a houseless man and am not free to give my pledge!"

Roshi backed his horse a few steps. Around Digen the murmured conversations burst into a roar. Roshi brought his stallion into the crowd in little, mincing, sideways steps. He faced Digen and said, for all to hear, "You came to us as a houseless refugee, and we sheltered you in good faith, only to be betrayed, as I have said, and now—now you admit that you gained entrance here under false colors!"

"He didn't know until Im'ran told us last night!" said Ilyana. "But he's laid down his office in Zeor, and last night he refused to go back with them and take it up again. If Roshi won't validate his pledge to Rior—I will be proud to accept it! Dual allegiance between parent and daughter houses must have some kind of legal precedent— and if not—well, what does Rior stand for if not establishing new precedents for others to follow?"

She was right. The word "rior" itself meant forepoint, the prow of a ship, or the leading edge—the cutting edge of a flying object—the vanguard of a movement. Audacious leadership had always been the hallmark of Zeor. What could be more fitting than the reuniting of Rior and Zeor? But—he had not truly refused to go back. He had merely put off making a decision that he simply could not make yet.

The surging conflicts within him were cracking him open along the stress lines that had just so recently healed. He began to feel the same sense of unreality, enervation, and hopelessness that he had felt during the trip by train and horseback from Westfield to Rior. He stood slumped, head bowed, and could not even feel embarrassed when his voice came in a strangled whisper.

"Ilyana—I can't—do it. I can't . . ." He was shaking.

Roshi guided his horse out in front of the group, strutting in triumph. "Since you will not pledge Rior and clear your name, then you will be confined within Ilyana's house —under sentence of banishment from the life of Rior until such time as you do offer me your pledge. And any who choose to enter your house of banishment will incur the same sentence of banishment. This is the official pronouncement of the Acting Head of the House of Rior."

Digen's whole body was shaking as if from palsy. Im'ran and Ilyana moved up on either side of him, applying their fields, but doing little good because his problem was not systemic or functional but purely emotional.

From astride his horse, Roshi said, "Touch him on pain of banishment!"

Immediately, Im'ran and Ilyana took Digen's hands and looked straight up at Roshi in silent defiance. Hogan, who had only half understood the conversation, and who had learned enough in six months to keep away from a channel in trouble, waited for Im'ran to explain before he, too, touched Digen.

All the people around them shrank back, falling silent. Roshi said, "Put them all in the house then—and if they— any one of them—emerges before Digen has publicly pledged Rior, the guards will shoot to kill."

The next morning, Digen watched from the window as the harvest crew moved in to finish his field. They were not permitted even to use the porches of the house while people were near. Every few days, Ilyana told him, somebody would pick up and fill their shopping list if they left it outside. But that was all that would be done for them.

Under the sheltering nager of his friends, Digen gradually emerged from the fringes of nervous collapse. They didn't urge him to come to a premature decision, and little by little they came to see just how deeply the issues affected Digen's ego structure, the whole integration of his personality.

They realized the limited usefulness of conscious, verbalized argument in such a situation, and most of the time they left him to private meditation, or merely provided silent, supportive companionship. But from time to time they would get into the deep philosophical waters that Digen trod for his very life, and they would argue for hours over tea and nuts.

Digen felt stretched tight between hundreds of opposing points—like a drumhead tuned to highest pitch. Sometimes he would follow the arguments to the relentless conclusion that he must try to escape and return to the Tecton—for the sake of thousands who would die if the Tecton collapsed. At other times he would become convinced that the Tecton way of life was indeed the disgusting travesty of the human spirit he had once glimpsed it to be. The entire concept of the householdings—that channels must shoulder the entire responsibility for transfer because renSimes simply could not keep from killing—would seem the fallacy underlying what had become an essentially evil way of life. It would seem obvious that the Distect precept —that in any transfer situation, the Gen and only the Gen was wholly responsible for anything that happened—was the only solid and obvious truth in life. *You can not separate authority from responsibility:* a fundamental maxim of Zeor. The power, the authority, always rested in the Gen—if he was master of himself, he could master any Sime.

Digen had seen this operating in Rior, and, seeing it, he had found that he'd never really believed it before. But now he did. Nobody would contest that an adult was to be held to account for his self-control. Therefore, in the most ultimate and fundamental sense, any Gen who got killed in transfer had simply committed suicide, out of sheer stupidity, most likely. He deserved exactly what he got—and more—if he accidentally hurt a Sime while he was about it.

There was no such thing as "the kill." There was no such thing as a junct, and the entire concept of disjunction, and conditioning Simes to channel's transfer, was such an abomination that it literally made his gorge rise.

At such moments he would vow to himself never to return to the Tecton. He could not lend himself to the support of such a hideous system and at the same time remain sane. He would arrive at this point, and start to go to Ilyana and offer to pledge Rior, repudiating all prior allegiances.

But then something would check his feet, stopping him and holding him in a kind of mental paralysis. And later, if he should happen to fall asleep, he would wake racked with the question: How can the Tecton's prevention of the wholesale slaughter of Gens possibly be immoral at any cost?

At other times he would wake with the question: How can human sacrifice possibly be moral, whatever the objective? For that was what the Tecton had demanded and would demand of him—his very life. All that he had found at Rior, all the health, happiness, satisfaction, and sheer vitality, would have to be given up so that the Tecton could totter onward for another generation or two, because that was all that Hayashi's machines could conceivably buy for them with the micklands in control.

How could he give up such goodness to create misery for millions? Could an evil way of life (the Distect) create good health, while a good way of life (the Tecton) created a living death for all who adhered to it?

Was there no logic to the universe? At first that was a rhetorical question, a question based on the unshaken certainty that the universe was always impeccably logical, meticulously clean of contradictions, and infallibly just.

But as his torment went on and on, unresolved, a tiny trickle of doubt crept across his soul like a stream of liquid nitrogen, burning cold. His hackles would rise and his tentacles extend in the chill grip of a shrieking, nameless horror the likes of which he'd never known.

A few days after their confinement, Digen was experiencing just such an episode of creeping terror while standing on the back porch, soaking in the noonday sun and inspecting the rocky cliff just yards behind the house. If there was no logic to the universe, there was no reason why that cliff shouldn't tumble down and crush them all. He couldn't take his eyes off it.

Behind him, Ilyana came out through the kitchen door to fling a washbasin of water out over the kitchen garden. She recognized the rigidly extended tentacles as a sign of fright, and propped the basin against the back-pantry door, watching him closely. After a time, she crept near, carefully respectful of the sheer power such a fright could summon in a Sime, a power even she might not be able to divert.

She fell into synch with him, drifting in that oh-so-natural way that he hardly felt as a Gen's touch. She managed to drain the intense charge gathered in him.

Digen wilted against the roof pole, panting.

She came into the curve of his arm like a whisper. After a while they sat down on the top step, curled together in a kind of weary mutuality.

Ilyana said, "You want to tell me what that was all about?"

Wordlessly, Digen shuddered in negation.

"Digen, you can't go on like this. You'll crack up so badly that nobody will ever be able to put you together again—I mean it, Digen—literal insanity."

"Does—does Rior have a Memorial to the One Billion? If I could go—maybe I'd feel better about it all."

"We do, yes. Under the main hall. Nobody goes there anymore. My father started using it as an arsenal years ago. It's filled with cobwebs and dusty old crates and stinking chemicals. Besides, we're confined here. You can't go anywhere."

"Yes," said Digen. "Ilyana? If—if ever I come to pledge Rior—I want it to be there, in your memorial."

Ilyana smiled. "I think that's a splendid idea." She thought about it awhile and said, "Digen? Did anyone ever tell you that you have a poet's soul?"

"I do? I'm not even sure I have a soul anymore."

She sighed, the inexpressibly weary sigh he had heard so often from her in Westfield. "I know the feeling."

He turned to look at her. "Now I know what you went through in Westfield."

"Yes. Most people go through their whole lives without ever really thinking through the implications of what they're believing and doing. I used to wonder if that isn't why—in the Tecton cities—people live so frantically fast. They don't dare give themselves time to think."

"With all the time in creation, I still couldn't see through this to the end. I know it must be obvious, but I can't see what I must do."

"Maybe there isn't a 'must do' in this case. Maybe for the first time in your life you have a real choice."

"That's a frightening idea."

"Look, Digen, start from the beginning."

"Does this thing have a beginning? It feels to me more like one of those slinky spring toys that's gotten all tangled up. An endless, interconnected spiral, and somebody welded the ends together to thwart the poor kid who wants to play with it."

"You sound like one of those Tecton channels suffering pretransfer depression. Of course it has a beginning. When the first Sime went through changeover, or rather, when the first Sime was born. The human race began to mutate. We're still mutating. The rate hasn't slowed down very much—but it's only been a couple of thousand years at the most, and that's not very long in terms of evolution. So, humanity is undergoing a process of change in which two paths are opening before us—and we have a genuine choice about which path to take. That's the choice you're confronted with—the Tecton or the Distect. Which is right? Which is better?"

"If I asked you that, you'd say the Distect?"

"The Distect way isn't just right and it isn't just better —Digen, it's the only path to the survival of our species."

"I don't see how you can say that. The death rate around here is nothing to brag about."

"But not in transfer. You've been here six—seven months? How many deaths in transfer have there been?"

"I haven't heard of any."

"There was one—a hundred-twenty-two-year-old Sime died of a brain hemorrhage during his transfer—but he died in bliss. The kill happens occasionally—but it's not a feature of life, and it never happens to the undeserving."

Digen thought of the children watching their parents enjoying transfer during the celebration. The Gens raised like that would go to their first transfer with such anticipation. And they would be rewarded. The ideal life? Then he thought of Ora's attack on Dula after he'd served Roshi in transfer. But that was personal. It wasn't the kind of thing that could start a Sime/Gen war.

"What about Zelerod's Doom?" asked Digen.

Zelerod was the mathematician who had predicted that, without something like the modern Tecton, the Sime population would grow so large that they would kill off all the Gens within one generation. World population figures now stood over three hundred per cent past Zelerod's

Doom. If the channels quit working and let the renSimes attempt personal transfer directly with Gens, each Gen would be able to give only one transfer and then would die. With the channel intermediaries, the world could support a population that was fifty per cent Sime if it had to—and they had a long way to go to reach that figure—because one Gen could support a Sime for his entire life.

"It wouldn't happen," said Ilyana. "Zelerod was a mathematician, not a sociologist or a psychologist, or even an expert on transfer theory. He was wrong, Digen, just wrong."

"How can you say that? His math was impeccable. It's convinced generations—"

"When has the majority ever been right? Sure they're convinced—because they don't think things through. Humanity has survived a lot of dooms. Our strength is in our diversity. Our strength is in our *minorities*—like us, here in Rior. We survive without channels. Somewhere out there Gens would survive and create their own houses and join the Distect and a whole new—and for the first time in history—right—chapter in the history of our species would begin. Those survivors would be different from anyone who had ever lived before—and their world would be a world without the sick, cruel, savage, repressed terrors of the Tecton—without the mickland-cringing-cowards. A world of nothing but emotionally healthy people."

Digen was bemused by the idea. He'd never heard Zelerod challenged before. "Utopia, Ilyana? Could it really happen?"

Ilyana pointed to the cliff face before them. "See that groove that's all discolored? That used to be a waterfall, and our kitchen garden is in the streambed from it—see?"

Digen traced out the lines, following her finger.

"Years ago, there used to be a mill here on this site, powered by the stream. Now, pretend that you're the very ground the mill was built on, and the mill is a part of you—something you conceived and built yourself. I come along and see that the waterfall has dried up—it's blocked up on the mountain and will never flow again. So I tear down the mill. Now, *feel* the shock, bewilderment, the blow to pride and ego that the ground must have felt."

She fed him the emotion, culled from all her own living experiences, and he felt it—the pain of destruction.

"Digen, the ground can't know that my plan is to rebuild —something new, something useful, something more suited to current conditions. But now the house is built and the ground feels fulfilled, satisfied, happy again. One day the house will be worn out and will have to be destroyed— so that something new can be built. Life is like that. Destruction precedes emergence of something better. Destruction is not bad. It only feels that way."

"But millions would die—horribly. Simes and Gens alike—not just feel like they're dying, but actually die. Who could be responsible for doing such a thing?"

"Not me. Not Rior, Digen. But we don't have to be. The Tecton is crumbling under its own weight. Let it go—let the Simes loose to find their mates. A hundred years already the Tecton has been holding back the pressure of this natural drive. Sure, there's going to be a lot of killing when that pressure is suddenly released. But with each passing year the pressure grows, and the destruction that must come when it is released gets greater and greater. Eventually—if we delay the Tecton's demise too long— that pressure will be so great that it will destroy all humanity. Call that—call that the Distect's Doom, if you want, but this one is real."

"How do you know we haven't reached that point already?"

"We better not have—because the Tecton can't last. It stands in defiance of all the most basic instincts. And it has fallen into the hands of the micklands, who use it to feed their voracious egos so that they won't have to face their own cowardice. Have any of man's structures built on such a foundation ever survived?"

"What makes you think the Distect is any better?"

"Rior, maybe, isn't. And right now 'the Distect' consists of only one house—Rior. But, Digen—the basic concept of the Distect is—well, you know that a parasite that destroys its own host dies. Simes who kill are parasites. And they'll die off eventually—when their hosts are all dead. Or— You don't believe that Simes really are parasites, do you?"

He stroked her arm. "The Sime/Gen relationship is symbiotic."

"But what's the premise behind the whole concept of the Tecton—keeping the incompetent Gens away from the Simes? The idea is that if they ever got together, the Simes would kill the Gens—that it is a Sime's *nature* to kill. That's the premise behind the Tecton. And it's wrong. You just said so."

"I did, didn't I?"

"What's so good about the Distect? The Distect is founded on the concept that it is *not* in the Sime's nature to kill Gens. Think about that. Doesn't it feel right? Doesn't the idea that you are not—by your nature—a killer—that your ego, your ethics, your morals, and your soul are not in danger from your bestial nature—feel good to you? You're not a killer. You don't have to be in conflict with yourself. You can live in harmony with yourself. Doesn't it feel good?"

He stroked her arm again. "Yes."

"Yet, back in Westfield, you spent your whole life fighting to keep yourself from killing. All that antikill conditioning that always cut your transfers short. Poor Jesse."

"Poor Jesse."

"I don't see how you could ever go back to that life. Can you—in conscience—support a system that does such things to people?"

"No."

"Then why not pledge Rior and the Distect?"

All during their confinement she had not asked him that question or any like it. When he had asked himself he had always found an answer. This time he could find no answer. There was just a gathering of heaviness in him that sapped all his energies.

"Digen? Digen, what's wrong?"

He shook his head.

Behind them, the screen door creaked open and Im'ran came out on the porch. As the fanir's nager swept over Digen, he recognized that gathering tension at the back of his skull—entran. Struggling to master it and to adjust to the moving Gen's field, he clutched at Ilyana. But something inside him went wrong. Speared by fiery cramps, he doubled over with a grunt.

Both Gens were at him instantly, which only doubled the cramps. Im'ran said, "Let me do it, Ilyana. You don't have the training." The steady, precise beat of the fanir's nager backed by all the concentration of a disciplined professional swept through Digen.

Ilyana said, "Get away from him! He's mine!" Her nager fragmented with alarm the moment he doubled over, and it was still incoherent as she divided her attention between Digen and Im'ran.

Ignoring Ilyana, Im'ran had come to total focus on Digen, narrowing and narrowing his attention until he could read Digen's problem. "Entran, Digen? Here—" And at once his field meshed hard and smooth against Digen's systems, ready for an outfunction.

Digen groped for Im'ran's hands, concentrating on his field, accepting his help. Bewildered, Ilyana faded back some distance to let them work. Im'ran made the contact, firm, steady, dead-true Tecton norm. It was such balm to Digen's nerves that when it was over he almost felt like crying. He straightened up, gulping air and throwing off the feeling.

Im'ran worked his fingers along Digen's laterals analytically. "This is the first occurrence since you did me?"

Ilyana said, "Yes, he's been fine. I can't . . ."

Digen shook his head. "No, it's the fourth episode. The other three were trivial, though."

"Digen!" said Ilyana. "Trivial?"

"There's a Zeor technique for it. It's good for the system."

Ilyana's gaze flicked from one to the other. "You were testing yourself! You're thinking seriously of going back!"

"No!" said Digen. "I—" He broke off, realizing that it was true. He'd gotten back into the Zeor disciplines not because he had to but because of a discomforting prick of conscience—and a self-doubt: *Can I still do it?*

"Well," asked Ilyana, "why did you choose Im'ran then?"

Digen looked at the fanir's hands, brown and roughened, against his arms. He felt so good—so safe—in the fanir's grip. *He's a product of the Tecton. Why did I choose him over Ilyana? Because I'm a product of the Tecton, too.* He raised his eyes to Ilyana. "Maybe you're right and I should pledge Rior. I saw it there for a minute. But," he said, glancing at Im'ran, "obviously, deep down inside, I still don't quite believe it. And I don't know why. I can't argue against you, but I can't accept Rior either."

"Ilyana," said Im'ran, "that's enough for now. Or you'll have him in another attack."

She looked at the two Tecton men for a moment. And then, without another word, she picked up her washbasin and went inside to make lunch.

Im'ran sat with Digen, sharing the spot of sunlight, without comment, providing the support that Digen's secondary system required with such finesse that Digen wasn't aware he was being supported. After a while the Gen said, "I'd expect one or two more hard ones like that, and then you should be back in secondary dormancy. But don't try it alone, Digen. That's foolish."

Disengaging with meticulous care, Im'ran left Digen to his spot of sun and his thoughts, saying only, "As One First—All Firsts. Even if you pledge Rior—you can still come to me for help."

Later, at supper, Im'ran started to apologize to Ilyana for intruding between her and her client. But the moment he used the Tecton word, that started the whole thing over again, Tecton against Distect—and it turned into a discussion that lasted well past midnight. At one point it escalated into a screaming match over the issue of whether the world should be run for the incapable majority or the capable minority. For a moment, Digen thought Ilyana and Im'ran would actually come to blows, but Im'ran apologized stiffly when he realized he was talking to his hostess.

Hogan came to the rescue with the comment that there could be no such thing as a government of laws but not of men. One good and just man was worth any number of good and just laws. But, in theory anyway, a good law could keep an incompetent fool like Mickland from doing too much damage. They all went to bed friends again.

There was a long stretch of days in which clouds thickened overhead and they never saw the sun. He knew that the storms of winter were coming. If he didn't decide now, they would all have to stay the winter—and still the roof wasn't repaired, wood wasn't stored up, and he had no energy for all the hundreds of little things that had to be done to keep Ilyana safe through the cold of winter.

One dawn brought with it a driving, pelting hail and sleet storm that sent the last of the harvest crews scurrying for cover. The storm lay heavily over everyone's spirits, especially Digen's, as he knew his time had run out. He had to make a decision.

They lived under artificial light for three days, hardly able to chip the back door free of ice to take out the waste and garbage. Digen spent most of the time sitting by the front windows, battling a growing anxiety due both to the decision confronting him and to approaching need.

The Gens in the house had long since given up trying to argue with him. Everything that could be said had been said several times over. They slept a lot, played games with elaborate rules, helped Ilyana with mending tackle or cleaning up the root cellar, and spent hours in the kitchen, concocting strange recipes. So Digen wasn't surprised when he noticed that he had been alone in the front room for hours.

He found Ilyana asleep in their room beside a roaring fire. He covered her gently, and from the ambient nager concluded that Im'ran and Hogan were in the kitchen— or was it the pantry? Yes, the back pantry, where there was no heat.

Curious at the strange twist to the reading he was getting, Digen went on through the kitchen and out the back door, then followed the nager into the back pantry.

There, by the dim light from the windows, he saw Im'ran standing by the door to the front pantry. And between him and Im'ran, Skip Ozik was sitting knee to knee with Joel Hogan. He heard just a snatch of conversation, underscored by the nager: from Skip, a pulsing of need with a kind of hopeless loneliness; from Hogan, a terrible wrenching sympathy and, as always, curiosity.

"Skip, I want to. But the only times I've ever felt selyn movement, it—it was terrifying. Digen says . . ."

"Digen! He's living in the past. Anyone who wants to do it can. It's that simple. I wouldn't hurt you for all the world—I just feel—it would be so perfect."

Digen saw their hands entwine, Skip's laterals just grazing Gen flesh. *He's serious!* thought Digen. *He's half into commitment!* The worst was that Hogan could not know just how deeply into it Skip already was.

Digen held his breath, wanting to scream out to Hogan "Don't move!" But just then Hogan felt the whirling draft from the door Digen had opened, and he turned. Skip, in the grip of reflex, pounced the moment Hogan moved. At the same time, Digen launched himself at Skip, preparing to offer transfer.

Digen lifted Skip's tentacles from Hogan's arms, sliding his own tentacles into place. But Skip yelled out in the shock of pure shen, and, realizing that Digen was prepared to serve, he wrenched himself away, rolling on the floor in agony, yelling, "No!" Hogan stood rigidly as if skewered by an electric current.

In a blur, Im'ran slid to his knees beside Skip and took him into transfer position, lavishing on the undeveloped channel all the skills and resources of a Donor. Digen turned to shield Hogan from the sight of the transfer, taking the Gen into his own arms. Hogan was stiff, not just from fright but from cold. His blood pressure was dropping and he'd begun to black out.

Picking up the Gen bodily, Digen said, "Let's get you in by the fire."

By the time Digen reached the door to the front pantry, the transfer was complete. Digen said, "Come on inside, both of you. It's too cold out here."

By the fire in the front room, Digen chafed Hogan's hands and feet. The Gen revived enough to look up and say ruefully, "You seem to make a habit of rescuing me."

Im'ran came in with Skip, and Digen swallowed a sharp reprimand to Hogan. He got up and fetched the kettle out of the fireplace to make tea. "How long were you two out there?" he asked Skip, handing him a glass.

"An hour," said Skip.

"You have to take better care of a Gen than that," said Digen. He handed Im'ran a glass, saying, over his shoulder, to Skip, "You enjoy it?"

"Im' is—smooth. You know that. All the Tecton Donors are like that."

"No," said Digen, offering Hogan a glass. "Im' is something very rare."

"Digen," said Im'ran; "I didn't plan that."

"I know. In a few weeks you'll have the whole underdraw thing to go through all over again."

Hogan said, "In a few weeks we could be back in civilization." He was stroking the sides of his wrists, where Skip's ronaplin had sensitized the nerves, and his nager held regret. He raised one arm to smell the sensitized area. He'd wanted to experience transfer—at least once—and he'd wanted it with Skip. He knew it would have killed him. He locked glances with Digen.

All the unresolved anxieties flooded through Digen. He had to take a definitive action. He had to put it all behind him or it would kill him. Hogan—a surgeon, and a fine one, a friend and a loyal one—an example of humanity's best—and he would have died under Skip's hands. Not because he was genetically defective. Not because he was unfit to survive. Because he was a cripple, like Digen himself. The Tecton existed for the sake of the joelhogans of this word, not for the farrises. The farrises could afford to take the punishment. The hogans couldn't.

He looked at Skip. "You've kind of been in all this right from the start. You've become a man through it all. Will you give me your word not to let what I'm about to say go beyond this room?"

"I've pledged to Rior, Digen—unto Roshi. I had no choice—I've nowhere else to go. I won't do anything against Rior."

"Nor I," said Digen. "Rior is too fine a thing to destroy. But—I've got to take my friends home. We'll require your help. Or— Did anyone see you come here? Are you accepting banishment being here?"

"I came to get your supply list. So many people are sick—there aren't any more guards on the house."

Digen cast about outside, noting that what he said was indeed true.

Ilyana, in suspended shock, had come from the bedroom to hear Digen's decision. Now she advanced into the front room, saying, "Sick? What do you mean, so many are sick?"

"Oh, everybody—dozens, anyway—all from those who were at the celebration—they're all coming down with the shaking plague."

"Shaking plague?" said Hogan. "How do you know?"

"Roshi was the first—and he knew right away. . . ."

"Roshi's sick?" asked Ilyana. "With shaking plague?"

Chapter 17

PLAGUE

"The shaking plague!" said Im'ran.

"That's what Roshi's been so afraid of all along," said Skip. "That's why he's been acting like this—with Fen —and with you—and everybody. But now it's happened and everybody knows it."

Together, Hogan and Digen said, "Now wait a minute." They looked at each other, and Digen went on, "How could he possibly anticipate an outbreak of something like shaking plague without taking cultures to screen every Sime in the valley?"

Lips compressed, Skip looked around at them all. "Well, he did swear me to secrecy when I went to work in the lab—but everybody else knows now, so why shouldn't you?"

"Knows what?" asked Ilyana.

"A few months ago—just before you came back—he discovered a mutant strain of the shaking plague among some routine cultures. It doesn't grow out on the usual culture plates in less than ten days."

Hogan asked, "Then how do you know it's shaking plague? It should only take twenty-four hours to grow out."

"That's what makes it a powerful weapon. Turned loose in the Tecton—with the channels vectoring it with every transfer and the labs not catching it at all—why, the Tecton is wide open, defenseless against this, but only those foolish enough to stick with the channels will die. The Distect was supposed to be immune because we stick with our own transfer mates. That's why he didn't want the celebration—because there'd been an accident in the lab, and he wasn't sure whether anyone had been infected. He tried to take all the possible carriers away with him—but then Digen played—and everybody—well, on Founder's Day you experiment."

Ilyana said, "I ordered the celebration."

Skip said, "He wouldn't tell you why. He knew you wouldn't approve the plan—Digen wouldn't. I didn't find out until this morning."

Numbly, Ilyana repeated, "I ordered the celebration."

Digen said, "And I played the shiltpron. Skip, what's the mortality rate on this strain?"

Skip shrugged.

Im'ran said, "You mean Roshi intends to infect the Tecton—on purpose—with this disease, and he doesn't even know the mortality rate?"

"He may know," said Skip. "He's too sick to tell."

Ilyana strode to the coat rack and snatched her rain jacket. "I'm going to my brother." She was halfway out the door before anyone moved, and then they all surged forward at once.

Slogging through the frozen-stiff muck to Roshi's house —a virtual copy of Digen's—they passed many houses with drawn shutters and an aura of illness. Digen was stunned with the magnitude of the epidemic that had struck overnight. But he realized that if the celebration had vectored it, then all those cases were reaching their incubation term at once. *Where did Roshi get it? The lab?*

They caught up with Ilyana on Roshi's porch. As she pounded on the door, it opened. Roshi's wife, Dula, stood there, her tentacles spread in an urgent demand for silence. "We have two sick ones here," she whispered.

Ilyana said, "Banishment or no banishment, I'm going to see my brother."

Dula wiped one fatigued tentacle across her brow. "Ilyana, you are Gen. You could catch it from him if you touch him."

"Digen can do whatever touching is necessary," said Ilyana. "Let us in, Dula."

Dula looked at them all. "The physician died this morning. You're the only medically trained people we have left." She opened the door and stepped aside, saying, "We have them both in the rear bedroom, where it is quiet and dark."

Stripping off rainwear, Digen said, "How long since he fell ill? Wait, you said 'them.' Is Fen also sick?"

"Of course. Roshi tried—after you transferred him—he tried to avoid Fen. But . . ." She shrugged. "Now we know what he was so afraid of."

Ilyana had gone straight to the bedroom door, unwinding her wet scarf. She stood with her fingers on the handle, listening to the conversation. Digen said, "How long ago did Roshi become ill?"

"He was one of the first. Three days ago, during the storm. And he knew right away what it was. He warned us all. He doesn't want to see you, Ilyana."

Ilyana eased open the door. Digen locked gazes with Hogan. "Seventy-two hours," he said. "Today is critical. Come on." Digen started for Ilyana, saying, "Wait, let me stabilize the fields or you might throw him into convulsions."

"Me?" said Ilyana, who knew she was the smoothest drifter Digen had ever met.

"You," said Digen, turning to Dula. "What medications has he been given? Do you have any antispasmodics?"

"He has refused the drugs. What little we have is to go to the Gens and the elderly."

"Digen," said Ilyana, putting a hand on his chest to stay his advance into the room. "You're going to treat them?"

"Yes, of course. And anyone else we can reach in time," he answered. And he realized that there had been no question about it in his mind since the moment Skip had first said the words "shaking plague." It was a certainty so solid within him that the creeping horror of doubt that had undermined his will all these days of confinement could not touch it. For the first time, he had something firm to grasp. *The universe may be illogical, but I am a physician—whether you call it channel or doctor, still a physician.*

He went on into the darkened room, grappling with the conflicting fields of Roshi on one side of the room and Fen on the other. Approaching Roshi's bed, he worked up a shielding nager for the Sime, and began examining him. Behind him, Hogan approached Fen in a businesslike way.

Ilyana crept up to Digen, very worried. Roshi was semiconscious but totally unaware of their presence. Digen let his hands drift over the Sime, laterals extended for a careful reading of body currents. Then, gingerly he touched

Roshi, palpating glands, abdomen, and neck. On the other side of the room, Hogan was finishing up the same ritual, with his bottom lip bitten tight between his teeth.

By silent agreement, the two doctors retired from the room for a conference. Any little noise or disturbance at this stage could throw one or both of the patients into convulsions—the shaking which characterized the final stage of the disease and which, in itself, caused death.

"What we require," said Hogan, "is complete blood transfusions to wash the toxins from them, heavy doses of antispasmodics, and a nice neat trach set standing by."

"Unfortunately," said Digen, "little of that is available." He turned to Ilyana. "With Roshi sick, that makes you Head of Householding, doesn't it?"

"Well, I hadn't thought—but yes, I suppose— Digen, Roshi's not going to die, is he?"

"I'll do my best for him—you know that." He turned to Dula. "He's got to have the antispasmodics, whatever is available. Something I noticed in transfer, and it's very prominent now, puts him in a very high risk group."

Tight and grim, Ilyana said, "I think he knew that all along. He doesn't want precious drugs wasted on him. Besides—the drugs themselves would probably kill him."

"What do you mean?" asked Im'ran.

Ilyana shot a glance at him, then turned to Digen as if for a difficult confession. "Here—in Rior," she said, "by our customs, our family name *is* Dumas."

And Digen knew what was coming.

"When your great-grandmother, Sectuib Muryin Farris, disappeared at the Battle of Leander Field—she didn't die. She was captured and brought here. Eventually, she married Jesse Dumas—a descendant of Hugh Valleroy. Digen, she's my great-grandmother, too—and Roshi's. So, by Tecton custom, our family name should be Farris.

I should have known! I did know, but I couldn't admit it.

"Well, aren't you going to say something, Digen?"

He could only see her dying as she gave birth to his child. Dully, he said, "And you did nothing to prevent this lortuen." *Life without her* . . .

"I don't have the allergies, or any of the other problems. It hardly shows in me at all. It will be all right for us."

And just why do you think you suffer from underdraw?

But aloud he said, "Dula, you don't have any Farris-neutral antispasmodics?"

Ilyana answered, "A fancy pharmacopoeia isn't part of our lifestyle."

In English, Hogan suggested that they find some substitute for the elements of a tracheotomy set, and start sterilizing them. Fen's wife, Ora, was in the kitchen, and Digen sent Hogan and Ilyana to find the requisite materials. He set Dula to copying instructions to be sent to other houses where people were sick. There was no way they could move the already stricken to a central location. And, Digen reflected, it wouldn't necessarily be good to have them together, because one Gen going into convulsions could set off Simes who might otherwise survive.

Digen went in to sit by Roshi and wait, refusing Im'ran's offer to help. A fanir was not an optimum choice in such an instance. And, as a Gen, he could pick up the disease from Roshi. Feeling utterly helpless, Im'ran went to assist in the kitchen.

Holding the fields steady for Roshi, Digen spent the time contemplating what he was going to have to do—and what it meant to him. The shaking plague had killed his family. He was very, very much afraid of it—little-boy afraid, he realized. And something else came to him: a repressed guilt over how glad he'd been that he had not gone out to battle it with his family. He'd been afraid of it even then. *Is this why I became a surgeon? To deal with such dangers at a distance?* He held out his tentacles to look at them.

Surgery. He was about to do surgery—a tracheotomy, one of the simplest of all procedures. It didn't take eight years of postgraduate study to learn it. There weren't even any major transport nerves between the skin and the trachea itself at the point of entry.

Under these primitive conditions, the patient might later die of infection—or might aspirate some blood and die of pneumonia. But the shaking plague was one of those diseases where the toxin in the blood and spinal fluid attacked the nerves, rendering them hypersensitive until, eventually, the patient went into convulsions and strangled to death. The Gen treatment simply bypassed the locked throat muscles with a small hole in the trachea.

A channel would lock into nageric synch and block each

convulsive nerve current, preventing the throat from locking.

To make the nageric link with Roshi, who was so dead set against all forms of channel's therapy—Roshi, who was a Farris channel!—was dangerous. Roshi would fight such a link with all his might. The only way Digen had managed to serve transfer for Roshi had been to play on his need and his total lack of training in controlling the need-based reflexes.

But Roshi had weaknesses even he did not suspect. There were tiny lesions throughout his vriamic node, which had probably given him a hellish changeover and which would surely kill him if he resisted channel's therapy, even considering the strange vitality he shared with all the Distect Simes.

So, Digen had no choice but to go with the tracheotomy. *At least in surgery the patient's subconscious can't rise up and slap you dead.* But surgery posed other problems. *Does Dula know what we're going to do? Does Ora?*

The Distect Simes had the same horror of cutting flesh as did the Tecton Simes—they merely rationalized it differently. Whatever the true basis of the phobia shared by Simes, Digen understood it. The rapid, traumatic loss of selyn triggers repressed fear of attrition.

Suddenly a jolt of dismay lanced through the walls, driven by both Sime and Gen nager—Dula and Ora. Quickly Digen blocked it from Roshi's perception, knowing that Im'ran had finally made the women understand why the knife had to be sterilized.

Will she let me do it?

By the time Hogan arrived with the impromptu instruments, Dula trailing in his wake, her nager had an ashen texture of horror burned out, of a leaden passage from one nightmare to another, beyond all sense of disaster.

She came to where Digen stood over Roshi and looked down at her husband. "No," she said, regaining herself. "No, don't touch him. Let him die if he must, or live if he can. By his own strength."

Digen, concerned that even the tiniest whisper might set Roshi or Fen into convulsions, motioned her to silence. Ilyana came to Dula, enfolding the Sime woman in the gentle, drifter's nager, and said, "He's my brother, too. Joel says it's simple, and Digen says it's safe. I've seen them perform miracles with their knives. Evil things can be made to serve good ends. Let my brother live, Dula."

So insistent was Ilyana's nager that Dula said gravely, "My mind tells me you're right. But I can't feel it." She turned toward Fen, fearful of approaching the Gen yet loving him scarcely less than she loved Roshi. Hogan was beside the bed, examining the Gen, sponging the fever-brightened skin with alcohol.

Im'ran said, "It would be difficult and painful for you to watch, Dula. And your pain would affect Roshi's chances of surviving. We'll call you as soon . . ."

Suddenly Fen stiffened and a strangled gurgle wrenched from him as his whole body went into spasm and his arms and legs vibrated to the intensity. As a well-trained team, Digen, Hogan, Ilyana, and Im'ran all acted simultaneously. Im'ran scooped Dula out of the room, and Ilyana moved to assist Hogan while Digen held the fields to protect Roshi.

With a quick stroke, right behind Ilyana's disinfectant swab, Hogan opened Fen's trachea. Each of the Gens was holding Fen still with one hand and working with the other. At the stroke of the knife Ilyana averted her eyes, but she didn't flinch. The moment it was over, she was handing Hogan the sponges and then the lubricated gauze packing as if she'd done this a hundred times, though she'd only been drilled verbally in the kitchen. Digen felt her shaking inside. Fen had been part of her family for too long, was too close to her. *She shouldn't be subjected to this—but who else is there?*

Roshi's system, despite all Digen could do, was trembling in response to his Donor's bone-cracking spasms. It was only a matter of time, Digen knew, and there was no point in further delay. "Ilyana, get Im' to re-sterilize the knife. I'm going to require it."

She nodded, but her teeth were clenched tightly. Fen was drawing air through the hole in his neck as Hogan applied artificial respiration to the locked chest muscles. Ilyana left with the instruments, and Digen's eyes met Hogan's, sharing a silent thought: *If only we had the drugs.*

Digen ached to cross the room and make full lateral contact with Fen—to still the spasms and ease the tormented nerves of the Gen. He was holding the screeching cacophony of Fen's nager at bay only by iron determination. And he knew this was only the beginning of a battle that would last for weeks and be fought in every house in the settlement.

He was steeling himself, summoning himself as he had always done by Zeor discipline to enter a channel's functional mode. He knew he could go the distance of this ordeal—however many weeks or months it would take—because he had once again begun his Zeor exercises.

Ilyana returned with a newly stocked tray, setting it on the stand beside Roshi's bed. "I'll help," she said.

"No," said Digen. "I don't want you exposed."

"I won't touch his arms."

"Not the slightest risk," said Digen. "I couldn't tolerate —even the thought that you might—I can manage alone."

Digen picked up the disinfecting sponge made ready in a blue glass soup bowl and turned to his patient, gripping the selyn fields tightly. The sensory shock of the cold liquid wash on Roshi's skin had to be carefully nulled to prevent convulsions.

Behind him, Ilyana clasped her hands in concentration, feeding her support to Digen in what had become an unconscious and mutual leaning upon each other. Digen let her lock on his systems and steady him to the task. He found, as he fit himself comfortably into the old, familiar work, that his mind stilled from the ceaseless and futile tail-chasing philosophical arguments and came to a burning focus of concentration. It felt good.

Through the newly carved pathways that made him junct, Digen let Ilyana's gentle strength flow into the job he was doing. His hands moved the knife in a soft caress, just above the sternal notch and well below the thyroid cartilage. The knife, well sharpened, parted the skin, with a shower of selyn sparks, and severed the superficial fascia and pretracheal muscles with a sensory *thrine* that felt to Digen as if he were cutting his own throat and made Ilyana's hands fly to her neck. At the anterior tracheal wall, Digen carefully incised the third and fourth tracheal rings.

Ignoring the bleeding, Digen passed the knife to the table via his handling tentacles while at the same time, with the fingers, he dressed the edges of the neat wound with the lubricated gauze. Ilyana picked the sterilized cannula from the soup bowl with salad pincers and handed it to Digen, handles first.

Their eyes met and held as Digen took the breathing tube and, without touching it, used the pincers to insert it carefully into the trachea. He did it so neatly that it barely scraped against the opened flesh and hardly disturbed the nager at all. The geyserlike plume of wasted selyn gradually collapsed and stopped as Digen worked to control the bleeding and superficial local voiding.

Only then did Digen realize that Ilyana had brought both him and Roshi into phase. Everything she did was so easy and natural—so healing.

Digen had worked with juncts—even junct channels like Skip—many times, but not since he himself had become junct. The durability of Roshi's system had somehow made the entire procedure much less of a feat than Digen had expected. The patient was breathing easily and was not any closer to uncontrolled spasm than he had been before Digen had started.

Across the room, Fen had fallen limp and, though unconscious, was breathing easily. Digen whispered, "Tell Dula it looks good for Roshi. I want her and Ora to come in now. We'll have to teach them how to keep these tubes clear, what signs to watch for, and what to do. Joel and I must go help the other victims."

Ilyana nodded and picked up the tray. At the door, she turned and looked from Fen to Roshi. She smiled through a veil of swiftly drying tears. "I'll have to go with you or they won't let you in the house." She slipped out the door.

Waiting, Digen recovered his inner equilibrium. He had done what had to be done with as little thought as possible. But somewhere deep inside, resonances had been awakened from a long sleep. For the first time since he'd left Westfield, memories, tactile, sensory memories of his time at the hospital, of his life as a channel, of all his hopes and dreams, of his entire self-image as *the* one uniquely able to bring a healing gift—surgery—in-Territory all came back to him, and it called him with a deep, powerful call —Unto Zeor, and Unto the Tecton, Forever.

But somewhere within him a still, frightened voice begged, "No, no, I don't want to go back!"

His left arm began to throb dully. He looked down at Roshi, still quivering slightly on the edge of total spasm but stubbornly avoiding it. His cousin by their common great-grandmother, also a Farris channel, and also—by his vriamic lesions—a cripple by Tecton standards. But Digen knew that if it were he himself on that bed, he'd not be surviving like that.

Roshi—junct pathways served by Fen as Ilyana served him—had lived his life junct, and it had given him an elasticity of constitution never seen in the Tecton Simes.

Digen's left outer lateral began to crawl with a prickly sensation, as if somebody were creeping up on him from the left. But Hogan was still far behind him, with Fen. He rubbed it away absently, caught up in his train of thought. For he could feel himself lying in Roshi's place, fighting off spasm after spasm, death lurking but one slip away, and knowing he was going to die.

In sudden, etched clarity, in high, stark relief, Digen saw that in all his work as channel, keeping Sime from direct Gen contact, he had been like a doctor deliberately infecting his patients with a slow-wasting sickness.

What had been done to him during his first year—the stealing away of his second and third transfers to implant conditioning that prevented the junct pathways from opening—the forced development of his secondary-system capacity—the arduous exercises to gain command of his vriamic node—*They have made of me an abomination!*

Trembling in the grip of a wave of self-loathing so strong that he thought only the mentally ill could experience it, he felt the distinct tactile sensation along his injured lateral that meant somebody was standing very close. Annoyed by the claim on his attention, he swung around, prepared to snap out a scathing rebuke. But there was nobody there.

Abruptly he flicked into hyperconsciousness, as if drawn by another's will, and there before him stood a blazing Gen image—or, no, it blazed in outline only. Within, it was marbled darkness like a Sime in attrition. His hackles rose, his mouth gaped in a silent scream, and his tentacles sprang out rigid in fright.

The figure vanished.

Digen's world flipped inside out and he was left way down in hypoconsciousness, seeing only with eyes, hearing only with ears. In this curious, flat, stark reality, he knew he had seen that nightmare figure once before. When he'd come to after his accident, there in the Sime Center infirmary room, on his newly blinded left side, it had stood regarding him thoughtfully, only to vanish when he caught it full in his senses. Something in him said that the next time he saw that figure—he would die.

Life is so short. He had spent most of his life living a lie, staggering through existence as a ravaged scarecrow letting the ravens snatch pieces of his substance whenever they chose. Here, in Rior, for a small march of days, he had become real, he had tasted life.

"Digen?" Ilyana had flowed softly into the room, seeing Digen's fright, which Hogan, his back turned, had missed.

Her field, as she approached him now, brought him gently back to duoconsciousness and a semblance of normalcy. He turned to her and, literally shaking, sank to his knees before her.

"Forgive me," said Digen, tears brimming around his eyes, "and forgive us all for what we've done to you."

Ilyana went to her knees, reaching out to Digen. "There's nothing to forgive."

Digen drew back his hands, afraid that contact might infect her with shaking plague. "I can never go back to the Tecton. Or to Zeor. I cannot live in support of such crushing evil as the Tecton."

At the doorway Im'ran pushed past Dula and came into the room, having heard most of it. "Digen!" he whispered, controlling his shock so that it didn't overwhelm Roshi. "Evil? Digen, no . . ." His throat caught and he couldn't go on.

Digen rose, bringing Ilyana with him. He could feel the penetrating thrum of the fanir's dead-true Tecton standard nager. Less than an hour ago, that trained regularity had been a delightful balm to starved nerves. Suddenly it made Digen feel soiled all over, inside and out.

An unborn sob twisting his upper lip into a trembling sneer, Digen forced words through clenched throat. "Get out of here. Get away from me and stay away. I can't bear the feel of you!"

Chapter 18

WAR AGAINST A MICROBE

The moment of shock lengthened to a silence stretched thin over the anguished nager in the room.

The faint whistle of air passing through makeshift tracheotomy tubes was the only sound. Digen could feel the prickly sensation all over Im'ran's skin as the Gen's blood pressure dropped, then steadied and rose. He could feel the jerky slide of Im'ran's eyeballs in their sockets as the Gen sought contact with Hogan, frowning as he asked, "What happened?"

Hogan's bewilderment was a faint undertone, barely perceptible against the two giant Donors, Im'ran and Ilyana, and the incoherent but strong nager of Fen. Hogan said, "Nothing happened! Nothing. He just . . ."

Digen, overwhelmed by the sudden and absolute reversal of his emotional responses to his friends, turned his back on them. "Get away from me, just get away."

Ilyana made an abortive gesture toward Digen. "They mean well," she said. "They just can't see it."

Digen held himself taut against it all, and she sensed his state accurately. She turned to the Gens, herding them toward the door. "Later. We'll talk about it later."

But they never did. There was no time for talk. As Roshi and Fen passed through the crisis and lived to have the wounds in their necks sealed, to take solid food and regain an awareness of their surroundings again, families all over the settlement begged for the help of Digen and Hogan.

Digen found he could work with Hogan as he had worked with any other intern or doctor at the hospital. Hogan's nager didn't make demands on him. And, though bewildered by Digen's sudden distance, the out-Territory Gen was professional enough to do the job without making emotional contact either with the patients or with Digen.

They lived in a miasma of death and ashen grief, fighting an inexorable rise in the daily death rate. Ilyana learned to do the tracheotomy herself and then trained Im'ran to assist her. Together they went among the sick, teaching families to care for the victims. They would work until, perhaps waiting for a meal or hot drink in someone's living room, they would fall inexorably into sleep. Pulling themselves awake for the next frantic emergency call, they would slog through mud, rain, or sleet to begin the numbing routine again.

Digen watched Ilyana spend herself for her house and people, the people who had pledged unto her personally and, through her, to Rior. He did not begrudge her the effort. He would have done the same, once, for Zeor. And at the moment he too was giving that same desperate, all-out effort to Rior, and so could not really criticize her. But he worried. His life was nothing without her. To lose her, before they had really and truly found each other, was too horrible to contemplate.

As time passed, Digen knew in a distant way that need was clamping down on his vitals again, that sometime soon he'd have to stop to take transfer. But always he and Ilyana worked separated by many houses and by a race against time to save as many lives for Rior as possible.

Hour after hour, day after day, patient after patient, Digen went on, doing what was necessary, trying not to think too much. At times he had little idea of whose house he was in or where he had to go next. He worked like an automaton, lucid only when a patient lay under his hands. When he came to see that patient again, the memory would jump to the fore of his mind and all the details would present themselves just as if he were making rounds at the hospital. But, between these moments, there was only fog, which, if it thinned even the slightest, revealed again the crystal knowledge that had come to him over Roshi.

Eventually, however, Digen found himself pausing in the same living room with Ilyana, and quite deliberately left alone. All the need, sidetracked and ignored for days, surged upward to claim him as she sagged under the weight of underdraw.

He never remembered physically moving across that room, taking her up in transfer, joining and drawing and giving and becoming alive. The soaring ecstasy of dizzy satisfaction, awakening, vitalizing his whole body and centering at the vriamic node with a delicious warmth also thawed his long-frozen mind, jolting him out of the deadening fog of not thinking.

Like a stroke of lightning, her selyn raced into those secret, long-denied passages in himself, touching off a cascade that awakened simultaneously all the levels and depths of his secondary and primary systems. Suddenly all the intimate sensations possible only to a developed channel swept through Digen.

It was a concrete touching of the essence of his soul. It was the tone of voice in which he had always said, "I am a channel. Let me through. I can help."

Help? No, destroy! Destroy. Destroy.

All at once he slammed hypoconscious, thrown into pure shen for the first time since Ilyana had taken him.

The wrenching shock flung him back to duoconsciousness, limp and hurting, his laterals hard knots drawn far up into the lateral sheaths, pressing torturously on his swollen ronaplin glands.

Ilyana had never had such a thing happen to her before. She hesitated, bewildered and off balance. Digen could see the blanched lips hovering over him as he lay on the couch. He could feel her heart beating counterpoint to his own. "Digen?" she said, hesitantly touching his ronaplin-slicked wrists, and stroking the tensed lateral orifices.

Need was still aching in him. She could feel it, and, in herself, the answering fullness. She sought his arms, probing the traumatized laterals, kneading them to pliability again. Little by little she coaxed them down to the orifices, operating on instinct and gossip she had heard concerning Digen's transfer problems.

Slowly and carefully Ilyana brought Digen back into transfer, letting the selyn flow build from the faintest trickle to the full, rushing draw that was so essential to Digen's well-being. Digen slid hyperconscious, letting it happen. He felt easy and secure in her grip, and was in no condition to help himself.

But as the selyn-flow speed peaked again, it drove into the junct passages, hitting again the strange secondary/primary awakening, and again Digen felt himself repelled by that secondary half of himself, repelled and disgusted to such a degree that he could not endure the full sensory impact of selyn motion in his secondary system.

He fought the abort, knowing he had to complete the transfer, knowing that the only way to do that was to let Ilyana do it for him. But at the peak flow, what he was doing jumped out at him in stark relief. He was *letting* her drive the transfer—as if she were a therapist, like Im'ran—as if it were possible to *let* a Gen dominate.

Face to face with this stubborn residue of his Tecton outlook, immersed in all the purest channel's sensations, it came to him: *I'll never be able to change!*

And again, without warning, he recoiled into abort, this time his whole body going rigid, locked as if in the throes of the shaking plague.

As Ilyana brought the slamming shen under control for him again, Digen gasped and said, "It's no use. I don't—I—just don't want to live anymore."

"I know what that's like," said Ilyana. "But you can't give up now. You wouldn't let me give up—I won't let you give up." She bent to kiss one lateral orifice and then to touch her ronaplin-smeared lips to Digen's, drawing all her skill into a fine wedge into his being.

Digen twisted aside, breaking the contact. "Don't. I can't take any more."

"You've withdrawn from Im'ran," said Ilyana. "But you can't withdraw from me."

Digen said nothing.

"If you die," she added, "I die with you. That's the way it is in lortuen."

"Most of the time," agreed Digen.

"Always," said Ilyana.

"If you insist, always." *But not in Zeor, not in the Tecton—not always. And maybe that's worse.* His life without her would be without light. He summoned himself. "But I'm not dying, at least now right now. I've survived on worse transfers. Let's just drop it."

"I can't just drop it. I have to understand what's going on in you. Those terrible frights you won't talk about—this aborting—I didn't unbalance on you, I know I didn't. . . ."

"No, you didn't." He rolled back and took her hands, overcome with inexpressible tenderness. "You're perfect. Too perfect for the likes of me."

"That's ridiculous—we're matchmates."

"I've been warped, though, warped by the Tecton into

something ugly and evil, warped before I was old enough to have a choice in the matter."

"It has to be that way," said Ilyana. "Channels can't be fully developed after their first year."

"Are you defending the Tecton?"

"No," she answered. "No, just the human struggle to survive—at any cost. We can't be blamed for our will to live."

There was a bleak, subdued tone to her nager. He took her hands and found them cold to his touch. "What's wrong, Yanami?"

She shook her head, putting all her feelings aside.

He kissed her gently. There was no sexual passion in him, after the beating his system had just taken, but it was a kiss of love nevertheless. She broke into helpless tears, falling into his arms, head against his shoulder.

Crying, she told him, "It's just that—after all the ghastly things we've done—the cutting and sewing, the submitting to your field control of the seizures, the sheer surviving of it all—Digen, Rior is *dying*."

"I don't think so. We're going to make it, I know. . . ."

She pushed away, shaking aside tears. "No. More of the Gens have been dying than the Simes. Lots of families are without a single Gen. And now . . ." She broke down crying helplessly again.

He rocked her back and forth, trying to will comfort into her, feeling distantly the frustrated sexual hunger in her, and aching because he felt no response to it. Perhaps the crying would ease her a bit.

Between sobs she blurted it all out. "You can't even take transfer from me—you don't even want to live—and Im'ran's dying too, after all he's done for Rior, without thought of himself—he's dying too!"

He sat up, still holding her tightly, and said over her head, "Im'ran's dying? What is it? What happened?"

"Oh, he keeps asking, begging, for you, and demanding that we don't tell you he's come down with the plague. But he won't let Joel near him. He's going to die, I can feel it."

"It's not just underdraw? The symptoms . . ."

"We've all seen enough of the plague to know the difference!"

"Im'ran." *Oh, what he must think of me!* "Where is he?"

"Just down that hall there," she said, pointing to a doorway across the living room.

It was a strange house Digen couldn't recall ever being in before. The rugs were purple, the walls hung with amateur oil paintings, the curtains hand-woven. Some family had put a lot of love into the house.

"Whose house is this?"

"The Stord place," answered Ilyana. "They're all dead."

Digen just stared at her.

"Im' and I were trying to save their last Gen. We sent the children to the central nursery. Their mother died giving birth this morning—she had the plague, too, and refused Im's offer of transfer. It wouldn't have endangered him, though—turned out he was already sick, but wouldn't tell anyone until he collapsed."

Digen struggled to assimilate it all.

Ilyana added, "I think that was this morning."

Now that his attention was drawn to it, he could sense Im'ran's distinctive nager through the triple-insulated walls. He went toward the back bedroom where so many had already died.

The first thing Digen noticed was the smell—not the smell of neglect, but of the hopeless struggle to keep terminal patients clean. Im'ran lay on the bed, wan and much thinner than Digen had ever seen him. Gaunt, like a Sime—in fact, "emaciated" would be medically correct. No Gen should be so thin.

Under the deep, outdoors tan Im'ran had acquired in his mountain trek lay a pallor of desperate illness, and over it all, fever cast an unhealthy flush. It had been over two weeks since Im'ran's transfer with Skip, and the Gen was solidly mid-field but not so high that he was feeling underdraw.

Digen approached the bed, steeling himself against that awful sensation of being soiled, which the Gen's nager had once given him. But, curiously, it wasn't there anymore. He wasn't a symbol of anything. He was just Im'ran again. *He was trying to kill himself. I should never have rejected him like that.*

He spread his hands over the Gen to catch every diagnostic nuance. Im'ran opened his eyes. "Digen?" His voice was a mere rasp in his throat, barely articulated.

"Yes."

"You came. I knew you would. As One First, All Firsts."

He had to stop to breathe, weakened so much that even that was a chore.

"As One First, All Firsts," Digen heard himself answer. They had qualified each other. There was more between them than just an oath. It was a bond—forever.

"Digen, whatever I've done to you—forgive me. I never meant to hurt. Never."

"You didn't do anything. Only I changed." *Didn't I?* Doubts churned and tore at him. *Oh, will it never end!*

From the doorway, Ilyana said, "Im'ran has fought valiantly to save Rior—because it was what you wanted."

Just behind her, Hogan said, "He won't let us help him, Digen."

"Im'," said Digen, "Ilyana tells me this strain seems more virulent to Gens. You must let them treat you."

"I can't. . . ."

"But . . ."

"I thought I could. I've been helping do it to so many. But—Digen, remember once I said I'd always trust a channel, not—a—surgeon. I—was too right about myself. I—can't."

Digen understood. Im'ran was the product of the Sime culture. He'd absorbed Sime phobias deep into his subconscious—and now he had crossed the four-plus barrier and was terribly sensitive to fields.

"Digen, promise me—don't let them do it. I'd rather die naturally. Promise me, by the bond between us if nothing else."

Digen could not say what he had to say. He could not tell Im'ran that the bond so sacred to him was the very symbol of all that Digen now loathed. In fact, Digen felt within himself the stirrings of that bond, a loyalty that was not just words or promises but an act, an experience shared and unique between them. And in that stirring, Digen knew again that he was a Tecton tool, molded in early life and unable to change, no matter how he came to understand and loathe himself.

Another bond, Im' and I both tools forged by the same hand to the same ghastly end.

He sat on the edge of the bed and took up Im'ran's hands in his own, scarcely knowing what moved him but afraid to think it through. He made a quick, violent lateral contact. "You have my promise."

Ilyana charged halfway into the room and stopped. Hogan said, "Digen!" But it was too late. He had exposed himself to the disease, and even Im'ran's shuddering attempt to pull away came too late.

"Get him a pitcher of water," said Digen. "Then go help whoever else you can. I'll be here awhile."

Their strangled and futile protests died unspoken. Water and other necessities were arranged for Digen—even, over protests, a trach set—all sterilized and ready. But even as the two Gens busied themselves with this job, Digen sensed that they had no intention of leaving. However, later on, a runner came to the door with the message that Fen and Ora were both sick again—and Roshi and Dula were frantic. This strain of the disease conferred little if any temporary immunity on its victims. Many Gens had survived the first bout only to die with the second. Hogan and Ilyana grabbed their coats and went.

It was just luck that Roshi had not unleashed the plague on the Tecton, thought Digen. Or was it? Digen no longer knew his own mind or his own motives. All his life he had been so sure of himself, so shidoni sure he had all the answers.

There are no answers, he thought. *Only questions.*

He was so weary, he envied Im'ran the exhausted slumber he had fallen into. He told himself that the fatigue was just the aftermath of the incompleted transfer with Ilyana. He wasn't in need, but he wasn't post- either. He'd lived that way for years and never minded. But he wasn't used to it anymore. *Living death, that's what it is.*

He thought of the crystal-clear health he had enjoyed here, and he wanted to cry. He knew that if he could cry he'd feel much better. But he couldn't. The brown numbness went too deep.

As he sat beside Im'ran, the fanir's nager penetrated, locking to him and bringing him into the Tecton standard mode. It drew Digen into a state of waking sleep somewhat akin to that which Im'ran had induced in him during their extended trautholo. His mind roamed free within itself while his body came to rest, and yet his systems kept vigil.

The Tecton—based on a vile perversion though it was —still held many many people possessed of an intricate and sublime goodness. Im'ran was one. Joel, despite all he'd lived through, had made himself another. Jesse Elkar, Mora Dyen, Inez Tregaskio, Ben Seloyan, little Enette, the receptionist, Dane Rizdel, and Chanet, Asquith, and Rin, and—and—yes, Bett, a Farris Gen, God help her, and the best sister anyone ever had.

And Im'ran—whose nager had made Digen feel filthy and sick. Imrahan ambrov Imil, the living pulse of the Tecton and all it stood for; Im'ran, who wished nothing more from life than to serve those who sacrificed so much so that the world could survive. Im'ran, whose highest and most secret ambition was to be good enough to pledge Zeor, who wanted most of all to give first transfer to a Farris channel, whose integrity remained unbreached even when it meant walking out on his own four-plus qualification and leaving the Sectuib in Zeor hysterical with post-syndrome.

Slowly, over a period of some hours, Im'ran's sleeping nager began to fragment and weaken, becoming chaotic under the attack of the nerve toxin. Digen was able to impose an order on the Gen's system via his own secondary system, which had become firmly set in the fanir's pattern.

As Im'ran's chemistry became progressively more disturbed, Digen had to exert a conscious control until, at some indistinct point, he began functioning in the channel's mode. Somewhere in the back of his mind was the concern that, as with Ilyana's transfer, he might suddenly become unable to function. But he knew that that had been psychosomatic. Physically he was in better shape than he had been in over ten years. And this job wasn't even a prime functional.

But it did take a certain concentration. It was all too easy to let the selyn-field-pulsing drift—and in the case of a fanir, that could be deadly to both of them.

Altogether, Digen found himself working to the limits of his own sensitivity, control, and concentration. Before the sun rose the second day, Im'ran came into crisis. Digen let the Gen's temperature climb to near Sime normal, knowing that this virtually guaranteed he would catch the disease himself, but knowing also that it was the best way to control the Gen's infection before it killed him.

Once, during a sunrise, the fields got away from Digen, and Im'ran went rigid, muscle locked against muscle, throat tightly closed.

Digen looked at the trach set so near his hand. With a savage jerk of a tentacle he knocked it to the floor, and plunged himself into deeper touch with Im'ran's inner flows. His own body went stiff, his throat clutching at his breath, and his heart faltering even as Im'ran's did. In a kind of frigid calm more suited to defusing a bomb than to any medical procedure, Digen brought all his Tecton and Zeor discipline to bear, and fought back, bit by bit, to control of the regular field pulse.

But he had lost the fanir's basal beat and could only approximate it from memory, engraving it on them both.

He felt again the creeping tingle along his left outer lateral. But he refused to look to his left, knowing that there was nobody there.

Alone in that darkened sickroom for four days and nights with Im'ran, as the Gen slowly regained his senses, beating off the infection, cleansing his system of the toxin, and fighting his way back to life, Digen found himself battling his way back to his own sense of life, self-worth, and even a flicker of hope to rebuild his integrity. *It had to be possible. Somehow, it had to be.*

He remembered the day when he was ten years old, standing on a windy hilltop, watching his dog chase rabbits as he came to the resolve to become the world's first Sime surgeon. It was the day his changeover had begun. And if he'd been given free choice, he would have taken the channel's training—and the conditioning—to become physician and surgeon.

On the fourth dawn, Digen raised the shades and opened the shutters on the starlit night, letting the natural progression of sunrise lighten the room gradually to accustom the Gen's nerves to outside stimuli again. And while the sun came up they talked, quietly, nostalgically, and randomly, in a kind of communion possible only between old friends.

Later on that afternoon, Ilyana and Hogan joined them for a meal. They were bedraggled and uncommunicative until Digen said, "How are things going out there?"

Ilyana just shook her head, but Hogan said, "We lost our last three patients. That assistant you trained—can't remember her unpronounceable name—has been doing a lot better with the Simes than we have. And their reinfection rate seems lower. Nobody has any real statistics, though. This place is disintegrating around us."

Mentally counting days, Digen said, "The original infections should all have run their course by now, and the secondaries should be coming out of it—people who picked it up nursing the sick. How many new cases today?"

Ilyana said, "Who knows? Maybe five, maybe ten."

"That's not so bad, if you can keep them isolated." He looked to Im'ran. "I can lend a hand this afternoon while Im' sleeps it off."

Im'ran nodded, picking listlessly at his soup.

Hogan was watching him, but he said, "I do think the epidemic has about run its course. The danger's not over yet, but we're on the downhill side, mopping up. Things are pretty well under control. If you want to stay here and get some rest, I think you can."

"You two are the ones who require the rest," said Digen.

"We got about four or five hours' sleep last night," answered Hogan.

"In how many days?" asked Digen.

Hogan shrugged. "I can use the experience in epidemiology."

Digen looked to Ilyana. "In how many days?"

She had been eating with a single-minded concentration, but now she met Digen's eyes squarely. "You're going to go to bed and stay there until I'm sure you're not coming down with it. And if I can, I'm going to get a solid transfer into you, build up your strength."

Digen shook his head. "No, I won't risk your catching it. Besides, it's not necessary. I'm all right. Really." He looked to Im'ran for support.

As Digen had told the therapist of the transfer abort, and something of the mitigating effect the work against the fanir's nager had had, Im'ran nodded. "I can believe that. If I were you, Ilyana, I wouldn't meddle with his systems at this point. Attempting a forcible rephasing on a Farris can be very tricky. And with Digen's system—in my professional opinion, you could do more harm than good."

In her fatigue, Ilyana flared resentment at the Gen, but it was brief. Her good sense came to the fore again, and she said, "But at least you're going to go to bed for five or six days."

Watching her gather and focus the ragged remains of her strength into that demand, Digen hadn't the heart to oppose her. But he said, "I really don't see what good that could possibly do. I don't keep countdown vigil."

"You don't what?" asked Hogan, following the Simelan conversation with difficulty.

Im'ran struggled to explain it to Hogan while Ilyana said to Digen, "The time to start fighting is now, not after the symptoms have appeared. You've been under too much strain, and your health still isn't as strong as you think it is. We should go home—and care for each other."

"You're frightened," said Digen, "and so am I. But I don't regret what I've done. I'm willing to live, again, Ilyana. Im'ran's given me that, at least. I'm not going to have any more trouble with transfer. And I'm not going to die. Not yet."

As they looked at each other in a long, silent communion, Digen heard Hogan say, "Im'ran, you have to eat if you expect to regain your strength."

Digen saw that Im'ran was holding his soup bowl out to Hogan to take away. It was hardly touched. Digen said, "What's the matter?" And as he got up and went to the bed, he probed the nager carefully.

Im'ran said, "It just doesn't taste right."

"Hmm?" said Digen, concentrating now.

"Sort of sour, bitter maybe."

Digen's eyebrows went up. "You should be hungry enough that anything would taste good."

"Well, I am, but it doesn't."

Digen said to Hogan, "Any other Gen patients react this way?"

"No. By this stage they're all ravenous."

"Hmm. Check his lymph glands."

Considering the reinfection rate, Digen didn't want to touch Im'ran and risk reinfecting him with the disease, which Digen himself might have picked up from him. It was difficult working without proper laboratory facilities.

Hogan said, "Negative—negative—and negative."

"Fever? Itching or burning of mucous membranes? Aches or pains?" Digen sensed none, but he asked the routine questions anyway. Hogan and Im'ran both shook their heads.

Im'ran said, "I seem to have trouble focusing my eyes, though."

Digen said, "Pull the shades farther down. How's that?"

"Not much help," Im'ran offered, peering about.

Digen said, "Close your eyes. Be quiet, everybody. Im', I want you to read me the ambient."

Im'ran concentrated, as if focusing on something very slippery. Sweat broke out on his upper lip, and Digen could feel the dark prickle of anxiety all over the Gen. At length, he said, voice tight with panic, "I can't!"

"Now wait a minute," said Digen. "Calm down. I know you can do it—just give me a first approximation." He was getting worried.

"Oh, I could *calculate* that—maybe one thousand fifty hyper-of-rotation with Joel in the saddle point."

"Good, now visualize it and read on me, second approximation."

"You're at—" He broke off in frustration, saying, "It just won't stand still. I can't focus!"

Digen bit his lip. "Take a quick stab at it."

"Somewhere in the upper seventeen—fifteen and a third, maybe?"

Way, way off for a Janir.

By this time Im'ran himself was getting scared. "Digen, what's wrong with me?"

"You're off true and you're fluctuating. The world isn't out of focus, your internal standard referent is vibrating around a displaced norm."

Im'ran went cold.

Digen was sorry, for a moment, that he hadn't softened the blow. You don't tell a man his legs have been amputated without preparing him for it. But Im'ran was a professional. He had known even before Digen had spoken.

After a moment of dead silence, Im'ran said, "How far off true?"

"Not far," said Digen. "I would have noticed sooner. In fact, even now I can't sense it. I sense your distress, that's all. To you it seems much larger than it is, because you've been so dead true all your life."

"The vibration?"

Digen concentrated again, comparing now with several minutes ago. He knew that he really should have a base of several hours before hazarding a guess, but on instinct he said, "It seems to be damped harmonic pattern, getting smaller and smaller rather than larger and larger. I expect you'll be all right."

"But permanently off true."

"You'll learn to compensate," said Digen. "Add or subtract a constant increment. You're still a fanir, no changing that."

"The bad taste in my mouth?"

"Your body's way of telling you something isn't quite right. I read something once about this. Supposedly, the new referent will become your norm, and your body will accept that. The distress symptoms will gradually disappear. But in the meantime, Im', you've got to eat, even if you don't want to. You're still very weak."

Hogan had been looking from Im'ran to Digen, scarcely understanding a word until Digen said, "You've got to eat." Then he handed Im'ran the bowl again. "You want, I'll heat it up," he offered.

Dazedly, Im'ran took the bowl, staring at the thick liquid, his lips curling in disgust. Suddenly, with an anguished howl, he flung the bowl across the room, turned away from them all, and began to cry.

Then all at once Digen knew what had caused this to happen to Im'ran. When he had lost control of the spasms that one time, he'd had to come back to an approximation of the fanir's base and rhythm, and he'd done it to the limit of his own resolution—leaving Im'ran off that tiniest increment and in the direction closer to Digen's own base—putting Im'ran now within range of an orhuen with Digen.

He stood helplessly by while the fanir raged, knowing with a sick guilt that he'd have to confess the moment the Gen calmed down.

Chapter 19

DIGEN'S OPERATION

Some days later, Digen said bleakly, "If I'm going to be sick, I'd rather it be in my own home."

They were seated around the dining table in Digen and Ilyana's house at the dawn of the tenth day after Digen's first exposure to Im'ran.

"He has a point," said Im'ran. "Rin once said that Wyner would have survived if they hadn't been using a ward setup."

"I don't believe that," said Digen. "You didn't know Wyner. He—Vira too, and Nigel—they were so much more sensitive than I am; I wasn't even trained to be Sectuib. I couldn't compete in their league." *Wyner wouldn't have brought you back off-true.*

"Rin said Nigel wasn't that much more sensitive than you are," said Im'ran. "And he died of it, too. Farrises in general are about as sensitive as some people get under the influence of the plague toxin. So I say we should listen to what Digen wants and do it his way."

Digen said, "I don't know why you're sticking by me after what I did to you."

Im'ran met his eyes squarely. "You did exactly what I asked you to do—the results are my responsibility." He looked at Ilyana. "But I didn't plan it this way."

The fanir was keeping himself rigidly apart from Digen by the strictest Tecton codes. Ilyana respected that intellectually, but deep down she couldn't help feeling threatened by the presence of another matchmate to her lortuen mate. Im'ran was desperately sensitive to her feelings, and they all wanted the whole, tense situation to be over with as quickly as possible.

Hogan said into the dead silence, "Didn't somebody just say Wyner died of primary entran, not the shaking plague?"

Im'ran said, "Primary entran complications as a result of shaking-plague complications—due to his sensitivity."

Digen stood, letting his chair scrape back. "I don't want to talk about my brothers. This is getting morbid." He went to the front window, looking out on the clear, cold mountain dawn.

Behind him at the table Skip Ozik—having somehow become part of the family since Roshi's illness—said, "Why don't you leave him alone!"

"Shuven!" swore Ilyana. "Two touchy Simes in the same room! Let's keep it down."

Im'ran, steeling himself inwardly, reached across the table to Skip. "You should let me help."

Skip winced, shuddering at the touch, and got restlessly to his feet. "No."

Hogan went after the boy, saying privately, "Why not? It will have to come to that eventually."

"You wouldn't understand. It's—" He looked over his shoulder at Im'ran, not wanting to be offensive. "It's just that we're—incompatible."

Digen thought, *Need will overcome that. It has to.*

Ilyana said, "Skip, you should have gone with Roshi." She looked toward the window. Somewhere down the valley the Rior Simes who were Genless were gathering to go raiding among the out-Territory Gen towns in the low foothills. For the first time in decades, Rior had been driven to—murder. But what else could they do? "Maybe," she said, "there's still time for you to catch up with them."

"You don't understand, either. I—I couldn't," said Skip.

"I know," said Hogan. Having himself been raised out-Territory, he better than any of them knew the stark terror the raiding Simes would bring.

"Oh, stop it, all of you!" snapped Digen, wrenching open the door and charging out into the cold air. It was too much for him. The crystal vision of the Distect that he had come to over Roshi was falling into a shattered ruin around the harsh reality of a raid of killer Simes, a raid that was the very antithesis of the Tecton and its house-holding base.

Ilyana came out after him, poised calmly to receive his storm of anguish. "You couldn't have prevented the raid, Digen. Too many Gens have died; too many Simes need—and—you might be sick."

"Killing, death, dying—is that all we can talk about? I'm sick of it! And I'm sick of being treated like a pregnant Gen about to give birth to twin channels!"

"Whew!" said Im'ran, coming up on Digen's right, opposite Ilyana. "Have we been that bad?"

Digen, caught between their two fields, squirmed. It seemed he had spent a lifetime pinioned thus between them, and with them fighting—albeit unconsciously—for control of his innards. He flung himself out of the net of unmeshed Gen nager, clinging to the roofpole, and turned on them. His knees were shaking, and suddenly he realized he was about to faint.

There was a careening blur as they helped him down the corridor to the rear bedroom. There was the smooth softness of the bed, long ago made ready for him just in case. There was coolness on his brow. Aching concern in the ambient nager.

I'm sick, he thought with a kind of hysterical shock. *It really happened. I've got it.*

Time whirled out of focus for Digen. There were brilliant little vignettes embedded in gray fog like jewels in a pudding.

Skip bending over him, Sime nager raking through him. "His temperature has fallen."

"Good," Joel's voice replying. "He's fighting it, then."

Another time, he was brought to by a sharp sound, like a pressure wave smacking into his whole body.

Wave after wave of Gen pain. Ilyana standing on one foot, clutching her ankle, biting her lip, one tear seeping under an eyelash.

She stubbed her toe in the dark, thought Digen.

The pain receding. She coming to sit by the bed, quietly at first, linking nagerically and therapeutically. Digen drifting with her, enjoying. Then, gradually, her bravery breaking down and the tears welling outward until she was crying softly but rackingly. If you die, I die too.

Digen understood why she was crying: not because she would die too but—because she would not die with him.

In the long gray murk after that, he remembered a strong compulsion to speak to her, something important he had to say. But by the time he summoned all his energies to articulate, she was gone.

He knew he had to live to tell her. But he couldn't remember what it was he had to say, what it was she had to know before he could die.

Im'ran was sitting next to him, carefully not touching. Yet, the nageric linkage was deep and clear. Digen didn't remember him coming or Ilyana leaving. It was as if one had turned magically into the other. He wanted to laugh at the idea of Ilyana turning into an off-true fanir but the desire slipped away unfocused. Dimly, he fretted that the fanir's nager wasn't ideal for treating shaking plague. But that too slipped away in a kind of languorous numbness.

Another time, Digen knew there were people in the room, whispering so low that they could barely hear each other. But the words were etched into him like blue fire.

"Digen, are you awake? Can you hear me?" *Joel was speaking. Digen sensed him as almost transparent, a ghost floating in bright gray fog. There was no nageric link at all—unreal ghost. But Digen was aware of the worried indecisiveness in the Gen—so very unlike Joel Hogan the doctor.*

Digen tried to say "Yes," but there was only an inarticulate hiss. He closed his mouth, then, realizing that it had been open and he had been breathing through it so long that his tongue and cheeks were dry, wooden.

Need—piercing, aching, driving need.

Hands and tentacles came about him and cool water dribbled between his lips. Rolling it about his parched tongue, Digen realized the need was not his own, but Skip's. At least he won't catch it. And he has good resistance. His case was mild, comparatively. He won't vector it.

"Digen." *The words came registering as sound.*

Digen managed to focus one eye. "Hmm."

Joel was saying, "His temperature is rising."

"It has to be now," *Joel said.* "In just a little while your sensitivity will spike, and if we cut then, it could kill you."

"Digen, I'm against it," *said Im'ran.* "Ilyana and I can hold you steady. I've worked it out on paper."

Skip said breathily and gently, "Quiet. He's raw inside."

Digen's first reaction was *no!* The great screeching horror of a knife actually biting into his own flesh, a knife held by a Gen hand, the whole thing picked up and amplified, fed back to him by Gen nager—the event leaped to life in his imagination, and he shrank from it. *No, not on me!*

His fear whirled up out of him, spinning and spinning into an almost palpable form, and it laughed at him.

The great surgeon! The great liberator of mankind! So now you know what you want to do to people. You expect more of them than you expect of yourself?

And something in Digen, a perverse artistic sense, said, *How fitting to die under the knife you so worshiped, or to live through it and know what it is.*

Joel was bending over him. "Digen, we'll require your cooperation. We have no local anesthetics left, and only a little alcohol for disinfection. You mustn't fight us."

Suddenly Digen was eager for it. He saw in this moment the convergence of all the threads of his life.

"Do it," said Digen.

Skip spun away from the bed, too caught up in Digen's mixed emotions to endure another moment. Im'ran knelt beside the bed, only his head, shoulders, and upper chest visible to Digen. The fanir's nager was bursting with arguments he would not voice. Slowly, a note of anguished resignation rose from him, then turned to an unquestioning loyalty.

"Yes, Sectuib," said Im'ran, head bowed.

The old title thrummed through Digen on so many levels that he could not name his reaction. He felt Im'ran had crowned him sovereign monarch. Deeper, there was the forlorn protest, No, Zeor is dead! And deeper yet, he knew this as Im'ran's way of saying that one cannot abdicate from one's genes. Sectuib in Zeor is Sectuib forever, made so by the pledges of generations, the Death of the One Billion.

A sense of panic rose to engulf Digen, the urge to protest that title driving him up and up to complete touch with reality. The fog lifted from his senses, the room about him aglow with the combined nager of Im'ran and Ilyana, a golden ruddiness that warmed and assured. Hogan was laying out his tray on the stand by the bed. Skip, next to the door, struggled to control his own need well enough not to disturb Digen; yet, because he had never had any training in vriamic control, he simply could not handle the fields. But he could read them out for the Gens. "Im', he's duo and scared witless."

"I've never been witless in my life," said Digen. The rasp of his own clogged vocal cords grated on his nerves. He coughed at the phlegm.

With all the air out of his lungs, abruptly, the sounds, sights, smells, and nageric textures burst in on him, amplified beyond endurance. His muscles locked against themselves, relaxed slightly, then locked again, harder, and again. He could not draw breath. Im'ran hissed, "Ilyana! Link!"

Im'ran had been doing his best to remain aloof from Digen, but now he brought Digen neatly under his control —off true, but solid and so close to Tecton standard that Digen sensed no difference. Ilyana dropped into link, hunting a bit, then steadying. Im'ran's quantized solidity held Digen firmly to one specific selyn-consumption pattern, and, through Digen, it held Ilyana from drifting.

Over his shoulder, Im'ran said, "Are we doing it, Skip?"

"I think so," he said.

The thrum and throb of the two Donors locked into Digen's system, shielding him from wild sensory inputs, collimating his inner flows, until the locked muscles began to melt loose and he drew a shuddering breath.

But, though he could breathe, his whole body shook with a palsied vibration he could not control. Saliva and oral selyn conductors poured into his mouth from aching jaws, his lateral orifices were bathed in ronaplin, and his breath came in little shivering gasps. But worst of all was the feeling of being torn, stretched, shredded between the two powerful Gens whose basal selyn-production rates were close enough to his own consumption rate that they each could be called matchmate to him—but Ilyana's was a hair's breadth high while Im'ran's was now an increment low.

It was like sitting between two violinists who are supposed to be playing in unison but aren't quite. Each ear heard a different note, and the notes met somewhere behind the eyeballs and sent a jangling cacophony down the whole body, shaking the teeth, grating under the fingernails, curling the toes.

"Stop it!" Digen gasped. "I can't stand it!"

"His sensitivity's way up," said Skip.

Digen tried to pull away from the Gens, and it was only

then that he realized they had each taken an arm and forcibly extended his laterals to make a contact.

"Hang on, Digen," said Im'ran in that neutral voice of the therapist. "We're going to have to block for you, or you'll never survive this. Joel, get going, if you're going to."

A knife floated into view. Digen recognized it as Hogan's favorite one, scrounged from the school's art department. It held the best edge, and was made all in one piece, so it could easily be sterilized. The blunt-nailed Gen hand around the knife was Hogan's, as was the whisper that screamed along Digen's nerves. "Flex his head back."

"No, no, I can't," Digen whimpered as Ilyana's hand came under his head. At the contact of her skin on his, Digen twisted, crying out, "Please, stop!"

Skip came behind Digen's head, spreading hands and tentacles on either side of his skull. "Hurry. Somehow, you two are *causing* the shaking. It's killing him."

Hogan brought the alcohol swab over with his other hand. His nager was steady, calm, and totally disconnected from the events taking place under his hands. "No. It's unpleasant, maybe, but he's breathing. And he wouldn't be without them."

A drop of alcohol fell on Digen's bare skin, burning cold. The shock of it died quickly, damped by the steady Gen nager.

"Ready?" asked Hogan.

Im'ran locked eyes with Skip, who nodded.

"Hang on," said Hogan, as he applied the alcohol wash to the base of Digen's neck. The two Gens, despite the nerve-racking dissonance, fielded the flooding shock of that cold wash, and Digen suddenly understood what they were trying to do for him and why it was necessary.

"Wait!" he gasped, and with all that was in him he worked to damp the palsied shaking, to still every vestige of resistance that had been causing it.

To Ilyana he gave control of his primary system, and to Im'ran he entrusted his secondary system. Cutting himself, thus, in half, utterly incapable now of imposing his own will on either system, Digen found the inner dissonance stilled, the muscular palsy dying down. Im'ran held his selyn consumption dead even, while Ilyana drifted off a hair and then came back under an increment, but limited in her wandering by Im'ran's steady pulse.

In a few gasped words, Digen tried to tell Im'ran what he was doing, but since it had never been done or even conceived of before, there was no vocabulary. Digen had no idea if he'd gotten his point across, but he knew the condition was unstable and could disintegrate at any moment.

He locked gazes with Joel. The Gen stood poised, nager totally detached, all emotion firmly distanced, awaiting Im'ran's signal. *He's only doing what I told him he had to learn to do to be a good surgeon.*

With all his courage, Digen said, "I trust you, Doctor." And he arched his head back, exposing his throat fully to Hogan's keen knife.

He saw surgery in a new light. It was a terrible insult, a violence done to the body to prevent the body from destroying itself, and it was acceptable only because it was temporary. *In a few days, there will be hardly a mark left and all functions will be restored.*

Each arm outstretched from his shoulders, his head pinioned back, his vriamic node itself beyond his control, his will floated free, unable to affect his destiny. He felt, for the first time in his life, in direct contact with the creative power flowing through the universe, and he simply submitted himself to it without whimper or protest.

Suddenly it was as if an intense white light had been turned on behind his head, above his line of sight—or no, somewhere above his eyeballs. It was so brilliant that it could not be *seen by* but only *seen*, for it swamped out all other sensory input. A living power touched him, and he knew the trembling fear that goes beyond awe into a kind of exquisite terror—the power no mortal can face and live.

For one flick of time he felt himself absorbed into that brightness, a part of it—a blinding expansion to infinity and beyond.

Then his sense of identity possessed him, and he squirmed away. *It's too much!*

Joel: *He fainted.*

Im'ran: *His chest muscles are hard as stone.*

Joel: *Keep ventilating him.*

Ilyana: *He's dead.*

Skip: No.

Joel: He's coming around.

Im'ran: Digen, can you hear me?

A wordless cry of relief from Ilyana:

His eyelids flickered.

Im'ran: We almost killed him.

Ilyana: Stay out of phase. I've got it now.

Im'ran: Come on, Skip, let's leave Ilyana alone with him. I'll take the next shift.

Joel: Right. He's breathing on his own again. You know what to do, Ilyana.

Ilyana: Thank God.

Digen: If you only knew.

Some intellectual part of his mind told Digen that the big black gaps in his awareness were the times he went into convulsions. Once, he felt Hogan's nager as the breathing tube was sucked clear, his throat swabbed out. Occasionally there would be a barely perceptible shift as Im'ran and Ilyana replaced each other. He thought of praying again—that they wouldn't catch the plague from tending him. But he was afraid to pray for something so trivial as life. *Are we not all immortal?*

Pearlescent gray fog swirled about him. A distant voice intoned a roll call. It had been going on, Digen realized, for quite some time. His feet hurt as he stood to attention, listening to the names. One flew out at him, recognized from a particularly lurid lesson—Feleho ambrov Zeor, inscribed by the hand of Klyd Farris, Sectuib in Zeor.

And on and on the roll went. He knew what it was now: the names of martyrs enshrined in Zeor's Memorial to the One Billion, the martyrs who gave their lives for the Zeor dream. And the voice reading off that honor roll was Orim Farris, Sectuib in Zeor—his very own father.

On Digen's right towered the slender form of his brother Wyner Liu, and on Digen's left stood Vira and Nigel. His mother hovered behind them. All around him, in a huge, invisible circle, were all the members of Zeor who had ever pledged, and every Sectuib who had ever stood for Zeor.

In wonderment, Digen whispered, "Wyn? Is that really you?"

The tall form, a bright ghost in the fog, said, "Yes, little brother. Be still now, this is the most important day of your existence."

"I died?"

"No, silly brother," said Wyn, and Digen flushed with a mixture of tingling nostalgia and embarrassment to be again Wyn's "silly but beloved brother." "Digen, today you are to receive Zeor."

"I can't be dreaming this," said Digen. "I don't even know what's done at a receiving."

"That's because you weren't an heir. Now hush and pay attention. You're about to find out."

Digen wanted to obey his brother. He had always obeyed Wyner. But he wanted the voice and the presence of his brother to continue.

Digen caught his lip between his teeth, and, feeling like a small boy, he snuck his hand into the big fist of his elder brother. He was inordinately gratified when his fingers were gripped in return by the warm flesh and soft tentacles. Then a nageric interlink rippled through him via that slight touch, the distinctive fluttery caress of Wyner's fields. It flooded him with all the aching loss he thought he'd buried somewhere during his teens. The raw grief, all new again, made this whole bizarre scene real to him in a tangible way.

Off in the mist, Orim Farris was saying, "All of these have died for Zeor, but the power of their lives burns brightly still. Digen Ryan Farris, son of Orim Farris, Sectuib in Zeor, and Diuio Scott, his wife and consort, step forward and become the vessel through which the power of death will brighten and grace the world of men."

Wyner's great hand propelled Digen out onto the featureless floor, misted in from all sides. Somewhere, he found a bubble of clearness, and there stood his father, as large as he had seemed to Digen as a boy. Orim was a lithe, beautiful Sime with all the classic Farris features, even to the stubborn cowlick of jet-black hair draped across his tall forehead.

As always, his father's presence was overpowering to Digen, and though he wanted none of Zeor or its heritage, he stood quietly as his father asked, "What is Zeor?"

"I haven't been prepared to answer that here."

"Yes—I know."

The clenched sorrow in Orim Farris almost choked Digen, but he managed to say, "Wyn always says Zeor is the common human striving for excellence."

"Truly spoken. But there is more. Zeor is the fueling force of life, which will not let us rest short of becoming the best self we may be. Zeor is the knowledge of the vast gulf between what we are and what we can be, the humbling knowledge of how far we have yet to go and the inspiring knowledge of what it will be like when we get there."

Orim came closer, though he didn't seem to move. "But there is much more to Zeor than that. To know Zeor, you must dive deep within yourself and come upon it within your own soul. It is a dangerous journey from which you may never return. And even if you do return, you will have gained nothing of value to you, but only to others. It is a journey which will change your soul as even death cannot change it. If you return, you will no longer be the same person you are now. Do you trust me to conduct you on this journey-of-no-return to Zeor and back?"

"Where Wyn has gone with you, I do not fear to follow."

But he was afraid as he'd never been in his life before. His only strength lay in the unseen multitude around them. They were Zeor, and he would do anything for them.

Orim Farris held out his hands, laterals extended. "Contact me," he commanded.

Gulping, Digen held out his hands, his own laterals twining about his father's. "To the grave and beyond, in search of Zeor and forever."

Selyn coursed into him, down the junct pathways that only Ilyana had ever touched. The sensation rose and rose until it possessed him, blotting out all else. He found himself drifting down a vaulted hallway toward a bright mirror. When he reached it, he shed his outer garments of seeming reality and went on toward another mirror, and through it to another.

At each station he met some new revelation, but in all that long journey downward and back he retained only three clear memories amid blurred impressions of the incomprehensible.

In one mirror, he saw himself from a new perspective. All that he had ever done in life, all he had ever thought *or felt, was designed to hide from himself knowledge of his basest fear: If I should ever really kill a Gen, I would* relish his terror and pain. I would. I . . .

He stood before that mirror, face turned aside, able to glimpse this self, this truest self of his own being, only from the corner of one eye. To pass through this mirror— to find what was behind this self—to search out and touch Zeor—he had to face this self and embrace it. It was the test.

He never knew how long he stood there struggling to look himself in the eye, naked of all pretense. But at last he did manage it. He learned: I am afraid of what I would do if I held any real power. That's why I ran away—from the Tecton, from Zeor, from myself.

And then he was through the mirror, stumbling down a long tunnel littered with the shattered remains of all he had ever been, sobbing the whole way, but never slowing.

He fetched up in front of another mirror, too bright to look into. For a long time he stood there, squinting sideways at it until finally he forced his eyes open and faced the light.

From what he saw there, he reeled backward in shock and lay senseless for uncounted time. His father's voice urged him up to confrontation again, and meekly he went to embrace the figure-marbled darkness like a Sime in attrition etched around by searing Gen fire—and he knew it as his own death, though he didn't know what that meant, except that this time it didn't terrify him.

He found himself kneeling in muck, a stinking sludge of foul waste. Digging in the muck with his hands, he uncovered a glittering, bejeweled chest in which he knew he would find Zeor, the thing he had come to touch.

He drew the chest up out of the ooze, and it came away perfectly clean. His father's voice said, "You will retain only what you are currently able to understand and benefit from. Nothing destructive will be brought back from this journey. But all of it—every bit—is now a part of you. It is not for yourself that you carry it, but for others. Open the box."

He opened it. Within, on black velvet, lay the Zeor crest ring he had stomped to shards beneath his heel in Westfield. He reached out to touch it, wondering what cruel trick was being played on him.

The ring sucked him into the box, and the lid shut him away in darkness, velvet-clad darkness.

He had scarcely begun to feel panic when he was caught up in Wyner's arms, cradled and protected, strengthened and bathed in that peculiar, fluttery nager which was Wyner's. "What is Zeor, little brother?"

"I don't know, I don't know!" cried Digen in despair.

"Silly little brother—you have become Zeor."

"That doesn't make sense!"

"Zeor is the focal point of a lens that can burn holes in reality. Does that make more sense?"

"No."

"Then take what you have become, and learn what it means to you." The mists swirled in, lighter than the velvet black, thinning lighter and lighter. Fading quickly, Wyner whispered, "And take care of Bett for us, silly brother, and tell her we are all well." Wyner's arms tightened around him, became solid and real to the touch, cool, smooth flesh, nager firming up to a steady, compulsive beat—a Gen beat, a fanir's beat.

"Digen?" A quivering voice, no trace of therapist neutrality.

His mouth felt stuffed with cotton and he hurt all over like one enormous bruise shot through with the screaming pain of strained muscles. His head throbbed, his neck was stiff, and he could barely swallow. But when he tried to say "Yes" he found air whispering over his vocal cords, and a sound did come out.

Im'ran's grip loosened, and suddenly he was the Tecton therapist again, distant, punctiliously proper, without a whisper of the emotional contact of Wyner/Im'ran, the confused dream image—fever hallucination—whatever it had been.

The shift was so abrupt that Digen gasped. *Wyn!* And, after that brief twinge of the old grief, he laid it aside.

Im'ran was holding a straw to Digen's lips. "Drink, just a sip now. Then I'll put you into your deepest sleep and you'll heal quickly."

Under Im'ran's deft ministrations, Digen plunged gratefully into the deep pit of real sleep.

Chapter 20

ILYANA ACTS

There was a space of days in which Digen faded in and out of wakefulness, then he plunged back into the healing sleep, from which he finally emerged early one night.

He was lying in a half doze when Ilyana came into the room, rousing Im'ran, who had fallen asleep in the chair.

"Is he awake yet?" she asked.

"I don't know."

Ilyana came to the bed. "Digen?"

She was very upset about something, Digen saw, but Im'ran's field blocked almost everything else. He rolled onto his back and struggled to sit up. The shades were up, moonlight pooling on the bedspread. "Ilyana? What's wrong?"

She hesitated, and he reached for her hand, but she drew back. "No, you might catch it from me again."

She wasn't showing any symptoms, so Digen said, "Maybe we'll all be lucky. Maybe it's all over."

"No, Digen," she said, brushing that aside. "It's Skip."

"He's sick?" said Digen, throwing the spread aside.

"No, no, he's decided—he's hysterical with deferred need. And—"

Digen grabbed her by the shoulders as if to squeeze it out of her faster. "He hasn't had transfer *yet?*"

Im'ran said, "I tried, but I just couldn't do anything with him, Digen. Ilyana was trying—"

Ilyana shook her head. "He only wants Joel!"

"That's insane," said Digen.

"He's out in the kitchen with Joel now, and Joel wants to try it, and—"

Digen swung his feet to the floor and grabbed a robe around himself as he went. His legs were unsteady, and his system fluttered ominously, but by the time he reached the kitchen doorway he had some command of himself.

Skip and Hogan were beside the sink pump. Digen felt Skip's laterals sliding into full contact as the young channel made lip contact, initiating the flow. For one insane moment, even Digen thought it was going to work. Joel seemed to be cooperating fully, glowing with an open sensitivity to Skip's plight, the likes of which Digen had thought never to see from his friend.

But then Hogan's nager burst into a screeching hysteria of Gen terror. As Digen began to move, he felt that terror bite into him.

I should never have permitted him to be my friend. People like Joel must never be allowed to associate with Simes. That's what the Tecton is for.

And then, abruptly, he was catching Hogan's body as it fell lifelessly from Skip's arms. The Gen had contained so little selyn that the brief instant of selyn flow had burned and drained him totally. Joel Hogan was dead.

At that same time, Im'ran came up behind Skip, raising a heavy crystal oil lamp. Skip, in the throes of vicious post-transients from the inadequate transfer, didn't sense Im'ran until the Gen was almost upon him. He turned to deflect the blow, but Im'ran seized Skip's arms, fingers biting deep into the swollen ronaplin gland, and as Skip folded in pain, Im'ran smashed the oil lamp over Skip's head.

Digen, still holding the empty corpse in his arms, cried out, "No!" But it was too late. Skip Ozik crumpled to the floor, his neck broken, life functions ceased utterly. In stunned silence Digen looked at Im'ran. He had heard of hysterical strength in Gens sometimes equaling low augmentation. He could feel it in the fanir, now beginning to ebb away and leave him weak.

Im'ran shuffled through the oil and the glass shards to reach out for the corpse Digen held, choking as he said, "He was in my keeping. I was responsible."

They sank to the floor together, supporting Hogan's body. The echo of Skip's kill was still trapped in Digen's nerves. *Skip craved Joel's fear, but he feared it too.* "He didn't want to kill him," said Digen.

"Now I'm a killer too, a fanir who's killed a channel."

Ilyana knelt beside them. She plucked up one of Hogan's scorched arms, running her finger along the dirty-looking mark that Skip's tentacles had left. "The world is full of joelhogans—isn't it, Digen?"

"Yes."

"He was—nobody could ask a man to be more than he was," she said.

"No, you couldn't," said Im'ran.

"There was nothing wrong with him," said Ilyana. "He just couldn't tolerate selyn flow. Not at all."

"No, he couldn't," said Im'ran. "And they've got a hundred just like him down there in that"—he broke off, his lip curling around the archaic word—"that *pen* they've built."

Digen looked up inquiringly, and Ilyana said, "The raiding party returned at sundown. None of them are in need anymore. They're playing the shiltpron and enjoying their captives."

Now that his attention had been called to it, Digen could sense the merrymaking in the distance. Ilyana said, "Skip could have gone down there and claimed a Gen for himself; they wouldn't have denied him. I wanted him to go, but he only wanted Joel—you know, you've seen how they were."

"I don't blame you, Ilyana," said Digen.

"But that wouldn't have made it all right for him to go kill some other Gen. They're all joelhogans down there."

"To one degree or another," said Digen. "I guess that's true."

Crying, Ilyana got to her feet and wandered out of the room. Im'ran followed her with his eyes, then started to get to his feet to go after her. Digen held him back. "Let her have some time to assimilate it. I know what she's going through." He picked up a bloodied fragment of crystal. "We'd better take the bodies to the kiln for cremating."

"It's not operating anymore. Besides, they didn't die of the shaking plague. Let's bury them properly."

Digen thought for a moment. "There's a nice place on the top of the hill over there. I used to tell Ilyana I wanted to be buried there—when things were bad."

Im'ran locked gazes with Digen, and what they shared then had no words.

As Im'ran straightened out Skip's frail body to heave it onto his shoulder, Digen's hand fell on the little silver medallion of the Final Donation Society around Hogan's neck. Grief burned away all capacity for tears. Im'ran paused, looking at Digen. "It—it meant a lot to him, you know. Digen, will—would you—could you take Skip's final donation. It would be Joel's, too."

Their eyes met, and without a word Digen bent to the grisly business of stripping the last selyn from the dead boy who had become a man under him and killed his best friend. *Out of Death Was I Born, Unto Zeor, Forever!*

When it was done, they hauled the beloved bodies out into the cold, standing under the moon, chopping fiercely at the stubborn, frozen soil to scrape out two lonely trenches facing east at the top of the hill. Shoulder to shoulder, the two men took out all their grief on the hardened ground as if the earth itself had wronged them and must pay for it. Each cracking thud of pick or shovel had a purging effect on them, and in the end, backfilling the graves over the bare bodies, together they came out of their pain and into a new, more barren reality.

Im'ran wanted to gather up their tools and head right back to the house. But Digen made him pause, saying, "We can't offer them burial in Zeor, but I'd like to observe our pledge-in-silence, anyway. Stay with me?"

He sensed that Im'ran wanted badly to say something important, but the Gen only nodded and stood back while Digen performed the one Zeor rite he could extend. It was the first time in his life he had performed that rite in which it seemed to have some piercing inner meaning.

At last Digen turned from the grave, oddly surprised to find the first stirrings of need in himself. It had been lurking there ever since he first came fuzzily awake, but only now did it claim his attention. Walking back toward the house in the firm luminance of Im'ran's nager, Digen said, "I thought surely Ilyana would come out with us." Digen had a moment's vision of Ilyana trying to clean up the oil in the kitchen, slipping, and getting hurt badly.

He stepped a little ahead of Im'ran to scan for her nager, but he couldn't isolate it. "Do you suppose anything's wrong?" asked Digen. "She's not in the house."

"From what I've seen of her, I'd say she surely can hold her own among any group of Simes or Gens. I wouldn't worry."

Im'ran suddenly stopped, cupping hands around his eyes to cut out the moonlight, and said, "Digen, what's that? There's no city out here to make a skyglow like that."

Digen, feeling the weakness of his recent illness, put a hand to Im'ran's shoulder to steady himself while he closed his eyes and scanned the distant part of the valley. "Fire! Two—no, four, six, seven houses on fire down there!"

Im'ran started to lunge past Digen down the path, but Digen caught his wrist and stopped him. "No, those are all abandoned—plague houses. Maybe somebody's idea of purification."

"But what if it spreads?"

"It's on the other side of the firebreak, and there aren't many trees near the houses—the fields are all in stubble. Don't worry."

Digen couldn't see Ilyana anywhere, but there were almost all the Simes and Gens of the settlement gathered in the main hall for the shiltpron party. He pointed toward the brightly lit building. "She must have gone to the party."

"To stop it, I bet."

Digen started off in that direction, but Im'ran stopped him. "Wait. Those are her people. We're the outsiders here. Best stay out of it."

Digen just looked at him.

"All right," conceded Im'ran. "So I have an ulterior motive. It's an old habit, worrying about my patients. Digen, you just got up from about the most serious illness you've ever had. I'm not going to let you go charging into that mess down there until I've at least gotten some of my trin-tea concoction into you."

"I couldn't stomach anything right now."

"I know, me either. But—if I do, will you?"

Digen made a weak, protesting sound.

"You can't hide it from me, Digen. Your knees are getting wobbly—or they will be in a few minutes. You haven't had any fluids worth mentioning in days. There's a limit to how far even you can stretch yourself."

Digen played his trump. "You don't want to be too close to me when I'm in need like this. You could disrupt my next transfer with Ilyana."

Im'ran whipped around in front of Digen, blocking the way. "Are you questioning my professional ethics? Or my competence?"

"I wouldn't dare," said Digen. And he meant it.

"Then come along home. We'll go down there together if Ilyana doesn't turn up by the time we've finished." He steered Digen onto the path toward the house. Digen went, saying, "Im'ran, you are a fiend."

"I know. It's part of the job description."

That's all it is to him, a job, thought Digen. But he vaguely remembered having dreamed—or was it real?—that Im'ran spent a tremendous effort keeping apart from him. *He's never had a matchmate before.*

Over a wild variant of the trin-tea-and-citrus-juice mixture Im'ran had fed him in the glade, Digen asked, "Skip's transfer didn't help you much, that time in the pantry, did it?"

Im'ran went through a medley of emotions as Digen watched. "No, you were right, Digen, a minor transfer just makes the next underdraw worse. But what else could I have done?"

"Nothing." Then, after a bit: "It wasn't your fault. It was mine, for the way I handled Joel all year at the hospital. I should have destroyed what little Donor's instinct he had left in him."

"I should have been able to handle Skip—he was a junct, an undeveloped channel. I should have—Digen, you have to know, he *promised* me—Unto Rior—not to try to induce Joel."

" 'An oath in need is no oath at all.' I don't blame him. Besides, he was attracted by the peculiar quality of Joel's fear. It's a craving it's awfully easy to get used to satisfying. But the Gens here in Rior don't fear, they dominate. So he had to go after Joel."

Drinking his tea, Im'ran said, "Do you—crave—Gen fear, Digen?"

"No. Ilyana's never given me that—I could never harm her."

"Then you're not really junct."

"Oh, but I am. I am. With this lateral scar, I could never complete a real kill and survive it. I have to be spoon fed. Ilyana—touches me—in a place only juncts have been touched. I'd do anything—anything—for that." His need was plain for Im'ran to see. He added, "And this may be my last such transfer—the last worth remembering."

"Digen! You're not going to get sick again!"

"No, Im', I've got to go back—to Westfield. I know that now. I've got to. But—Ilyana can't and won't and I don't want her to. I can't explain it to you, Im'. Just believe me, it would be altogether too horrible an experience to ask her to live through twice."

"But, Digen—you're not talking about breaking lortuen while both of you are still alive?"

"That's impossible. Even for me that's impossible. But with your help I think I could survive long enough to solve Rin's equations."

"I can offer her an equal chance at death from a pregnancy, or the shaking plague—it may not be over yet."

He was talking about a double-suicide pact and they both knew it. Im'ran said, "It hasn't come to this yet, Digen. Surely there's got to be another way."

Digen shook his head. "No, I have to go back. There's another thing." He glanced toward the hill where they had just buried two close friends. He took a deep breath, steeling himself as for a confession. "I want to inscribe them in Zeor's Memorial to the One Billion. It's important to me, Im', I can't explain why."

Im'ran knew what that meant. Digen was saying that Zeor would live again, that he would pass it on to an heir before he died—and if Ilyana refused to return and pledge Zeor, then that heir would probably be Mora's child by Digen—raised as Im'ran's own.

With this bleak vista opening before him, Im'ran was shaken. He reached across the table to grip Digen's wrist. "Digen, I won't let you die. Understand that, good. *I* won't permit it."

Digen put his hand over Im'ran's, letting one lateral-tentacle tip just brush the Gen's finger. "I do understand, Im', I do." There was a moment of that all-too-close nageric linkage between them.

Im'ran grew uncomfortable, and Digen withdrew the contact, taking up his glass of tea again. Im'ran said, "Digen, you've been fighting this battle between going back or staying—since we came. Maybe even before Joel—and I—came. One day you're ready to do one thing. The next day you've got to do another. That day Roshi was sick—the first time—you swore to Ilyana you could never go back. Now—Digen, what's changed your mind?"

Digen thought about it for a space. It was hard to put such an impelling feeling into words. "Nothing's changed my mind, Im'. What I said to Ilyana—what I learned over Roshi—it's still true. All my life I've given my allegiance to Zeor and to the Tecton—on blind faith. Now I know what they really are. I know the fallacies underlying them. I'm still just as revolted as when I first saw those fallacies."

He met Im'ran's gaze. "With Skip—and Joel—I saw the Distect in truth—and—choice is forced on me. Im', the world hasn't changed—I have. When you came, I didn't have the strength to force myself to go back. Now I do. And if I don't use it, I'll never be able to live with myself."

With all the trained perception of a therapist, Im'ran inspected Digen. "Yes—you have changed. But—I couldn't say how."

Digen swirled the tea in the bottom of his glass and drained it. "You were right, I feel much better now, but I'm still in need. I'm nervous about Ilyana, too—she was terribly upset, and if she's gone down to try to stop that party—"

"Well," said Im'ran, putting the two empty glasses neatly together in the middle of the table, "let's go find her."

The party was in full swing when they reached the main hall. The moon threw the shadow of the silo across the open yard. The wide double doors were held back by hay bales, and inside, among the Simes wildly drunk on shiltpron music, a makeshift corral of hay bales had been set up to contain the captured Gens.

The prisoners were a dispirited lot, suffering from exposure and prolonged terror, but they had been well clothed and fed. Their collective nager was strong but, to Digen, not particularly attractive. His need keened for Ilyana, and he found her up on the stage, confronting Roshi, her anger worn like a crown of light.

In the loft, and all around the main floor, Simes stood guard with rifles aimed at the captives. Ilyana was saying, as if for the twentieth time, "It's better to let yourself die of attrition than to cause a death."

Roshi said, "It's easy for a Gen to say that."

Someone in the crowd of Simes said, "The Tecton has corrupted her!"

"No!" she yelled back. "Listen to me. Some Gens just can't tolerate transfer—"

"It's their own fault," yelled another Sime.

"Not always," Ilyana answered the one in the audience.

"How else has Rior ever grown, or survived?" asked Roshi. "We're offering them a chance to join us, a chance at real life. Isn't what we have worth the risk of death to gain?"

"Yes, it is," said Ilyana, still talking to the audience, "but wouldn't it be better if eighty or ninety of these people could survive and join us—rather than the ten or twelve who might make it at the most?"

"Ilyana, don't talk foolishness," said Roshi. "We'll have to raid until we build our numbers up again."

"No," said Ilyana. "If you do it again, you'll be caught —or traced back here. And that will be the end of Rior— forever."

She turned back to the audience. "The Tecton is crumbling. Rior is mankind's last hope. But we are the leading edge of mankind's progress—our methods cannot be the brute-force methods of the majority. We must cut a new pathway—not *back* to the days of freeband raiders preying on the helpless Gens and becoming addicted to the savor of Gen terror—you've all had a taste of that and you can feel how it could trap you. We must go onward to something new."

Cynically, Roshi said to Ilyana while addressing the audience, "And just what do you propose as something new to replace transfer with?"

"You think that because I'm a Gen I don't know what need is? Have I not served each and every Sime of Rior in pledge transfer when I accepted your oaths Unto Rior? Can anyone who has known my touch doubt that I know the meaning of need?"

Thers was a murmur from the audience, which she silenced. "I've been very ill this last year. But, through it all, I've learned a lot. I've seen the twisted travesty of the channel's body used to good ends. Most every Sime here who has survived the plague is alive now because of Digen's touch—*as a channel*. Let him help us survive while we train these Gens to our way. He can teach them to serve us—we can only terrify them to death. Digen has saved Rior once—let him do it again."

With lip curled, Roshi said, "Rior does not bow to the channel's touch!"

A cheer went up.

Roshi took their approval between his hands and proclaimed, "The only ones fit to pledge Rior are the ones who survive transfer without a channel's intervention. The unfit Gens must die. Ilyana, have you forgotten that the Tecton saves the unfit to breed? The human race is still in the process of mutating. Save enough of the unfit, and the whole race will be unfit."

Ilyana turned on him. "Unfit? Roshi, you are unfit. I am unfit. There is no strain among us that is less fit to survive than the Farris strain."

"But I am alive, and so are you."

"Only because I brought Digen Farris—a surgeon *and* a channel—to Rior. You and everyone else here would be dead of your own stupid scheme to kill them with disease if it weren't for Digen—and Joel. And Im'ran. Think about that. The Tecton reached out and saved you from the fate you stupidly planned for them." Her anger was growing beyond her control.

"Not so stupid," said Roshi. "It would have killed only those who couldn't divorce themselves from dependency on the channels—the very thing about the Tecton that Rior stands against. Rior itself would have been immune because we keep our contacts within our own families. But you had to parade your tame channel in that—that—cloak you made for him, on the only day when such behavior is sanctioned—and you did that against the expressed order of the Regent in Rior!"

"And I'm glad that I did—even though it killed most of my friends—because if I'd known what you were doing, Roshi, on our father's grave, I swear, I would have killed you with my own hands!"

The power of her underdrawn nager went into that oath and every Sime in the room became drenched in cold sweat, knowing that she would have done it and what it would have done to her.

She turned to the audience. "Since the Battle of Leander Field—since Muryin Farris came to us—it has not been Rior's way to attack and destroy. It is enough that we stand proudly as an example of the best life man can live. That is what you pledged to me when you pledged Unto

Rior. And that is what my life stands for, as Sosectu in Rior. I stand before you now, well and in my strength, and ask—no, I demand—that you set aside the Regency and place Rior back in my hands. By our charter, no Sime can be Head of Householding Rior."

Roshi strode to the edge of the stage. "A vote, then, sister? Very well, all in favor of being ruled by a Gen, say so."

There was absolute dead silence save for a timorous noise or two from the few Gens scattered among the majority of Simes.

Roshi said to Ilyana, "Our great-grandmother was a fool. And to the audience, "Those in favor of the Regency?"

A roar went up, and when it was over Roshi said, "Then things shall remain as they have been this past year."

Ilyana, the anger compressed now to a dull burning coal, said, "If you reject Muryin, then you also reject Hugh Valleroy and all he stood for, because Muryin returned us to his original principles. And if you reject those, then you also reject Rior itself and stand foresworn."

There was an uncomfortable rustling in the room, but no movement to change the vote. Ilyana was flying in the face of the deepest Sime instincts. Roshi, whatever else he might be, had led these Simes in a raid and had blooded them. He had shared their need and the fulfillment of it. There were few bonds stronger than that.

Over her head, Roshi spotted Digen standing in shadow by the doors, perceiving even at that distance Digen's need matching Ilyana's replete nager. "She's off her head again, Digen, come and take her. You both need it."

Ilyana twisted around, aware of Digen for the first time. Even across the sea of Gens and Simes, their nageric linkage operated to phase them perfectly. The strain of the distance between them made every Sime squirm with sympathetic need.

A pathway opened before Digen, leading to the stage, but before he could step out, Ilyana said, her anger shrinking to a focused point within her, leashed and controlled now as Digen had never seen it before, "Then let the House of Rior be razed to the ground and its remains cursed for a hundred years!"

With a patronizing exasperation, Roshi muttered, "Underdraw . . ." and made as if to help his raving sister off the stage. But she wrenched her elbow away and jumped down, striding away without a backward glance. It was the first time since Digen had known her that she had made an exit in anger in which she didn't leave every Sime literally stunned senseless.

As she stalked past blindly, Digen caught her up in his arms, motioning Im'ran over between them and the crowd. On the stage, Roshi had the shiltpron player stroking up a soothing rhythm. Digen, already melting into the edges of trautholo, found all his prepared words evaporating from his lips, unspoken. She needed him now, not just in transfer but for all the strength his own ordeal had given him. He wanted to pour his strength into her as he drank of her nager.

But she allowed them only a moment's joining, and then, with that sure, instinctive control, she broke the trautholo with an utterly painless flick of her nager.

Dizzy with it, Digen fought to gather himself together and asked, "Why . . . ?"

"I know, I know, Digen, but I have something I must do downstairs." She deftly extricated herself from Digen's grip, her surface a wispy gentleness, her core a banked furnace of undischarged anger. She couldn't serve transfer in that condition. Reluctantly Digen let her go.

She gave Im'ran's wrist a little squeeze. "Take him home for me, Im', and keep care of him."

Digen came out of his daze to find Im'ran stationing himself at his left, staring after her. "What's downstairs, Digen?"

"I don't know. Storerooms, the armory, some offices— oh, their memorial. She could use an hour or so there right now. She's just buried her house." On their flight from Westfield they had stopped at a public memorial, where Digen had laid to rest his own house. "She'll come when she's able. This is something she has to do alone."

Digen looked to the shiltpron player, who had raised the tempo back to the raucous, provocative level. "Let's get out of here, Im'. That's vile."

On the paths under the trees, it was so dark that Digen had to guide Im'ran by the elbow. The fanir's nager was grave, brooding. Digen said, "Talk to me. Keep my mind off—things." He guided Im'ran's fingers along the soft, swollen ronaplin glands. "I've never been so high intil in my life, and I'm not used to denial anymore. I've fallen out of discipline. That's some admission from the Sectuib in Zeor, huh?"

"The Sectuib in Zeor? Digen, Ilyana will pledge to you now—she'll come back with us, and everything will be all right." As he spoke, Im'ran leashed Digen's need and brought it under firm control.

Digen paused at a bend in the path, shaking his head. "She's got a long way to go before she can pledge the opposite of Rior. Believe me, I know that path backwards and forwards now. It may require more strength than she has in her, after all she's been through."

"You made it. She will—somehow."

"I wish I could believe that, because—she's all I have left of value in my life. Except you—and the Tecton will take you away the minute we get back."

"Yes, I suppose so."

Down in the valley, houses were still burning brightly. One collapsed in a shower of sparks, some catching in the stubble of harvested wheat.

"You realize," said Digen, "we'll have to prevent them from raiding again."

"Yes," said Im'ran, "of course. We'll think of something."

At that moment the main hall blew up.

Gouts of fire burst upward, bulging the walls outward, sending roof and walls flying like stick kindling. The flash and roar reached Digen and Im'ran a split instant before the furnace heat washed over them and a rain of burning sticks came down out of the sky to set trees, underbrush, and houses afire. A second explosion and then a third rent the air, a veritable geyser of fire leaping upward and outward from the hall.

Digen screamed.

The moment of Ilyana's death ripped through him as if his nerves had all been torn out by the roots. He screamed and screamed, as if his own body were a burning torch. And he never felt himself hit the gravel.

Ilyana's arms under his laterals, her lips against his, nageric linkage more firm than ever in life. "I'm sorry, Digen, I'm sorry to leave you like this. But Zeor is still pledged to you. You must go back, bring Rior's ideals to

Zeor—to the Tecton—finish the job, Digen—finish it for both of us. We must not fail."

She thrust him inexorably away from her and flashed past him, her voice fading—*"Unto Zeor, and Rior—Forever!"*

Digen felt himself falling, falling, falling into a black pit of death and torment. Falling and falling, screaming out, *"Ilyana, don't leave me! Ilyana!"*

Falling and falling, his screams inarticulate, his panic boundless, Digen raked out to every side to save himself. Something . . . pushed back. Something bounded him, limited him, caught and held him steady.

With a shock, he was in his body, numb and bewildered, his heart pounding with fear, but he held firm. The fanir's nager linked hard and deep into him as never before. Digen's throat, raw with spent screams, rattled once more, and then, Im'ran made full lip contact, all barriers flat open to Digen's draw, all Digen's laterals secure to Im'ran's fields.

Selyn began to flow, without Digen's active will. The sensation was instant balm to each cell it touched, and it awakened a blaze of selyn hunger in every cell of his body. He drew then, full out on pure instinct. A moment, and then the flows unbalanced and Digen shook all over with incipient shen, but before the tension had fully gathered, the flow righted under Im'ran's will, fed across Digen's scarred lateral with perfect synchrony. Digen drowned again in the glory— *He can see!*

And this time Digen didn't stop short of his full-capacity draw. Im'ran supplied every dynopter Digen could take with a comfortable margin left over. But, strain as he might, Digen could not get the flow to divert into the junct pathways, burning and aching though they were.

Im'ran gave him an orhuen consummation transfer in the strictest Tecton style, and held firm against all Digen could do.

He came out of it with his handling tentacles digging crushingly into Im'ran's arms, shaking the Gen so hard that their lip contact broke off. There was blood against the Gen's teeth from Digen's ferocious straining for that one last bit, the junct touch.

Im'ran waited patiently for Digen to pry his own tentacles away from the contacts. Digen, stiff with strain and gasping audibly, dismantled his grip while all about them trees had begun to blaze. The very air reverberated to death cries, a nageric pall rising from the towering flames at the center of the conflagration. Ash sifted down all around them.

Digen caught his breath, choking, and touched the Gen's bruised forearm. *I did that.* "I'm sorry." *He gave me his all, and it's not—quite—enough.*

A burning branch fell behind them and Im'ran flinched, saying, "Let's get out of here."

Digen shook his head. "You go. I can't move."

Im'ran got his shaking legs under him and struggled to stand. He reached down and took Digen's hand, to pull him to his feet. The moment their flesh met, the nageric static of orhuen postreaction snapped like static electricity discharging. Swearing, Im'ran pulled at Digen's coat until he had the channel on his feet.

Tilting Digen's limp body into a fireman's carry, he heaved him up to his shoulders and made for the outskirts of the settlement. Somewhere down that long tunnel of fire and ashes, out of the valley, down the cliffside path, through drenching waterfall and across the open forest, Digen lost consciousness. The oblivion was the greatest blessing ever bestowed, for it wiped away the insistent liturgy in his head: *Why didn't he just let me die?*

Chapter 21

THE WAY HOME

Digen woke to the sun on his face and the quiet chatter of a mountain stream nearby. He lay wrapped in blankets on the gravel of the stream bank. A little fire burned inside a ring of rocks, water boiling in a small camp pot. He was alone.

Ilyana. No, she's dead. She's dead. She's dead.

Inside himself, he felt the raw ends of the uprooted lortuen—but somehow they'd been sealed—"cauterized" was the English descriptive that came to mind. After a while he recognized it as a Zeor technique he had so long ago taught Im'ran. *She's really gone—dead.*

Im'ran? He felt a shiver of fear at being alone in this condition.

There was still the afterimage of Im'ran's nager. Looking about, Digen picked up the Gen's distinctive pattern coming toward him along the stream bed. In moments, he was in sight and then kneeling beside Digen.

"Can you move, Digen?"

Digen drew the cold air deep into the bottom of his lungs and forced his gluey eyes open. He flexed his arms and legs, finding the weakness and near paralysis of the postlortuen break almost gone. He sat up, kneading the back of his neck. "Apparently I can."

"Good," said Im'ran, looking at the high mountains all around them. "Because this is where they caught us before. We can't stay here. But—we had to get our camp gear, as much as they left intact."

Digen too scanned the mountainsides. "There's nobody up there in the guard stations now."

Im'ran shrugged. "There must be some survivors. Not everybody was in the main hall. They'll be in a vengeful mood. But—maybe we'll have time for some breakfast." He held up what he'd been carrying. A naked rabbit car-

315

cass. "I'm going to roast it. You'd better move upwind if the smell's going to get to you."

Digen swallowed his gorge. He had lived many years among the carnivorous Gens out-Territory. Meat was a natural food to them. It surprised him how quickly he'd lost his conditioning. And then it surprised him that Im'ran had managed to overcome an in-Territory upbringing to such a degree.

"Don't look at me like that, Digen. I wouldn't be here at all if—Joel—hadn't taught me this."

"We owe him a lot," said Digen.

"Yes," said Im'ran, then shook himself. "It's over."

Im'ran busied himself spitting the carcass. Digen noted the sooty smoke still pouring from the valley hidden away above them. "You carried me all that way?"

"Believe it or not, you walked part of the way, but I don't think you were really conscious."

"I don't remember—except flashes. A weird bush. Didn't we fall down a shale hill?"

"Nothing broken, though. Before we leave, I want to bathe your legs again in the stream. We've both got a lot of scrapes and bruises under the film of soot."

Digen pushed himself to his feet, feeling the shredded cloth of his trousers scrape over raw skin. He ambled upwind as the rabbit fat dripped, smoking, into the fire. He felt so weak that he had to sit down on a log, wrapped around and shivering in the blankets. After a bit, Im'ran handed him a steaming tin cup.

"Tea?" asked Digen, smelling it.

"Sort of. It's a little raw. We found a trin bush after our supplies were washed away in a flash flood, the one that killed our third packhorse. I kind of improvised. Joel never cared much for trin."

Digen sipped. It wasn't bad. "It's an acquired taste."

There was a long silence while Imran ate his roasted rabbit, feeding Digen bits of dried fruit and a handful of nuts. Then, as Im'ran began striking camp, kicking the fire out, making backpacks of the sparse equipment, Digen felt strangely as if he had come from the moment on the front porch when he'd fallen ill with the shaking plague directly to this moment, and all that had gone between had been only nightmare. "Did it really happen, Im'ran—all of it—all of them, dead?"

Im'ran stopped what he was doing and went to Digen. He knew that the channel had been in shock, and the death of a lortuen mate could easily throw him into a mental breakdown from which he'd never recover. "Yes, Digen. It all happened. It was real."

"The Distect is dead, then. Zeor has to live. It has to, Im'."

Im'ran went down on one knee at Digen's feet. "Zeor has never been in danger. It has a life of its own, apart from the existence of you or me. But we can't exist apart from Zeor, Digen, neither of us."

Digen frowned, puzzled by Im'ran's choice of phrase. "Neither of us?"

"I've left Imil, Digen. I retrieved my pledge from Asquith before we left on this search, though it cost me everything I owned. Maybe I shouldn't have let you introduce me as companion in Imil up there. Because I'm not anymore. I'm houseless."

Digen understood then. Im'ran hadn't wanted anything personal between them to affect Digen's decision to go back. Imrahan—pure Tecton, through and through, and satisfied to be so.

"Bett was ready to accept my pledge, provisionary, as Acting Head of Householding—but I wouldn't. Digen, you are my Sectuib—if you'll have me, stained by killing a channel, lying to you by omission, losing the Gen I was assigned to protect."

"Im'ran—" Helpless, Digen just shook his head. "Aren't we all stained by misdeeds, aren't we all imperfect, crippled? Is that an excuse not to swear ambrov to Zeor?"

"Zeor stands against all these things."

"Zeor is not the pledge to be perfect—it's the pledge to never cease struggling toward perfection."

Im'ran, reaching for a deeper nageric link, touched Digen's hand. A small discharge of static flung their touch apart. Fretfully, Im'ran said, "What *is* that!"

Digen looked at the finger Im'ran had touched.

"Im'ran—Im'—you mean you didn't know what you were doing? Oh, Im'ran, how could any Sectuib refuse the house pledge of his own orhuen partner? How?"

"Orhuen?" said Im'ran blankly. "Oh. Oh! I didn't mean—"

Digen said, "It's the only reason I'm still alive, so don't

apologize." Digen looked at his hands, making a sour face. "Well," said Digen, "if you can stand it long enough to pledge—I'm game." He grinned, a fierce challenge to the universe, and seized Im'ran's hands for the pledge.

Im'ran sucked breath between his teeth at the touch, and tossed his head as if to clear it.

"Unto the House of Zeor," said the Gen, "I pledge my heart, my hand, my substance. And unto Digen Farris, Sectuib in Zeor, I pledge my life, my trust, my undying loyalty. I commit my life, my substance, and my children, Unto Zeor, Forever!"

"Unto Imrahan ambrov Zeor, I pledge my substance, my trust, my undying loyalty, in my own name—born from death—and Unto Zeor, Forever!"

What is the Tecton?

Like surgery, the Tecton is a necessary evil, tolerable only because it is transient.

"OUT OF DEATH WAS I BORN—
UNTO ZEOR, FOREVER!"

Digen Ryan Farris
Sectuib in Zeor